THE
PHOTOGRAPHER

Kevin Marsh

Published by Kevin Marsh

ISBN 978-1-78222-812-7

Book design, layout and production management by Into Print
www.intoprint.net
+44 (0)1604 832149

Dedication

To my brother Ian who I don't see enough, but I know he enjoys reading my books.

Acknowledgements

I would like to thank Mark Webb at Paragon Publishing for all his help and guidance in getting this novel into print. With the initial proof reading, Maria did a fantastic job ironing out the wrinkles and my mum Lyn who sorted out some of the gamma and other oddities. To everyone else who offered support and advice I thank you. Any remaining errors are purely down to me.

Chapter One

AN ICY LUMP FORMED AT the base of her stomach and it refused to budge. He had made it quite clear what would happen if she refused him and she had no doubts that he would carry out these unspeakable things. To avoid torture and gain her freedom was simple, all she had to do was agree to his demands.

Lowering herself down onto the filthy mattress, she pulled her legs up under her chin and hugged her knees tightly then taking in her dank surroundings, she began to sob.

Gatwick airport was busy. A crowd had gathered along the luggage conveyor and when the first bags appeared, Matthew Cunningham stepped forward. Immediately he was nudged aside by a woman who despite her advanced years could hardly contain her excitement.

"We always tie a bright yellow ribbon around the handle of our bags," she told him, her mid west accent giving away her nationality. "Me and my husband are on our first trip to Europe."

Matt glanced down at her and smiled politely, she took this as a sign to continue.

"Dwight said that we should start in London, but I insisted on Paris. Don't you just adore Paris?"

Before Matt could reply, a cheer went up as a huge case sporting a yellow ribbon trundled past on the conveyor. A man wearing a Stetson hat and a brightly coloured shirt fought his way to the front of the crowd and wrestled it to the ground before flashing his wife a triumphant smile.

Not long after, Matt's bag appeared partially hidden behind a bright pink case so stepping forward, he rescued it before it passed him by. His second piece of luggage, an aluminium framed studio case was nowhere to be seen. He waited patiently and watched as people around him claimed their property then left. Strangely, several bags ended up at the end of the conveyor, which had now stopped, but his case was not amongst them.

Matt frowned and checked his watch. His train was due to leave in just twenty minutes and still he had to make his way to the platform. There was little time for delay but before he could continue his journey, he would have to report his missing case.

"Can I have your name please sir?" The young man behind the counter asked politely.

Matt handed over his travel documents.

"So," the man said staring at his computer screen. "You have just arrived from CDG; that's Charles De Gaulle airport." He made eye contact and smiled.

Matt stared back willing him to get a move on.

"It says here that your luggage, consisting of two items were loaded onto the aircraft," he paused and squinted at the screen, "a leather overnight bag and an equipment case."

"I have my flight bag," Matt glanced down at his feet, "but there's no sign of my studio case."

"I have a loading reference number here, let me make a quick phone call." Reaching behind him, he grabbed a cordless phone and punched in a number then after a brief discussion, he turned back towards Matt. "Your case has not been left on the aircraft or in the cargo area. All baggage is loaded onto trolleys before going into the hold," he explained. "If it's a particularly bumpy flight, bags can sometimes become dislodged from the trolleys."

"I see," Matt nodded and made a show of glancing at his watch.

"I'll check with lost property for you, sometimes bags picked up in error are handed in."

His fingers danced across the keyboard and the computer screen changed then after a few seconds he shook his head. "There's nothing here that matches the description of your case." Reaching for the phone again, he continued. "I'll just see if it's there but not yet been added to the system."

Matt sighed and standing back rolled his eyes. Why didn't he make the call in the first place? It had been a long and eventful day, which had now become even longer with the loss of his studio case and to make matters worse he was about to miss his train.

His assignment in Paris had not ended well, the timetable became impossible mainly due to the models he was working with. One of the girls had been particularly difficult which resulted in them having to do an early morning shoot. Now it seemed with the loss of his case containing two very expensive cameras and lenses, his mornings work was gone too. He had not yet downloaded the pictures to his laptop, his work was still on the memory cards inside his studio case. Because of the stress of the impromptu photo shoot, he had forgotten to activate the feature on his camera that would send the images directly to his laptop.

"No, I'm afraid your property has not been handed in." The sound of the man's voice cut through his thoughts.

"So what happens now?" he snapped, "there is some rather expensive equipment in that case."

The young man was tempted to mention travel insurance but wisely kept his thoughts to himself.

"There is a reference number on your ticket that relates to your luggage which I'll now log as missing. We will of course continue to search for your property and contact you by email or text if it turns up."

Matt doubted his sincerity.

"In the meantime I'll give you some forms to fill in so you can make a compensation claim. If you prefer, these can be completed on-line." Glancing up, he raised his eyebrows and waited for Matt to reply.

"So that's it?"

"I'm afraid there's nothing more that I can do, all the details are now on the system." His eyes flicked from Matt to the computer screen and he was tempted to add that dozens of bags disappear mysteriously every year, but again he chose to keep his thoughts to himself.

"Give me the forms," Matt snapped angrily. "I've missed my train so I may as well complete them now."

Much later, he arrived at Victoria station and emerging into the cool night air did nothing to improve his mood. Earlier he had called Libby, his girlfriend to tell her that he was delayed. He had not yet worked out what he was going to tell his client. What a fool he was not to have downloaded the images from his camera the moment the assignment ended, it broke all the rules of his work ethic, but then he did not expect to lose his case. The memory cards were loaded with images of past jobs, not the sort of thing that would interest a stranger. He really should have deleted them after saving them to files on his computer. There were even some personal photographs.

"Matt," Libby called out. "You walked right past me," she scowled before hugging him. "I've missed you so much."

"I'm sorry," Matt replied ruefully, "it's been one of those days."

"Well you are here now." Linking her arm through his she led him along the pavement. "I managed to leave the car behind a friends flat, it's impossible to find a parking space around here."

She was thankful they did not live in central London, as far as she was concerned the costs outweighed the advantages.

"How was your trip, why are you so late?"

Matt told her about the early morning session and the loss of his case at Gatwick.

"That's awful." Peering at him over the top of the car, she opened the driver's door. "So being surrounded by the most beautiful women in France was no compensation then?"

Matt stared at her then pulled a face. "Don't you believe it," he groaned. "The English models were babes, I've worked with them before, but the French girl was a complete nightmare."

"Poor you," Libby pouted sarcastically as she climbed into the driver's seat.

"Paris would have been so much more fun with you."

"Oh how sweet of you to say that," she looked at him and smiled before starting the engine. "You know that I would have come with you if it wasn't for these impossibly tight deadlines I've been forced to work to."

Libby was a fashion journalist. Her job involved writing features for some of Europe's top fashion magazines.

"I'll take you to Paris before the summer," Matt promised. "Perhaps we could go in May for your birthday."

"That would be nice," Libby replied as she pulled away from a junction.

Matt sat quietly for a few minutes.

"It's a shame about your cameras, but you do have them insured."

"I'm not bothered about that, it's the images on the memory cards that concern me."

"You have them backed up though."

"Well, that's the thing. I didn't have time to save them after this morning's session."

Libby glanced at him and frowned. "Is that going to be a problem?"

He told her that the morning shoot was the highlight of the week, the best costumes reserved for the finale.

"They probably form the most important part of the catalogue. You know what Veronique is like, once she finds out that I've screwed up..."

He did not have to spell it out. Veronique Moreau was one of Europe's top fashion icons with boutiques in every major city. Her company produced nothing but the best in haute couture and her clients were the rich and famous. She would not be impressed.

"Oh Matt, try not to worry. As soon as we are home, you can relax. Try to forget about work. Tomorrow is another day."

Chapter Two

"I CAN'T BELIEVE HOW REASONABLE she was." Matt said blinking rapidly as he glanced at Libby, his phone still in his hand. "In fact she hardly raised her voice and even proposed a solution to the problem. Can you believe that?"

"Perhaps she isn't the ogre that people take her for." Libby replied, although she guessed the woman might have an ulterior motive. Most of her friends thought Matt gorgeous, so why would Veronique be any different.

"She promised to email me some of her own photographs from the early morning shoot. Of course I'll have to work on them."

"I'm glad she didn't give you a hard time, it's hardly your fault. Anyway, you might be pleasantly surprised, her photographic skills may be much better than you think."

"I doubt it, the camera she was using was not much better than a cheap mobile phone."

Libby giggled and reaching out brushed his arm with her fingertips. "You'll be fine, you are a master at image manipulation. I'm confident that you'll be able to do something quite marvellous with her pictures."

"I had better make a start on what I've got before Veronique sends me her photos"

Turning to his computer, he waited until Libby sat down. Their office was a converted bedroom, which they had transformed into a well appointed work space. They each had their own desk and computer station. Filing cabinets lined the back wall and they shared a rack of shelves that groaned under the weight of resources and files.

"What are you working on?"

"I'm preparing to do a piece on a celebrity wedding," she told him. "A woman called Emilia Sykes is organising the whole thing. She has a shop called White Lace and Promises. A great name for a bridal shop don't you think?"

"A Carpenters fan obviously."

Libby was interested in writing the article for two reasons, the fact that it was a celebrity wedding was cause enough, but she wanted to know more about Emilia Sykes. Her research told her that Emilia had not been in business for long, but in a short space of time had managed to put together a very impressive portfolio. She was either very lucky or had an amazing strategy for success and Libby was certain that the editor of any fashion magazine would be interested in running her story.

"I'm going to be conducting the initial interview later this afternoon but first I want to discover more about Emilia. She has a very impressive website by the way."

Libby was hoping that he would take the hint. They had been together for over three years now and she would like nothing more than to celebrate their relationship in marriage.

"I will of course be taking my camera, but if I'm to persuade her to use us as official photographer and reporter for the celebrity wedding, then I might need a little help."

She was an accomplished photographer, but on occasions, Matt had supplied the visual effects for many of her articles. They made a great team and to have his name accredited to her work was a prospect that could hardly be ignored.

Libby pushed open the door of White Lace and Promises and a little bell tinkled charmingly overhead. The perfectly restored Georgian facade gave way to a series of open plan rooms each pleasantly proportioned and she felt as if she were stepping back in time. The air was delicately perfumed and Libby found herself surrounded by the most beautiful things. Remaining perfectly still she was captivated, reluctant to break the spell.

"Libby Ellis?"

The sound of her name brought her back to reality and she watched as a young woman strode confidently towards her. Emilia Sykes was nothing like she had expected. Dressed in a floral striped print swing skirt from the 1950s and a pink bolero cardigan over a plain white blouse she looked elegantly fresh. Her strawberry blond hair hung loosely around her shoulders and her lips were painted cherry red to match her nails and shoes.

"Hello Emilia." Libby smiled as they shook hands. "What an amazing shop, I'm completely lost for words."

"Oh I do hope not as by trade you are a wordsmith!"

They laughed together and looking around, Libby tried to take in everything at once but failed dismally.

"I could spend hours in here, there are so many beautiful things to see."

"That can sometimes be a problem," Emilia replied dryly then she explained. "As soon as you think that everything has been agreed, the bride or one of her bridesmaids will spot something else and our well made plans unravel and we have to start all over again."

10

"I can imagine." Libby sympathised, then after a moment she said. "What a lovely skirt. Are you into the whole retro thing?"

"No not really but I do love well made clothes." Stepping back, Emilia swung her hips and the hem of her skirt danced around her legs. "Sometimes I'm lucky enough to pick up original items, but my wardrobe consists of a combination of authentic and modern retro copies. I like to mix and match."

"Well it certainly works," Libby said approvingly. "You will have to give me a few tips."

"Would you like some tea or coffee? I was about to put the kettle on."

"Coffee would be most welcome thank you."

Libby followed Emilia into a tiny office situated at the back of the shop and slipping out of her coat, draped it over the back of a chair.

"How long have you been here?" she asked as Emilia spooned coffee into a cafetiére.

"Just over eighteen months now. I started my design business when I was a student and sold stuff on-line."

Libby knew from her research that Emilia had studied fashion and design.

"How long were you trading before you set up this shop?"

Emilia looked up from what she was doing and frowned. "Please take a seat, let me move some of the clutter out of your way."

Reaching into her bag, Libby took out an electronic notebook and placed it on the desk in front of her.

"To answer your question," Emilia continued, "it was during my first year at university. I began by selling off some of my own clothes. Money was incredibly tight, I had no idea how expensive it was to be a student." She smiled and placed a mug off coffee down beside Libby's notebook.

Libby nodded sagely, she knew what that was like.

"It wasn't long before I ran out of stuff to sell," Emilia laughed and squeezed in behind her desk. "I was literally in danger of selling the clothes off my back." Picking up her mug, she took a sip and smiled at the memory. "It was then that I began trawling through vintage clothes shops and second hand market stalls looking for anything that I could sell on. I would often buy something and alter it, embellish it with some adornment or other but as my course progressed, I became more adventurous. At the same time I enrolled on an evening dressmaking course then I began to design and make clothes for the market."

"This all sounds fascinating," Libby said enthusiastically. "How did you make the transition from on-line retailer to a wonderful shop like this?"

"When I graduated I was just about earning enough from my business to afford the rent on a little flat in Brighton where I lived for a while. The vintage scene is brilliant there, but as my business expanded, I found myself designing bridesmaid's dresses and accessories. There was such a demand that my vintage labels had to take a back seat. I did however incorporate a retro look into many of my bridal designs."

"So did you outgrow your flat? I assume that you were working from home at the time."

"I'm afraid I did. Brighton is a fabulous place to live and work but most of my business was here in London so it made sense to move."

"In reality then you were forced into taking a shop."

"Yes indeed but the moment I saw this place I fell in love with it. I didn't want an ordinary high street outlet, I was looking for something a little different, a shop with soul you might say."

"Well this place certainly has that." Libby agreed.

Emilia laughed. "True, but it's far from perfect."

"Why do you say that?" Libby's fingers hovered over the keys of her notebook.

Emilia thought for a moment before answering.

"This is a fabulous location which attracts the right kind of person." Her frown deepened. "Oh that sounds terrible, I'm not a snob by the way, what I mean is that if it wasn't for my wealthy clients I could never afford a place like this."

"I can understand that," Libby nodded as she continued to type furiously, then she asked. "When did you decide to move into organising the complete wedding package?"

"It was several months ago. I have always been interested in doing that and when an opportunity arose I took it."

"It must be a huge undertaking, organising an entire wedding on top of all your design commitments and the day to day running of a shop like this."

"You are right there." Emilia gave a little laugh. "It's true that we organise everything, the bride's dress, the bridesmaid's outfits and accessories not to mention the flowers and the venue."

"Wow," Libby's eyes widened at the enormity of it all.

"It's not as bad as it sounds though," Emilia admitted. "Each wedding takes between twelve to twenty four months to organise, so in theory we have plenty of time to get it right."

"Still, it's an enormous undertaking."

"I don't do it all by myself," Emilia told her. "My brother Ben is responsible for a lot of the organising. His job is to interview the parties involved and agree the type of wedding and the venue, which leaves me to concentrate on designing the dresses and outfits."

"Don't tell me that you actually make the dresses yourself?"

"No," Emilia laughed. "My skills are in the design. I leave the dressmaking to the professionals."

"I read somewhere that you are interested in expanding the design side of your business, create your own label. What's that all about?"

Emilia told Libby about her plans to revive her retro ideas.

"I actually make up some of my prototype designs and wear them myself, it's a great opportunity to try things out. This skirt for example is my own work."

"How marvellous, I just adore that style. I'm so tempted to ask you to measure me up."

Libby realised this was not going to be a simple assignment. The magazine that she was writing for wanted a single article, but clearly it was far more complicated than that. She would have to sit down with the editor and work something out.

When she broached the subject of celebrity weddings, Emilia was very discreet. She was willing to discuss general arrangements but would not disclose personal details or give Libby the names of her clients. She was however interested in meeting Matt to explore the possibilities of using his photographic services.

Chapter Three

STEALING THE CASE FROM THE airport had been an easy task. He knew that it contained technical equipment but when he opened the lid, he was surprised at the quality of the cameras inside. He knew nothing about photographic equipment but could appreciate using kit like this.

Prising a camera carefully from its resting place, he weighed it in his hand. It was reassuringly heavy, the cold hard casing familiar to his touch. It reminded him of a weapon, but this was an infinitely more powerful tool. It was designed to capture a moment in time and hold onto it forever.

Tucked into one of the pockets he found what he was looking for, a little plastic case containing memory cards. These should tell him everything that he wanted to know.

Booting up his computer he waited patiently as it ran through its start up program then inserting the first memory card, images began to appear on the screen. These were mostly pictures of models parading the latest fashions, but he studied them carefully in an effort to identify their location. He wanted to know where Cunningham had been and whom he worked with. Ejecting the card, he inserted the next. Many of the girls featured were the same only wearing different costumes. A number of the photographs had been taken in a studio. He made a note, he would have to find out where that was located. Did Cunningham own it himself or did he work with others?

Matt completed manipulating the first of Veronique's photographs and looking intently at the screen he nodded with satisfaction. Libby had been right, Veronique seemed to have a natural flair for photography. He had no idea of her history; perhaps she had studied the subject. He smiled then getting to his feet stretched his arms above his head. The muscles across his shoulders and neck were beginning to ache, this was an occupational hazard associated with staring for too long at a computer screen. Suddenly he heard the front door open.

"Matt," the sound of her voice drifted up into the stairwell. "Are you there Matt?"

He stepped out onto the landing.

"There you are," she said shrugging off her coat. "How are you getting on, did Veronique send you her photographs?"

"Yes she did," Matt replied as he made his way down the stairs. "I'm just going to make a cup of tea, would you like one?"

"That would be lovely." She kissed his cheek before squeezing past.

"How was your interview with Emilia Sykes?"

"Her shop is absolutely amazing." Libby enthused then she told him all about it.

"You intend to write a series of articles?" He glanced at her over his shoulder. "I thought you were supposed to be presenting your editor with a double pager including glossy images."

I couldn't possibly do Emilia justice with a single feature," she explained. "Her business is far too complex."

They carried their tea up to their office and the moment she sat down Libby began to sort out her notes. She wanted to draw together her ideas while still fresh in her mind, she also intended to come up with a plan before taking it to her editor. She would have to provide another interesting editorial to fill the space reserved for Emilia's article. It would be impossible to put together a proposal, convince her editor to run a series and have the first draft ready before the deadline of the next edition.

Matt was alerted to an incoming message, so moving to his computer station he cancelled the screensaver and clicked on the email icon.

"It's another message from Veronique," he said. "No images this time just a few lines." He read it through before turning towards Libby. "She has another assignment for me, this one is in Brighton and Salisbury." Pausing, he turned back to the screen. "It says here that she has a brand of beachwear and wants to do a shoot on Brighton pier. She also has some other ideas and intends to use Salisbury cathedral as a backdrop."

"Sounds interesting," Libby replied. "At least she hasn't dumped you over your incompetency." Putting her hand over her mouth, she stifled a laugh.

"That's not funny, besides Veronique adores my work."

"True," Libby mumbled once she had stopped sniggering. "Does she say when the assignment is likely to take place? It's not the best time of year to be modelling beachwear outside of the studio."

"No, but I did overhear some gossip the other day. It seems that Veronique wants to use the same girls. One of them mentioned a job in Brighton next week."

"As soon as that," Libby swivelled her chair round. "Will you be ready to go to Brighton next week? You have a lot of work to do here preparing her current portfolio."

Matt frowned and ran his fingers through his hair. "It should be okay," he replied unconvincingly, "providing nothing else turns up in the next few days."

"Emilia Sykes wants to talk to you about her celebrity wedding."

"Well, she can probably wait, that wedding is months away yet."

"Middle of August."

"Not as far away as I thought then. I'm surprised that she has not yet appointed a photographer."

"Me too, but I guess she's not too worried. Photographers will be clambering over themselves for the opportunity to cover such a high profile wedding."

Chapter Four

HOURS OF STUDYING THE PHOTOGRAPHS yielded satisfying results. These were professional images of both male and female models either on location or at some indoor venue including a photographic studio. A number of them however were quite different. These were informal snaps of architecture, country lanes and artistic arrangements of ordinary things that revealed something of the photographer's character. Several of the images caught his eye. Cunningham had a partner, a stylish woman, clearly a girlfriend of substance. They were an intimate couple that much was clear from her body language and the way she looked into the lens of the camera. The models were interesting enough, but this woman caught his imagination. Ideas began to fill his head and using the internet it was not long before he discovered more about them both.

Matthew Cunningham was a respected photographer that much he knew already. There was a website, a useful source of information, not only did it provide a profile but also an email and social network address. From this, he found out about Libby Ellis. She was a thirty two year old freelance fashion journalist and as he probed deeper, he came across the publications that she worked with. This was the information that he was looking for and by studying both Cunningham and his partner, he began to come up with a plan.

Detective Sergeant Isobel Woods was a member of the Criminal Investigation Department based at the Metropolitan Police Headquarters in the City of London. Highly respected by her colleagues, she maintained an impeccable work record and it was her goal to reach the top.

"DS Woods," Detective Chief Inspector Simon Wyman invited her into his office. "Sit yourself down."

Rhyming Simon, as he was known was the Senior Investigating Officer looking into the recent disappearance of a young woman. He was juggling several cases and needed DS Woods to join his team.

"I've already cleared it with the Chief," he told her, "so I would like you to work on this."

He pushed a slim buff coloured file across his desk. "This is all we have at the present time I'm afraid. A twenty seven year old woman by the name of

Kelly Spencer was abducted from her place of work during what appears to have been a robbery."

"The filling station," Woods said as she looked up at him. She was familiar with the incident; it was current news around the station.

"Correct, the felon got away with a lot more than just the weeks takings."

"You don't think she was in on it then?" Woods asked the obvious question.

"I don't believe so."

"There must be CCTV images."

She knew that filling stations with twenty four hour shops were likely to operate a reasonably decent security system.

"Correct again," Wyman smiled.

Opening the file, Woods studied several black and white images of a man dragging Kelly Spencer from behind the counter. She appeared genuinely terrified and Woods was satisfied that it could not have been an act.

The man was dressed in army combat fatigues, he also wore gloves and a balaclava that covered his face.

"What do we know about Kelly?" Woods asked.

"She is a single mother, a local woman who lives in a bedsit close to her place of work."

"How old is the child?"

"Almost three I believe."

"Have social services been informed?"

"No need, I visited the bedsit myself. The little boy was being cared for by a neighbour, but we managed to contact Kelly's sister who agreed to look after him until his mother returns." He reached for a sheet of typed paper before going on. "The sister's name is Caroline Ensley and her address is here."

Woods nodded thoughtfully before asking her next question.

"Where did our man leave his car?"

"He parked it out of shot. He must have done his homework, he knew exactly where the cameras were situated."

"What about forensics?"

"We haven't got their report back yet, but I don't expect there to be much."

Woods chewed at her bottom lip as she considered her next question.

"Do we have uniforms on the street?"

"Yes, officers are still carrying out door to door inquires and we have signs posted at either end of the road appealing for witnesses to come forward."

"Constable Yearsley up in surveillance could probably help. I've used his services before," she said thoughtfully.

Wyman was aware that she had been instrumental in tracking down the killer of a number of musicians recently. It had been a high profile case involving the cellist Mia Ashton.

"Can I leave this with you DS Woods? We need to get things moving. There has been no word from the abductor and given Kelly's circumstances we can probably rule out a ransom demand."

Woods realised from bitter experience that if demands were not made within the first twenty four hours then it would most likely turn into a murder hunt.

Chapter Five

MATT PUT THE FINISHING TOUCHES to the portfolio before attaching it to an email. Libby had been right, the photographs that Veronique Moreau had sent to replace the ones he had lost were remarkably good. Her work contained elements of artistic expression and she had made clever use of light. The images were crisp and clear and once digitally enhanced it was almost impossible to tell they were not his own.

Suddenly his computer alerted him to an incoming message, it was Veronique again with details of his next assignment. Quickly he scanned the email, it confirmed the location, date and time. He would be working with the models from the Paris shoot including the French girl that had caused all the problems. He just hoped she would be a little more accommodating this time. When he had finished reading, he added a reply linking it to the message he had compiled earlier, then checking the file containing the portfolio he clicked on the send button.

It did not take long for Veronique to respond, she wanted him to make a couple of minor adjustments but it was nothing more than he expected. Usually he sent his client a file with their digitally manipulated images, these would then be used by their own editorial team when putting together a glossy publication, but with Veronique things were different. She preferred to send him the storyboards that made up the pages of her fashion magazines. He knew which images she wanted to use and she relied on him to attach them to the relevant pages. What made his job more difficult on this occasion was that some of the editorials were missing. Spaces had been set aside for the accompanying photographs but he had no idea what size images were required. He would have to make an educated guess and leave it to others to make adjustments later when going through the editing process.

"Would you like a cup of tea Matt?" The sound of Libby's voice drifted up the stairs.

"Yes please," he replied.

A few moments later, she appeared at the door carrying two steaming mugs.

"All finished?"

"Yes," Matt nodded. "Just replied to Veronique's request for changes."

"She was pleased then?"

"So it seems. I've had a lucky escape, don't you think?"

"Lesson learnt I hope." Libby shot him a lopsided smile and holding onto her mug, blew gently across the surface of her tea. "You won't make that mistake again."

He looked at her and grinned ruefully.

"Have you been onto the insurance company about your missing cameras?"

"Yes," he rolled his eyes. "They want copies of all the paperwork including details of the claim I intend to make against the airline."

Libby grimaced and sipped at her tea.

"Don't forget about this evening," she said, looking at him sideways. She knew that it would have slipped his mind. "Raymond Duval's."

"Oh yes of course, the French restaurant. No I haven't forgotten," he lied.

She stared at him for a moment before saying. "I've got my outfit organised. The venue is a bit upmarket, so I hope you intend to make an effort."

She knew that left to him he would probably turn up in jeans and a jumper. They had never been to this particular restaurant before but it had great reviews and Libby was looking forward to spending a romantic evening with Matt, besides, she had something important to discuss with him.

"I'm off to Brighton on Monday," he told her. "Veronique has just sent confirmation."

"How long will you be gone?"

She knew that he would stay on location. It would be impossible to commute given the unsociable hours that he would be expected to work.

"Three days as planned providing all goes well."

He logged onto a social media website and typed in her name then searching methodically through the list he found what he was looking for. Libby Ellis had a profile page, it was not set to private so scrolling through the details, he discovered more about her. Most of the articles on her page were work related, it was a professional platform from which to promote her business. Her biographical section was interesting and featured a selection of images. He recognised Matthew Cunningham, but was not particularly interested in him just yet.

Working through the website he found a link to a social media site then clicking on it was redirected. More photos appeared and glancing through some of the comments, he came across something that caught his attention. It never ceased to amaze him just how much personal information people would post in a public forum. It seemed that she would be attending a restaurant later that evening. Looking past the computer screen he stared up at the wall and his eyes narrowed. He knew the restaurant and its location, he also knew exactly what he was going to do.

Reaching for one of the cameras, he fitted the lens and peered through the viewfinder then, he studied the panel of buttons on the casing and worked out how to use the long distance night setting facility. Turning back to his computer, he touched a button on the keyboard and the image on the screen changed. He could now see what was happening in one of the cells further along the corridor. Kelly Spencer had not moved, she was still sitting cross-legged on the mattress. The plate of food he had taken in earlier remained untouched but the water bottle was almost empty. The tiny surveillance camera in the corner of the cell provided a surprisingly clear image; its wide angle lens covering most of the room. Luckily, it was too small to be noticed, almost invisible against the bare concrete wall. He smiled as he stared at the woman. Perhaps it was time to pay her another visit.

Chapter Six

DS Woods made what she hoped would be her last phone call of the day. She had worked beyond her shift and although the hour was late, someone would probably still be there to answer her call.

"All done," was the reply to her request. "We can send it over to you first thing in the morning."

"Any chance of emailing me a copy now?" If her request was honoured it would probably mean her staying even later.

A few minutes later, it arrived in her mailbox and opening up the file, she skimmed through its contents. The prints lifted from the garage where Kelly Spencer worked were not a match for anyone on their system. She knew the abductor was wearing gloves that much was clear from the CCTV images so no surprises there. SOCO did however manage to pick up fibres that came from standard army issue fatigues, but this was not much use to her. Clicking on another image, she found details of a size eleven boot print found behind the counter. This could not belong to Kelly.

The report was detailed, revealing more about the footprint pattern. There was hardly any wear on the sole, so the boots must be new. Had they been purchased recently or simply not seen much use? Pictures of footwear associated with that particular sole pattern were included, these resembled the type of boot used by the military. There was also a list of high street outlets where footwear like this could be found. These would have to be checked, if a pair of size elevens had been sold within the last few weeks and a card was used to make the purchase then she could get details of the owner. Equally, they could have been bought on-line. She had seen enough so closing down her computer, Woods reached for her bag and left her office. There was nothing more that she could do until the morning.

Libby and Matt arrived at Raymond Duval's restaurant and were shown to their table in a romantic alcove lit by candles. Libby was enchanted and glancing around, could not stop smiling. This was everything that she imagined and more. She had heard great things about this place but nothing could prepare her for the greeting they received at the door and the relaxed ambience of the restaurant.

"This is so lovely," she purred breathlessly.

A waiter, hovering unobtrusively nearby held back until the right moment then he approached their table and presented them with complimentary cocktails.

"Is that a Josie MacDonald?" Matt asked and reaching for his glass, indicated towards a painting on the wall.

Libby turned to face the watercolour.

"The Cairngorms I think."

Josie MacDonald was a local artist who specialised in landscapes. Just over a year ago, she had completed a tour of the Scottish Highlands creating a number of watercolours featuring mountains and wild landscapes. Whilst in Scotland she witnessed a brutal murder at Spey Bay in Morayshire. The killer then targeted her and several of her friends leaving Josie lucky to escape with her life. The newspapers had been full of it at the time, but Libby chose not to dwell on the subject, instead she lost herself in the beauty of the painting.

"You are right," she said spotting a signature in the bottom right hand corner. "Doesn't she exhibit regularly near here?"

"Yes," Matt nodded. "She works closely with Timothy Granger. We'll have to check out his gallery, go along to one of their exhibitions."

Libby agreed then reaching for her glass took a sip before scrutinising him critically.

"You look very smart," she began. "I'm so glad you decided to wear that tie."

She had bought it the previous year for his birthday and this was the first time she had seen him wearing it. Before Matt could answer, a waiter visited their table and they made their choices from the menu.

Couples or small groups enjoying each other's company occupied the tables in the main part of the restaurant. Everyone was talking in hushed tones but occasionally the sound of laughter would rise above the soft music playing in the background.

Their meal arrived and to their delight, they experienced a wealth of tastes and textures, the wine that Matt had ordered to accompany each course was perfect. Libby was impressed, she knew that he was interested in wines but had no idea that he was such an expert.

They talked and laughed over a variety of topics during their meal but inevitably, much of it involved work. Libby wanted to talk to him about their future together and her own expectations and leaning back in her chair, she absentmindedly fingered the stem of her glass.

"I want to talk to you about something."

Matt looked up.

"We've been together now for several years," she began softly, "I'm not getting any younger."

"You're hardly an old maid," Matt told her doing his best to look serious.

"I'm thirty three years old this year and my biological clock is ticking. I want to settle down and have a family."

"Is this you telling me that you are pregnant?" Matt teased.

"No, of course not," she frowned, "but I do think it's time we thought about getting married."

Matt knew how important marriage was to her, she would never consider having a baby until he had put a ring on her finger. He was tempted to remind her that they were settled, they were buying a house together and had established their own businesses. Studying her from across the table, he could no longer keep a straight face. He loved the way she pouted with frustration and in the candlelight, she reminded him of a beautiful but spoilt child.

"Was that some kind of marriage proposal then?" He couldn't help himself. "It's not even a leap year!"

"If I wait for you to ask I will be an old maid." She glared at him sternly but was unable to hide a glimmer of humour.

"You know that I promised to take you to Paris in May."

She nodded her head but remained silent, waiting for him to continue.

"Well, I have reserved us a table in the restaurant at the top of the Eiffel Tower." Reaching across the table, he took hold of her perfectly manicured fingers. "I thought it the perfect place to propose, but if you'd rather me get down on one knee now..."

"Oh Matt," she screeched, "Paris will be perfect." Luckily, no one seemed to notice her outburst. "A promise of a proposal will have to do for now." She squeezed his fingers happily.

She was still grinning when the waiter arrived with their coffee. She was amazed at how things had turned out, she expected Matt to come up with all kinds of objections. Although their conversation had not gone quite as planned, she had the result that she wanted and could almost feel the engagement ring on her finger.

Raymond Duval appeared. Having finished in the kitchen it was his custom to mingle with his guests and share a nightcap or two.

"Mademoiselle, Monsieur, good evening." He greeted them warmly as he approached their table.

Libby was enchanted, Raymond made her feel like the most important woman in the room.

"Our meal was simply amazing," she told him. "For us this is a very special occasion."

Raymond moved closer eager to hear more.

"You are too kind," he smiled, "my little restaurant is made special by young lovers such as yourselves."

His French accent drove her wild and she couldn't resist telling him about their plans.

"Magnifique!" Raymond threw his hands into the air and danced on the spot. "Paris is such a romantic city, the perfect place for people to express their love for each other. The Eiffel Tower eh, a good choice Monsieur."

He shook Matt's hand vigorously before turning to Libby then he kissed her gently on both cheeks continental style.

"Champagne," he said stepping away from their table. "We should all have champagne."

To their amazement, Raymond ensured that everyone in the restaurant had a glass then he got them up on their feet before proposing a toast to the happy couple. Libby's cheeks burned but she was overjoyed at his generosity. She couldn't have planned for a more perfect evening.

They emerged from the restaurant and hidden in his car he raised the camera and steadied it against the window before taking a round of quick fire snaps. A taxi was waiting for them so he decided to follow and half an hour later, it stopped outside their home. Driving past slowly, he smiled. He now knew where Libby Ellis lived.

Chapter Seven

"DS WOODS." SHE SPOKE TO the sales assistant as she entered the shop and reaching into her pocket, produced her warrant card.

"Good morning, I'm Steph, Stephanie Potts." The young woman responded calmly, quite unfazed by the appearance of a police officer. "How can I help you?"

"I understand that you sell this type of boot."

Pulling a colour print from her folder, Woods placed it on the counter between them.

"Yes we do," Stephanie nodded her head. "We keep them in stock because they are a very popular line."

This was more promising. The first two shops that Woods had visited were unable to help.

"Have you sold any recently?"

"I'll have to check on the system, but I should think so." Turning towards the computer Stephanie began typing on the keyboard. "Everything that goes through the till is recorded on here," she explained.

Columns began to appear on the screen but from where she was standing Woods found it impossible to read.

"Ah, here we are a pair of size nine brown boots sold last Wednesday." Stephanie looked up triumphantly.

"No," Woods grimaced. "I'm looking for a pair of black boots, size eleven."

Turning back to her screen Stephanie continued her search.

"Several pairs were sold last month," she said over her shoulder," but not in that size. We usually see an upsurge in boot sales especially when the weather turns nasty. Ah, a pair of black size elevens, sold on the twenty first of January."

"That's almost two months ago," Woods replied thoughtfully. "Was it a cash or card transaction?"

Glancing back at the screen Stephanie said. "The customer paid by credit card."

Woods smiled, she was hoping for a paper trail that would lead her to the abductor.

"I don't suppose you remember making the sale?"

Stephanie looked at her and laughed. "I can hardly remember the day before yesterday let alone two months ago." She checked the calendar kept beneath the counter. "The twenty first was a Saturday, we have a lot of customers in at the weekend."

"Do you have CCTV footage for that day?"

"I doubt it, not for January." Reaching for the telephone, she continued. "I can check with my boss."

Woods nodded but was certain of the outcome. Shops like this would probably only keep a thirty day record, that much she had learnt from working with PC Yearsley.

Gathering up her notes, she thanked Stephanie.

"I'll leave you my card, if you remember anything please don't hesitate to call me."

She realised this was unlikely. The purchaser had chosen the busiest day of the week to visit the shop, safety in numbers she thought as she headed for the door.

Walking back to where she had left her car, Woods arranged her thoughts. She would have to telephone the credit card company but decided to leave that until she was inside her car, the noise on the street was deafening.

The details that she needed were on the copy of the till receipt, but she wanted more information. Using her phone, she logged on to the internet and found the website that she was looking for. It was several minutes before she made the phone call but the person she was talking to was reluctant to release information without proof of her identity. Although standard procedure, it was frustratingly time consuming so Woods reminded them that she was conducting a police investigation.

"Could you please email me a copy of the paperwork?" she asked before ending the call.

Starting her car, Woods hoped that by the time she returned to her office the information would have arrived.

The train pulled into Brighton station and the crowds of people milling about never ceased to amaze him, it was almost as busy as Victoria. Leaving the platform, Matt made his way down the hill heading for the seafront. His hotel was just a short walk from the pier and he wanted to check in and dump his bags before running into Veronique Moreau. He was intending to get some shots of the pier and the arches along Madeira Drive. The light was perfect so he should make the most of the good weather but he did not get far before a taxi pulled up at the kerb beside him.

"Matt." A young woman called to him through the open window. "I thought it was you, we must have been on the same train from London."

Charley Baker was one of the models that Veronique liked to employ. She had been part of the team in Paris and he had worked with her many times before.

"Would you like a lift? I guess that we are both heading for the same hotel."

Not wanting to appear rude, Matt reached for the door handle and Charley slid across the seat. He would rather have walked, he loved browsing the little individual shops in the Lanes.

"Okay, thanks," he said climbing in beside her.

"How did the shots turn out from the Paris trip?" she asked casually as the taxi pulled away.

Matt told her that everything was complete and Veronique had some brilliant images for her magazine. He chose not to tell her about the work he had lost.

"I think this assignment is for a different magazine," she told him.

Matt was aware that Veronique owned or was at least part owner of several magazines. The last assignment was for one of her boutique publications, but the objective of this photo shoot was to produce resources for a fashion magazine.

"I take it that both Melissa and Pascale will be working with us again?" Matt asked in a conversational tone.

"Yes," Charley nodded enthusiastically. "Mel is already at the hotel, she texted me earlier, but I don't know about Pascale."

The French girl was not a popular member of the group.

"She may well be travelling with Veronique seeing as they are both coming from France."

Secretly Charley was Matt's favourite. Pascale may be the prettiest but she lacked the social niceties that the other girls possessed. At first, he thought it was because she did not speak English very well, but he was wrong, she was aloof and often quite rude.

"I hope the French contingent will be on their best behaviour," Charley murmured and Matt laughed. They both knew how difficult Veronique and Pascale could be.

"You don't think they are related do you?"

This time they laughed together.

The taxi pulled up outside the hotel and Melissa Miles ran out to meet them. Holding her luscious hair back from the chilly sea breeze, she shrieked a greeting as Charley appeared.

"Let's get you booked in," she said holding onto her friend's arm then she continued excitedly. "I'm eager to get into town. It's been a while since I was last in Brighton."

Matt following on behind couldn't help but notice the admiring looks the two young women got from several male onlookers.

Chapter Eight

THE MORNING STARTED WELL FOR DC Woods, but the moment she returned to her office events took a downturn. Waiting on her desk was a note informing her that DC James would be joining her, he was her least favourite colleague. She had worked with him before on the murdered musician's case. Her good friend DI Terry Ashton had led the hunt for the killer until his daughter Mia Ashton became a target. James's loyalty became compromised when certain accusations were made about Ashton and his daughter and Woods found it difficult to forgive him for that.

The second blow of the day came when she turned on her computer and logged onto her emails. A message from the finance company told her that the card used to purchase the boots had been stolen that same day. A man named Montague Holmes reported the theft to a police station in north London and attached was a crime reference number. Accessing the system, Woods found the file and read the incident report. On the afternoon of January twenty first Mr Holmes reported the theft of his wallet containing his driving licence, credit cards and a small amount of cash. It was removed from his coat pocket whilst it hung over the back of a chair in a cafe. A station sergeant, whose reference was also attached, had taken the short statement.

Woods sat back in her chair and let out her breath. It would have been too much to hope for, Kelly Spencer's abductor using his own credit card to make the purchase. Reaching for a pen, she jotted down Mr Holmes details. He would have to be interviewed again, but it was unlikely to yield a result so not wanting to waste her own time, she decided to delegate the job to DC James.

Libby was missing Matt already. She had dropped him off at Victoria station earlier and was now on her way to a lunchtime meeting. Matt had only just returned from an assignment in Paris and now he was off again. The previous evening however had been perfect and now she had something to look forward to. She could hardly believe it when Matt had not only promised to take her to Paris, but he was going to propose as well. This was her dream come true.

Pulling at the door to the department store, she turned to smile at a man wearing an army camouflage jacket. Reaching out he held the door open for her then, as she went towards the escalator, she failed to notice him just a few paces behind.

Julia Peters was a brightly dressed young woman who could not resist the temptation of a cream cake and today was no exception. Licking her sticky fingers, she sighed contentedly and reached for her teacup. The moment Libby appeared Julia raised her hand and began to wave vigorously above her head.

"Julia," Libby said as she approached the table. "It's lovely to see you again."

Shrugging off her coat, Libby draped it over the back of the chair before sitting down.

"I've got a large pot of tea, I hope you don't mind Earl Grey." Julia made no attempt to pour. "So, what have you got for me?" Wasting no time, she got down to business.

"As you are aware," Libby began, then reaching for the pot she filled her own teacup. "I went to see Emilia Sykes at her shop White Lace and Promises and carried out an initial interview but I really can't see how we can do her justice with just a single article." She went on to present Julia with a proposal for a three part serial.

"Your brief was to get an exclusive of the celebrity wedding that she is organising." Julia reminded her.

"I will, but at this stage she is reluctant to trust me with the details. I feel that by offering her this kind of exposure in the features section of the magazine, she will become more inclined to reveal her business."

Julia sat back in her chair and scrutinised Libby through half closed eyes.

"I suppose it could work," she said after a short pause. "This feature will obviously focus on weddings and the planning involved but do you honestly think that you can keep it going for more than one issue?"

"I'm sure we can, readers love this kind of thing." Libby began to outline the details of her proposal.

This was her pitch to secure a regular feature followed by an exclusive covering of the celebrity wedding. They could use Matt to produce the photographs, she didn't need to remind Julia that his name credited to the magazine would be quite a coup.

"You make a fair case." Julia admitted. She liked the idea especially if Matt Cunningham was willing to produce the images. "Of course I will have to put it to the committee, but you will have my full backing. What do you suggest we use in the meantime? You won't have time to put the first article together for next month's issue."

"I will have completed the preliminary draft, but you are right. We are too close to the deadline."

Libby suggested a number of alternative articles; she had several in reserve and Julia asked her to send copies of everything she had. The women continued with their meeting completely unaware that on the other side of the room a man was taking photographs of them. Checking the time on his commando style watch, he hid his camera away in his bag before getting to his feet. He would have to be on his way, he had business of his own to take care of.

Chapter Nine

THE FOLLOWING DAY THE WEATHER was perfect. The sky over Brighton seafront was cloudless, clear and blue it stretched all the way to the horizon. The only thing that marred this holiday atmosphere was the chilly breeze coming in off the sea.

Peering through the viewfinder from his spot on the pier Matt focused in on Charley and Mel. They were both wearing swimsuits and looked as if they were enjoying a day at the seaside. He would have to be quick, capture their frolicking at the water's edge before they became too cold to continue. Between shots, they kept warm with hot drinks and thick coats. The make-up team were fighting a losing battle; the wind whipped constantly at their hair and no amount of spray would keep it in place.

Pascale was talking to Veronique as they sheltered in the lee of a windbreak. Soon it would be the French girls turn to charm the lens of his camera. Today she was modelling a brightly coloured bikini that harped back to the seventies. Her only accessory was a huge floppy sunhat that required pins to keep it in place, but still she had to hold onto it as she made her way across the pebbles to the spot chosen for her session.

"This is madness, why do we have to do summer shots on a day like today?" One of the make-up girls complained.

Once they moved off the beach and onto Madeira Drive, things improved. The spaces beneath the arches offered shelter and once lit with powerful lights became as cosy as a suntrap. People gathered along the road curious to see what was going on and Matt was amazed to see Veronique happily answering all their questions. She was even willing to allow some of the spectators to take photographs of their own. This was most unusual as only official photographers were supposed to take pictures. It was not uncommon for a competitor to muscle in and expose a new range by posting images on the internet before the official release date or worse, copy the designs and use them as their own. Matt was under pressure to complete all of the outside shots by the end of the day. Tomorrow they would spend the morning in the studio before moving on to Salisbury.

It was almost time to stop for lunch and it wasn't long before one of the crew announced that he was off to buy fish and chips. They had seen a cafe further along the beach beside a crazy golf course. Tables and benches were set up on a concrete hardstanding and currently there was enough seating to accommodate the whole team.

"What is it with the English and their fish and chips?" Veronique laughed. "I thought the favoured dish these days was Indian curry."

"You are right," Matt agreed. "In London fish and chip shops are becoming a rarity."

He lowered himself down onto a bench at one of the tables and was handed a polystyrene tray piled up with food. Veronique squeezed in beside him and stole one of his chips.

"Good work this morning," she said, "we did well. Most of what I need is done so an hour or two is all that's required to complete the day."

Matt raised his eyebrows as he popped a hot chip into his mouth.

"The girls are working well together despite this biting wind." Veronique continued, as she linked her fingers around a steaming cardboard coffee cup.

"We have been lucky," Matt agreed.

The weather in Paris had been dull the previous day when Veronique boarded the Eurostar but now looking up at the blue sky overhead she smiled. They discussed the previous job including the technical changes they had made to the photographs and script before it went to print. Neither of them mentioned the work that was lost, Veronique was clearly relieved that they achieved everything she required for her magazine.

Looking away Matt studied the pier, it was magnificent in the afternoon sun. Libby would love it here he thought and he wondered what she was doing now. She would either be working in their office or out to lunch with a client. He realised that he had no idea of her schedule, so wrapped up in his own work he had little time for anything else. Suddenly he felt guilty at not taking more interest in what she was doing.

"What are you thinking about?" Veronique touched his arm lightly. "You look so sad."

"No not sad," he replied and turning to face her, he told her about the trip he was planning with Libby.

"The restaurant at the Eiffel Tower is very good," Veronique nodded approvingly, "but you are obliged to reserve a table well in advanced. It is a very popular venue. If you have a problem be sure to let me know."

Matt realised that she probably knew the owner.

They went back to work and within a couple of hours were done. Matt had all the shots that Veronique needed and the models were happy to get back to the hotel and soak in the warmth of a hot bath.

On the pier, a man was peering through the viewfinder of a professional looking camera. He was amazed at the quality of the view, the girls he focused on looked as if they were just a few metres away. He recognised them from the pictures he had seen on the memory cards and holding the camera steady, he took a few shots of his own. The models were not the only people he was interested in, he also took pictures of Veronique and Matt.

DS Woods looked up from where she was sitting as DC James bowled into her office, he didn't bother to knock. Blinking at him with tired eyes her mind was elsewhere, not only was she working on the disappearance of Kelly Spencer, but she also had a number of other problems to solve.

"Nothing much to report," James began. "Mr Montague Holmes was unable to give me any more information. He doesn't remember seeing anyone suspicious at the cafe on the morning his wallet was stolen."

Woods nodded and chewed at the end of her pen. There had been no word of the abducted woman and talking to her sister Caroline Ensley, had revealed very little. She confirmed that Kelly was not currently involved in a relationship and could think of no one who would want to harm her. The father of her child was not on the scene, he was working abroad and had no contact with either Kelly or their son.

"It looks like this abduction was completely random," Woods sighed. "Kelly was simply in the wrong place at the wrong time." She dropped her pen onto her desk before going on. "The CCTV report that I requested from PC Yearsley also failed to come up with anything. The man we are looking for is as cunning as a fox."

James smiled and sat down wearily.

"I've been going through some of the old records looking for similarities, but all we have to go on is a boot impression and army camo gear. Our man must either be a retired serviceman or has a fetish for army clothing."

"Maybe he wears that stuff because it suits his line of work. He probably thinks it makes him appear anonymous."

Woods was tempted to look up all the Army and Navy stores in the area, but what good would that do. The man they were looking for had probably not purchased his clothing recently, he may have had it for years. If he was a retired serviceman it could even have been issued to him.

"Talk to the owner of the filling station again. I want to know why his place was targeted. We also need to find out who Kelly saw regularly, where she went on a daily basis and who her friends are," pausing she took a breath and frowned. "She doesn't seem to socialise much, but there must be someone that she is close to."

"Her neighbour looks after the child when she is working a shift." James said but Woods knew this already. "She told me that Kelly rarely has visitors to her flat, not even her sister."

"It seems that the two of them are not particularly close."

"Perhaps you are right," James glanced up at her. "Look, maybe there is no connection. The guy who took her planned to rob the service station. It could be that Kelly gave him a hard time so he decided to teach her a lesson."

Woods shook her head. "I can't accept that, he must have planned the whole thing. You can't just take someone against their will, he would have prepared a secure holding place first. If she is being held close by then someone must know about it."

"Perhaps she is dead and we just haven't found the body yet."

Woods glanced at him but made no comment.

Chapter Ten

CLIMBING TO HER FEET, KELLY walked around the tiny room again. She hated it, the air was cold and damp, it smelled musty and old and reminded her of a prison cell. The walls, once painted white were now peeling, the grey plaster beneath showing through. In the corner was a stainless steel toilet and hand basin, en-suite facilities that thankfully still functioned. Above that was a tiny barred window. It was little more than a slit in the wall, a narrow strip of glass covered in years of grime offered little in the way of light, but at least it offered a sense of time.

The door was a solid mass of sheet metal and rivets, clearly designed as an impenetrable barrier. A slot served as an access point and when the cover was pulled back, plates of food or water bottles could be passed through. It also provided a window for communication although to her dissatisfaction this was mainly one way.

It seemed strange that he should leave her bottles of water. The hand basin had a cold tap, but perhaps the water was not for drinking. She did her best to maintain basic hygiene but was in desperate need of a change of clothes. Kelly had no idea who was doing this to her. At first, she thought it a misunderstanding and she would be released when he realised that he had kidnapped the wrong person. She had no money and there would be no one willing to pay a ransom. He refused to answer her questions, in fact, the only time that he had communicated with her was to explain what would happen if she failed to do as she was told.

Sitting down on the mattress, she thought again of Callum her little boy and the same questions ran mercilessly through her head. Who was looking after him and what must he be thinking. A deep sadness weighed heavily against her chest, but her tears failed to flow. She had already cried them all away.

Swallowing noisily, she stared at the plastic bag on the floor. It contained a single apple, the last of her supplies. It seemed a long time ago that he had passed them through the hateful slot in the door. Kelly frowned and biting at her bottom lip attempted to count the days. She had lost all sense of time, the filthy little window did its best to remind her, but it was in vain. She was frightened and tried hard not to imagine the consequences of being stuck in this God forsaken place.

He stopped just outside Brighton at a superstore. He was aware that the others had gone to Salisbury the previous afternoon. This much he had discovered from studying a social media site, but he had little interest in following them. He had what he came for.

Going into the store, he inserted the memory card from the camera into the photograph processing machine and selected the images that he wanted before hitting the print button. It was all too easy he thought. People were basically stupid, easy to manipulate, in fact he could make them do anything that he wanted.

With the newly printed photographs in his hand, he went in search of the stationary section where he picked up a pack of envelopes. Next, he purchased a book of postage stamps before returning to his car. Going through the images, he studied each one in turn anticipating the reaction they might have. They were harmless enough, but would have the desired effect.

The address label was already printed so reaching for the document case on the passenger seat beside him, he found what he was looking for. Next, he slipped the photographs into an envelope before attaching the label and a stamp then he left his car for a second time. Retracing his steps, he went to the entrance where he had seen a post box.

The weather in London was not so good, the sky was grey and thick with clouds and rain soaked the pavements. Peering out of her window Libby sighed miserably. Her thoughts never far from Matt, she had called him earlier that morning and he reassured her that although overcast, Salisbury was dry. Luckily, rain had not yet reached that part of the country.

The feature that she was working on was going well and she had arranged to meet up with Emilia Sykes for a second interview. During their initial conversation, Emilia had answered all of her questions and Libby promised to send her a copy of the first draft. Turning away from the window, she pressed the send button on her computer keyboard and fulfilled her promise.

Julia had decided on a feature for the next edition of her magazine. This was to replace the piece that she was asked to produce on celebrity weddings. A fifteen hundred word composition called 'Second Time Around' was perfect. Interestingly it profiled the fashions that women chose to wear when marrying for a second time. They had discussed the piece at length and there were a just few minor changes that Julia wanted to make. She also wanted Matt to check his stock of images and come up with something they could use.

An hour later and the changes had been made. Libby drafted up an accompanying email, included a couple of images of her own before sending it. Julia would have no idea that Matt had not produced them himself and it wouldn't be until the magazine was published and the credits announced that all would be revealed. Suddenly an email appeared in her mailbox. It was from Emilia. Her feedback was positive she liked what she saw. She also said that she was looking forward to their meeting the following day.

Chapter Eleven

THE RAIN ARRIVED IN THE early afternoon. At first, it was a fine mist, which soon developed into something more substantial. They had already modelled the evening wear in the make shift studio that had been set up at the hotel and Matt, who had got up early, managed to capture a number of shots of the cathedral before the weather closed in. He now had most of the elements he needed to work with on the computer. If they were forced to abandon the shoot then all would not be lost. It was amazing what could be achieved with digital manipulation.

The models were huddled together beneath a collection of huge umbrellas in the shadow of the cathedral. The attention from hair and make-up artists was constant, this was the third costume change of the day and with each outfit, a new look had to be created. The girls looked stunning, but it was a time consuming process.

Charley was the first to appear in front of the camera and stepping carefully onto the tiny dais sheltered from the elements she smiled at Matt. This would be her final session of the day.

"We have a problem," she said as she struck her first pose.

Moving from behind his camera, Matt eyed her critically.

"Do I need to ask?"

Charley rolled her eyes before tossing her head and staring seductively into the lens. Working quickly, Matt made a few adjustments before capturing the pose.

"Pascale is playing up." Charley moved into another position then placed her hands on her hips.

On the next pose, she informed him that Veronique was attempting to humour the French girl. Matt sighed and studied Charley again. She was very good at her job and hardly needed his input. Pascale by comparison was an amateur who resented being told what to do. Working with her could be a frightful experience and often a long drawn out process, but with the weather closing in, time was not on their side and tempers were in danger of being frayed.

Melissa was up next and the contrast between her and Charley was remarkable. Together out on the town it would be hard to tell them apart, but here in front of the camera their individual styles were evident. Melissa was also a professional model but there were times when she needed guidance. She appreciated his prompts and a kind word went a long way. She liked Matt and enjoyed working with him. She loved to tease the camera and secretly hoped that Matt liked what he saw. She knew of course that it was his job to flirt with all the girls, but she liked it all the same.

"Lovely Mel," he approved then lowering his voice seductively, he said. "Shock me with your sensuality."

This time her smile was genuine as she tossed her magnificent tresses and pouted woefully for him.

The target readers would hardly appreciate the work that went into producing these glossy images. It was Matt's job to draw their attention to the evening wear, but it was also the clever use of accessories that helped set them apart. This of course included the skills employed by the models and the illusion they created.

Finally Pascale appeared. She looked gorgeous and again quite different from the others. Striking her first pose, she lost her frown replacing it with a smile that lit up her face. Her eyes smouldered mysteriously and her small teeth were just visible as she parted her perfectly painted lips. Veronique watched her every move, determined not to allow this girl to spoil the shoot. The weather was becoming worse and she wanted to finish up as soon as possible.

Whatever Veronique had said to Pascale worked. The girl moved seductively and with passion and did everything that Matt asked of her without complaint. There was a moment when he thought it would all go wrong, but Veronique would have none of it. When at last the final shots were taken, she smiled with relief and called an end to the session.

Chapter Twelve

STANDING OUTSIDE THE HOUSE WHERE she lived he waited for her to appear. It was odds on that she would have to go out at some point so he kept watch. He was beginning to learn her routine; whenever she went into the city, she used public transport. It was far easier to travel around London by bus or train. He had scouted the roads earlier, searching for surveillance cameras. There were plenty situated along the main road, but here in a nice area like this there was little use for electronic security. There were however, plenty of neighbourhood watch signs on display and he realised that curtain twitching was likely if a stranger was detected. Sensibly, he left his car some distance away, an unidentified vehicle in the street would certainly raise suspicions.

Cunningham must have remained in Salisbury over night, he thought shifting his weight from foot to foot. Who could blame him, he grinned lecherously, surrounded by so many beautiful women opportunities were bound to come his way.

Suddenly she appeared and easing back into the shadows, he watched as Libby closed the door firmly behind her. Descending the short flight of steps to the pavement, she turned right and walked quickly towards the end of the street. He waited for a moment then checked left and right before emerging from his hiding place.

At the main road she paused, waiting for the traffic to pass she stepped off the pavement and headed for the tube station. It would be easy to take her, he could move in at any time but that was hardly the point of the game. He liked to watch them first, build up a picture of their daily routine, learn as much as he could about his prey before pouncing. It was surprising what he could discover about people's lives. The woman he had taken from the filling station had no idea how much he knew about her. He knew where her sister lived, he also knew that she had a small son, intelligence like this could be very useful.

She disappeared from view at the entrance of the tube station so increasing his pace he closed the gap between them. She was now just a short distance ahead and edging closer he was beside her by the time they arrived at the platform. An announcement informed them that the train was on time and would be arriving in just under one minute. Casually he studied her as they waited side by side and he approved of what he saw. She looked very smart and businesslike. Her hair lifted gently as the air moved through the tunnel then suddenly the train rumbled along the platform its breaks squealing noisily as it came to a stop. People spilled out the moment its doors opened then the waiting crowd surged forward. Once on the train, she took a seat but he chose to remain standing and curling his fist around the bar above his head, braced himself as the train began to move.

Thirty five minutes later they arrived at her destination. Following on behind, he observed her carefully as she rode the escalator towards the exit. She was certainly classy and he liked what he saw. From her website, he learnt that she was a successful writer, her business taking her into the world of fashion. This was probably why she was so well dressed he thought.

Leaving the main road that headed into the West End, she stepped into a side street and it was not long before she stopped outside a Georgian fronted shop. From the window display, he could see that it was a bridal shop.

"Hi," Emilia said the moment Libby appeared and dancing across the floor, she went to greet her visitor.

Today she was dressed in a 1950s sleeveless swing dress, the floral print vibrant, the pink detachable sash around her waist matching the colour of her nails and lips.

"Wow, is this another of your creations?" Libby asked as she stepped back.

"No, this one came from an on-line retro clothing shop. It's new, a reproduction I'm afraid."

Pushing his face up against a small square windowpane he watched as the women embraced. They soon disappeared into a room at the rear of the shop then stepping back, he observed the artistic window display. Marriage was not something that he had considered, but the incredibly lifelike mannequin staring back at him gave him an idea.

Three hours later and Libby was back in her office. Matt had not yet returned from Salisbury, but had telephoned earlier. He managed to get a lift with some of the lighting crew and reassured her that he would be home soon.

Libby was delighted with her second interview, now she had enough material to complete the next instalment that she was working on. Emilia Sykes had been less guarded this time and seemed happy to tell her more about the celebrity wedding. She even told her that her brother Ben was due home soon from a short break in Europe. He was responsible for coordinating the weddings and Emilia promised that he would tell her about his role in the company when he returned. He would have to get permission from the celebrities involved before their names could appear in her article.

Libby was certain that she had guessed their identities but decided to say nothing.

The letterbox flap on the front door rattled followed by a dull thud as mail hit the doormat. Getting to her feet, Libby went down stairs. It was time to put the kettle on so going into the kitchen she sorted through the letters separating hers from Matt's. It was mainly statements and bills but there was also a white envelope addressed to her. Exploring it with her fingertips, she slipped her thumb under the flap and tore it open. Tipping out the contents several photographs spilled onto the worktop and she frowned, there was no accompanying note. Going through them carefully, Libby studied the pictures. Some of them featured Matt and Veronique at the photo shoot in Brighton. Putting these to one side, she turned to the others. There were shots of her and Matt leaving the restaurant they had been to just a few days before. There were even photographs of her and Julia at the cafe where they held their meeting. Turning away, she reached for the kettle. It had just boiled so pouring hot water onto a teabag waiting in a mug she added a splash of milk. What was this all about she thought, why would someone take these pictures and send them to her?

The sound of the front door opening startled her and she almost spilled her tea.

"Hello, Libby."

Matt's voice cheered her so abandoning her mug she moved quickly along the hallway and hugged him tightly.

"Wow, what's all this?" he asked delighted at the reception.

"I've missed you so much."

"I've only been gone a few days," he replied staring at her lovingly.

"I know," she groaned, "but it seems like you have been away for ages. No sooner had you returned from Paris then you were off again."

Holding onto her, he nuzzled her neck. "Well, I'm home now."

"Would you like some tea," she asked not wanting to let him go. "The kettle has just boiled." Taking him by the hand, she dragged him towards the kitchen.

"I would love a cup of tea, but can I take my coat off first?"

She laughed when she realised that he had not even had chance to close the front door.

"What are these?" he asked nodding towards the piles of photographs on the counter.

"I have no idea. They came in this morning's post."

Reaching for the envelope, he studied the postmark and discovered that it had been sent from Sussex the previous day.

"There was no accompanying note," she told him. "At first, I thought that someone you were working with must have sent it, but then I saw these." She pointed at the images before continuing. "Who would be taking pictures of us coming out of a restaurant?"

Matt had no idea and his frown deepened as he studied the photos.

Chapter Thirteen

MATT SPENT THE AFTERNOON WORKING at his desk. The images from the photo shoot had been downloaded from his camera automatically and now working at his computer, he was going through them critically. Those that needed editing he moved to a separate file. Luckily, most of the photographs required little or no creative retouching, but he knew that Veronique would insist on him image compositing. This involved using several photographs to create a single image. He would use his early morning shots of Salisbury cathedral and the surrounding area for this purpose. The hastily erected shelters had protected the models and their costumes but lacked dramatic backdrop, this is where his skills with photo editing came in useful. Brighton however was quite a different story. Although chilly, the cloudless sky and brilliant sunshine ensured almost perfect conditions. Flicking through the images on the screen, he studied Charley and Melissa fooling around on the beach. It was impossible to tell that it was not a scorching bank holiday weekend in August.

Libby, with her back to him was also working. The sound of her fingers dancing over the keyboard confirmed that she was composing her next instalment for Julia's magazine. The atmosphere in their office gave way to perfect working conditions. Matt loved it when they were together like this, each focused on their own projects. They shared a similar work ethic and a burning desire to succeed.

He thought about their plans to visit Paris, he knew how much it meant to Libby. She was desperate to get married and start a family. He was ready for the commitment and the responsibility of being a father, but he also realised the huge changes and sacrifices they would have to make. Secretly he would rather wait a little while longer, but Libby was right. They had been together long enough to have forged a deep and lasting relationship. He loved her dearly and would do anything for her, he was also aware that it was different for girls. What she said was true, her body was telling her to get a move on.

"What's wrong?"

The sound of her voice startled him out of his thoughts.

"Nothing," he replied almost too quickly. "Just thinking about work," he lied.

"When does Veronique want the finished portfolio. Has she allowed you sufficient time to put it all together?"

"Yes, of course. I have a couple of weeks before she will start to get jumpy."

Turning to face him, Libby smiled. She loved the phrases that he liked to use.

"What do you think about those mysterious photographs?"

"I really don't know," he replied honestly. Receiving them through the post had obviously upset her more than he realised. "They seem to have been taken using a good quality camera," he continued, "but the paper they are printed on is nothing special."

"Do you think we should tell someone about them?"

"Tell who, the police?"

He watched as a shadow of worry invaded her face.

"What could the police do?"

He was right, a crime had hardly been committed.

"We may have a stalker," Matt realised that she needed reassuring. "Perhaps it would be a good idea to be a little more vigilant when we go out."

"Yes," she nodded, but deep down she felt that something was very wrong.

Changing the subject, she told him about her meeting with Julia who was interested in accepting a series of articles about Emilia Sykes. This was in addition to the piece that she was supposed to be writing on the celebrity wedding.

"It should keep me busy for a while," she smiled triumphantly. "Julia even wants to use some of my stock articles so now it seems I have a regular slot in her magazine *Fashion Today*."

"I don't know how you do it," Matt laughed. "The poor woman asks you for an article and you come out with a series."

"Well," Libby shrugged, "who knows how long it will last. I'm quite happy to take on as much as I can get."

"And why not?" Matt agreed. "Make a name for yourself while you can."

They were both aware of how difficult it could be in their line of work. Editors were always on the lookout for the next best thing and there was the constant risk of being knocked into obscurity by an up and coming young writer.

Caroline Ensley left her flat pushing the buggy occupied by her nephew Callum Spencer. From the front seat of a car parked across the road a man with a camera was busy taking shots. Caroline, quite unaware, walked hurriedly past heading in the direction of the park but little Callum could see what was going on. The man inside the car was dressed like one of his soldiers but instead of a rifle, he was pointing a camera at them.

Chapter Fourteen

SLOWLY HIS PLAN WAS COMING together. Most of the elements were in place, but he was becoming impatient, growing tired of watching and waiting. He wanted some action. His only error was his timing, perhaps he should have waited before abducting the first girl. He was not worried about the authorities, he had been careful but the woman was a liability. She needed maintaining and would have to be ready to carry out his orders, but then a few weeks in solitary confinement should make her more pliable.

Moving along the corridor, he studied the bare brick walls. It had been years since they had seen a coat of paint, this place reminded him of an underground facility in Afghanistan where troops were held prisoner by rebels. Those had been desperate days so pushing these unwelcome memories aside, he stopped at the cell door and opened the flap.

Kelly Spencer was curled up on the mattress but she jumped to her feet the moment he appeared.

"What do you think you are doing," she screamed, "leaving me for days on end without proper food and fresh water?"

That was not true, he had provided sufficient apples to keep her from starving. Ignoring her outburst, he pushed the plate of readymade stew through the slot.

"Why am I being kept here like this?" Pressing her face up against the door, she glared at him. "My clothes are disgusting, I need to change them."

"Take them off and I'll see they are washed."

Snatching the plate, she turned away and inhaled deeply. This was the first decent food she had seen in days and the rich aroma made her stomach rumble in anticipation.

"You're wrong if you think I'm going to hang around here naked while you wash my clothes. Provide me with something else first."

He stared at her, she was beginning to annoy him with her demands. She definitely needed to be taught a lesson but now was not the time. Slamming the cover back into place, he turned and retraced his steps along the corridor.

The following morning Matt was up early. He was determined to get ahead with his work. Once Veronique had selected the images she wanted to feature in her magazine she would expect him to help with the editing process.

"Breakfast is ready." Libby called from the bottom of the stairs.

She had agreed to make tea and toast while he worked but insisted on him eating at the kitchen table. She hated having empty plates and crumbs left all over the desktops in their office.

"Thank you," he said as he sat down and biting into his toast his head was still full of photo editing but Libby would soon change that.

"Are you working in the office today?" he asked.

"No, this morning I have to see Julia. I emailed her some stuff last night and now she wants to discuss it with me."

"Can't she do that over the telephone?" Matt scowled as he looked up at her.

"That's what I thought, but you know what she's like." Libby nibbled at her toast and chewed thoughtfully before going on. "It will probably be a complete waste of time, but it's important to keep up that customer client relationship."

Matt nodded in agreement. He knew all about that, Veronique Moreau could also be quite demanding at times.

"I should be back by mid afternoon at the latest." She paused to sip at her tea. "I thought I might check out the shops, catch up on what's being displayed in the windows."

Matt grinned, what she really meant was that she intended to go shopping so he would have the office to himself for most of the day.

"You be careful, keep your eyes open for our illusive stalker."

She knew what he was doing. By playing down the potential threat, he was hoping to put her mind at ease.

The city was as busy as usual. The weak springtime sun had managed to penetrate the gloom drawing most people out from their offices and coffee shops were doing a roaring trade. Libby swept past the security guards on the door and entered the building that housed the offices of *Fashion Today* then going to the reception desk, announced her arrival. Although now a regular face, she was still required to sign in before accessing the offices above.

"Libby," Julia exclaimed the moment the lift doors parted. "Welcome, it's so good to see you."

This seemed to be her standard greeting and Libby wondered if it was sincere or simply a mantra that she repeated to every visitor.

"I've had a look at your first draft," Julia said, leading the way into her office. A printed copy lay on her desk where she had been busy with a red pen. "Just a couple of things I need you to look at," she continued, sounding like a schoolmistress.

They discussed the article at length, clearly Julia was happy with what she saw.

"This piece goes into more detail regarding the development of the bridal shop White Lace and Promises," Julia began and Libby watched as she fiddled with the end of her pen. "It's interesting in its detail but how does it lead our readers into the world of celebrity weddings?"

"As you are aware the third and final piece will highlight the work that Emilia does in arranging weddings in general, this will allow us to deliver the full story of the upcoming celebrity wedding in the following edition."

"Okay," Julia nodded, "that works for me. We are working to a fairly tight schedule but I'm confident that you are up to speed with this." She tapped an elegantly manicured finger on the papers in front of her.

"Absolutely," Libby replied. "I have another interview arranged with Emilia later next week. Her brother Ben will be available to give me details of all the wedding packages they offer."

Julia nodded again before saying. "I've selected a couple of your other articles that I would like to use. I'll email you the details later. I have some ideas on how you might follow them up in future editions."

Libby smiled, it pleased her that Julia was thinking ahead, including her in her plans.

"Right," Julia said. "I think we are done here. Let me have the amended script back as soon as possible. The next thing we'll need to discuss is suitable images to accompany next month's piece."

"Matt is on standby," Libby assured her, but secretly was intending to produce images of her own.

He was waiting for her across the road in a stolen van. Having followed her into town, he realised that she would probably be some time at her present location, so taking a chance, he left his post in order to steal a vehicle. It had not taken him long and confident that she was still inside the building, he waited for her to appear.

Libby turned left as she stepped out onto the pavement and headed towards the shopping area. He did not expect that, the van was facing the wrong way. He cursed. He thought that she would be returning to the underground station so pulling out into the traffic, he indicated before making a U-turn. This was an illegal manoeuvre but what the heck, he was driving a white delivery van.

Moving slowly along the road, he used his powers of observation to pick her out amongst the crowds. His army training had prepared him for situations like this. Swinging into the kerb, he activated the hazard indicators then reached for the papers on the passenger seat. The people operating the CCTV surveillance cameras would probably assume he was searching for his next drop where in reality he was observing her in the door mirror.

She walked past and again he admired her. She seemed to float along the pavement, hardly needing to deviate as she avoided oncoming shoppers. Pulling away again, he drove further along the road before stopping but this time when he searched his mirror she was gone. Cursing louder this time, he realised that she must have taken the side road running between the buildings so selecting reverse, he revved the engine and backed up into the oncoming traffic. A car horn blared and someone shouted an oath but ignoring them all he turned the wheel and edged into the narrow street scattering pedestrians as he went.

She was a little way ahead so driving slowly he eased past before stopping. There were no shops here, the surrounding buildings were home to offices. There was only one surveillance camera, it was fixed to the corner of the building overlooking the junction ahead.

Pulling a baseball cap onto his head, he jumped out and keeping his head down, made his way quickly to the back of the van. She was just a few metres away when he pulled open the rear doors then, checking over his shoulder he could see they were alone. Reaching into his pocket, he gripped the hilt of a knife and slowly pulled it out, concealing it against the underside of his arm as he turned towards her.

"Excuse me love," he called out.

Libby stopped and peered at him. She could see his smile but his eyes remained hidden beneath the peak of his cap.

"I wonder if you could help me." He stepped towards her.

Libby glanced nervously at his van, parcels were stacked up neatly inside but there were no logos or markings on the side.

"I can't find my next drop," he continued holding out a piece of paper.

Instinctively she moved closer for a better look.

"Get into the van," he hissed as he grabbed her.

Libby cried out but before she could scream louder, he clamped his hand over her mouth and from the corner of her eye, she saw the blade of a knife. It was hard and cold, pressed firmly against her throat.

"Do it," he said louder this time and shoving her forward she almost lost her balance.

His arm went around her waist as he lifted her off her feet and kicking out wildly, she tried to wriggle free but it was no use. He was too strong and his knife ensured that she did as she was told. Lifting her up over the step, he threw her into the van and as she crashed into a cardboard box, he slammed his fist against the back of her head and her world went black.

Chapter Fifteen

MATT TRIED HER PHONE AGAIN but still it went to voicemail, why wouldn't she answer? It was getting late, it was almost dark outside and he was beginning to worry. Libby must have finished her meeting with Julia hours ago. Automatically his fingers worked the numbers as he dialled the editor's office but the phone just rang. They must have closed for the day.

Staring out at the courtyard garden at the back of their house he wondered what to do next, then turning away from the window he went to Libby's desk. She kept a little book with telephone numbers and a list of contact names in her drawer. Most people programmed their phones with their contacts but Libby liked to maintain a written record, she loved using a pen and adored notebooks. Opening the drawer, he found what he was looking for and flicking through the pages soon had the numbers he wanted.

"Julia, it's Matt Cunningham. Is Libby still with you?"

"Matt," Julia replied surprised to hear his voice. "No, she left my office hours ago, why what's up?"

"She hasn't come home yet and I can't seem to get hold of her," he paused before going on. "Did she say where she was going once she had finished with you?"

"No, I'm afraid not. Did she arrange to meet up with friends or something?" Julia asked trying to be helpful.

"She told me that she would be home by mid-afternoon. She did say something about having a look at the shops."

"There you are then," Julia sighed. "She has probably met up with someone and lost track of the time."

Matt frowned. It was unlike Libby to go off without leaving him a message and why wasn't she answering her phone?

"Okay Julia," he mumbled, "thanks anyway."

"Look, try not to worry. I'm sure she will turn up soon with a plausible explanation."

Matt disconnected the call and tried Libby's number again.

An hour later and he had exhausted her list of friends, none of them had heard from Libby and weighing the phone in his hand, he looked at his watch again. It was almost eight o'clock and now dark outside. He thought about the package they had received through the post. Libby was worried that someone was following them, but surely that was a crazy idea. There must be some other explanation regarding the photographs. Suddenly he felt apprehensive, perhaps she was right, maybe it was time to contact the police.

Libby's head was throbbing mercilessly. Her mouth was dry and when she opened her eyes, she could see nothing. Seized with panic she thought that she was blind then shapes began to emerge from out of the darkness. She was in some kind of room, the air was damp and cool against her skin. Struggling to sit up she discovered that her wrists were bound but what shocked her most of all was that her clothes were missing; all she had on was her underwear.

It was almost impossible to move her arms but luckily, the rope binding her wrists was not so tight that she could not wriggle her fingers. At least blood continued to circulate into her hands. She had no idea what was going on. Where was this place, who was doing this to her? Thoughts to which she had no answers whirled around inside her head and lying back in an effort to alleviate the discomfort, she groaned.

Later, the lights came on and screwing up her eyes, she tried to turn away, bury her face into the mattress but the rope binding her wrists tightened. A mechanism bolted to the ceiling whirred slowly dragging her upright. Fighting against it was no use so scrambling to her knees, she glanced around looking for something with a sharp edge. Perhaps she could cut herself free. Moments later, she was up on her feet and pulling frantically at the rope in an effort to reverse the motor but it was impossible. The winch stopped as her feet came off the ground leaving her dangling helplessly. Pain shot through her arms and across her shoulders, she cried out in agony. Suddenly he was there standing in front of her and through the fog of discomfort, she tried to focus on his face.

"Who are you," she croaked dryly. "What am I doing here?"

Ignoring her questions he stared at her approvingly then reaching out, he touched her. She tried to move away but as she wriggled, the rope tightened and she cried out again.

His hand was hot against her skin and running his fingers down over her ribs, he traced her curves until he came to her hip. His face remained expressionless as he stared at her, his deep brown eyes burning menacingly into hers.

Libby's mind was reeling with shock. It was becoming difficult to breathe. The weight of her body suspended by her arms tightened her chest and soon it felt as if her lungs were on fire. Panting, she did her best to remain calm.

He moved away and she closed her eyes with relief then she heard the sound of rapid clicking. She knew what it was immediately, he was taking photographs and when he was done, he checked the little screen on the back of the camera and smiled with satisfaction. Slowly he reached down and picked something up from the floor. It was her clothes and rolling them into a ball, he glanced at her once more before leaving. The winch above her head began to move, lowering her until her feet were firmly on the floor but then it stopped. At least now, she could breathe, support her body weight but her legs were shaking madly and she wondered how long it would be before they gave out completely.

He had answered none of her questions, in fact he had said nothing at all. Swallowing back her tears, she forced her mind to work. It must have been him who sent the photographs. Why had he done that and what did he want with her?

Chapter Sixteen

MATT WAITED FOR ANOTHER HOUR but still there was no word from Libby so shrugging on his coat, he reached for the envelope containing the photographs and left the house. He had to get out, do something positive so he decided to go into the city, trace the steps that Libby had taken earlier that day. He was also going to the police but first he wanted to see the office block where Libby had her meeting with Julia.

The building was quite unremarkable, no different from those around it and looking up he felt no connection. He was hoping to pick up something, a clue perhaps. Maybe a light would be on at one of the windows and Libby would still be there but the building was dark, cold and empty. Julia had told him that Libby left her office hours earlier but he wanted to see for himself. Moving away from the entrance Matt wandered along the pavement; Libby must have done the same as she made her way to the shops.

Stopping at a side street, he turned to peer into the darkness and shuddered at the emptiness. During the day, this place was bustling with office workers and shoppers, but now in the hours of darkness, it was gloomy and foreboding almost as if something sinister was lurking in the shadows. He shuddered, his mood taking on the atmosphere of the street then turning away, he headed deeper into the city. He was determined to report Libby's disappearance to the Metropolitan Police.

The desk sergeant took down his details and asked the nature of his visit and once he had carried out his initial assessment, he decided to pass this one up the line. Given the fact that a woman was missing and a package of photographs were involved it would need investigating further.

Detective Constable Wallis collected Matt from the waiting area and led him along a brightly lit corridor lined with empty offices and interview rooms. It was unusually quiet but in a couple of hour's time, these rooms would be alive with activity.

"Take a seat please sir," DC Wallis smiled encouragingly.

They introduced themselves and Matt told him why he was there. The detective listened carefully then reaching for his file, pulled out an official looking form and began to fill it in.

"I need to take down a few details," he said once he had written Libby's name and address. Having done this many times before he tried not to look bored or sound patronising.

"When did you last see Miss Ellis?"

Matt told him that she had left the house just after breakfast and he described what she was wearing.

"Apart from the photographs, was there anything else bothering her?"

"No," Matt shook his head. "She was in a buoyant mood and looking forward to her meeting with the editor of the magazine *Fashion Today*."

DC Wallis asked him about her work and Matt gave him the details and when they were finished, Matt checked the completed documents, reading through his statement of events.

"Now," Wallis said looking up at Matt, "what happens next is I'll go away and check our system, see if what you have told me about Miss Ellis rings any bells." He paused before going on. "In the morning if she if she is still missing, we'll need to carry out a routine search of your home and the office where Libby works. Are you happy with that Mr Cunningham?"

"Yes of course, I'll do anything to help."

"Someone will telephone to let you know when we'll be coming but don't worry," he grinned, "it won't be like a police raid, no flashing lights or battering rams. Your neighbours won't even know we are there." Gathering up his papers, he got to his feet. "I would like to hang onto these," he said indicating to the package of photographs.

When Matt arrived home just after midnight he was exhausted. The interview at the police station had upset him more than he thought possible. It seemed that something final had taken place, confirmation that Libby was actually missing and not simply detained at work. Pushing open the door, he almost expected to see her there waiting for him with a plausible explanation, but the house was empty and still. On the mat underfoot was an envelope and stooping to pick it up, he closed the door behind him before going into the kitchen. Turning the envelope over in his hand, he found no address and suddenly his stomach lurched. Tearing it open, he emptied the contents onto the work surface. Four glossy photographs spilled out and he gasped with shock. At first, his mind refused to take it in, but slowly he accepted the reality of what he could see. Libby looked terrible, her face was pale and streaked with tears, but what shocked him most was seeing her strung up by her wrists and wearing nothing but her underwear. She appeared to be some kind of dungeon. Desperately he searched the images looking for anything that might tell him where she was but the cold brick walls in the background offered no clues. The pictures were taken from different angles but each one told the same story. She was distressed and clearly in some pain. There was no evidence that she had been beaten but the fact that she was almost naked worried him immensely.

Reaching for his phone, he began to dial DC Wallis' number but then he discovered a message scrawled on the back of one of the photographs.

Go to the police and you will regret it.

The warning was clear enough and breathing deeply, Matt ran his fingers through his hair. What was going on, what had they got themselves into? With shaking hands, he slipped the photographs back into the envelope. He had seen enough and it sickened him, but he would have to remain calm, decide what to do next.

Chapter Seventeen

DS WOODS ACCOMPANIED BY DC James entered the building where Libby Ellis lived and worked. It was an ordinary 1930s semi situated in a quiet street just thirty minutes from the centre of London.

"Have you heard from Miss Ellis since you reported her missing?" Woods asked once their introductions were over.

"No," Matt shook his head sadly.

The detectives followed him into the living room where they sat down then, pulling a file from her bag, Woods went through his initial statement. She added notes of her own as they talked, all the while forming an opinion of the man they were interviewing. She believed in first impressions and on this occasion had a good feeling about Matthew Cunningham. She was convinced that he was genuine, there was nothing in the room to suggest anything other than a loving relationship. Photographs of Libby adorned the walls, professionally presented in frames or transferred onto canvas and the atmosphere was calm and welcoming.

"Could we see where Libby works?" Woods asked.

Matt led the way up to the office they shared. Woods was impressed, it was a well organised workspace. Libby's desk and computer faced the wall and going through her things, the detectives began to build up a profile of a woman who appeared to be a very capable and organised individual.

"Here is a list of Libby's contacts," Matt presented DC James with a printout.

"Does Miss Ellis keep a diary?" he asked.

"Oh yes, both electronic and a traditional diary." Reaching into a drawer Matt pulled out a journal and handed it over then turning to Libby's computer he accessed her files.

"You know her password?" Woods observed.

"Of course, we have no secrets."

James sat down and began to cross-reference the entries from the diary to those on the screen then he wrote down the names of those he would like to talk with.

"Do you need to access my computer?" Matt asked.

DS Woods was busy going through files in the cabinet beside Libby's desk. "That won't be necessary," she stopped what she was doing and looked up at him, "not at this stage of our investigation." Suddenly her phone rang and excusing herself, she stepped out of the room.

Matt could hear her clearly her voice coming from the landing at the top of the stairs.

"We are almost done here," she said before pausing briefly. "Get uniform to check it out and make sure they leave a detailed report on my desk." Finishing her call, she returned to the office. "Is there anything more that you can tell us?"

Matt thought carefully before answering. The threat he had received earlier weighed heavily on his mind but he decided to keep it to himself for the time being.

"If you think of anything else or if Miss Ellis contacts you then be sure to let me know immediately."

DC James finished what he was doing and folding the sheet of contact names into his pocket, got to his feet. "All done," he said with a nod of his head.

Matt accompanied them both to the door and thanked them before asking what happens next.

"We'll need to contact the editor of the magazine that Libby met with yesterday and I would like to talk to some of her friends."

Matt's smile failed to hide his concern.

"Try not to worry Mr Cunningham," Woods touched his arm lightly. "We'll speak again soon."

He watched as they left the house. He knew what they were, he had a nose for authority and there was no mistaking this pair. Cunningham had been warned about going to the police but clearly had chosen to ignore his threat. He would have to be shown the error of his ways. Disobedience like this would always have consequences.

DS Woods decided to let James interview Julia Peters by himself. He telephoned the editor's office and discovered that she was available to see him as soon as he could get there. Woods had other things on her mind, once she had learned a little more about Libby Ellis she would know which of her friends to approach. First, she wanted to check the files, see if there were links with other women who had disappeared recently. She was working on several cases and DCI Wyman was pressing her for a result on the Kelly Spencer abduction.

A report was waiting on her desk when she arrived back at her office. It contained the details of a stolen delivery van that was found abandoned not far from the offices of *Fashion Today*. Scanning the document quickly she put it to one side. DC James could deal with it when he returned.

He was angry and throwing himself down in front of his laptop, he activated the camera that overlooked her cell. Libby was standing with her legs slightly apart and her head slumped forward. Zooming in, he scrutinised her carefully. She had no idea that he could see her and he smiled. He thrived on having such influence over people, he was a master of manipulation and soon Cunningham would feel the force of his power. He would ensure that the photographer never disobeyed him again and looking at Libby, he knew exactly how he was going to achieve that.

The door suddenly flew open and he appeared. In his hand, he carried a camera and a short bladed knife. This was terrifying enough, but the way he looked at her almost drove her over the edge.

"Cunningham has let you down badly," he began, his voice a whisper that was barely audible. "He failed to carry out my orders so now you are going to pay the price."

The knife pierced her skin but she felt no pain, the agony of hanging by her arms for so long made sure of that. The cuts were not deep, just surface lacerations. He knew exactly what he was doing. The trick was to maximise the effect whilst causing minimum injury. It was a shock tactic designed to create the illusion of massive haemorrhaging and soon her torso and thighs were covered in nicks that would bleed profusely for a short time.

Libby clamped her eyes shut and focused on breathing. She was petrified and gasped as he carried out his hateful work. Occasionally he would stop and using his camera recorded the grisly scene.

Kelly picked up the clothes that had been pushed through the flap in the door and running her fingers over the fabric could feel the quality of the cloth. Holding the blouse up to her face, she breathed in the faint aroma of perfume. It was expensive, she knew that much and wondered where they had come from. Slipping out of her stale shirt, she shrugged on the blouse. It felt good against her skin, but was a size too large. The skirt was the same, it hung loosely over her hips but at least was an improvement on the filthy slacks that she had taken off.

From his little command centre he observed her every move. The image of her cell filled the screen and switching between cameras, he had a perfect view of both women. He left Libby sobbing but he had no choice, Cunningham had disobeyed his orders so must be taught never to do it again.

Kelly sat down on the mattress and reaching for her own clothes folded them carefully, then suddenly without warning, the door crashed open.

"Get up," he growled menacingly as he stood over her.

She followed him along the corridor to the adjacent cell. Opening the door, he stood aside and gestured for her to enter. Kelly could hardly believe her eyes. A woman was hanging by her arms, her body covered in blood and Kelly swore an oath as she took in the scene.

"Clean her up," he demanded tossing her a rag then, standing back he leaned against the wall.

At first, Kelly was unable to move. She was reluctant to touch what she believed to be a corpse. There was so much blood, the injuries looked terrifying, but then the woman groaned so moving forward she moistened the rag at the sink and gently began to sponge the wounds.

"Can you let her down?" Kelly pleaded once she had recovered from the initial shock.

Without answering, he went out into the corridor, activated the winch and watched as Kelly helped lower the woman onto the mattress.

"You are okay," she whispered encouragingly. "I will do what I can."

Kelly soon realised that the wounds were not life threatening and when the woman was more comfortable she turned to their captor and said.

"Surely you are not going to leave her like this."

"Like what?"

"With open wounds for one thing and what about her clothes?" She wanted to ask for a first aid kit or some balm to help sooth Libby's skin. She worried about the chance of infection and scarring.

"If you want to give her clothes back then feel free," he paused before going on. "Make up your mind now before you go back to your own cell."

Swallowing noisily Kelly felt awkward. It shocked her to realise that she was wearing this woman's clothes, but she was not about to take them off.

"Can you at least find her a blanket? Surely she has been humiliated enough."

He stared at her, unable to believe her concern for a total stranger. Her outburst angered him. What did she know about humiliation? A filthy cell like the one he had experienced in Afghanistan would teach her a lesson or two.

Chapter Eighteen

DC JAMES MOVED SILENTLY THROUGH the incident room where DCI Wyman was addressing his team. They were investigating a series of aggravated burglaries linked to a gangland killing so keeping his head down, he went towards the office where DS Woods was situated. The last thing he wanted was to be spotted and have his workload increased.

"Izzy," he said the moment he entered her office.

"DC James," she responded tartly, clearly not a fan of his familiarity.

"I've just got back from interviewing Julia Peters, the editor of *Fashion Today*." He told her and realising his error, went on quickly. "You'll have my written report shortly."

"Good," she nodded. "Could you have a look at this and tell me what you think."

Pulling up a chair, he sat down as she slipped a slim folder across her desk. The report contained details of the recovered delivery van and scanning the pages, he sucked air noisily through his teeth.

"The vehicle was discovered dumped not far from where it was stolen," he said reading the closely typed script. "This is also the area from where Libby Ellis disappeared."

"Coincidence?" Woods studied him intently.

"There could be a connection," he admitted. "Both incidents took place at about the same time; nothing would surprise me in a city like this."

She knew what he said was true, but they had a duty to check it out.

"We need to trace Libby's movements from the moment she left her meeting. Get PC Yearsley in surveillance to have a look at the cameras in the area. We may as well see what this van was doing in the vicinity at the same time. It should be fairly easy to spot on CCTV."

They stared at each other for a moment, both having the same thoughts.

"It's possible that this vehicle was used to abduct her," James said thinking aloud. "I'll phone PC Yearsley, give him the heads up."

It was almost an hour before James managed to visit the surveillance suite.

"Yearsley, how goes it loafing around up here?"

The young police officer was sitting in front of a bank of computer screens and he glanced over his shoulder as James appeared.

"Zeus, God of the sky looking down on mankind."

"Stupid bugger!" James replied and squatting down beside him asked. "What have you got for me?"

Yearsley typed in a command and suddenly the image on one of his screens changed.

"Here's your van," he began. "It was taken from Westminster road at eleven eighteen and twenty minutes later it stopped outside this address where it waited for twelve minutes."

James eyes widened as he recognised the building that housed the editorial offices of the magazine *Fashion Today*. Yearsley noticed his reaction and waited for an explanation.

"We are investigating the disappearance of a young woman and this is the address where she was last seen."

Running the film slowly they watched as the van drove away then it performed a U-turn in the road.

"Why carry out a manoeuvre like that?" James whispered. "Can you focus in on the entrance of that building just before the van pulled away?"

Yearsley performed his magic and the huge glass doors leading into the building appeared clearly on the screen. A moment later, Libby Ellis stepped out onto the pavement.

"That's the woman we are looking for," James said excitedly. "Can you monitor her progress?"

Making a few adjustments, Yearsley accessed a number of CCTV cameras and they tracked Libby as she made her way along the pavement. The white van appeared and pulled up at the kerb then as she drew level, it drove away only to stop again further along the road. They lost sight of Libby as she stepped into a side street then suddenly, the van reversed dangerously into the traffic before turning off the main road.

"This is more than just a coincidence," James mumbled.

Yearsley tapped busily at his keyboard in an effort to find a camera that covered the side street, but he was out of luck.

"The only camera I can find is situated at the end of the street overlooking the junction onto the main road."

They watched as the nose of the van came into view. It was stationary for almost two minutes before it took off at speed.

"Where did she go?" James leaned closer to the screen.

"We should have a view of her exiting the side street," Yearsley told him but the pathway remained empty in both directions.

"She either went into one of the buildings or was forced into that van."

"It did take off rather rapidly," Yearsley agreed.

James returned to Woods office clutching a number of printed images. She was alone when he arrived, so pushing open the door he briefed her on what he had discovered.

"Get someone round to that side street," she told him. "We need to establish if Libby Ellis visited one of the offices there."

He agreed but wondered why she didn't ask him to carry out that task.

"Do we have the van parked up in our compound?" Woods looked up at him.

James was not sure, so reaching for the telephone on her desk Woods made a quick call.

"It's been returned to its owner," she told him then regarding him thoughtfully, she continued. "Get onto the delivery company and see if we can have it back. Forensics ought to take a look."

James returned to his own desk in the incident room where he phoned the delivery company. Luckily, the vehicle was still there its undelivered load being checked. Next, he arranged for a forensics team to meet him at the depot.

Shrugging on his combat jacket, he prepared to leave the room that served as his office or command centre as he preferred to call it. He had produced the images on paper this time using his own printer. He didn't want to use a public photo printing machine, these images were far too graphic. It would definitely raise suspicion if he was seen printing them off.

He decided to take the tube, it would be easier to blend in, disappear in the crowds if necessary and an hour later he arrived at the street where Cunningham lived. Facing the house, he checked to see that it was clear before crossing the quiet suburban road then he climbed the steps leading up to the front door.

Matt was in his office when he heard the flap on the front door rattle. He frowned and glanced at the clock on the wall, the post had been delivered hours ago so getting to his feet, he went out onto the landing. Standing at the top of the stairs, he could see a white envelope on the doormat below and the hairs on the back of his neck bristled. He had received a package like this before. Racing down the stairs, he pulled the door open and looked both ways but the pavement was empty. Cars were parked along the street as usual and scanning each one carefully could see nothing out of place. Turning his back on the outside world, he stooped to pick up the envelope before returning to his office where he tore it open.

At first, the images reminded him of a side of meat hanging in a butchers shop but as he looked closer, he realised what he was looking at.

"What the hell!" he gasped and thinking that she was dead, collapsed into his chair.

It was several moments before he could look at the horrifying pictures again. Reaching out with shaking hands he touched one of the prints and shuddered then suddenly his phone began to ring. Libby's number appeared on screen and in his haste to answer the call he almost cancelled it.

"Libby," he cried.

"Not exactly," a man's voice replied.

"Who is this?"

"I warned you about going to the police."

"What. Where is Libby, what have you done to her?"

"She is still alive, it looks worse than it is."

"What do you mean?" Matt was confused and could hardly believe that he was having this conversation.

"If you want to see her again you will have to learn to do as you are told."

"Are you completely insane?" Matt shouted into the phone. "Where is she?"

"You need to calm down, her life depends on it."

"What? This is madness."

"That may be so, but she has suffered nothing yet. Believe me, I can make it a whole lot worse for her."

Matt was speechless, he wanted to smash the phone against the wall and pretend that none of this was happening.

"Do not speak to the police again and be ready to carry out my instructions. I will contact you again soon."

The line went dead.

Matt stared at the images in front of him and could hardly believe they were real. He was an expert at photo manipulation, perhaps these were the result of a twisted imagination, but as he studied them, he realised that he was wrong. The close ups of her face revealed a cruel mask. Libby's eyes were huge and haunted, her mouth a thin line of suffering and the blood, there was so much blood. He had to believe that this man was capable of anything. It was so unfair, Matt thought as he went over the conversation in his mind. He would never have gone to the police if he had received the warning in time. If only he had stayed at home the previous evening. The package containing the threat had arrived when he was out. This misunderstanding had resulted in torture. Libby would not be in this state if it were not for him. It sickened him to think that this man had been watching their house, seen the detectives as they left. He shuddered at the thought, he should have listened to Libby when the first set of photographs arrived. She had been right to be worried.

Chapter Nineteen

HIS TELEPHONE RANG SO SNATCHING it up he growled. "Hello!"

"Matthew," the voice on the other end enquired. "Are you okay?" Veronique immediately noticed the strain in his voice.

"Oh, sorry," he replied in an attempt to sound normal. "I was expecting someone else."

"You have a problem?"

"No, nothing like that, I'm just a little bit busy at the moment, distracted." He laughed nervously.

Veronique accepted his excuse but was not entirely certain that he was telling her the truth.

"How are you getting on with photo editing?"

"Making progress," he reassured her.

Matt wondered why she was calling. She was not in the habit of checking up on him unless there was some kind of emergency.

"I'm organising a small party for the crew and models who have worked with us recently," she explained. "I would of course like to invite you and Libby."

"We are both quite busy at the moment," he replied.

"It will be held at my West End boutique." She chose to ignore him. "The models from the Paris shoot will be there so please bring a camera. I am going to use this as a feature for my boutique magazine. Libby could write something."

Matt did not have the energy or inclination to argue. Clearly, no was not the right answer so he made all the right noises and when she was gone, he tried to focus on his work whilst waiting for the telephone to ring again.

The flap in the cell door opened with a shrill clatter and he passed in a plate of food.

"Hey, before you go, what about the other woman?"

His face appeared at the opening and he waited for her to continue.

"Do you have food for her too?"

He raised his arm so she could see the plate he was holding.

"How can she possibly feed herself with her hands tied together?"

"Don't worry, I'll see to it."

He was about to move away when Kelly decided to push him further.

"What about some clothes, surely you don't intend to leave her in her underwear. It gets quite cold in here especially during the night."

She watched as he frowned and thinking that she had said too much stepped away from the door.

"You have a point," he replied. "I'll see what I can do."

The flap closed noisily then he was gone.

He paused outside the door before inserting the key into the lock. Kelly was right, he should try to make her a little more comfortable. A shadow passed over his face as he thought about Afghanistan. Some of their captors had shown compassion, bringing them hope in the form of extra rations or more water, but it was all part of the process, the Good Cop, Bad Cop routine.

Leaning against the door, it swung open on hinges that complained. She was still curled up on the mattress in the same position that she had been in earlier so stepping forward, he placed the food down on the floor beside her. He paused then reaching for her arm, forced her onto her back. Libby cried out in alarm and tried to pull away but his was an iron grip. Closing her eyes tightly she waited for the onslaught to begin.

He looked down at her and studied her face. She was an attractive woman, the type that he would normally be drawn to. Cunningham did not deserve her, it was because of him that she was in this situation. If only he had listened then things might have been quite different.

The rope binding her wrists was tight and he struggled to loosen the knot, but after a few moments, it fell away.

"There," he said, "you should be a little more comfortable now."

Rolling away from him, she drew her legs up and hugged them tightly. Her hands were cold and lifeless and as she forced her fingers to work, they complained stiffly.

He coiled the rope neatly and hung it up on a hook beside the winch above her head, then reaching into his pocket he pulled out her phone. As soon as he turned it on a ringtone sounded alerting them to several unread text messages. Ignoring the alarm, he selected the camera mode from the icons that appeared on the screen then leaning forward, he began to take pictures.

She hugged herself tighter and buried her face into the mattress.

"I just want some pictures to send to your boyfriend," he laughed cruelly. "Let him know that I'm treating you well." He was compelled to touch her again but resisting the urge, he stood back and continued. "Your wounds are healing nicely." He took some more pictures then he moved away.

Libby didn't hear him leave but he was only gone for a few moments before he returned carrying a thin grey blanket.

"Best I can do I'm afraid," he tossed it down beside her.

The door banged shut and opening her eyes she feared that he might still be there but she was wrong. Reaching out she forced her stiff fingers to work, the blanket was not as rough as it looked and pulling it towards herself she breathed a sigh of relief.

Taking the tube into central London, he was going to send the pictures he had taken to Cunningham. Using the girl's phone was a stroke of genius, there would be nothing to trace back to him. Activating it back at base had been risky. If the police were monitoring it, they would not have had time to triangulate its position but he was taking no chances. It would be much safer to use it away from his lair.

Pressing the power button, it came to life to a serenade that alerted him again to unread messages and now several voice mails had arrived too. Ignoring this, he searched the memory looking for the photographs he had taken earlier and once he found the file, he attached it to an email and sent it to Cunningham. He would allow him time to reflect before making his call.

The pictures arrived and linking his phone to his computer screen, Matt opened the file. Several images appeared and going through them carefully his stress levels began to soar. Libby was lying on a filthy mattress and the expression on her face was one of absolute terror. Several of the pictures were close ups showing that her wounds were clean and the healing process had begun. He tried to view the pictures objectively looking for clues but again there was nothing. In fact, there was less in the background than he had seen in the previous photographs. At least her hands were free but he could see the marks where the rope had done its work.

What did this madman want?

Matt tried to work, occupy his troubled mind but it was useless. Images of Libby filled every space inside his head leaving no room for anything else. He could hardly concentrate knowing that she was suffering so moving away from his computer, he tried to work out what had led up to this moment. He had been busy in Paris, nothing that he could think of had gone wrong, everyone he came into contact with were friendly and helpful, besides he had worked with most of them before. His Paris trip was followed by the Brighton assignment. It was practically the same team, familiar faces. Veronique liked it that way, everyone knew what they were doing but most importantly they were used to her working preferences.

The only difference between the two assignments that Matt could see was the man doing this was also on location in Brighton, there were photographs to prove it. There was nothing to suggest that he had been there in Paris. They had received the first photographs in the days between the two assignments. He picked up a pen and absentmindedly began doodling on a pad. The pictures of Libby and Julia had been taken during the same period and he frowned. Working through Libby's movements, he came up with nothing. Her world consisted of reporting on women's fashions and more recently writing articles about Emilia Sykes and her bridal shop. She had not yet begun to write about celebrity weddings so there could be no sinister connection there.

He was aware that Emilia's brother was closely associated with the cellist Mia Ashton and it was not so long ago that musicians were being murdered. Mia had been caught up in it but the case was resolved with the death of the murderer. Surely, there could be nothing there to influence current events.

Suddenly his phone rang and startled out of his thoughts he reached for it and glanced at the screen. It was Libby's number.

"Cunningham." The voice began loudly. "You have seen how well I'm looking after your woman and if you want it to stay that way I suggest you do exactly as I say."

Breathing heavily, Matt remained silent but then with an effort he said.

"I understand."

"The little dark haired model you worked with in Brighton, what's her name?"

Matt's frown deepened as his mind raced, he could hardly think clearly. There were a number of dark haired women but then he realised who he meant.

"Pascale," he whispered.

"Pascale what? She must have a surname."

"Dominique, her name is Pascale Dominique."

"Is she French?"

"Yes."

There was silence for a moment. Matt was confused, he had no idea why this man was interested in the French model.

"The older woman, the one you are working for, is she French too?"

How did he know about Veronique?

"Well," he shouted when Matt failed to answer quickly enough.

"Yes, she is French."

The silence continued.

Matt wanted to ask him again where he was holding Libby but he didn't want to say anything that would cause her more harm. He knew what this man was capable of and he shuddered.

"The little French girl Pascale, I want her so you are going to get her for me."

"What?" Matt exclaimed loudly. "What do you mean?"

"If you want your woman back then you must give me something in return."

Matt's stomach tightened then he caught his breath. "You expect me to abduct a woman and hand her over to you?"

"Of course," came the reply.

"How am I supposed to do that?"

"I'm sure you will come up with something but I'm prepared to help you. I will contact you again once you've had time to think it over."

The phone went dead and Matt stared at it in disbelief. He felt sick with anxiety and his hands were shaking badly.

Slipping the phone into his pocket, he grinned. He had given Cunningham enough to think about for the moment. Too much information at this point may push him over the edge. He had seen men driven crazy by too much stress. He would contact him again once he had worked out the best way forward. The plan would have to be simple, unlike himself Cunningham was undisciplined, he had no military training.

Chapter Twenty

THAT NIGHT MATT FOUND IT impossible to sleep, thoughts of Libby gave him no peace. Reaching out, he hoped that she was there in bed beside him and all this was just a terrible dream. Rolling over he buried his face into her pillow and as her scent washed over him, her image appeared out of the darkness and he gasped. He would give anything to have her back safe and warm.

The words the man had spoken echoed around inside his head; his demands were outrageous but what choice did he have? The implications if he refused to carry them out weighed heavily on his mind, but he simply could not imagine handing Pascale over to this monster. He would have to alert the police. If he could speak to Detective Sergeant Woods, it might be possible to work out a plan that would lead to this man's arrest before he could harm Libby further. It all sounded so simple but then images of her tortured body brought him back to reality.

Detective Chief Inspector Wyman called Woods and James into the incident room the moment they arrived at work. He wanted an update on their progress.

"We now have two missing women," Woods began and picking up a marker pen, she wrote their names on an evidence board before attaching photographs of the victims.

"Kelly Spencer was abducted just over a week ago and Elizabeth Ellis, known as Libby disappeared the day before yesterday."

"Are the incidents linked?" Wyman asked and standing in front of the board, he studied the images of both women.

"They don't seem to have known each other," James told him, "but we can't rule out a connection."

"What about the delivery van?" Wyman turned to face them.

"It seems likely to have been used in the abduction of Libby Ellis," Woods told him but before she could go on James took over.

"We've had our people checking the offices in the street where she was last seen and we can rule them out. She did not have an appointment with anyone there."

"The forensics report," Woods continued, eying James sharply, "turned up no fingerprints other than the drivers, but they did recover a number of fibres from the driver's seat and from the back of the van."

"Fibres and a footprint were found at the service station where Kelly Spencer works," Wyman said thoughtfully. "Any similarities there?"

"It's early days yet, but I'll get onto forensics, see if they can come up with a match."

"If we are looking for a connection between these abductions then this could be it. We know that the man who took Kelly Spencer was wearing a camouflage jacket." Wyman said.

He didn't need to say more. If the fibres in the van matched those found at the service station then it was likely that the same man took both women. Wyman reached for the marker pen that Woods as holding and began to make a list.

"We need to go back to basics," he began. "Speak to the sister again see if she can tell us more about Kelly's day to day movements. Also, see the owner of the service station. I want to know if there was a regular customer to the forecourt wearing army gear in the days leading up to Kelly's disappearance. Maybe our man checked out the place before making his move."

Woods crossed her arms and leaned back against a table. She was fuming, what did he think she had been doing? They had already gone through this, the reports were stacked up on her desk.

Tapping the pen against the board, Wyman continued. "We need to connect the fibres found in the back of that van to Libby Ellis. We have CCTV evidence of her leaving the office where she had her meeting so we know what she was wearing at the time of her abduction."

James was busy making notes but Woods couldn't wait for the meeting to end. She knew exactly what needed to be done, Wyman was clearly trying to undermine her authority.

"Get onto forensics, then go and see Caroline Ensley. Is it worth having another word with Matthew Cunningham?"

"Not at the moment," Woods shook her head. "We are still going through files that we took from his office and I'm happy with what he's given us so far."

"Okay Izzy," Wyman paused then staring at her thoughtfully he added. "Don't let him stray too far."

DS Woods led James back to her office, her mood far from happy. She realised this was a wasted emotion but she couldn't help herself. Simon Wyman annoyed her immensely, she liked most people, but he was definitely not one of them. Perhaps she should stop comparing him with her previous boss DI Terry Ashton. She had known Terry for years and they had worked well together. Wyman was a good detective but he could be overbearing and patronising at times. It was as if he had no faith in her ability. This did not bode well as she was trying to prove herself capable of holding down the position of Detective Inspector. The job should have been hers when Terry retired but promotion had not come her way, Detective Chief Inspector Simon Wyman had appeared instead.

"We need to make a plan," she said closing the door behind them.

"Wyman is not happy with our progress," James stated the obvious.

Woods glared at him then taking a deep breath, she sat down at her desk.

"I'll telephone forensics, get them to look at both sets of fibres. I feel certain that those found in the back of the van will match the coat that Libby Ellis was wearing."

"I'll see you in the car park in ten minutes then." Sensibly, James decided to say no more.

Caroline Ensley lived in a Victorian terrace near Croydon. The building had seen better days but inside the rooms were clean and filled with a collection of mismatched furniture that could only have come from charity shops. In places the carpet on the floor was threadbare but that did not seem to bother little Callum Spencer who was playing with his toy cars, pushing them along an imaginary road. He seemed content enough living with his aunt.

"He's a good boy," Caroline smiled as she invited them into the living room. "He missed him mum at first of course but he's more settled now."

"Resilient little buggers," James said inviting a dirty look from DS Woods.

"We need to go over some of the information that you gave us earlier, but first is there anything else you can tell us?" Woods asked.

"I've told you everything that I can think of. I'm not familiar with Kelly's friends but I have given you a list of those I do know."

"Did your sister have a new boyfriend?" James asked bluntly.

"Not as far as I know, she would have told me if she was seeing someone new."

"Is she a regular visitor to pubs and clubs?" he continued.

"Not on her wages," Caroline laughed, "besides, what would she do with Callum?"

At the sound of his name, the little boy looked up and smiled.

"Army man, army man," he said in a singsong voice.

Woods asked several questions of her own urging Caroline to give her a clear picture of a typical day. She wanted to know what Kelly did and who she saw.

"My sister rarely went out of an evening, apart from work of course. Her neighbour took care of Callum when she was not there."

"Did she have any enemies," Woods asked, "anyone with a grudge perhaps?"

Caroline stared at her and frowned, she couldn't imagine anyone disliking her sister.

"I don't think so," she replied realising how unhelpful that sounded. "As I said before, my sister and I have unfortunately drifted apart."

It was the first time she had acknowledged the fact. Since the birth of Callum, Kelly had become distant and Caroline realised then just how much she missed her sister.

"What about past boyfriends, Callum's father for example."

This question jolted Caroline from her thoughts.

"Callum's father, well he is someone I've not thought of in a long time."

"What can you tell me about him?"

"His name was Tom, but I can't remember his surname. He was an army officer, a right posh sod too. As soon as he discovered that Kelly was pregnant she was no longer good enough for him."

"Can you tell me what regiment he was in?" Woods glanced at James who was busy scribbling notes.

"I have no idea," Caroline laughed. "I only met him once and that was enough. I don't know what Kelly saw in him to be honest, it was clear that he was just using her. He was from a completely different background, Kelly would never have fitted into his neat little world, but she couldn't see that. Anyway, the inevitable happened and he was posted away or whatever happens to soldiers."

"Do you know if she keeps in touch with him?"

Caroline shook her head. Sadly, she had no idea.

Army man, army man." Callum said again as he parked his toy cars neatly in a line.

Woods watched what he was doing and frowned thoughtfully then leaning forward she asked.

"Is the army man in a car Callum?"

The little boy turned towards her, his expression full of importance.

"Where is the car?" she prompted gently.

"The blue car," he pointed at the row of toy cars on the floor before repeating. "Army man."

Woods looked at Caroline.

"Do you remember seeing a blue car parked outside your house?"

"There are always cars in the street."

"Have you seen a man recently dressed in a camouflage jacket?"

Caroline leaned back in her chair and chewed at her bottom lip as she searched her memory.

"Army man in car with a..." Callum paused and screwed up his face, he did not have the words to describe what he had seen so he mimed an action.

"Did the man have a camera?"

Shrugging his shoulders, Callum put his thumb in his mouth and stared at her blankly.

Reaching for her phone, Woods logged onto the internet and found a picture of a camera with a telephoto lens then, showing it to Callum he nodded his head vigorously.

"Good lad," she said squeezing his shoulder gently.

"What do you make of that?" James asked as they drove away.

"A man wearing a camouflage jacket must have been taking pictures of them as they left the house."

"It's the jacket again," James said. "It must be our man."

"Why would he want pictures of Caroline?" Woods frowned as she changed gear.

"It could have been the boy's father," James surmised.

"If it was, then why didn't he just knock on the door and ask?"

"Perhaps he knows what Caroline thinks of him."

"I don't think it was the father," Woods shook her head. "There is something far more sinister going on here."

"I can't see either of them being in any immediate danger." James said as he noticed her expression. "Our man goes for young women not children."

"I suppose you are right," she agreed. "I don't think our abductor is Callum's father, it doesn't make sense. Why would he kidnap Kelly?"

Chapter Twenty One

MATT HAD CONSUMED ENDLESS CUPS of coffee in an effort to stave off the effects of a sleepless night and now his senses were heightened by caffeine. Pacing the floor in agitation his thoughts kept coming one after the other until eventually he stopped and stared out of the window. He saw nothing of the little courtyard garden that Libby loved so much, then reaching for his phone, he knew that he should speak to the police, tell them everything but by doing that, he could make it worse for Libby. Having seen the pictures of her injuries, he was convinced that the madman was capable of anything.

Matt growled with frustration, he couldn't afford to take that chance, gambling with Libby's life was not an option. If he did as he was told how could he be sure that it would secure her release. His eyes focused on the window and he studied his reflection in the glass. How could he possibly involve Pascale? He might not think much of her as a person but she was as innocent as Libby and equally as vulnerable. She hardly deserved to be drawn into this nightmare but what else could he do. He loved Libby dearly and would do anything to keep her safe.

Suddenly the phone rang and as it vibrated in his hand, he almost dropped it.

"Cunningham, we have to talk." The voice was annoyingly calm and persuasive. "How do you intend to deliver the girl?"

Unable to respond coherently, his heart hammered painfully as he stuttered.

"Calm down man," he snapped, "you must have given it some thought. The sooner you start to think like a criminal the better it will be for Libby."

Matt hated the way he used her name with familiarity, it was as if they were old friends.

"What do you expect me to say?" he managed before taking a deep breath.

"Where is Pascale now?"

"In London I think."

"Has she not returned to France?"

"No, there is a party here in town. I guess she will be attending." His admission was automatic.

"A party eh?" he said thoughtfully. "What kind of party?"

"It's a social gathering of all those who worked on the recent fashion shoots."

"Will all the models will be going to this event?"

"Yes." Matt could hear the excitement in his voice so was reluctant to say more. He could hardly believe that he had told him this much already.

"I take it you have an invitation."

Suddenly Matt could see an opportunity that might work in his favour.

"Libby and I have to be there, we are working you see. She is interviewing several of the guests then writing an article for a fashion magazine."

"How do you expect her to do that?"

"If you let her go and we attend together then no one need suspect a thing." he spoke quickly outlining his plan. "I can get you in there then introduce you to Pascale."

Laughter was his response. "Do you think I was born yesterday?" he laughed again and when he calmed down, he continued. "Libby remains where she is until you have delivered Pascale Dominique."

Matt swallowed noisily and was about to argue his case but he did not get the chance.

"This is what you are going to do," he said asserting his authority. "Bring the girl to me then we'll work out an exchange."

"I ask you again," Matt snapped. "How do you expect me to do that?"

His sigh was audible, he was tired of Matt's negative attitude. He thought about the woman curled up on the mattress inside her cell. Perhaps Matt needed another incentive.

"Tell me what to do." Matt whispered, sensing the unspoken threat.

"That's better, now listen carefully."

He began to reveal his plan and Matt thought it best not to interrupt.

"Are you particularly friendly with this girl?"

"No," Matt admitted.

"That is unfortunate, it will probably make your job a little more difficult. You must win her trust, be affectionate, make sure she has a good time, because when the time comes to leave she must go with you."

He went on to explain the finer details.

"I will give you something to help make her a little more pliable."

"You think it will be as simple as that?" Matt shuddered.

"For your sake it had better be. I will provide you with the drug, all you have to do is to carry out your part. If you fail then you will never see Libby again."

The connection was broken and he was gone.

Leaning over the kitchen sink Matt retched then reaching for the tap, splashed cold water over his face. The shock of it against his skin brought him back to reality. Once Libby was released, he would tell the police everything then do what he could to help get Pascale back.

His phone rang again and reaching for it with wet and trembling fingers it fell to the floor. Luckily, it remained in one piece so snatching it up he pressed the receive button.

"Hello."

"Matthew?"

It was Veronique.

"You sound strange, are you okay?"

"Yes," Matt replied. Controlling his emotions was an effort but he went on. "I'm fine."

She began by telling him about the arrangements for her party and he did his best to take it all in.

"Everyone will be there. Now tell me, how are you getting on with my photographs, have you got anything to show me yet?"

"I'm still working on the initial edits," he lied.

He had not been able to concentrate on his work since Libby disappeared but he had to tell her something. Veronique would want to see results very soon.

"Can you send me what you have done so far? We may be working to a revised schedule."

She did not go into details but Matt guessed that it was because of the foul weather they had experienced in Salisbury.

"I will have something for you by the end of the day." Matt promised.

It was unlike her to worry. Veronique relied heavily on his ability to create images digitally but as the models were still in London, perhaps she was thinking about getting them back into the studio for another photo session.

"Send me what you have later then we'll discuss it further at the party tomorrow evening."

The call ended leaving him staring at his phone. He had to pull himself together, concentrate on his work. Veronique must not discover that anything was wrong. Luckily, he'd made good progress before Libby disappeared so all he had to do was check through what he had done so far before arranging it in a portfolio.

DS Woods sent DC James to talk to the owner of the service station. She had carried out the initial interview herself but thought it best if James continued with the questioning.

A PC appeared at her door, he knocked twice before entering. "From forensics," he said efficiently before handing over a file.

Sitting back in her chair, Woods began to read. The fibres found in the back of the van were made of pure wool and the handwritten notes in the margin suggested that these had come from a heavy garment such as a coat. There were traces of colour showing that the wool had been dyed pink. Woods reached for the CCTV prints of Libby leaving the office where she had attended her meeting. She was wearing a three quarter length coat but the images were in black and white. Next, she consulted her notebook; it confirmed that the colour of Libby's coat was pink then turning back to the report, she continued to read.

A page of technical information explained the different types of camouflage patterns used in British military clothing. DPM or Disruptive Pattern Material commonly known as Woodland Camouflage was the colour pattern designed to be effective in woodland. It was widely used by the military with jackets and trousers readily available to civilians through army surplus stores. MTP or Multi-Terrain Pattern was a six colour pattern intended to replace the woodland and desert design. MTP was used in the Afghanistan theatre of operations where a wide range of patterns was trialled and evaluated against DPM. In 2010, MTP combat uniforms began to be issued to forces employed in Afghanistan. The fibres found in the van and at the service station were consistent with the MTP type.

Woods stared at the report thoughtfully. Their man was wearing the latest MTP designed combats, so it seemed likely that he could be or was recently a military man. What was his connection with the army? Caroline had told them that the father of her sister's child was an army officer. Unconsciously Woods tapped her fingernail against the desktop, at least now they had confirmation; the same man had abducted both Kelly Spencer and Libby Ellis.

Chapter Twenty Two

MATT WAS EXHAUSTED HAVING SPENT another sleepless night worrying about Libby. His anxiety was heightened by the fact that it was the day of Veronique's party and he was expected to carry out a heinous crime. He spent more time than usual in the shower in an effort to wake himself up and now, clutching a mug of coffee, he sat down in front of his computer. Strong coffee was the order of the day, but it would hardly help his nerves. He needed to remain calm, it would not do to draw attention to himself at the party, it was important to appear relaxed and normal. He would of course have to come up with an excuse for Libby's absence. Veronique will not be happy, she was expecting Libby to write an editorial covering the event. Perhaps he should telephone Veronique, warn her in advance but then she might insist on talking to Libby herself and demand her phone number. He sighed miserably and ran his fingers through his damp hair.

Several emails were waiting for him and as he read the first, another one arrived. His heart began to beat faster and his stomach tightened, it had been sent from Libby's phone. Using the mouse, he moved the cursor and double clicked on the message then as it opened his eyes widened.

Rohypnol-DFSA-Drug Facilitating Sexual Assault, was the title.

Sitting back in his chair, Matt did not want to read further and it was several moments before he could summon the strength to continue.

You will be supplied with a number of pills that dissolve in liquid. Be aware, these should not be used in drinks such as white wine or champagne. A dye is present in this drug and will turn the liquid a bright blue. It is therefore recommend that it be dissolved in dark drinks only, but even this may turn cloudy. Under the right circumstances, subdued lighting, or a party atmosphere where alcohol has already been consumed, it should remain undetected.

When enough of the drug has been administered, the girl should appear drunk. At this point, you must get her to leave with you before she becomes unconscious.

Matt stopped reading. The message underpinned the severity of his involvement. It went on to explain that he would receive further instructions later that afternoon. This was a serious crime and he should contact the police, but Libby's life was in danger and he could not afford to take the risk, besides, this may be his only opportunity to get her back.

DS Woods met DC James in the incident room. It was quiet, a couple of DCI Wyman's team were working at their desks, but they were able to compare notes without being disturbed. James began by telling her that his meeting with Kelly Spencer's boss had been a waste of time.

"Okay," Woods sighed as she slipped the forensics report across the table towards him. "We may have something here."

Getting to her feet, she turned towards the evidence board and began to create a timeline as James read the report.

"So, the delivery van was used to abduct Libby Ellis."

"The forensic evidence is conclusive," Woods nodded, "but first we need to rule out the possibility that someone from the delivery company may have driven that van whilst wearing an army combat jacket."

Reaching for the telephone on the table, James said. "I'll get onto that right away."

A few minutes later, he had the answer.

"It's company policy that all delivery drivers wear a uniform, they also confirmed that the van has not been used recently by staff at the weekends."

Woods stared at him thoughtfully and fiddled with the marker pen.

"We need to know where it went after it left that side street. Get onto PC Yearsley, see if he can trace its movements using both CCTV and roadside cameras." Woods turned back to the evidence board and folding her arms, studied it before saying. "I'm wondering given the forensics report if our man is or was military."

"He might wear the latest in camouflage but that doesn't necessarily make him military." James pointed out. "All that stuff is available on the internet."

"We should at least check to see how many soldiers left the service last year." Woods continued to study the board. She also wanted to track down Callum's father but without a name, it would be an impossible task.

Turning to the computer James typed in a command then reading from the screen, he looked up.

"During 2017 almost 10,000 soldiers left the army."

"As many as that?" she turned to face him. "What about medically discharged?" She waited as James searched for the information.

"According to this, during 2016/17 there were as many as 2000 personnel medically discharged."

"Is there a figure for those suffering from Post Traumatic Stress Disorder?"

"For the same period the number drops to 176."

"Perhaps our man falls into that category."

"That's a huge assumption," James replied, glancing up at her.

"Just thinking out loud," she said defensively and moving away from the board, she continued. "Our man could have had a rough time in a war zone and returned with a grudge of some kind."

"We can't assume that either," It surprised him that she could be thinking this way. "We need a hell of a lot more proof before we can go accusing ex servicemen of crimes like this."

"You are right," she acknowledged.

"I'll see what PC Yearsley comes up with. If we can find out where that delivery van went..." He didn't need to say more. Tenuous though it was, this was their only lead.

At three o'clock that afternoon, Matt was at his computer. Miraculously he had been able to do some work and for an hour or so had immersed himself in manipulating photographs for Veronique. Suddenly his phone rang, it was the call he had been dreading.

"Cunningham?" the voice demanded.

"Yes, it's me."

"Don't talk just listen. Be at the multi-storey car park at Oxford Circus at 19:00 hours. The car you are looking for is a blue Ford." He read off the licence plate number and told him that he would find it on the first floor on the east side of the building.

"The keys will be hidden up the end of the exhaust pipe, the drugs are in the glove compartment. When the party is over deliver the girl to the car then leave her there."

The call was disconnected.

Glancing at the clock on the wall, he had plenty of time but then he thought of something. If he was to get there early, he could wait until the car was delivered to the car park then perhaps catch the man in the act. Again, he considered calling the police, they would have the resources to cover all of the parking area, but he couldn't bring himself to do it.

Going into the bathroom, he washed and shaved before dressing for the evening then selecting a compact but good quality camera, he left for the tube station.

Just over an hour later, he arrived in Oxford Street and made his way quickly towards the car park. It was a huge building, far bigger than he imagined but orientating himself on the eastern side, he pushed through a door and made his way to level one. Emerging from the stairwell, he got an almost overwhelming sense of space. Hundreds of cars were arranged in neat rows and walking along the narrow gangway that snaked through the parking area, he realised that it was an impossible task. He would be lucky to see the arrival of the car, there were several ramps leading up to multiple parking zones. Corners and columns obscured his view; he had underestimated the job.

Turning another corner he stopped as a car passed by slowly then he saw it. A blue Ford bearing the registration number that he had been given. Matt stopped and surveyed the area looking for movement but the place was deserted. The car had been left well ahead of the rendezvous time and the chance of spotting the driver was gone.

Moving slowly towards it, Matt studied every aspect of the vehicle. If he looked carefully then perhaps he could pick up some clues as to where it had come from but he was wrong. There was nothing to indicate where the car had been kept. Placing his hand lightly on the bonnet, it was cold so must have been there for some time. Edging towards the rear of the car there was just enough space between the bumper and the wall for him to bend down and retrieve the keys. Pressing the remote, the indicators flashed twice and the locks released, then opening the driver's door he looked in. The interior was spotless, the carpets in the footwell looked new and there were no personal items in the pockets of the door or on the dashboard. Climbing in, he reached for the glove compartment, it was not locked and as it opened, he found a little plastic bag containing a number of olive shaped grey pills. Matt sat back in the seat and frowned, how was it possible that these tiny pills could cause so much misery and anguish?

Stuffing them into his jacket pocket, he checked behind the sun visors and beneath each seat before moving into the back. The car was parked too close to the wall to enable the rear door to open so folding the seats forward he reached into the luggage space but there was nothing, the car was clean.

Climbing out he readjusted the seats and leaving it as he had found it, he closed the doors then, pressing the remote he stood back. The car park was silent, there was nobody around so pulling the camera from his pocket he took several photographs including a close up of the number plate. These might prove useful later.

Checking his watch, it was almost two hours before the party was due to begin and the boutique was only fifteen minutes walk away, it was far too early to arrive. Slowly he retraced his steps to the pedestrian stairwell wondering all the time how long the car had been there. He had told the madman about Veronique's party the previous day, but why deliver the car so early? Perhaps he was a lot smarter than he thought.

Chapter Twenty Three

THE PARTY WAS IN FULL swing when finally he arrived. Stepping in off the street, he was greeted by an easy mix of well dressed people enjoying champagne and soft music. Matt paused and taking a deep breath straightened his shoulders then he spotted Veronique. She had seen him arrive so calling out his name she made her way towards him.

"Where is Libby?" she frowned.

"I'm so sorry but she sends her regrets. Her mother was taken ill suddenly so she had to drive down to Kent."

"You didn't go with her?"

"No," he could hardly believe that he was spinning such a web of deceit. "Libby insisted that I come here tonight, she will telephone me with news later."

Veronique smiled sympathetically before saying. "Come, let's get you a drink."

Linking her arm through his, she led him across the floor towards the bar set up at the back of the shop. Matt was amazed at the transformation, all the stock had been removed creating an open space that was slowly filling with guests. Photographers brandishing expensive cameras were busy searching for that perfect pose and the young models were willing to oblige. Matt wondered why Veronique insisted on him being there.

"Don't worry," she said reading his thoughts. "They are mostly students from the local art college seeking work experience. I like to help out where I can, it's good PR working with the local community."

The mix of students was cosmopolitan, many of them from overseas, foreign students studying in the UK.

"If you create a photographic record," Veronique said thoughtfully, "perhaps Libby could work from that."

Clearly, she was thinking about the editorial that she wanted Libby to write.

"Are Charley and Melissa here?" Matt asked as she handed him a drink.

Glancing around the room she gestured vaguely towards a group of people and following her gaze, he realised that he had not yet spotted Pascale.

"I like the portfolio that you sent me last night," she told him. "I don't think we need to take extra shots in the studio, just continue to be creative with what you have."

Taking a sip of champagne, Matt nodded at one of the male models he recognised then suddenly someone shrieked his name. Charley moved quickly towards him and he couldn't help thinking how stunning she looked. Reaching out, he took hold of her hands before kissing her cheek then she hugged him less formally. Of all the women he worked with Charley was his favourite.

Veronique took the opportunity to slip away but before she went she left him in no doubt, they would be speaking again later.

"Are you on your own?" Charley asked.

"Yes," Matt replied turning his attention to her. "Libby, my partner, couldn't make it tonight."

"You sound sad," Charley pouted. "Come over here and join us."

Going around the circle, she introduced her friends, some of whom he knew already.

"Don't worry you will be quite safe with us." Melissa smiled as she moved closer.

Matt noticed the look on her face as she glanced towards Veronique. Clearly, something was going on between the women.

"Are you involved in the Italian job?" Charley asked.

He was aware that Veronique was planning a photo shoot in Rome but this was the first time he had heard it referred to as the Italian job.

"I'm not sure," he laughed, "she hasn't told me much about it yet."

"Me neither," Melissa snapped.

Stepping away from the crowd the three of them continued their conversation.

"Veronique told us to keep our diaries clear for the first two weeks in June, so I guess from that we are on the team." Charley said excitedly.

"She told you to keep your diary clear," Melissa hissed then Matt realised why she was so upset.

"Has Pascale been invited?" he asked and as Melissa's frown deepened, he realised that he had asked the wrong question.

"I'm not sure," Charley replied quickly and glancing around searched for the French girl.

"She is here somewhere," Melissa told him and Matt studied her as she took a sip from her glass.

Although similar in many ways Melissa could be so different from Charley. Her complexion darker she was not so delicately boned. She was a confident young woman and not afraid to voice her opinion. Matt liked her style, the two women complemented each other and he enjoyed working with them.

The drugs in his pocket bothered him and he wondered how he could possibly administer them. It would be no use slipping them into champagne, he remembered the warning he had been given. He had no idea how many pills he would have to use before the drug took effect and silently he cursed himself for not finding out. He wondered what Pascale was drinking, everyone in the room seemed to be holding champagne glasses, but then the evening was young.

"There she is," Charley said spotting her colleague and as if hearing her name, Pascale looked up and smiled.

"She looks so different," Matt remarked in amazement.

Her long dark hair was braided into a French plait and neatly rolled up around her head, it was the perfect accompaniment for the medieval style gown that she was wearing. Matt would never have recognised her, he had not seen her like this before but he thought the dress suited her petite frame perfectly.

"Trying to impress Veronique," Melissa hissed tartly.

Lifting his camera, Matt couldn't resist taking several shots.

"You know what she's like," Charley said softly. "They both blow like the wind, I swear they must be related."

"Perhaps they come from the same region in France."

Listening to what they were saying, Matt doubted that was true. Pascale came from a rural area in central France and Veronique was a Parisian born and bred.

"Pascale is so different from us." Melissa continued.

"Of course she is and there is nothing wrong with that."

"No I suppose not," she looked at Charley and wrinkled her nose, "but you know how rude and unreasonable she can be at times."

Charley laughed and was tempted to say more but she didn't want to spend the evening talking about Pascale. Turning to Matt she asked how the photographs from their last shoot had turned out.

"Incredibly well considering the circumstances," Matt replied. "I'm having to do quite a lot of technical and creative retouching but it's going well so far."

They talked easily for a while and Matt began to relax in their company but he could not lose sight of the task that he was expected to undertake. Time was running out and still he had to get close to Pascale. He wanted to move into her circle but clearly, both Charley and Melissa had other ideas, they wanted him all to themselves.

Suddenly Veronique appeared at his side.

"There is someone I would like you to meet," she told him and smiling sweetly at his companions, stole him away.

"You can't spend the whole evening gossiping with them," she glanced sideways at him. "I need you to take pictures. I have a room upstairs that has been set up."

"I've only brought a compact camera," he replied, "you should have warned me about what you had in mind."

"Don't worry, I'm sure that you will be fine. There are some aspiring young models upstairs who would benefit greatly from your experience. I would like you to help Pascale, show them what it's like to work in the real world."

He was hardly prepared for that. Playing nursemaid to a bunch of students whilst so wound up was not his idea of fun but at least he would be closer to Pascale.

The room was decorated impressively. A huge pleated curtain draped against one wall helped to create a photographic atmosphere and a sheepskin rug thrown on the floor completed the illusion. Some basic lighting hung from frames overhead and Pascale was busy with a number of budding models demonstrating poses for the camera.

Veronique called everyone to order before introducing Matt. Several of the students were delighted, clearly familiar with his work.

"Pascale has already told you how to behave in front of the camera," Matt began, "so perhaps I can start by explaining what is expected from a professional model."

When he was finished, Matt left Pascale to organise the models while he worked closer with the young photographers. Checking their cameras, he then showed them how to get the best out of the people they were working with. He demonstrated what he wanted them to do by photographing the first student model. He talked to her constantly as he used his camera, telling her how to move, how to look into the lens and even what to think. He explained that by doing this, he hoped to capture the perfect picture.

After a while, he stepped back allowing the young people to get on with their work and glancing over his shoulder, he could see Pascale holding an empty glass.

"Would you like some more wine?" he asked stepping up beside her and reaching for a bottle of red, poured some into his own glass.

Staring at him, Pascale held out her glass then turning away, she said something in French before going to the aid of a model.

Reaching into his pocket Matt took out the plastic bag and shook a couple of pills into his hand. Next, he filled her glass with red wine and hesitating, had no idea how many to drop in. He decided on one, given the fact that the drink could turn cloudy, it would be wise to be cautious.

He waited for Pascale to finish talking before offering her the glass then he watched nervously as she took a sip. There was no reaction, she obviously detected nothing so he breathed a sigh of relief. Twice more over the next hour, he repeated the procedure.

"Matt," Veronique called. "Could you come down now?"

He was reluctant to leave Pascale. She was talking animatedly to a group of girls who were about to work together. She was a little louder than usual and not quite as coherent but then everyone in the room were the same; most of the bottles standing on the table were empty.

Veronique briefed him on what she wanted him to do as he followed her down the stairs to the party below. Charley and Melissa were first to pose in front of his camera then systematically he began to work the room. Forty minutes passed in a flash then a commotion drew his attention.

Pascale was standing unsteadily at the bottom of the stairs her face flushed, her eyes bright. Veronique was talking to her harshly in French and from the tone of her voice; it was obvious that she was not happy.

"Is there a problem?" Matt asked as he came to stand beside them.

"The silly girl has had too much to drink."

Pascale attempted to defend herself but Veronique would have none of it.

"I have called a taxi, you are to go to your hotel and sleep it off."

"My car is not far away," Matt told them. "I will make sure she gets to her hotel safely."

"There is no need, a taxi has been called."

"Who will take care of her?" Matt persisted. He had to persuade Veronique to let him take Pascale back to her hotel.

"I will instruct the driver to see that she gets to her room."

"No, we can't do that. Surely we have an obligation to ensure her safety."

Veronique glared at him and he felt awkward.

"Perhaps Charley or Melissa can accompany me?" Matt tried again.

"You are right," Veronique agreed reluctantly. "Please get her coat from the cloakroom."

Matt sighed with relief as he left the women standing together. All he had to do now was find a way to get rid of their chaperone then deliver Pascale to the car park.

When he returned with her coat, he discovered they had left without him.

93

Seized with panic he stumbled out onto the pavement and stared along the road but it was too late, the taxi was gone. He had no idea where Pascale was staying and now the opportunity to complete his task was lost.

"Charley has gone with her," Melissa said softly as she appeared beside him.

"Do you know where she is staying?"

"I think it's the Waldorf."

The sound of Veronique's voice invaded his thoughts. She was standing with a bunch of students who had decided to leave and he watched helplessly as they climbed into the waiting taxis.

"I will have to go to Pascale's hotel." Matt said. "I still have her coat and bag."

"Don't bother, she can collect them tomorrow."

His mind was racing, he had to get Pascale to that car park. Libby's life depended on it.

Chapter Twenty Four

SOMETHING HAD GONE WRONG AND watching from across the street he waited to see what would happen next. The French girl Pascale had already left but still there was no sign of Cunningham. Leaning against a shop window, he was not concerned about street cameras, no one knew who he was besides, he would probably not even be noticed.

A constant flow of taxis arrived to carry guests away, the younger generation were on the move, off to another party or nightclub. He did not care about them, his interest lie in the older age group. Pushing his hand into his pocket, he curled his fingers around Libby's phone. He was tempted to use it, send Cunningham a message, a reminder of the consequences of failure but he decided to wait.

Suddenly Cunningham appeared with Veronique Moreau at his side. He knew this woman influenced his business, she was one of his professional contacts and may prove to be useful. Another taxi arrived but this time a young woman climbed out and a conversation began. Pushing away from the window, he moved closer for a better look. This was one of the models from the photo shoot in Brighton, he recognised her, he had taken pictures of her himself. Ideas began to flood into his head and he smiled. Their conversation ended and he watched as Cunningham kissed both women affectionately before turning to hurry away.

Matt was in turmoil. He hated himself for what he had done to Pascale but he had no choice. He had not been confident from the start and now the evening had gone terribly wrong. He would have to try to put things right. He glanced at his watch. It was just after ten thirty and at least a twenty minute walk to the Waldorf Hotel where Pascale was staying. He could take a taxi but he needed time to think. Suddenly his phone began to ring and pulling it from his pocket he didn't need to check the screen, he knew who was calling.

"Cunningham, what's going on?"

Matt stopped walking and held onto the phone tightly. "I couldn't stop her from leaving without me." He realised how lame that sounded but it was the truth.

"So what are you going to do about it?"

"I'm on my way to her hotel now. I will see if I can speak with her, try to persuade her to come out with me."

"How many pills did you give her and how much did she drink?"

Matt had no idea how much drink she had consumed but he had given her three pills over the course of an hour. The man laughed silently, the girl would probably be unconscious by now so the prospect of him talking to her was highly unlikely.

"You know what will happen if you fail."

"Give me another chance, don't do anything to hurt Libby." Matt pleaded but it was no good, the connection had already been broken.

Running his fingers through his hair, he cursed. He should go directly to the police, tell them everything but that would be the wrong thing to do. He knew nothing about this man or where he had taken Libby. He needed more information before going to the authorities.

Matt found the hotel but the night manager would not give him Pascale's room number. He agreed to telephone her room, but there was no answer so he refused to do any more.

Returning to his lair, he was furious. Cunningham was pathetic, he needed something more to focus his mind and he knew exactly what he was going to do. Thoughts of Afghanistan crept into his head but pushing them aside, he grabbed a camera from the desk in his command centre before heading towards the cells.

Libby Ellis had not moved, curled up on the mattress she was holding onto her blanket tightly. The food and water he had left earlier was untouched. When he appeared, she screwed up her eyes in an effort to block out his image and she whimpered nervously.

"Stand up," he growled but she remained where she was.

"Get up," he shouted louder this time but still she refused to move so grabbing her by the arm, he hauled her roughly to her feet.

Crying out, Libby clutched at her blanket and stumbled away from him.

"Come with me."

Reaching out he pushed her along the gloomy corridor.

"Stop," he commanded.

Looking to her right she saw another cell door. Fixed to the wall was a digital touch pad and reaching over her shoulder, he punched in a series of numbers before the door clicked open. The cell was much larger than the one she had just left. In the middle of the floor stood a steel table and Libby's eyes widened when she saw the leather straps, these were obviously used as restraints. She failed to notice the wooden frame standing against the wall behind her.

Suddenly he grabbed her and as he lifted her off her feet, she began to scream.

Chapter Twenty Five

KELLY KNEW THAT SOMETHING WAS very wrong; she could feel it. The oppressive atmosphere that engulfed this place had changed. He had not yet delivered her breakfast. It was hardly hotel service, but at least breakfast usually came with a hot mug of tea. A noise from outside her cell made her sit up then she heard the sound of a key scraping in the lock. As a rule, he would slip back the panel in the door and push her tray of food and tea through.

"Come with me," he said as the door swung open.

Kelly did not argue, she welcomed every opportunity to get out of her squalid little cell.

The door to the adjacent cell was open and the woman was gone. Kelly frowned, she had heard nothing earlier, she would have known if something had happened during the night. Her mind raced as she searched for a possible explanation.

"Stop." The voice that interrupted her thoughts demanded obedience. She watched as he entered a series of numbers into a digital touch pad.

"Don't try to remember the code. It's changed regularly, besides this system relies on facial recognition."

The door opened and she almost stumbled as he pushed her inside. Steadying herself as the door crashed shut behind her the first thing she saw was a metal trolley. It was the kind of thing that would be found in a mortuary then turning away, she gasped.

"Oh my goodness!"

Behind her against the wall was a wooden frame and the woman was tied to it. Her only items of clothing lay shredded on the floor along with her blanket.

"What has he done to you?" Kelly groaned.

Stooping to pick up the blanket, she covered her before moving closer. Kelly was appalled. The woman's eyes were red and swollen, her cheeks stained with tears and where she had been struggling, her wrists and ankles were raw, chafed by the ropes that restrained her.

"Oh you poor thing," Kelly said at last and laying her hand softly against her cheek the woman realised that she was no longer alone. Her eyes flicked open and she shuddered but as they focused, her terror turning to relief.

"Did he hurt you?"

Kelly realised this was a stupid question of course she was hurt. Psychologically she must be devastated.

"Did he rape you?" she whispered almost afraid to know the truth.

Libby remained silent as Kelly loosened the ropes at her wrists and ankles then she began to massage the life back into her limbs.

"No," Libby replied at last.

"My name is Kelly."

"I'm Libby." She looked at Kelly and realised that she was wearing her clothes but she said nothing.

"Why did he do this to you?" Kelly asked, convinced that she had been sexually assaulted and was in denial.

"I have no idea. He came for me during the night." Unable to go on she sobbed then began to tremble violently.

Holding on to her Kelly rocked her gently as she would a child quietly whispering words of comfort.

"He didn't touch me," Libby insisted once her sorrow had passed.

"Why would he tie you to this contraption?"

"He took photographs." Fresh tears began to fall silently over her cheeks.

"Oh Libby."

Kelly was horrified and it upset her to think how terrified she must have been. Words were unnecessary as they held on to each other. Libby had been through a brutally terrifying ordeal and was exhausted.

"You are wearing my clothes," Libby whispered as she eased away from Kelly.

"I'm sorry." Kelly gasped awkwardly. "I had no idea who they belonged to when he gave them to me." She didn't know what else to say.

He returned to his command centre and sitting down at his desk, turned towards his computer. He might have used the camera high up on the wall of the cell to see what the women were doing but he could imagine the scene. Instead, he thought about Matthew Cunningham. The man had let him down badly and would now have to pay the price for his failure. The photographs he had taken were already in a file on his computer.

It had not been necessary to touch the girl, the threat was enough to send her half mad and the images of her tied naked to the frame would have the desired effect. Cunningham could imagine the rest. Using the keyboard he sent the file to Libby's phone, he would send it to Cunningham from a different location. He was still wary of the fact that the police might be monitoring her phone. He was tempted to send them straight from his computer but the police had the technology to trace his machine, he was not yet ready to risk that.

Chapter Twenty Six

DS WOODS WAS SITTING AT her desk studying the photographs that Matthew Cunningham had given them. They appeared harmless enough, shots of Libby Ellis and himself leaving a restaurant together. There were however a number of pictures featuring them both with other people, Libby and her editor enjoying coffee together and action shots of Matthew Cunningham at work on location. It was obvious that none of the people featured were aware of being photographed and as far as she was concerned, this was a direct attack on their privacy.

Woods could find nothing to implicate Cunningham in the disappearance of Libby. She was duty bound to investigate this line of inquiry but was convinced that he was innocent. They now had evidence that a man wearing a military style camouflage jacket had abducted both Libby Ellis and Kelly Spencer. She wondered why there were no pictures of Kelly. She knew that a man was seen using a camera outside Caroline Ensley's house but again there was no photographic evidence. Woods sighed and scratched her head thoughtfully. Matthew Cunningham was a professional photographer so was there some kind of link there, something that she had overlooked. Picking up a pen, she made a note on a pad.

The last person to see Libby was Julia Peters, the editor of *Fashion Today*. Woods knew that Libby was a freelance fashion journalist who wrote articles for various magazines but was currently working for *Fashion Today*. Turning back to the photographs, she found the shots of the women together at the cafe. Maybe there was a clue here, she thought, a pattern or sequence in the pictures that she had not yet found. Perhaps all the women featured were potential victims, they appeared connected in various ways, but with the exception of Kelly Spencer. Where did she fit in? Woods made another note on her pad.

Laying the photographs out on her desk, she pored over them again searching for anything that might tell her what was going on but after fifteen minutes, she gave up. Perhaps the message here was simple, no aspect of these people's lives was private. The abductor could observe them whenever he wanted and would prove it with his camera. Pushing the photographs into a neat pile, she reached for a file and began to scan a report. DC James had conducted the initial interview with Julia Peters and had put together a comprehensive and surprisingly well written account. He may be incredibly annoying at times but at least he could write a decent report. When she had finished reading, Woods realised that they still had very little to go on. Whenever she thought they were about to make a breakthrough it would frustratingly lead to nothing and now was no exception. She had been in situations like this before and sitting back in her chair thought about her trusted colleague DI Terry Ashton. Together they had worked through many problems and invariably managed to come up with the answers. They used to work well together and she missed him more than she cared to admit. She was tempted to telephone him, tell him about the case, encourage him to come up with a few suggestions but that would be unethical. Terry no longer worked for the Force. He had retired recently and was now supporting his daughter the cellist Mia Ashton. Woods smiled as thoughts of her old friend and colleague filled her with hope.

Suddenly DC James appeared at her door.

"Morning," he said cheerfully. "Mind if I come in?"

"Of course," she replied indicating to an empty chair.

"What are we up to today?"

Clearly, they were equally as clueless.

"DCI Wyman will be chasing us for answers again soon I guess."

"I'm sure he will," her smile faded as she studied him thoughtfully, then she made up her mind.

"I would like you to chase up PC Yearsley. See if he's had any luck with tracing the movements of the white van from the moment it picked up Libby Ellis. We need to know exactly where it went."

"Sure," he nodded eagerly then his eyes strayed to the files piled up on her desk.

"As you can see, I'm still trawling through statements and the stuff we took from Libby's office. I'm trying to find a link between her and Kelly Spencer." Looking up she frowned before going on. "Perhaps we should track down Kelly's parents, see if they can remember the name of Callum's father."

"Ah," James looked troubled as he fumbled in his pocket for his notebook. "Both her parents are deceased. It was a question I asked Caroline Ensley in my initial interview."

"Oh," Woods replied wondering why she had not read this in one of his reports. Perhaps he was not the comprehensive author that she gave him credit for.

"I've been thinking," he said as he fiddled with his notebook. "It should be possible to track both Kelly and Libby's whereabouts using their mobile phones."

Woods stared at him before replying. "That's assuming they have their phones with them and they have a signal. Their abductor would of course have confiscated them." Matthew Cunningham had already told her that he had not received any calls or messages from Libby since her disappearance. "I believe that the phones need to be operating in order to track their signal. I will chase up the surveillance team for more information."

Chapter Twenty Seven

PASCALE WOKE TO THE SOUND of her phone ringing and rolling over she waited for it to go to voicemail. Her head was spinning mercilessly and her throat was parched so there was no way she was going to answer it. Events of the previous evening were unclear and difficult to recall but in flashing moments of lucidity, snapshots of the party came back to her. How she managed to become so drunk was a complete mystery, it had never happened before. Unlike her British colleagues, she was not in the habit of drinking excessively. Pulling herself up into the sitting position, she reached for the glass of water perched on the bedside table and drank greedily before glanced at the time on her phone. It was almost midday and she cursed silently. She had missed the meeting with Veronique who was going to inform everyone about their next assignment in Rome.

Pascale groaned miserably and touched her fingers to her hair. It was still tightly plaited but was now a little untidy so with trembling fingers she began to work it loose. Her dress was hanging on the door of the wardrobe and closing her eyes, she tried to remember who had brought her back to the hotel. She had no memory of leaving Veronique's party so groaning again she swung her legs over the side of the bed and headed towards the bathroom.

Her stomach complained angrily as she stared at herself in the mirror. Her face was pale and there were shadows beneath her eyes, she was horrified and vowed never to drink again. Leaning over the sink, she splashed cold water over her face but a wave of nausea stole her strength and she collapsed onto the toilet seat. Holding her head in her hands, she waited for the sensation to pass. Clearly, the day would have to be conducted at a slow and delicate pace so it began with a long soak in the bath.

Matt was trying to work, put the finishing touches to a number of images but it was proving impossible. He usually found composing digitally enhanced photographs satisfying but all he could think about was Libby. Saving his work to a file, he leaned back in his chair and sighed wearily. Events of the previous evening gave him no peace. He had failed to deliver Pascale to the car in the multi-storey car park and he could only imagine what this would mean for Libby. He had not yet heard from her tormentor and with the uncertainty of waiting came psychological misery.

His phone began to ring and startled out of his thoughts, he snatched it up and pressed it against his ear.

"Hello Matt, it's Julia, Julia Peters."

"Oh," he replied doing nothing to disguise his disappointment. "Julia, hello."

"Have you heard anything yet from the police?" she asked undeterred by his lack of enthusiasm.

"No, not much." Uncertain of what she might know already, he was reluctant to go on.

"The police interviewed me the other day," she confided in him. "I was warned against talking to anyone about it but I don't suppose you count. I've heard nothing since and we are all desperately worried here at *Fashion Today*."

"The police have spoken to you?" Matt was surprised, he had no idea that she had been interviewed.

"Sure, didn't you know?"

"No. They have seen me a couple of times, including a visit here to our office but I've heard nothing more."

"Well," she huffed, "surely you of all people should be kept in the loop."

"Perhaps they have nothing yet to report." He couldn't tell her that Libby would be in even greater danger if he were to contact the police.

"I know people," she was saying. "Perhaps I could find out how the investigation is going."

"I'm not sure that would be a good idea." Matt replied a little too quickly.

"Why," Julia asked suspiciously. "Is there something you would rather I didn't know?"

"No, of course not. It's just that I don't feel comfortable prying into police business."

"Oh come on Matt, this is Libby we are talking about and it seems to me that the police are keeping you in the dark. Don't you think you have the right to know about everything that is being done to find her?"

"Yes of course but I'm certain they know what they are doing."

"Well I don't know about that. I simply can't sit back and do nothing. I'm determined to find out what happened to Libby." She paused, waiting for her words to make an impression then she said. "What's more, I would really appreciate your help."

Matt swallowed noisily and held the phone closer to his ear.

"We need to help her Matt," Julia insisted.

He wanted to agree, share everything that he knew with her, but how could he do that when he had been warned about going to the police?

"What is your problem Matt, don't you want to find her?"

"Of course I do, I'm out of my mind with worry."

"Then let's do something about it."

Julia was not the police and he desperately needed someone to confide in. She seemed an unlikely ally but Libby held her in high esteem.

"Let's meet up and discuss this further." He surprised himself with a sudden rush of optimism. "Are you available this afternoon?"

"I could be later," she replied and suggested they meet at a wine bar close to where she worked.

When their conversation was over, Matt stared blankly at the computer screen. He would have to decide just how much to tell her. How far should he go, would it be wise to include his part in the plot to kidnap Pascale? What would she think of him then?

Chapter Twenty Eight

DC JAMES MADE HIS WAY up to the surveillance department situated on the top floor. He had already warned PC Yearsley that he was on his way and his colleague told him that he had some interesting information to pass on. The department was busy, a hive of noise that was quite uncharacteristic for an area that was usually quiet and calm. Whenever James came up here he was reminded of a library, but today it was quite different, something big must be going on.

"Don't worry about them," Yearsley said as he ushered James into his computer room then closing the door behind them, the din of progress became muted.

"Don't you ever wish that it was you at the sharp end?"

Yearsley looked at James and grimaced. "Not in the slightest, I'm happy here surrounded by my screens where like an ageing General I can conduct the battle from the safety and comfort of my chair."

James was not convinced, he preferred the hands on approach. Being in the middle of things as they kicked off gave him a thrill and he tended to ignore the dangers. It didn't seem right, employing cameras and computers to catch criminals. Whatever happened to traditional policing?

"I've had some luck with your white van." Yearsley began as he sat down in front of the huge computer screen.

"Now that will make the boss happy," James grinned as he pulled up a chair and sat down beside his colleague.

"I'm not sure about that," Yearsley mumbled as his fingers danced over the keyboard.

Suddenly the screen came alive with images of the streets of London.

"Here is your van exiting the side street."

They watched as the vehicle nosed into view then it turned onto a main road and sped away.

"The next sighting is along the Embankment."

A series of stills appeared, static images that traced its progress east.

"We know it didn't go far but unfortunately I can't tell you where it went exactly. I lost sight of it in Whitechapel but managed to pick it up again on its return journey."

"So, he must have made his drop somewhere in Whitechapel."

Yearsley simply nodded in agreement then he highlighted another image. "This was taken as the vehicle approached a camera along Upper Thames Street."

The van was coming towards them, the head and shoulders of the driver clearly visible through the windscreen but as Yearsley zoomed in, the quality deteriorated alarmingly.

"Can that be cleaned up?" James asked as he peered at the screen.

Yearsley worked feverishly, minimising images and opening files and when he was done, he leaned back in his chair and waited for the program to complete its work.

"This might take a few moments," he said as they watched expectantly.

When it was finished, there was an improvement in quality but the features of the driver remained blurred. They could just make out his facial expression as he negotiated the traffic. His dark hair was cropped short and he was wearing a camouflage jacket.

"It's the best I can do I'm afraid."

"Good work," James said. "That's our man all right and this time he's not wearing a hat pulled down over his face. Could I have copies of all those images?"

"Of course, I can email you the entire file if you want."

"Yes please but can I have a hard copy of this one?" he nodded at the screen. "DS Woods will be thrilled to see him."

The printer behind them began to whirr.

"Oh yes," he said as if remembering something important. "We need to monitor mobile phone calls and signals. Who do I need to talk to about that?"

Yearsley glanced at him. "I'll get someone to contact you shortly."

James returned to Woods office to find it empty. The files she was working on lay open on her desk and the coffee in her mug was cold. Turning his back on her office, he went to the desk he was using in the incident room and sitting down at his computer, he entered his password. The file he had requested was already there so double clicking the mouse, he opened it and took another look at the images. A message arrived shortly after, minimising the files he accessed his emails. It was from a woman called Fiona Richardson, one of PC Yearsley's colleagues. She was available to see him right away, so heaving himself out of his chair, he began the long journey back up to the top floor.

Fiona Richardson was a petite redhead who stood barely five feet tall. She was in her early thirties but passed for someone much younger. She no longer found it flattering to have to prove her age when out for an evening on the town.

"DC James," she smiled as he appeared at her door and rising to her feet, she held out her hand.

James stared at her approvingly and wished that his heart would stop hammering. He had just climbed several flights of stairs for the second time that morning and was now regretting not having taken the lift.

"PC Yearsley tells me that you might have a job for me," she said as they shook hands.

"Yes," he replied breathlessly and wondered why he had not seen her around the station before.

Recovering quickly from his exertions and this unexpected encounter, he briefed her on the case that he was working on. Leaving out the details, he gave her enough to understand the nature of his request.

"We can track public handsets over a targeted area," she told him when he was finished.

James nodded his head and waited for her to continue.

"The system that we use intercepts SMS messages and phone calls by secretly duping the phone into operating on a false network."

"That sounds interesting," James smiled.

"You need to be aware of how it works in order to understand the limitations." She realised that he was probably unfamiliar with the technology.

"Can you track a mobile phone and pinpoint its position?"

"It's not as simple as that." Sitting back in her chair, she folded her arms before going on. "Our system works by emitting a signal over an area of approximately ten square kilometres. It forces mobile phones to release their unique IMSI and IMEI identity codes which can be used to track its movements in real time."

He had no idea what she was talking about but he loved the sound of her voice. His heart began racing all over again but this time it was not down to exertion. He had never been out with a redhead before so decided not to let this opportunity pass him by.

"IMSI?" he asked lamely when he realised that she was waiting for a response.

She began to explain that phones have a unique identity installed at manufacture and this is what helps in tracking devices over the mobile network.

"In most cases when you turn off a phone, even if you don't remove the battery it will stop communicating with our system. In that case it will only be traced to the location in which it was powered down."

"So we can't use it as a tracking device?"

"Not unless it remains switched on. It seems that in the case you have described it's likely that the phone is powered down once it's been used to transmit a message."

James realised that even if they did manage to get a fix on its position, by the time they got there the device and the person using it would be long gone unless of course the abductor was foolish enough to transmit from his lair.

"I can give you the make of the phone, the network it employs and its number."

"That's all useful information," she smiled again.

"How about your number?" he grinned cheekily as he looked up at her. "If I give you mine will you give me yours?"

"Nice try," she replied dryly. "You have my email details and of course my office extension number. Quite enough to be going on with don't you think?"

James nodded ruefully. He thought that she might be flirting with him but was not at all convinced, it could easily have been a rebuff.

"You will let me know of developments?"

"Of course," she said, as he got to his feet.

Chapter Twenty Nine

IT WAS LATER THAN PLANNED when Julia arrived at the wine bar. She had been unavoidably detained at the office.

"I'm so sorry." She murmured as she shrugged off her coat.

"There's no need," he smiled reassuringly as he watched her sit down. "I quite understand and I've been well catered for." He nodded towards the empty glass standing on the little wooden table that separated them.

Julia took a few moments to relax then she began to tell him about her day. Talking to him easily it was as if she had known him for years. Matt was amused but he reserved judgement. Libby had told him that Julia could be quite difficult at times, she liked to get her own way.

"So, what are you drinking?" she asked eventually eyeing his empty glass.

"No, please allow me," Matt insisted as he got to his feet. "I'm drinking Shiraz but what would you prefer?"

"Shiraz would be divine."

"Well, in that case I had better order a bottle."

Julia watched as he dodged his way to the crowded bar. The place was noisy with executives enjoying a glass of something before making their way home to the suburbs. She couldn't help thinking how lucky Libby was to have a man like Matthew Cunningham. She had thought about this before and now having met him was convinced. Not only was he handsome he was in possession of an impeccable reputation. His photographic expertise was widely sought after and she wondered how it was that Veronique Moreau managed to monopolise him as much as she did. His coat was hanging over the arm of his chair and she noticed a buff coloured file hidden beneath it. What secrets were hidden there she wondered.

Matt was surprisingly quick, carrying a bottle of red wine and a glass he weaved his way back to where she was sitting.

"That didn't take long," she smiled.

Matt did not reply, he filled her glass first before pouring wine into his own then he sat down. This was one of her favourite places, the staff knew how to take care of their wine and although popular, it was the perfect place to unwind at the end of the day. Soon the mad rush would be over and they would be able to talk more easily but for now, she was happy to sip at the contents of her glass and observe Matt from across the table. Earlier he had sounded troubled and although she hardly knew him, her instincts told her that he was being guarded. It could of course be his way, but it aroused her interest further.

"What do you think of Veronique Moreau?" she asked suddenly. "Do you enjoy working with her?"

The question caught him unawares and he wondered what it was that she really wanted to know. Julia was not in direct competition with Veronique but there were similarities in their work. Veronique's editorial was hardly a main stream publication, it was designed exclusively for her boutiques and dedicated to fashion.

"So, you have heard nothing from the police?" she changed the subject. He was obviously uncomfortable talking about his work so expertly she guided him onto the conversation that was the purpose of this meeting.

"No, they have been surprisingly quiet," he said before going on to tell her about the police visiting their house and office. "They took away a number of files."

"Really," her eyebrows disappeared beneath her fringe. "Why would they do that?"

"I have no idea," Matt replied before admitting they had also removed Libby's laptop.

"I guess its standard procedure. When someone disappears suddenly like that, the police are obliged to build up a complete personal profile." She didn't like to remind him that it was often the partner or spouse who was considered the prime suspect.

"Do you think her kidnapping was a random act, Libby in the wrong place at the wrong time or is there more to it than that?"

Matt hesitated for too long and Julia got her answer. Sitting upright, she leaned in towards him.

"Someone has been following us," he admitted, "taking photographs of us together."

"Really?" her eyes widened with interest. "How do you know there are photographs? Did you see someone with a camera?"

"No, we didn't see anyone, but we have evidence."

"So you do have photographs," she persisted, glancing briefly at the file under his coat.

"No," Matt replied shifting uncomfortably in his seat. Suddenly he felt awkward. He was having a conversation that he thought he could never have and in just a few minutes, Julia had managed to get information out of him.

How did she know about his file, was he that transparent or was she particularly perceptive? He would have to be more careful. "The police have those photographs."

"You said they are images of you and Libby."

He nodded before telling her about the time they had visited the restaurant. "It was as we were leaving that the pictures were taken."

"So someone must have been waiting for you outside."

"Yes," he nodded his head again.

"They must have known you were there, followed you earlier, or had prior knowledge of your plans to visit that particular restaurant."

"I suppose so." He had not given it much thought.

The police had asked him similar questions but at the time, he was unable to process the implications.

"There are more photographs," he added, "these include other people." He described the images of him working in Brighton.

"Were there any of Libby on her own?"

"No, not on her own." He told her about the pictures of herself and Libby at a cafe.

"Really, there are photographs of us together?"

"Yes, I'm afraid so."

"The police didn't tell me that." She sounded surprised.

"I gave them the photographs before they interviewed you."

"Maybe that's why they chose to speak to me. I thought it was because I was the last person to see Libby." Draining her glass, she swallowed noisily then she asked. "Have you any idea who might be doing this?"

"No, honestly I don't." He reached for the bottle and re-filled her glass.

"Well, I assure you that I can think of no one who would do such a thing," she told him, her eyes straying once again to his file.

Matt watched her carefully and tried to assess her motive. At first he thought that she might be fishing for a story, a sensational scoop for her magazine but as the police had told her not to discuss the case it was unlikely that she was thinking about publishing. She seemed genuine enough and it only reinforced his need for an ally. Julia and Libby were not just colleagues they were friends so she was the ideal candidate, someone with whom he could share the burden of truth. He made up his mind and reaching for his file, he said.

"This came through my door the other day."

Placing her glass carefully on the table Julia reached for the envelope and opened it. She gasped in horror when lifting out the printed images then sitting back heavily in her chair took a closer look. Libby was hanging by her wrists in what appeared to be a squalid little room and shockingly was dressed in nothing but her underwear.

"Have the police seen these?"

"No, I was warned against going to the police."

"What do you mean?"

"I was told that if I did then Libby would suffer the consequences."

He decided not to reveal the other pictures, Julia had seen enough to realise the gravity of the situation.

"What does he want?"

"I have no idea."

"Have you received a ransom demand?"

"No," he replied miserably.

He could hardly tell her about the man's demands or his part in drugging Pascale. Suddenly his phone alerted him to an incoming message and he stiffened. Julia noticed his reaction and realised this could be something important.

"Aren't you going to respond to that?" she asked after a few moments.

Slowly he produced his phone from his pocket and with trembling fingers pressed a series of buttons. This was what he had been waiting for and he knew that it was going to be unpleasant. A crowded wine bar was hardly the place to receive a message like this and he was tempted to get up and walk away.

Julia watched as he struggled with his emotions. This was no ordinary text message that much was clear, it had to be something to do with Libby.

"Are you okay?" she asked and getting to her feet, went to stand beside him. "Is it about Libby?"

Matt said nothing, he simply looked up at her and Julia could see that he was stunned. He did not resist when she took his phone then as she looked at the image on the little screen, she gasped.

Libby was tied down to some kind of rack, she was naked and completely at the mercy of whoever was doing this. There were several more images and as she scrolled through Julia became even more horrified. It was hard to believe that it was real.

"What the hell is going on?" she demanded.

Matt was unable to respond, he was leaning forward with his head in his hands.

"We have to find out who is doing this to Libby." Julia told him forcefully. "Do you hear me Matt?"

Slowly he lifted his head and stared at her, his face grey with shock. His expression was murderous and when they made eye contact, she almost looked away. She could only guess at what was going through his mind. He would need time to come to terms with this new horror, only then would they be able to discuss the way forward. Reaching out she took hold of his hand and squeezed it tightly in an effort to convey warmth and hope.

"Come on," she whispered, "let's get out of here."

Once outside, she led him towards the embankment where a chilly breeze was coming up off the river. Here there were not so many people so linking her arm through his, she held onto him. Under different circumstances, she would have enjoyed the pretty lights that lit the promenade. The bridges that spanned the Thames were magnificent, their illuminations reflecting romantically from the surface of the river but she saw none of this.

"Jesus Matt, I didn't appreciate just how serious this is."

Matt had still not said a word and as they walked, Julia glanced sideways at him. This time his face was not so pale, the fresh air seemed to be reviving him, but he still looked haggard and decades older than before. She wanted to take hold of him, hug him tightly until all this unpleasantness had gone away but that was impossible. The images of Libby burned fiercely into her brain and her imagination gave her no respite. Undoubtedly, he was thinking the same. These photographs sent a powerful message.

"Look, I have a friend who works in surveillance. Maybe she could help us to find who is doing this."

"How do you imagine she can do that?" He sounded bitter and drained of hope. "We have nothing to go on."

"We do," she reassured him. "He sent you that file by email so there must be a way of tracing it, find out where it came from."

Matt thought about it before replying. "He uses Libby's phone to send me messages but whenever I try to return the call it goes to voicemail."

"He obviously turns it off once he has sent it," she thought for a moment before going on. "I'll speak to my friend, see if it would be possible to track Libby's phone. That will be a start."

"Did you say she works in surveillance?"

"Yes, she used to be freelance but now operates with the police."

"She would have the means to track people then, devices that can be used to listen in on conversations or track vehicles."

"I suppose so. It's all a bit beyond me I'm afraid."

Suddenly he stopped and turned towards her.

"I have something that I must tell you."

He blurted it out and in shocked silence she listened. It was impossible to judge him, she realised that he had been given no choice and she understood just how difficult it must have been for him.

"I failed to deliver Pascale into the hands of this man, that's why Libby is suffering so much."

"Oh Matt, how awful." Julia could hardly believe what he had just told her. "The poor girl must have felt dreadful this morning, those kind of drugs can make you quite ill." Her comment did nothing to salve his guilt. "How well do you know her?" she asked as an idea began to take shape.

"Pascale is one of Veronique's models. I have worked with her on a couple of occasions."

"She is not a friend of yours then?"

"No, definitely not a friend. Do you honestly think that I could have done this to her if she was?"

Julia studied him thoughtfully but said no more. She would have to think her idea through very carefully before discussing it with him.

Chapter Thirty

"DS Woods, what can I do for you?"

Woods had requested a meeting with her boss DCI Wyman but he was heading up a busy day and could only spare her a few moments in the corridor. She knew exactly what had to be done but required his backing before putting her ideas into action.

"We have managed to track the van used to abduct Libby Ellis. It took her to Whitechapel but unfortunately we have no idea where it stopped."

"Whitechapel," Wyman said thoughtfully as he glanced at the surveillance images that she was holding.

"The area of Shoreditch to be more precise."

"Well that narrows it down then," he retorted. "So how do you intend to proceed?"

"I would like to mobilise local officers, increase the footfall in that area."

"Where do you suggest they begin and what do you suppose they will be looking for?"

His patronising attitude was not lost on Woods. She knew that he didn't care for her and he resented the fact that she was actively seeking promotion. She had no idea why he felt this way, she had done nothing to upset him. Wyman had transferred to the Met from the other end of the country, they had no previous history, she had never met him before.

"We should target the main route through the area," she said calmly, "begin at Dock Street, Leman Street then move on into Commercial Street."

"That's a huge area to cover and being a main route it's likely to be very busy. I doubt that our abductor is operating from there. Don't you think he would prefer somewhere a little less crowded, a back street perhaps?"

"I agree and fully expect to discover something off the main route but as the van was not in Shoreditch for long, his hideout must be close by."

Wyman frowned and stared at her for a moment before saying. "Leave it to me, I'll get back to you, but it's unlikely to be today." Checking his watch his frown deepened. "Have a word with the Metropolitan Police Services, their SNT could probably help get the ball rolling."

Woods sighed heavily and watched as he hurried away along the corridor. The Safer Neighbourhood Team would probably be a good start. They worked closely with the authorities and had impeccable knowledge of the area but it was not what she had in mind. It was her intention to mobilise officers from the local police stations.

Returning to her office, she carried out a little research of her own. Being unfamiliar with this part of London, she decided to consult the internet and tour the streets virtually from the comfort of her chair. Once she had compiled a list of likely hideouts, she was going to check them out for herself. This was likely to be a huge task, far too big for her and DC James alone, they would need the support of local officers, but only Wyman could sanction that.

They had been locked in the cell that Kelly christened 'the torture chamber' for almost twenty four hours and being surrounded by such frightening contraptions did nothing to raise their spirits. Food was in short supply but at least they had water. Like her own cell, there was a tiny hand basin with a single cold tap and a toilet in the corner. There was no privacy but she was becoming accustomed to that.

Libby seemed to be recovering from her ordeal although understandably was subdued and clearly still in shock. Kelly was full of admiration, she was convinced that subjected to the same treatment she would have lost her mind. She did not understand why Libby was being so badly treated, what had she done to deserve such punishment? The brutality had begun the moment she arrived. During their time together, they had learnt a little about each other. Kelly told her about her son Callum and in exchange, Libby described her life as a fashion journalist. Kelly was amazed, she knew very little about the subject and was full of questions.

"So Matt, your boyfriend, is a photographer?" She had never heard of Matthew Cunningham so was unfamiliar with his work and reputation.

Libby told her all about Matt and Kelly listened with growing interest.

"He is a fashion photographer."

"Wow, so he gets to meet loads of beautiful models."

"He does although not all of them are as perfect as you might think."

"What about locations, do you go with him to all those wonderful places?"

Libby smiled at her naivety.

"He does get to visit some glamorous cities like Paris, New York and Rome for example but I rarely go with him. You have to understand that he goes to these places to work, he doesn't always have time to go off on sightseeing trips." She decided not to mention that working outside often meant enduring inclement weather. "He does have other interests," she added. "He likes to photograph architecture and bridges."

"Oh," Kelly looked at her and pulled a face. She couldn't understand why anyone would be interested in bridges.

"Do you think our man is a photographer?"

Libby frowned at the suggestion. How could their captor possibly share an interest with Matt? "I doubt it," she whispered. "He simply uses images to intimidate and humiliate." She shuddered and a tear escaped from the corner of her eye. She worried that Matt may have seen the latest pictures and she was mortified. What must he be thinking? She began to sob again.

Kelly had more questions but clearly, Libby was in no state to answer. She was far more fragile than she thought. Kelly experienced confusing emotions. She was dismayed at what Libby was going through but at the same time was relieved that she herself was not the focus of his attention. She wanted to know why he was doing this. What was there to gain by humiliating Libby in such a way? She could not understand why they were locked up in this depressing place. There was no reason for it. She had no money and could think of no one willing to part with cash to secure her release. She had Callum that much was true but in reality, she was nobody in a world full of strangers. Kelly sighed, locked up for a long period in such stressful conditions was troubling her more than she cared to admit. Her confidence was slowly being undermined but she had to remain strong for Libby.

Chapter Thirty One

MATT WAS STARING AT HIS computer. The images sent to his phone were now on the screen and in the privacy of his office, he was attempting to view them objectively. This was the only way it could work, block out the reality and convince himself that it wasn't Libby. He had to decide if they were genuine or made up compositions, digitally enhanced arrangements designed to shock.

Libby was tied to what could only be described as an instrument of torture. He had never seen anything like it before. Her suffering seemed real enough, the compromising position in which she was held implied that rape may have been part of her ordeal but he could not allow himself to believe that. The images were real enough, he was convinced of that. These were the most alarming to date and clearly, Libby was being made to suffer because of his failure. If he had delivered Pascale as instructed then none of this would have happened. The message was clear enough he would not fail again.

Suddenly his phone began to ring.

"Cunningham, how are you enjoying the picture show?"

"What have you done to Libby, where is she?"

"You don't have to worry, she is being taken care of."

"If you harm her...",

"There is nothing that you can do to stop me. I can do anything." He paused, allowing his hateful words to sink in. "Now listen. To avoid further unpleasantness you will deliver the French girl to me."

"How do you expect me to do that?" Matt shouted in frustration.

"At the end of your road you will find a black taxi cab, the keys are in the ignition. The girl is expecting to be picked up in twenty minutes so you will go to the hotel where she is staying and collect her. On the dashboard, you will find instructions. Follow them carefully to the location I have selected. When you arrive all you have to do is walk away leaving her locked inside the cab."

"What?" Matt cried. "How do you expect me to do that?" He waited for an answer but it was no good, the connection was broken, the caller had gone.

Matt stared at his phone and his hand began to shake. He now had less than twenty minutes in which to carry out this hateful crime. Images of Libby tied helplessly to the frame threatened to overwhelm him and he could almost hear her screams. Glancing briefly at the computer screen, he knew what he had to do and this time he must not fail so getting to his feet, he reached automatically for his camera.

The cab was parked at the end of the street exactly where he was told it would be and reaching for the door, he looked around anxiously before pulling it open. Slipping into the driver's seat, he started the engine. The light on top of the cab was not illuminated, so as he made his way into town was spared being hailed by prospective passengers.

Pascale was waiting on the pavement outside the hotel and as Matt approached, his stomach tightened. Surely, she would recognise him so sinking lower into his seat, he avoided making eye contact as he pulled up at the side of the road. He did not have to worry, Pascale climbed into the back of the cab and arrogantly gave him her destination before sitting back.

Pulling away from the kerb Matt sighed with relief. Her cool attitude might work in his favour this time, but he wondered how long it would be before she realised that it was him. The traffic was surprisingly light as they headed along the Embankment. The location written on the pad was somewhere in Whitechapel, but he was not familiar with the area. Fortunately, the directions were clear enough but designed to give nothing away. Although hand written, an analyst would be unable to build up a character profile from this.

"Where are we going?" Pascale called out.

The knot in his stomach tightened. He did not expect her to realise so soon that they were heading away from Veronique's boutique.

"This is not the right way," she insisted.

Hunching his shoulders against her protests, he resisted the urge to glance in the rear view mirror. He was amazed that she had still not recognised him.

Leaning forward, Pascale tapped against the glass partition that separated them.

"You are going the wrong way," she said louder this time. "You must turn around."

Matt continued to ignore her. The little red light on the dashboard told him that the rear doors were locked, Pascale could not escape. She didn't know it yet but she was already a prisoner. He could of course pull over, turn around and drive her to safety but images of Libby burned into his brain, he couldn't let her down again.

Pascale began beating at the glass with her fist.

"If you don't stop immediately I will call, the police."

In her hand, she held her phone but it was a useless threat. She had never been to this part of London before so could not tell the police where she was.

The roads were full of black cabs and without the licence plate number, the police would have no way of identifying them.

Swinging off the main road, Matt drove into a side street as directed. Here grubby terraces and small industrial warehouses replaced the glamour of the city but finding a place to park was impossible. Cars lined both sides of the narrow street, manoeuvring was not an option so stopping at a junction, he bumped up onto the pavement and prepared to abandon the vehicle.

Pascale pulled at the handle but the door would not budge and she became frantic in her attempt to escape. Matt hurried away, he felt terrible leaving her like this. It was his intention to find a place to hide then photograph the abductor as he appeared but unfortunately, it was already too late. The sound of an engine revving alerted Matt to his error and as he spun round, he automatically brought his camera up and began taking pictures but all he got was images of a rapidly receding taxicab. Stumbling to the side of the road, he dry retched before collapsing onto the pavement. A passer by stared at him but did nothing to help. Matt could hardly believe what he had done. Pascale was innocent and did not deserve to be drawn into this terrible business. He could hardly imagine what terrors awaited her but at least it might draw unwanted attention away from Libby. All he could do now was demand her release, he had carried out his part and it was a fair exchange.

Fiona Richardson was surprised when a signal from the phone she had been asked to monitor appeared on her computer screen. Initiating the program, she stared at the information coming in. A call was made to another mobile phone so reaching for a pen, she copied down the number. It lasted for just under sixty seconds then the signal was lost. Working the keyboard, she triangulated the coordinates then sitting back in her chair, she smiled with satisfaction as a location was revealed then, reaching for her telephone, she called DC James.

Chapter Thirty Two

THE CAB PULLED SHARPLY TO a stop and as it had rocked over the pavement, Pascale was thrown sideways. She was furious and continued to scream obscenities in both French and English. The driver, a different man this time ignored her just like the first and when he got out, she watched helplessly as he unlocked a huge padlock that secured a tall pair of panelled gates. The man was stocky and muscular, his hair cropped short against his head and he wore a military style camouflage coat. Once the gates swung open, he returned to the cab and drove into a small courtyard then getting out for the last time, he secured the gates before releasing the locks on the cab doors.

"Who are you?" she hissed as she scrambled out and glancing around she shuddered. Her surroundings reminded her of a prison. "What do you think you are doing, why have you brought me here?"

He remained silent, content for the moment to listen to her outburst then suddenly he grabbed hold of her arm and pushed her towards a doorway.

"Take your hands off me," she screamed, the sound of her voice echoing around the courtyard.

"Get in there." He nodded towards a door that stood open.

"I will do no such thing." She stared at him defiantly and dodged nimbly out of his way as he reached for her. "If you touch me again I will scratch your eyes out."

His face creased with merriment and as he shoved her, she almost lost her footing. Recovering her balance, she turned on him and carried out her threat raking her nails over his cheek but retribution was swift. Her arms were twisted violently up her back and as pain shot through her shoulders, Pascale cried out. Kicking backward, she hoped to make contact with his shins but he anticipated this move and tightened his grip. The agony of the increased pressure was unbearable and Pascale screamed.

"Carry on like that and I will break your arms," he hissed.

With him so close behind her and in the confines of the gloomy corridor, she was helpless. There was no room to manoeuvre, it was impossible to fight back. He admired her spirit. She was a lively creature, not quite what he had expected. She may be beautiful but she possessed a foul temper and he was looking forward to softening her up a little.

Finally, they arrived at a cell door and holding her against the wall, he pushed his face up close to hers.

"In there," he whispered, his breath hot against her cheek and with a final shove, she sprawled across the floor.

The door slammed noisily behind her and breathing heavily, she was shocked at the violence of this extraordinary turn of events. Raising herself up from the cold concrete floor, she stared fearfully at her surroundings. The room was tiny and offered no comforts. A steel framed bed covered by a thin mattress stood against a wall and in the corner was a small hand basin and toilet. There were no windows, the only light coming from a bulkhead light fixed to the wall above the door. Pascale shuddered and sobbed with disbelief, she had no idea who this man was or what she was doing there. Rubbing the soreness from her arms, she moved slowly towards the door then taking hold of the handle, tugged at it but it would not budge. It was made of steel and held together by large rivets. A narrow strip that resembled a letterbox flap was sealed from the outside and above that, a peephole stared back at her blankly. It reminded her of a door leading to a dungeon and her stomach lurched as realisation set in. She was a prisoner. Sitting down heavily on the mattress, she groaned. Why was this happening to her? She was supposed to be meeting with Veronique at the boutique to discuss the Italian trip and from the tone of the telephone conversation, this was clearly her last chance. She groaned again and going over the taxi journey in her mind, searched desperately for a clue as to what might be going on. Luckily, her bag was still slung over her shoulder and reaching for it, she fumbled for her phone. With trembling fingers she scrolled through her list of contacts looking for Veronique's number then pressing the call button she listened desperately for a ringtone. Nothing happened and staring at the small screen, she could see there was no signal so throwing it down, she cried out in frustration.

Returning to his control centre, he accessed the camera in her cell. She was a magnificent specimen and he watched as she searched through her bag. He should have taken that from her, there could be all kinds of weapons concealed in there, nail scissors, files or a sharp handled comb. He would have to take care when returning to her cell. The phone would be of no use, the signal could not penetrate the thick walls.

Her dark good looks fascinated him, she stood out over the other models. When he had first seen her in Brighton, he knew that she would become part of his plan. Reaching for the light switch he flicked it off plunging her cell into darkness, it was time to start softening her up.

Turning his attention to another monitor, he stared at the other women. They had been left for long enough, perhaps he should move them into a double cell. This was something that he should consider but for now, he decided to leave them where they were.

DC James went to the email that Fiona had sent him earlier. She had alerted him to the message and now as he opened the file he began to digest the words that appeared on the screen.

"What have you got there?" Woods asked as she passed by his desk.

"Fiona up in surveillance has managed to track a signal from Libby Ellis' phone."

"That's brilliant."

"Don't get too excited, she could only locate its position once the phone had been turned off."

Woods leaned towards him and read the message on the screen. It contained the number of the recipient and staring at it thoughtfully she said.

"That number, does it look familiar to you?"

James looked again and shook his head, it meant nothing to him.

Disappearing into her office, Woods returned a moment later carrying a folder.

"Would you believe it?" she looked at him incredulously. "That number belongs to Matthew Cunningham."

"What about the location?" James said jabbing his finger at the screen. "Isn't that the street where he lives?"

Chapter Thirty Three

"SO YOU CAN DO IT?"

Julia was sitting at a table in her favourite wine bar again but this time in the company of her friend Fiona.

"Of course, I can track mobile phones." Sparing Julia the technical details, she chose not to elaborate.

"Can you wire people, put a miniature microphone on them so as to listen in on conversations?"

"Yes," Fiona replied nodding her head slowly, wondering where this conversation was going. "That is possible."

"What about a bug or something to track a vehicle?"

"What is this?" Fiona laughed before reaching for her wine glass. "You must have been watching too many TV dramas." Sitting back in her chair, she regarded her companion with interest.

"A friend of mine is in a spot of trouble and could really do with our help."

Julia filled her in with the details and when she was finished, Fiona realised that she had heard this story before. Obviously, Julia was unaware that her friend was under police investigation.

"I can do all of the things that you have mentioned." Fiona told her when Julia was finished. "But you do realise that it's against the law to hack into someone's business."

"Even if a crime has been committed?"

"Well yes it makes no difference. If this is a police investigation then what you are suggesting would be tricky."

"Not if you were to take the job on privately."

"You know very well that I don't do that kind of work anymore. In case you haven't noticed, I now work for the police."

"Yes," Julia waved her hand dismissively in the air, "but technically you could take on the job."

"Look," sitting forward Fiona lowered her voice before going on. "The problem is, the situation you have described is something that the police are currently working on."

"Oh," Julia's eyes widened. "He told me that he was ordered to have nothing to do with the police."

"Really, by whom?" Fiona put her glass down on the little table and stared at her friend.

"If I tell you, you must swear to keep it to yourself, the life of someone may depend on it."

Fiona frowned, eager to hear more. If this was true then it was far more serious than she thought.

"My friend Libby has been abducted and her boyfriend Matt is doing all he can to find her. The kidnapper threatened that if he goes to the police then Libby will suffer the consequences."

Fiona raised her eyebrows in alarm. DC James had told her none of this, the only details she had been given were relating to a phone that belonged to a man they were interested in speaking with.

"Let me get this straight, your friend Libby has been abducted and could be in danger."

"Yes," Julia nodded, "I've seen the evidence."

"What do you mean?"

Julia told her about the images that Matt had shown her.

"Do the police know about this?"

"Of course not, I've just told you, Matt can't go to the police. He did initially and I believe that he gave them some photographs from an earlier incident but the latest images he's had to keep to himself." Julia shuddered at the memory of the pictures.

"So Matt is convinced that he can find his girlfriend Libby without help from the police." Fiona could hardly believe it.

"He does yes, that's why he needs our help."

DC James really should be informed of this latest development, Fiona thought. Withholding this kind of information was not a good idea especially given the circumstances. She would be in serious trouble if he found out that she had passed confidential details of an ongoing police investigation to a third party, but there must be something that she could do.

Matt was beside himself with guilt and pacing the floor in his lounge, he tried desperately to come to terms with the crime he had just committed. He reminded himself that he had done it for Libby, a mantra designed to right the wrong but still he was not convinced. Sitting down heavily in his favourite armchair, he tried to relax but it was impossible. Taking a deep breath he held onto it, then letting it out slowly he closed his eyes and rested his head back against the cushion. Images of Pascale panic stricken in the back of the cab haunted him mercilessly and he could still hear the sound of her cries. He had never liked her much, she was often rude and difficult to work with, but she did not deserve this. Opening his eyes in an effort to chase away the demons, he thought of Libby. She would soon be free, he had kept his part of the bargain, all he had to do now was wait and everything would be fine.

Through all of this, the voice of doubt nagged at him. Could this man be trusted? Was it his intention to release her? Had he even agreed to hand Libby over once he had Pascale?

His heart began to race again then suddenly the doorbell rang. Dragging himself to his feet, it was an effort to move then the doorbell chimed again.

"Mr Cunningham," DS Woods smile greeted him as he opened the door. "Do you mind if we come in?"

Matt was stunned to see the detectives standing there.

"Of course," he muttered, "please come in." Standing back, he allowed them into his home, before peering nervously along the street.

"Can I get you some tea or coffee?" he asked once Woods and James had settled.

"No thank you." They answered in unison.

Sinking heavily into an armchair, Matt did his best to sound calm and rational. "What can I do for you?"

Woods thought it strange that his first question was not requesting news. Most people in his situation would regard a visit at this stage of a police investigation with anxiety, fearing the worst.

"Have you heard from Miss Ellis lately?"

The question stunned him and it took a moment before he could answer.

"No," he replied.

The detectives glanced at each other before going on.

"How do you explain a telephone call made from Miss Ellis' phone to your number earlier today?"

James held out a piece of paper and automatically Matt took it but the trembling of his fingers blurred the numbers.

"Well Mr Cunningham," Woods prompted him. "That is your number?"

"Yes it is," Matt admitted.

He hardly needed to see it in print. When he looked up his distress was clear. "The abductor called me," he whispered.

"You spoke to the man doing this," James asked incredulously. "When were you going to inform us of this development?"

"I couldn't, I was told that if I had further contact with the police then Libby would suffer."

"You believe this do you Mr Cunningham?"

Matt stared at him and swallowed noisily.

"What did he want?" Woods asked softly then eying her partner, she leaned forward.

"He told me that it would not be good for Libby if I spoke to you."

"You have told us this already," she reminded him. "Why would he say such a thing, there must have been more."

"I don't know what he wants, he hasn't told me yet. I suppose his calls are designed to intimidate me."

"Calls?" James snapped. "Are you saying there have been more?"

Matt realised that he was being drawn in. He wasn't thinking clearly so was in danger of revealing more. If he was not careful, he would incriminate himself. He was convinced they knew nothing about Pascale, it was too early, she had probably not been missed yet. He also believed that he was safe. The man doing this would be unaware of this police visit because presumably he was busy with Pascale.

"Yes, he has telephoned before and sent messages by text."

"Do you still have these messages?"

"No," Matt replied a little too quickly. He did not want them to see the correspondence relating to Pascale.

"Can you explain why the person you spoke to made the call from this street?"

"What do you mean?"

"We know that whoever called you was standing not far from here."

"I had no idea," Matt replied, the blood draining from his face. It must have been when he delivered the taxi.

"Has he been here to your house Mr Cunningham?"

The question disturbed his thoughts and he paused before answering. "No but I guess he delivered the package of photographs himself, the pictures that I gave to you." He realised now that their house must have been under scrutiny for some time, how else could the man have known their movements?

"Have you received any more photographs?" Woods watched him carefully and when he hesitated, she knew the answer.

"Yes," he whispered unable to deny the fact that he had.

"Do you still have them?"

"Yes, they are on my computer."

"Can we see them please?"

Leading the way up to his office, Matt accessed his files. Luckily, he kept the images separate from the other correspondence so selecting the one that he was willing to reveal he opened it. A picture of Libby hanging from her wrists and dressed in nothing but her underwear filled the screen.

"Bloody hell!" James exclaimed. "When were you going to tell us about this?"

"I couldn't, don't you understand?"

"Can you send me that file please Mr Cunningham?" Woods said firmly, it was an order not a request.

Doing as he was told, Matt sent her an email but he was not about to reveal the latest images of his girlfriend tied naked to a wooden frame.

Chapter Thirty Four

"Izzy, we have another missing person." James called out from across the incident room as DS Woods walked towards her office. "It's a woman," he continued as he glanced at his notes, "a French woman by the name of Pascale Dominique."

"Who reported her missing?" Woods turned to face him, ignoring the fact that he had used her Christian name.

"Someone called Veronique Moreau. She owns a fashion boutique in the West End."

"Do we know from where the girl went missing?"

"The Waldorf Hotel, that's where she is staying."

The information he had was limited, it would be their job to fill in the details.

"Okay, we had better pay the boutique a visit before going to the hotel."

Piccadilly was as busy as usual and of course, there was nowhere to park so swinging her car into the kerb, Woods bumped the nearside wheels up onto the pavement and activated the hazard flashers. Although it was illegal to leave a vehicle there, she displayed a police notice that she kept in her glove compartment on the dashboard. Climbing out, she spotted a parking enforcement officer already making his way towards them.

"He'll be disappointed when he spots that," James remarked.

"Probably won't stop him from slapping a ticket on though, I just hope he doesn't have it towed away."

Pushing at the door of the boutique, Woods was impressed by the elegance of the clothing on display. The price tags however excluded her as a serious client and all she could do was dream of owning such luxurious items. After a moment, the spell was broken and as she announced their arrival DC James watched captivated as the young assistant went to inform her boss.

"Down boy!" Woods whispered under her breath. She knew exactly what her colleague was thinking.

An elegantly dressed woman appeared from an office at the back of the shop. It was impossible to predict her age and as she walked towards them she exuded the confidence that Woods associated with hugely successful women.

"Veronique Moreau," she introduced herself, her French accent beguiling then wasting no time she ushered them towards her office. It was obvious who they were, even in plain clothes. It would not do to have two police officers loitering on the shop floor.

"What makes you so sure that Pascale Dominique is missing?" Woods began once the pleasantries were over.

"She was due to arrive here earlier this morning to attend a meeting. I sent a taxi to collect her from her hotel but she failed to turn up."

"She has only been missing for a few hours." James pointed out.

"That is true," Veronique stared at him intently, "but she has no friends here in London and would not go out on her own in a strange city."

He glanced at Woods who took up the questioning.

"Do you have the name of the taxi firm that you called?"

"Not to hand but I will get someone to give you the details."

They watched as Veronique sat down at an ornate antique desk then, picking up a fountain pen she unscrewed the cap and scribbled a note on a pad.

"Have you tried calling Pascale on her mobile?" James continued. It was the obvious thing to do but he was obliged to ask.

"Of course but each time I try it simply goes to voicemail."

"Have you contacted the hotel?"

"Yes, I spoke to the concierge who assures me that he saw Pascale waiting in the foyer for the taxi to arrive."

James made notes of his own.

"She was there one minute then gone the next. The taxi arrived but she was no longer waiting." She was sounding more like a concerned parent than an employer.

"Was Pascale working whilst staying here in London?"

"Yes, we have just finished a fashion shoot and she is due to return home in a few days time. Pascale lives in the Limousin region of France." Veronique went on to tell them about the party she hosted. "I often do this after a successful shoot, it's nice to get the crew together and have a wonderful time."

"Are you based here?" Woods asked glancing around.

"No, my headquarters are in Paris, this is just one of my little shops."

Woods would hardly have described it as little, an area like this in such a prime location must cost a fortune to run.

"Could we have your details and the address of your headquarters in France?"

Veronique made another note on her pad.

"We need to start building up a profile of Pascale," James began. "Do you have a recent photograph of her?"

"Of course, she is a model." Veronique indicated to a magazine. "This is a copy of my boutique publication and voila, this is Pascale."

She tapped a perfectly shaped fingernail on the front cover of the magazine and reaching for it, James could see three young women smiling back at him. They were dressed in fashions from Veronique's own label.

"Pascale is the dark haired girl," she told him.

Veronique continued to answer the questions that Woods put to her as James perused the magazine. Pascale featured on several of the pages as she modelled a range of clothing. She was a very attractive girl, her dark looks and petite frame excited him. She was definitely a woman he would like to meet. At the top of one of the editorials, he discovered a name that was familiar to them so leaning towards Woods, he made her aware of it.

"Matthew Cunningham," she said astonished to see his name in print.

"Yes," Veronique confirmed. "He is the photographer that I prefer to use, in fact all the images in that magazine can be attributed to him."

"Where was the location of your last shoot?"

"It was in Brighton and also Salisbury Cathedral."

Veronique looked at the detectives and wondered why their questions had suddenly taken a different direction then she frowned as she saw something pass between them. Woods was thinking about the photographs that Matthew Cunningham had given them. He told her that he had been working in Brighton recently and if she was to check, she felt sure that she would find pictures of the same women featured in the magazine.

"These other models," she said glancing at the magazine. "Did they accompany you to Brighton?"

"Not all of them, but those with Pascale on the front cover did."

Taking the magazine from James, Woods studied the faces of the women before asking.

"Can we please have their names and contact details?"

Another note was added to Veronique's pad.

"Do you mind telling me what the meeting that Pascale missed was about?" James asked his final question.

"Oh that," she eyed him before going on. "It was to discuss our next assignment. I'm planning a photo shoot in Rome next month, it is to illustrate my autumn collection and Pascale is one of the models that I would like to have on my team."

"Will Matthew Cunningham be going along as photographer?"

"Yes I should hope so."

Not once did the detectives mention Libby Ellis. Veronique had heard rumours that she was missing although Matt had not confirmed this himself. It was something that she meant to discuss with him. Libby and now Pascale, she thought. He knew them both and she wondered if this was a coincidence or was there something more going on.

"I will ask someone to get this information for you." She smiled and getting to her feet waved the pad above her head as she ushered them towards the door.

Outside, Woods stared at her windscreen and muttered an oath. A parking ticket had been stuck to the glass and she knew just how difficult it would be to remove without leaving a sticky mess.

"Take the reference number of the officer who did this," she snapped, "pass it on to uniform. Make sure they give him a hard time."

He couldn't resist a smile as she began to peel the plastic cover from the windscreen.

Chapter Thirty Five

HE PICKED UP HIS CAMERA and made his way to her cell, it was time to make the model pose. Pushing his face up against the peephole in the door, he assessed the situation. Pascale was lying on the bed wrapped in her coat. Her bag was on the floor beside her and he could see nothing that could be used as a weapon, so it was safe to go in.

Pascale stirred at the sound of the key turning in the lock and swinging her legs over the side of the bed, she got to her feet.

"What is the meaning of this?" she demanded the moment he appeared.

"I want to take some pictures of you," he said pushing the door shut behind him. "You know what to do."

She said something in French that he did not catch and folding her arms across her chest she stared at him rebelliously.

"If you don't do as you are told then your situation will become a lot worse. I can assure you of that."

"Why am I here?" she asked ignoring his threat.

"You are here because I desire it."

"Because you desire it," she spat furiously. "Who do you think you are to desire it?"

"I am all you have. I am your link between life and death. You are now my plaything and you will do as you are told. We shall see how well you perform before I decide what is to be done with you."

Pascale could hardly believe what he was saying. Unaccustomed to being spoken to like this she made a serious error of judgement; she doubted his sincerity.

"You are nothing to me," she hissed, "now let me out of here before you regret it."

He laughed cruelly and she backed away. Ordinarily she would have stood her ground, rely on common decency to prevail but suddenly there was something about him that alarmed her.

"Now, are you going to do as I ask and allow me to take my photographs?"

"You will do no such thing," she snapped holding her head up defiantly.

This was definitely the wrong thing to say and before she had a chance to react, he pounced. He overwhelmed her completely and in seconds, she was reduced to helplessness. What could have been a relatively pain free session had just turned into something infinitely more unpleasant.

DCI Wyman called a meeting in the incident room and as DS Woods and DC James arrived, he studied them intently.

"DS Woods," he began when everyone had settled. "Would you care to get the ball rolling?" He wanted answers.

Turning to face her colleagues she was about to begin when Wyman made a comment.

"You had two missing persons, now you have three so won't you tell us what the hell is going on."

Woods glared at him before looking away, she refused to be intimidated by this man.

"A twenty six year old woman by the name of Pascale Dominique is the latest victim."

She activated the remote control that she was holding and an image of Pascale filled the screen on the wall behind her. "She was picked up from outside the Waldorf Hotel where she is staying." She went on to tell them about the black taxicab. "We have confirmation that a taxi was stolen from the city centre yesterday morning when a driver left it momentarily unattended."

"These vehicles usually carry some form of tracking device which enables an operator to track their movements," someone commented.

"That's true," Woods nodded her head in agreement, "but in this case it seems to have been disabled."

"So you have no idea where it went." Wyman stared at her.

"That's not entirely correct. We tracked the cab using CCTV to Whitechapel before it went off line."

"Whitechapel," Wyman repeated thoughtfully. "Isn't that where Libby Ellis was taken?"

"Yes sir, it is also the area that I want to focus on. I have contacted SNT as you advised but have heard nothing from them yet." She paused and stared back at him boldly, willing him to acknowledge their recent conversation. Her request to move in on Whitechapel had been ignored, he had obviously failed to take her seriously.

Wyman turned away and studied the map that was pinned to the board. "Get onto Shoreditch, Holborn and Paddington Green nicks, see what uniforms they have to spare. Send them a brief and get them out onto the streets."

"We know that the abductor has been in contact with Matthew Cunningham." Woods said, changing tack. "He has been withholding information because he received a warning advising him that if he spoke to us then it would have a negative impact on Libby Ellis."

Using the remote, she changed the image and as Libby appeared on the screen a shocked silence filled the room.

"Do we have details of the specific treatment that she might have endured?"

"No sir, naturally Cunningham was reluctant to go into details."

"Do you think he has more information to share with us?"

"Yes I do," she replied and stepping forward she continued. "If these threats are real then we have to tread very carefully. We can't be seen to do anything that would put Libby Ellis in even more danger."

"What about Kelly Spencer." Wyman asked. "Is there any news about her?"

"No sir, there has been nothing."

"If Cunningham is communicating with this man then perhaps we can use him to get us information about Kelly."

Woods frowned as she considered the consequences of his proposal. "It would be a risky move, I doubt that he even knows about Kelly Spencer. It may rouse suspicion if he suddenly starts asking questions about her."

The meeting went on as they discussed all aspects of the case. The evidence board was updated with details about Pascale Dominique and a plan of how to proceed was made. The investigation was gaining momentum but the pressure was about to rise even further.

Chapter Thirty Six

HOLDING HER BREATH, SHE LISTENED to the ringtone and when he finally answered, she announced. "Matt, it's Julia."

He sounded down as he responded.

"What's the matter?" she asked. "Have you heard from Libby's abductor?"

"No, it's not that," he replied. "The police have been here and they know that I have been speaking with the man doing this."

"Really, how did they find out?"

"They have been monitoring Libby's phone."

Julia thought about her friend Fiona.

"What did they say to you? Are they going to charge you with withholding information or something?"

"No, I don't think so. I explained that I was warned against making contact with them but I get the impression they have not finished with me yet."

"Look, I might be able to help." She decided not to mention the fact that Fiona worked for the police. "I have spoken to my friend who specialises in surveillance and she has agreed to lend me a tracking device. All we have to do is persuade your colleague Pascale to offer herself up to the abductor. Obviously, she will be wearing the monitor so we'll know where she has been taken then, we can inform the authorities."

It was a naive but simple plan that might have worked if Pascale was not already a prisoner.

Julia was astounded by what he said next, no wonder he sounded so low.

"I can't believe that he actually got you to do his dirty work," she said her voice full of recriminations.

"I had no choice," he defended himself bitterly. "The latest image that he sent was truly disturbing so I had to do it. I can hardly forgive myself." He whispered this last remark shamefully.

"Okay," Julia replied her tone softer this time. "We may have lost this opportunity but something else is bound to come our way."

Matt closed his eyes and shuddered, he could hardly face the prospect of committing another crime. As far as he was concerned, a deal had been done and it was only a matter of time before Libby was released. Julia on the other hand did not share his optimism.

"You can't mention a word of this to the police," she warned him.

"I do realise that. I would be locked up for what I've done."

"I dare say they will want to speak to you again especially as you know Pascale."

"I guess so," he whispered miserably.

He was expecting them to turn up on his doorstep at any moment. It was true, he had connections with Pascale, they had both been at Veronique's party and it would not take the police long to discover that he had gone to the hotel where she was staying.

"What are you going to do Matt?"

"All I can do is to wait for him to make contact again. Surely now he has Pascale, Libby will be set free. I can't see that he will expect me to carry out more of his crimes."

"Let's hope you are right. Let me know the moment you have any news."

Julia needed time to think. Her original plan, tenuous though it was, was all they had and now the opportunity to put it into action was lost. She knew nothing about Pascale Dominique but she felt truly sorry for the girl.

Kelly woke up suddenly from a fitful sleep. He had come for them earlier and marched them back to their own cells where he had left food. She had not eaten in over twenty four hours and was ravenous. Exhaustion had threatened to claim her but tearing open the packet, she wolfed down the sandwich before curling up on the mattress again. It had been impossible to sleep in the torture chamber but away from those disturbing instruments, she was now able to close her eyes and rest.

The noises that disturbed her now were both distant and alarming. Someone was crying out and it did not sound like Libby. After a while, the screaming stopped but the sound of sobbing became momentarily louder as a door opened then slammed shut, after that she heard nothing more.

Going straight to the command centre he connected his camera to the computer and downloaded the images he had just taken, he then saved them in a file. Moving closer to the screen, he studied his handiwork. They were really rather good, he thought with satisfaction. Pascale may have been an unwilling participant but this was no barrier to him achieving his goal. Cunningham would have seen nothing like this before, the thought filled him with excitement and he couldn't help but laugh.

Sitting back in his chair, he took his time selecting a number of images that told the story of her ordeal then attaching them to an email, he carefully typed a message before pressing the send button. It was the first time he had used his own computer to communicate with Cunningham but after some research, he was confident that the police would not discover its location.

Matt had just finished talking to Julia as the email arrived and going to his inbox, he braced himself before opening it. Images of Pascale filled the screen; her features set in defiance and her fists clenched as if to defend herself, but the pictures told a very different story. She was unable to fend off the level of violence and dominance imposed on her by this brute. Clearly, her punishment had been severe. He knew her well enough to understand that she would not give up easily. She would have done everything in her power to avoid such an unpleasant ordeal. Like Libby, her wrists were tied preventing her from resisting then the process of humiliation had begun. Each picture told part of a story and when the display ended, there was nothing left to imagine. Her skin was red and sore her body bruised, the expression on her face was one of total shock.

His fingers shook as he closed the file and sitting silently, Matt stared at a blank screen.

"What have I done?" he groaned as realisation set in.

Chapter Thirty Seven

"I WANT YOUR PEOPLE TO check all abandoned buildings in this area," Woods said as she addressed the small team at Shoreditch police station then she handed over a file containing the details.

"Do you realise just how large an area you are talking about?" the officer in charge looked at her incredulously.

"Coordinate with the other stations in the borough. I don't expect your team to tackle this alone."

"Well that's a relief," he responded.

Ignoring his sarcasm, she went on to explain what she was looking for. "In that file you will find details of the abducted women along with my notes relevant to this case."

Consulting her diary, she arranged to return later that week in order to review and address the situation with the team on the ground.

"I can't stress how important this is," she remarked unnecessarily.

They were both aware that abduction cases like this invariably turned into murder hunts.

"We'll start right away," he told her. "I'll get officers out to the old Whitechapel train station first. Refurbishment and modernisation works are still ongoing but there are still plenty of people who may have seen something."

They discussed a number of ideas and options before finally she got to her feet. It was her intention to mobilise as many officers as she could before the day was over. This was mundane police work that could have been conducted over the telephone, but she wanted to become acquainted with Whitechapel so what better way to do that than meet the officers she would be working with. With the backing of DCI Wyman, the responsibility for driving this case forward was hers alone.

DC James and PC Yearsley were in the surveillance dept and James was hoping to bump into Fiona Richardson.

"CCTV imagery is rather sparse I'm afraid," Yearsley told him as they settled in front of his workstation. "We don't always manage to capture complete pictures with every camera," he explained and using the keyboard, he accessed the hotel security system and a view of Pascale appeared. She was standing on the pavement just outside the main doors waiting for her taxi to arrive. "She is rather a stunner," Yearsley remarked even though he was looking at a grainy image.

"You've not seen the glossy fashion magazine," James nudged him with his elbow and grinned. "She's a French model," he added as if this would somehow make a difference.

Yearsley smiled then began to flick through a series of captured stills. "Look at these," he said sharpening the contrast of the screen. "When the taxi arrives you can just make out the shadow of the driver. Now look at this one," he continued as the next image appeared. "It's as if he has shrunk into his seat. If I were picking up a stunner like that, I would be out of that cab in a flash holding the door open for her."

"I see what you mean, it's almost as if he's hiding from her. Now why would he do that?"

Yearsley glanced up at him but made no comment.

"Can you do anything to clean up the picture of the driver?"

"No, I'm afraid not. I ran it through a filter program earlier but it did no good at all."

"Is there nothing else that can be done to give us a better picture?"

"Unfortunately not," Yearsley shook his head then he said. "I can only guess at the route that he took into Whitechapel but none of the roadside cameras have revealed anything."

"Okay," James thought for a moment before asking. "Do you recognise the face of the delivery van driver?"

He was aware that Yearsley was known as a 'super recogniser'. Part of his job was to remember faces that he had seen on CCTV footage.

"I'm afraid to say that I have never seen him before."

Coming from Yearsley, James was satisfied that he could not be wrong.

"I ran his profile through the system but came up with nothing. There were a couple of potential matches but I managed to discount those. Your man I'm afraid remains a mystery."

"Have you seen your colleague Fiona lately?" James slipped the question in casually.

"Fiona, only in passing. Why?"

"She's a babe," James giggled like a teenager. "I've never been with a red head before."

Yearsley swivelled his chair round to face him. "Well, for your information word has it that she prefers the company of women."

"Really, do you mean she's a..." he didn't get to finish what he was saying.

"I'm afraid so."

"Bloody hell, I can't believe it. What a waste."

Yearsley just about managed to keep a straight face. He knew the rumours about Fiona were untrue but he couldn't resist winding him up. James had a reputation for being a womaniser and Fiona would probably thank him for it.

Later that afternoon DS Woods and DC James held a meeting with Matt at a cafe on the other side of town.

"Thank you for agreeing to meet us like this," Woods said as they settled at a table away from other customers.

"To be honest I was expecting to be questioned further."

"We appreciate the pressure you must be under and realise that it would be unwise to come to your home again or ask you to attend the station. I hope you took the necessary precautions in coming here today. The last thing we want is for the abductor to know that you are talking to us."

"Yes, I just hope my efforts to avoid being followed worked."

"We know that you are acquainted with Pascale Dominique," Woods began. "We also know that you both attended a party hosted by Veronique Moreau recently. Can you tell us what happened at that party?"

Matt frowned but remained calm as he gave his view of events. "Pascale and I worked with a group of student photographers and models." He went on to tell them about their interaction with the students. "She was in pretty good spirits and seemed to be enjoying herself."

"Would you say that she was drinking heavily that evening?"

Presumably, they knew about the state she was in when she left the party but they could have no idea that it was drug related. "We did consume quite a lot of wine," he admitted.

"Does she usually drink to excess?"

"No, I don't think so. I've never seen her like that before." He noticed a look that passed between them. "She is rather small so I guess it wouldn't take much to get her drunk."

"Was that your intention Mr Cunningham to get her drunk?"

The attack was unexpected and sitting back in his chair, he stared at DC James before asking.

"Why would I want to do that?"

"We know that you don't like her much so maybe it was to discredit her in some way."

"Pascale can be rather difficult to work with sometimes," Matt admitted, "but I wouldn't go as far to say that I dislike her."

"I understand that the other models find her a little challenging at times." Woods added.

"It's true that she is not the most popular woman in the group."

"Did she take anything else at the party apart from alcohol?"

The question surprised him and he wondered if they knew about the Rohypnol after all. They would not have had an opportunity to check the glass that Pascale used because everything was cleared away the moment the party ended.

"No, there's no way that she is a drug user if that's what you are implying. Veronique would definitely have none of that kind of behaviour. She selects her models carefully and monitors them very closely."

"Why did you go to her hotel after the party?" James asked.

"She left without her bag and coat. I was concerned so decided to return her property and make sure she was okay."

"In the middle of the night," James snapped, "when you knew full well that she was inebriated and was most probably sleeping it off."

"You could have left it until the following day." Woods remarked with a little more compassion.

"I'm sure you are right," Matt smiled weakly, "but as I just said, I was concerned. Perhaps I wasn't thinking too clearly, I'd had a few glasses of wine myself."

DS Woods made a note on a pad. Matt had not realised that she was making notes and this made him nervous so he remained silent as he waited for her to finish.

"Do you know a woman called Kelly Spencer?"

Matt pulled a face and thought for a moment.

"No, I don't think so."

"Does Libby know this woman?"

"Not as far as I know, I don't remember her mentioning that name before."

Woods dropped this line of questioning and moved on.

"Do you have any reason to visit the Whitechapel area?"

The question hit him like a blow from a hammer but he did his best to conceal his reaction. Had someone seen him when he abandoned Pascale and the taxi?

"No but Libby and I go to an Indian restaurant in Brick Lane occasionally. We have not been there recently."

"So it's not somewhere that you visit regularly."

"No," he shook his head, reluctant to say more until he knew where this line of questioning was heading.

"Do you have any friends or colleagues who live or work in that area?" Woods persisted hoping that her questions might trigger something that would help in her search for the abductors lair.

"I'm afraid not."

They continued to ask him about his photography and the models he worked with.

"Both Charley Baker and Melissa Miles also appear in the photographs that you gave us." Woods wondered if a pattern could be emerging here.

"We were all there in Brighton and Salisbury. Do you think they may be in some kind of danger?" Matt couldn't bear the thought of Charley being drawn into this.

"Perhaps not," she reassured him. "However, given the fact that you are connected to two of the abducted women, we have to be concerned for the others."

Two of the women, he thought, why did she not say both of the women? This implied that more people were involved. Was this why she asked him about Kelly Spencer?

"Do you have anything else to tell us?"

"Not that I can think of," Matt replied avoiding eye contact with the detectives.

"Are you certain?" Woods persisted.

Matt realised that she suspected he was holding back. There were things about Pascale's abduction that he could not reveal, to do so would implicate him and he would probably be arrested. Reaching into his pocket he pulled out a memory stick and sliding it across the table he said.

"On there you will find a file that I was sent this morning. It concerns Pascale Dominique."

Chapter Thirty Eight

BREAKFAST CONSISTED OF AN APPLE, a banana and a lukewarm mug of tea and the moment she was finished, the cell door opened.

"Come with me," he said, gesturing for her to follow.

Further along the corridor was the torture chamber and she watched as he entered a code into the electronic keypad then as he peered into the face recognition camera she became apprehensive.

"Don't worry," he mumbled sensing her unrest. "I'm not going to do anything to you."

Reluctant to go in she hesitated at the door.

"I want to show you something that's all."

Suddenly his hand was at her back and she felt a gentle pressure as he manoeuvred her forward then the door closed behind them.

On a table in the middle of the room lay a body. At first, she thought it was real then she realised that it was a dummy, the type used for first aid training. Beside the table was an assortment of knives and as she pressed herself back against the door, she realised that he was watching her closely.

"Don't think about doing anything foolish," he said. "If you were to stick me with one of those knives you would never get out of here."

"I know," she looked him in the eye. "The door has a face recognition thing on it and I would need to enter the right code."

"Indeed, if the correct code is not entered after three attempts the computer will shut down and it will be impossible for you to get out. This room would become your tomb."

Kelly shuddered and thought about Callum, her son.

"Shall we make a start?"

Moving towards the table, he reached for one of the knives and weighed it expertly in his hand then he glanced at Kelly.

"No need to worry," he said as her eyes widened with fear. "I intend you no harm." Placing the knife down carefully, he turned to the dummy. "Now for a short lesson in anatomy," he continued. "This part of the chest is called the sternum or breast bone." He glanced at her again to make sure he had her attention.

"The heart is slightly to one side of the sternum; it is located here and is about the size of a clenched fist." Turning towards her, he smiled and pointed his finger at her left breast.

"You don't need to tell me where my heart is," she snapped, shying away from his touch.

"I have been trained to kill by delivering a blow to the heart. It's no good using a wide bladed knife, so we use a dagger shaped like this." Reaching for the knife again, he picked it up. "It's what we call a Style's dagger."

Kelly stared at it as he held it out to her.

"Don't you like the look of it?" he asked when she refused to take it. "A weapon like this could save your life."

"I would rather not know what it's capable of." She shuddered before turning away.

"You had better pay attention because the life of someone close to you may depend on it."

Turning back towards him, she searched his face for an explanation.

"Got your attention now have I?"

She thought of Callum again, he was the only person that she truly loved.

"It's no use trying to stab someone like this." Lunging with his knife, he stuck it into the dummy's chest.

Kelly was visibly startled and as she cried out he laughed.

"The sternum is designed to protect the centre of the chest. The ribs also form a barrier that can deflect the blade away from its intended target. Penetrate the heart and the victim will die."

He paused again, delighted at her reaction.

"He may not die instantly but it won't take long."

Withdrawing the blade from the dummy's chest, he came to stand beside her.

"Now, hold the knife firmly like this." He demonstrated by placing the tip of the blade at a shallow angle just below the sternum then he continued. "Aim for the left shoulder and slide it in."

She was surprised at how easily the blade disappeared all the way up to the hilt.

"There will of course be some blood but most of it will be contained in the chest cavity as the blade penetrates the pericardium. Do you know what that is?"

Kelly shook her head, her eyes still fixed on the hilt of the knife.

"The pericardium sack surrounds the heart, penetrate that and you will cause a cardiac tamponade. This means that the cavity surrounding the heart will fill with blood and as the heart becomes compressed, it will fail causing unconsciousness followed by death. This process can take several minutes and if the victim is aware of what's happening just imagine the thoughts going through their head."

Kelly wanted to vomit and clamping a hand over her mouth, she staggered away. Ignoring her distress, he withdrew the knife and held it out to her.

"I want you to have a go."

Kelly shook her head and backed further from the table horrified at what he suggested. The thought of stabbing someone was more than she could bear.

"Think of the person you love the most. How far would you go to save their life?"

She remained rooted to the spot.

"What would a mother be prepared to do to protect her son?"

"Callum," she whispered her heart aching with concern. "What about my son?" she asked louder this time.

"If you refuse to do as I ask then I'm sure that I can arrange for something unpleasant to happen to him."

"You don't know my son," she cried. "How can you possibly know anything about him?"

"Oh I know plenty," he assured her. "I know that he is currently living with his auntie Caroline. Would you like to see the photographic evidence?"

"You have photographs of my son?"

"Oh yes and of your sister. She doesn't look much like you does she?"

Kelly almost collapsed and reaching out, placed her hand against the wall. It was several moments before she had the strength to look at him. He was still standing by the table with the knife in his hand watching her carefully. Now was her chance she thought as adrenaline began to surge through her veins. If she were to take the knife and plunge it into his chest then Callum and her sister would be safe. Her instinct to protect her child was powerful but if she did manage to kill this man then she would never see her son again. These thoughts rushed through her head as slowly she reached for the knife.

He watched as she fought her demons. He knew what she was thinking and it amused him.

"Now," he said calmly. "Just as I showed you."

Moving behind her, he placed his hands on her shoulders and guided her gently towards the table.

"You see the mark I made just under the sternum, now you have a go."

He moved her hand, positioning the blade.

"Think of Callum," he whispered into her ear.

Suddenly the blade disappeared all the way to the hilt.

"Good, now slide it out and do it again."

Time after time, the blade slipped effortlessly into the dummy and Kelly felt nothing. Divorcing herself from reality, she refused to acknowledge the fact that he had shown her how to take a life.

Kelly had no memory of returning to her cell. She was lying silently on her mattress covered by the thin blanket waiting for the warmth to return to her numbed body. How did he know about Callum? She had been so careful not to mention him, she had said nothing about her son. She was confused and even more terrified than before. He had not touched her physically as he had done with Libby, but her torture was psychological and now her nightmare had just been taken to another level. Suddenly the door opened and Libby appeared. At first, Kelly thought she was dreaming, Libby was still pale with shock, her eyes red from sobbing but now she was wrapped in a coat.

Libby stumbled unsteadily towards her then lowering herself down onto the edge of the bed, she forced a smile and whispered. "He told me that he was going to move us into a cell together."

Kelly nodded as a lump formed at the back of her throat.

"He gave me my coat so now you can keep my clothes." Libby smiled again.

This time it was Kelly's turn to weep.

Chapter Thirty Nine

"WHY DIDN'T YOU TELL ME the truth about Libby?" Veronique looked hurt as she sat down. She had summoned Matt to her office and now she wanted answers.

"I was advised by the police not to say a word," he told her. "Their investigation was in its infancy. How did you find out anyway?"

"You know how it is," she looked at him. "Once a rumour gets started everybody finds out."

"I'm sorry that Pascale has become a victim of this dreadful business."

"Do the police think she was taken by the same man?"

"Yes I'm afraid they do."

"I wonder what she has done, I mean why not one of the others?"

Matt did not care to think about the reasons why, he was just relieved that it was Pascale and not Charley or Melissa. He hated himself for thinking this way but it was the truth.

"How are you coping?" Veronique asked.

It was a double-edged question. She needed reassuring that he would deliver the completed photographs for her magazine by the agreed deadline.

"You don't need to worry about me," he smiled weakly.

"I could get someone else to complete the final digital arrangements."

"There's no need."

She was happy with what he had produced so far but she realised that he must be under considerable pressure.

"The work is a welcome distraction," he went on quickly, "don't even consider bringing someone else in." He sensed that she was still not convinced, it would take more than a promise. "I will send you everything that I've done so far as soon as I get back to my office. I assure you, most of it is complete."

"Okay," she smiled, holding her hands up in defeat. "If you are sure then I will leave the arrangements as they are. I will of course have to bring someone in to write the editorials. Will you be happy working with someone else?"

What choice did he have? Libby was supposed to produce the article based on his input and images but now in her absence Veronique would need another writer to take on the task.

"Of course, who do you have in mind?"

She mentioned a couple of names but no one that he knew.

"Is it the right time to talk to you about my planned trip to Rome?"

Matt looked up, he appeared interested so she continued.

"I'm going to organise it for the end of next month, the weather may have improved by then."

Matt nodded but made no comment. Surely, the weather in Rome at this time of year would be perfect.

"I would really like you to be on my team Matt."

"I'm sure that will be fine. Libby will come too and perhaps we'll stay on for a while, make a holiday of it."

Veronique smiled again, there was nothing more to say. She just hoped that he was right and it would turn out well for them both.

Pascale was furious, she had never been treated so badly before. Her clothes were ruined and all she had to keep out the chill of night was a filthy blanket. Her wrists were sore, the skin chafed by the rope used to tie her down and her ribs were tender from the beating she had received. He would never touch her again, she was certain of that. Gently she rubbed at her bruises. She would kill him before he got the chance. When she was younger she helped her father slaughter pigs on the farm so it would not be too difficult to do the same to him, all she needed was a knife. She had already searched her cell but found nothing that could be used as a weapon. He had taken her bag and phone along with everything else she had.

She lay in the darkness for what seemed an eternity going over all the gruesome options. There were many ways to kill a man and slowly she began to formulate a plan.

Suddenly the light above the door came on and screwing up her eyes, she waited for them to adjust. It wouldn't be long before he arrived so she would have to be ready. The flap in the door shot open and he peered in. Pulling the blanket tightly around herself she was poised, adrenaline coursing like fire through her veins. She knew exactly what to do, but her plan was about to be ruined. She had to think of something quickly as he pushed a bowl of cereal and a lukewarm mug of tea through the flap.

"The toilet is blocked." The words tumbled out of her mouth without too much thought but she was happy with the response.

His face re-appeared at the flap, so hauling herself up off the bed she held onto the blanket and went to stand by the door.

"Something is wrong, it does not work properly."

"Victorian plumbing," he replied.

Pascale did not understand, her focus was on the task ahead and dancing nervously on the spot, she waited for him to open the door.

Watching her carefully he hesitated as he considered his options. It would hardly take a minute to have a look but he would need tools in order to fix the problem.

"I will come back," he said as he closed the flap.

Pascale cried out in frustration, she was ready but could feel her chance slipping away. Pacing the floor, she hugged herself and pulled the blanket tighter around her shoulders, but she did not have to wait long. Once he had delivered breakfast to the others he went to collect his tools then he returned to her cell.

At the sound of the key in the lock, her muscles tensed as she prepared herself. Standing back, she watched as he walked in. He said nothing as he turned to lock the door behind him. She would have to do this quickly, make use of the first opportunity before he realised there was nothing wrong with the toilet. She made her move when he crouched down to lay out his tools. Letting the blanket fall from her shoulders, she wound the flimsy material of her bra into a tourniquet then pushing her arms up over his head she wrapped the twisted material around his neck and pulled with all her strength.

He reacted immediately and standing upright, she was hauled off her feet. Curling her legs around his waist she held on, gripping tightly whilst applying as much pressure as she could to the stranglehold. The animal sounds that he made were terrifying but she would not let go. It was like riding a raging bull as he bucked and jerked around the room and she just about avoided his clawing fingers as he reached back over his shoulder. With his other hand, he pawed at the tourniquet and managed to slip his thumb beneath the material. Pascale was losing her grip, so twisting the ends tighter she felt the material stretch.

He roared again, a half strangled scream of pure anger and as his muscles tensed, she forced her knees up under his ribs and held on as he charged backwards. Suddenly lights flashed inside her head and pain rippled along her spine as he crushed her against the wall. She lost her grip and screamed out in frustration as he pitched her up and over his shoulders. Landing awkwardly on the concrete floor the wind was driven from her lungs, then for a few agonising seconds, she lay there stunned by violence and pain.

He was standing over her his face red with fury, his chest rising and falling angrily. It was all over, she had lost the fight. He was far too strong, further resistance would be futile.

"Get up," he hissed as his fingers probed at his throat.

Unable to move, fear and discomfort kept her immobile.

"Get up," he said louder this time then gripping her arm savagely, he hauled her to her feet.

Pinning her against the door, he held onto her while he fumbled for the key then as the door swung open he dragged her screaming along the corridor. The door to the cell next door was open so forcing her in she stumbled and fell against a steel table. At first, she thought this was some kind of gymnasium; equipment that she did not recognise filled the space but she did not have time to look closely.

He was there behind her and before she could avoid him, he lifted her up and slammed her against a wooden frame. For the second time in just a few minutes, the air was forced from her lungs and she was stunned. Before she could react, he secured her ankles and wrists then standing back to admire his work he smiled with satisfaction. Pascale moaned pitifully and her expression changed from defiance to fear, her naked breasts rising and falling rapidly as she sobbed. He realised then that he should have his camera, Cunningham would need to see this.

Chapter Forty

DS WOODS WAS GOING THROUGH the report that PC Yearsley had put together. She had been staring at the grainy CCTV image for the last few minutes but it was impossible to make out the features of the taxi driver. She was however convinced, this was not the man who abducted Libby Ellis.

"Who are you?" she whispered as she compared the photographs.

His was a smaller, neater profile. The driver of the van had been wearing a cap, but it was clear that his hair was cropped close to his scalp while the taxi driver had a full head of hair.

An idea was beginning to take shape so reaching for the computer keyboard she pulled it towards her. If the man they were searching for was military, then maybe he was a deserter. Typing the words into a search engine, she sat back in her chair and waited for the results to appear on the screen. Several headings arrived in the form of a list so selecting the first one she opened it.

AWOL – Absent Without Official Leave, was the title and reading the paragraph that followed she discovered that Ministry of Defence Records show that 17,470 incidents of AWOL have occurred since the Iraq invasion of 2003.

Looking up from the screen, she frowned. The figure was a lot higher than she imagined, but then it did cover a fifteen year period. She read on.

Two thousand soldiers went AWOL in 2017 and by the end of the year, three hundred and seventy five remained at large. She wondered what drove soldiers to do this when if caught it could lead to a lengthy custodial sentence. She continued to read, learning that in most cases these incidents were caused by domestic circumstances, family problems rather than a wish to avoid military service. Post Traumatic Stress could also be a factor. She had first-hand knowledge of this. When joining the force as a PC in training, one of her colleagues, an ex army serviceman joined at the same time. At first, there was no indication of a problem, he hid it well but as time went on and after a particularly harrowing case, his mood changed. His life began to unravel and eventually he broke down. Post Traumatic Stress Syndrome was diagnosed and unfortunately, it ended his career with the police.

Woods had seen enough, so closing the page she began to consider what she had learnt. Once the army had decided to pursue an absconder, the local police forces were notified. When posted absent, a serviceman's unit makes contact with the Service Police Crime Bureau, SPCB, which is operated by the Royal Military Police, RMP, listing the individual as missing. The SPCB then informs the relevant Home Office Police Forces and a notification is passed to all forces where the absconder is known to have an address.

Woods knew this information was on the Police National Computer System, PNC, but without a name, a search would prove difficult. Perhaps she could work backwards. It would be simple enough to check the PNC for a list of addresses in the area where absconders were known to have lived. If the man they were searching for was holding the abducted women in the Whitechapel area then maybe he was a local man with knowledge of the neighbourhood. It might be a long shot but it was worth investigating.

Woods accessed the system and found dozens of names listed at addresses across the London Borough of Tower Hamlets. Tapping her finger against her chin, she sighed. These were names of British soldiers having gone AWOL in the last five years. They were all local men and any one of them could be the man they were looking for. She could of course be wrong, he might not be from this area at all, even if he was he might no longer be a resident or have family contacts living close by.

Hitting the print button, pages began to spew from the printer. It was a start, she told herself, something positive that could be passed on to the local stations. Each address would need to be checked.

Matt was also working at his computer. He had sent his file of work in progress to Veronique as promised and she came back to him with positive criticisms that required only minor changes. He could only focus for short periods at a time, his thoughts were constantly straying to Libby. It was impossible to stop worrying about her and images of her suffering haunted him mercilessly. There had been nothing more since Pascale had been abducted, he should have heard something by now. Matt was becoming even more despondent, he was convinced that once he'd handed Pascale over, Libby would be set free but now realisation was beginning to set in. He sighed and pushed these dark thoughts away before turning back to his computer. He must remain positive, so finding the next image he began to work.

A few hours later and the digital imaging was almost complete, all that remained now was the written editorial. He would of course have to set up the storyboard, lay out the text to suit his images before Veronique would give her approval. It would then be included with the other articles that made up the magazine before being sent to the printers.

Suddenly a message arrived in his in box and hesitating for a moment he held his breath, expecting the worst, but it was from Charley. She had heard about Libby and was concerned, her lengthy email was full of sympathy and questions. It went on to include details of their next job together and she apologised for talking about work but Matt appreciated the importance of an opportunity like this. Charley had a contract with a lucrative cosmetics company. She modelled the latest make-up products and perfume and her face appeared on posters and advertising boards. Matt had been asked to produce the photographs for the latest advertising campaign. The two day photo shoot was planned to take place in a London studio early the following week, it was short notice but he was expected to confirm his availability. This was the kind of work that he wanted. The organisation was well known and paid well, besides it was always a pleasure to work with Charley. On a job like this, she would look stunning and it would be his responsibility to ensure that both Charley and the products were displayed to perfection.

Matt composed his reply assuring her that he was coping and that he was looking forward to working with her the following week.

Chapter Forty One

DS WOODS FELT AS IF she had taken a giant leap forward. Progress was being made on a case that had all but stalled and now her reputation was on the rise again. Her theory about an absconder seemed credible and given what they already knew about him, pieces of the puzzle were beginning to fit together. Uniformed officers from the Whitechapel police stations were doing a great job and with the information they had gathered, the search was about to be opened up across the London Borough of Tower Hamlets. The Whitechapel constabulary would continue their search for the abductor's lair while others in the Borough would be tasked with checking addresses known to be associated with absconders. Her investigation was about to become widespread with her job turning into an administrative role. She would be responsible for sifting through and collating the information that came in, liaising with the different departments and directing the officers on the ground. With the lack of a Detective Inspector on the case, she would have to step up and take control. She was more than capable, this was her chance to show the Chief that she was ready for promotion but she would have to watch her back. DCI Wyman had it in for her and would no doubt do his best to discredit her at the first opportunity.

Woods wanted to speak to Matthew Cunningham again. She was convinced that he was withholding information so was not finished with him yet. He was in communication with the abductor and she was determined to use this to her advantage. It was her intention to get DC James to organise an observation team. If the abductor was monitoring Cunningham's movements then maybe they would catch him in the act.

DC James appeared at her office door and caught her looking pensive.

"Have there been any further developments with the surveillance team?" she asked when she realised he was there.

"Nothing yet," he replied, "but I could pop upstairs and ask if you like."

Woods guessed that he was interested in a woman working in that department, he would no doubt have a hotline to her desk.

"No need, an email or phone call will do."

He looked disappointed and opting for a phone call, went off in search of a quiet desk.

Kelly took the top bunk in the cell that she now shared with Libby. It offered little more space than a single cell and the washing and toilet facilities were far from private. It was however an improvement on spending hours at a time locked up on their own. Libby seemed to be recovering from her latest ordeal in the torture chamber and now they could take comfort in each other's company.

Libby was from a completely different background to Kelly. She was infinitely more educated having attended a private school for girls before going on to university. Her parents lived in a fashionable part of London and her father had used his contacts to help boost her career in fashion journalism. Kelly could hardly imagine the lifestyle that Libby enjoyed but she liked to listen to stories of her time as a student and more recently her work. In return, Kelly recalled events from her own childhood. Libby listened with interest to tales from the other end of the social spectrum. Kelly's observations were often earthy and amusing but the deprivation that she had endured could sometimes be quite heartbreaking.

Kelly had left school at fifteen and regretted not having achieved much. She realised now the importance of education and wished that she had taken more interest in her own academic development. Life for her was never easy but she strived to improve her lot by working hard and keeping out of trouble. An opportunity once came her way in the form of an army officer. He was well above her class but she adored him and hoped they would have a future together. He told her that he loved her and promised that things would be very different. Her life did change dramatically but not in the way that she expected.

Suddenly the flap in the door clattered open and he peered in. Libby was startled and turning away, pulled her blanket tighter around her shoulders. Kelly stared at him defiantly as the key rattled in the lock then the door swung open.

"Get up," he said looking at her. "I have something that I want you to do."

Doing as she was told, Kelly swung her legs from the top bunk and slipping to the floor, touched Libby's shoulder gently before whispering.

"Don't worry, I won't be long."

She followed him along the gloomy corridor and soon realised they were going towards the torture chamber. Perhaps he was going to give her another demonstration in murder.

Stopping by the door, he went through the security procedure then as the lock clicked he pushed it open. He made no attempt to enter so she went in alone and as the door slammed shut behind her, her eyes widened with shock. A woman was tied to the wooden rack. Her long dark hair hung loose and knotted between the slats and bruises covered her naked body.

"What the hell..." Kelly exclaimed as she moved closer.

The woman cried out in fear and turning her face away, strained at the bonds that held her down.

"It's okay," Kelly said, gently placing her hand on the woman's arm.

This simple act of human contact settled her frantic nerves and she became still.

Kelly could see that she was beautiful. Beneath her bruises, her skin was smooth and lightly tanned and she could detect traces of expensive perfume. She obviously took great care of herself.

The woman turned her head to face Kelly. She had been crying and her make-up was a mess. Words of anguish poured from her mouth and although Kelly could understand none of it, the meaning was clear. Suddenly she switched from French to English but her accent was strong and she spoke quickly.

"The filthy English pig," she spat. "He raped me."

Her face crumpled and she sobbed uncontrollably then battling with her emotions, she became still.

Kelly was shocked, she could hardly believe that it was true then reaching out, she took her hand and squeezed it reassuringly before loosening the ropes that secured her wrists. The ugly marks were an indication of a sustained struggle, the attack must have been brutal.

"Will you untie my legs?"

Kelly moved to the foot of the rack and made a start on the knots that held her ankles. The evidence of rape was clear and her breath caught at the back of her throat. Pascale raised her head and could see where she was looking.

"The filthy pig. I will kill him for what he has done to me."

As soon as she was free, Pascale staggered unsteadily to her feet and Kelly held onto her until she found the strength to support herself.

"Thank you," she whispered. "My name is Pascale. You are a prisoner here too?"

"Yes," Kelly replied before telling Pascale her name.

She looked around searching for something that she could use to cover the woman but there was nothing; even the dummy had disappeared along with the collection of knives. That was a relief, she did not want to see anything like that again. Pascale stood beside her with her arms folded across her body.

She was trembling but it was not particularly cold, Kelly realised that it must be the effects of extreme stress and shock.

Slowly and reluctantly, Kelly began to unbutton her blouse. It was a size too big even for her so would swamp Pascale who was much smaller, but at least it would cover her nakedness and help to restore a fragment of her dignity.

"Here," she said shrugging it from her shoulders. "I will try to get you a blanket when he comes back."

Wrapping herself in the thin material, Pascale folded her arms then as she looked up, they made eye contact. "Merci," she whispered.

Kelly thought that Pascale was about to break down again. After what she had been through, she would not blame her if she did but she was wrong.

"We are not alone." Kelly said awkwardly, not knowing what to say.

All she wanted to do was wrap her arms around Pascale and comfort her, but she got the impression that the French girl was not like that. Although devastated, she appeared to possess an inner strength and seemed able to cope on her own.

"There are more?" Her eyes widened at the news.

"One more as far as I know," Kelly added.

"What does he want from us?"

"I have no idea."

"Where are we, what is this place?"

Kelly looked around and shook her head miserably, it was a hopeless situation and what he had done to Pascale frightened her even more.

Chapter Forty Two

HIS PHONE BEGAN TO RING. He had left it on his desk in the office so bounding up the stairs he raced to answer it.

"Hello, Matt."

"Julia, good morning. How are you?"

They exchanged pleasantries, Julia thinking that he sounded a little brighter. The last time they had talked, he was down and she had been worried about him.

"Any news of Libby?"

"No, nothing."

Suddenly he was not quite so upbeat. He had already told her about his part in the abduction of Pascale Dominique but she chose not to mention that. She was still shocked, but it would do no good to dwell on his crime.

"Listen, Libby was writing a piece for my magazine about Emilia Sykes. She owns the bridal shop White Lace and Promises."

"Yes, that's right. I remember her telling me about it."

"She was going to provide photographs for the article. Did she speak to you about that?"

"No, she didn't mention it to me."

Julia suspected that Libby was considering taking photographs of her own but she chose to keep this to herself.

"Would you mind doing a few images for me?" she paused before going on. "Emilia has been on the phone asking why Libby is not responding to her calls and messages. Of course I told her nothing, I said that she has been called away on family business."

"What exactly are you looking for?"

Julia explained what she had in mind. "Libby has already discussed this with Emilia so she knows exactly what to expect."

"So the photographs will be taken at her shop?"

"Yes that's right. Libby told me that it would be easy enough. Apparently the lighting is perfect inside the shop so you won't have to cart loads of equipment across town."

"When do you want me to do this?"

He was already committed to working with Charley the following week.

"Can you do it right away? This afternoon or tomorrow would be perfect.

I'm in no hurry but apparently Emilia is working to a very tight schedule. Perhaps you could give her a call."

Matt did just that and half an hour later, clutching his camera case, was on his way across town.

A man dressed in a camouflage jacket appeared from the shadows. Eager to see where Matt was going, he unclipping the lens from his camera and dropped it into his pocket then followed him towards the train station. He enjoyed playing these little games calling them 'Trivial Pursuit'. He smiled at the analogy. He had been trained in covert operations and was amazed at what people got up to. It was surprising what information came his way. He had several ideas that included Matthew Cunningham but for the moment had no firm plans. He was content to wait, observe and see what opportunities presented themselves.

The route took them across London and it was not long before he realised where Cunningham was going. He had come this way before when following Libby Ellis. They had ended up at a little Georgian fronted bridal shop.

Matt hurried inside eager to meet Emilia Sykes. Libby had told him so much about the woman and her extraordinary style.

"Emilia?" he asked as he stepped into the shop.

"You must be Matt," she replied sweeping across the floor towards him.

Matt was impressed, Emilia was wearing a retro designed dress made up of bright yellow panels. Her hair was dyed red and matched the ballet slippers on her feet. Reaching out he took her outstretched hand and as she drew near, he caught her scent. He had no idea what the fragrance was but she smelt marvellous.

"I'm so pleased to meet you at last," she smiled. "Libby has told me all about you."

"Has she indeed," Matt laughed.

"Sorry to hear that she was called away. I hope everything is okay."

"Yes," he replied remembering what Julia had told him. "She had to go to Kent, take care of her mother for a few days."

"Oh, nothing serious I hope. I wondered why she was not answering my messages and that explains it."

She offered to make coffee so left him to set up his camera. Emilia had organised everything, the items that she wanted photographed were already laid out so all he had to do was take the pictures.

The man outside waited patiently. He caught a glimpse of the woman that Cunningham had come to meet and regretted not being ready with his own camera. She appeared very interesting indeed. He studied the shop front. The nearest CCTV cameras were further along the main street. There were no other security devices set up above the door or along the window bays and none of the neighbouring shops appeared to have a surveillance system in place. The alarm looked simple enough and the locks on the doors would keep out all but the most sophisticated burglar. The entrance to the shop nestled between two bay windows made up of tiny panels of Georgian glass. Standing in the left hand bay was a lifelike mannequin wearing an exquisite wedding gown and lifting his camera, he took several pictures focusing particularly on this display. He also managed to get shots of the interior through one of the little glass panels. An idea was beginning to take shape based on something that he had thought of earlier.

Cunningham appeared at the door so retreating quickly along the street, he glanced back over his shoulder. Luckily, he was not seen, Cunningham was busy taking photographs of the shop, standing in exactly the same spot he had occupied just a few moments earlier. The woman was there beside him and not one to miss an opportunity he lifted his camera and focused in on her.

Forty minutes later Matt was on his way home. It had been an easy assignment and Emilia Sykes was charming. She had taken his mind off Libby for a while but now it was back to reality. His pursuer was off in the opposite direction but ironically, both men were sharing the same thoughts. They were equally happy with the photographs they had taken. Matt had even persuaded Emilia to pose for him. He was not sure if Julia would approve but he decided that he was going to produce a number of portraits of Emilia. There was no harm in promotion shots, besides he knew that Libby wanted to add Emilia Sykes to her business portfolio. Libby was also hoping to become involved in the celebrity weddings that Emilia was hosting. There were plenty of business opportunities here for them both.

The moment he returned to his lair, he went straight to his command centre where he did two things. First, he loaded the images from his camera to his computer, then selecting a file he attached it to an email before sending it to Cunningham.

Chapter Forty Three

MATT DID NOT SEE THE email until the following day. Like an explosive device planted to cause maximum effect, it waited patiently to be opened. Going into his office, he glanced at Libby's desk. The space that her computer once occupied was empty and her shelf was clear of files. A few solitary pens and a pencil with a chewed end stood in a tin mug plastered with the inscription, *too much Ego will kill your Talent*. Matt smiled, Libby loved that quote. She had bought the mug from a little shop in the Cotswolds where they had stayed for a few days the previous year. He could not remember the name of the village, but he was sure that Libby would. He could hear her now chastising him for his lack of memory and sadly, he turned away and sat down at his computer. Powering it up, he waited for the icons to settle on the screen then he got to work. He was going to check through the photographs he had taken of Emilia Sykes at her shop before sending them to Julia. He also wanted to put the finishing touches to the images for Veronique before allowing her to see them. Later that day he was scheduled to meet the writer who was going to produce the editorial that would complete the article for Veronique's magazine. He had a busy day ahead.

The computer alerted him to an unread message sitting in his inbox so going into his emails he opened it. Inside sat a collection of jpeg images but no accompanying message and before he could gain access, he was required to send confirmation of receipt. From the reference at the top of the screen, he could see that it was from the abductor and as soon as he responded, the man would know that he had opened the file.

His fingers trembled as he hesitated. These could be photographs of Libby and he was reluctant to look. Almost involuntarily, his fingers strayed to the mouse then with a click, the first image filled the screen. Throwing himself back in his chair, he cried out. Pascale was staring back at him her face a mask of anguish and despair, clearly an unwilling participant in a performance that stripped away her dignity.

After his initial shock, Matt began to look closer. The injuries she had suffered suggested a violent struggle but most alarming of all, she was naked. The following series of photographs left nothing to the imagination, each image describing in minute detail the extent of her torment. She was completely deflated, her natural poise and confidence gone, the shock and disbelief of her situation told of a woman driven to breaking point.

A sob rose up from deep within his chest. He had never seen Pascale like this before. He was responsible for her terrifying ordeal and the guilt would remain with him for the rest of his life. Taking a deep breath, he fought for control. He wanted to turn away, close the file, pretend that it did not exist, but as he stared at the woman on the screen, he begged for her forgiveness. It could easily have been Libby looking back at him and he hated himself even more for the relief that he felt knowing that it was Pascale and not Libby. Climbing to his feet, he paced the floor in an effort to stabilise his thoughts. This he could not keep to himself he would have to inform the police.

DS Woods was at her desk when her phone rang.

"Isobel Woods," she spoke clearly then she heard the caller sob.

"Can I help you?" she asked her voice softer this time. There was another pause so checking the caller's number on the tiny screen her eyes widened.

"Mr Cunningham, is that you?"

"I've had another message," finally he managed to speak, his voice trembling with emotion.

"Is it Libby?" she asked responding to his distress.

"No, not Libby, it's Pascale Dominique." He told her about the email he had received.

"Can you forward it to me please Mr Cunningham?"

Doing as she asked, Matt turned to his computer and closed the file before sending it. A few seconds later, it arrived and as she accessed the information, Woods understood the reason for his distress.

"Mr Cunningham, are you still there?" He did not answer but the sound of him breathing confirmed that they were still connected. "I've got your email, stay by your phone," she ordered, "I will call you back shortly."

The moment the call ended the phone vibrated in his hand.

"Hello," he said lifting it up to his ear.

"Cunningham, did you enjoy my little picture show?"

At first he could not answer, the frozen lump at the centre of his chest prevented him from speech.

"Cat got your tongue or are you still admiring the little beauty on the screen?"

His impertinent tone angered Matt.

"You won't get away with this," he almost shouted.

"Who is going to stop me?"

Matt gripped the side of his desk, he had to remain calm, it was not a good idea to antagonise this man. Images of Pascale played over inside his head and it frustrated him to think that he could do nothing to stop him.

"When are you going to release Libby?"

"Oh, I wasn't aware that was the deal," he sneered. "You are ruthless offering up your friend so easily in order to save your Libby."

Panic threatened to undermine his hard fought calm and Matt gasped.

"You don't have to worry she is quite safe, but her continued comfort depends on you entirely. I wonder," he paused, stretching out the silence. "How far would you be prepared to go in order to ensure her safety?"

The call ended abruptly.

DS Woods continued to study the computer screen. Frustratingly, clues as to where the women might be held eluded her. Ignoring the despicable content, she studied the background. The walls were dull, paint peeling in patches told of decay, clearly, the building was old and neglected, but apart from that, there was nothing to help reveal its location. The contraption that Pascale was tied to was constructed of wooden planks and by zooming in for a closer look, Woods could find no evidence of a manufacturers tag or label. The rope securing her was unremarkable and offered up no clues either. DC James appeared at her door but luckily could not see what held her attention so completely.

"Sarge," he said remembering just in time not to use her Christian name. "I've just had a message from Fiona in surveillance. Cunningham received a telephone call just a few minutes ago, it was made from Libby Ellis' phone and originated from the Shoreditch area."

"Do we have a definite location?" she looked up at him, her eyes wide with anticipation.

"No, I'm afraid not, the call was not long enough, but it came from within the search area."

Rising from her chair, she went into the incident room and studied the map pinned to the wall.

"Both the delivery van and the taxi were lost in Whitechapel," she said thoughtfully, tapping her finger against the map.

"It's a huge search area," James added needlessly.

"Officers have been checking out various locations including the old train station and neighbouring railway arches."

"There must be hundreds of places around there that would make a perfect hideout but surely it's only a matter of time before we winkle him out."

"Time is what we are short of," she reminded him thinking of the pictures she had just received. James had not seen them yet, he was in for a shock.

Chapter Forty Four

THE DOOR TO THE TORTURE chamber opened and Pascale jumped to her feet. Kelly, sitting on the floor beside her made no effort to move.

"You disgusting filthy pig," Pascale spat, her heavily accented words charged with revulsion.

He simply grinned at her, his posture that of the victor. He had complete power over them and could make their lives as unpleasant as he liked.

"Get up," he said his gaze lingering on Kelly.

Without her blouse, she felt vulnerable under the weight of his stare and climbing slowly to her feet, she crossed her arms across her chest.

Pascale was on the balls of her feet, fists clenched in an attitude of aggression. Kelly could feel her anger and it frightened her. Her hostile attitude could easily make their situation a whole lot worse.

"Let me go this instant," Pascale cried and moving forward courageously squared up to him. She believed that she had endured the worst and there was nothing more that he could do to humiliate her further.

"You are going nowhere," he said towering over her. He had dealt with tougher women in the past.

Undeterred by his reply Pascale screamed before launching herself at him. She clawed at his face but he was ready for her onslaught and holding her at arm's length he began to laugh. This riled her even more so she pressed on with her attack. Leaning to one side she wriggled free of his grasp and lashed out again. She was a lightweight compared to him but he underestimated her ferocity and determination. With nails extended, she clawed at his face again this time raking his cheek and blood appeared like jewels against his skin. The sting of her assault enraged him and he lashed out catching the back of her head with his fist.

Kelly looked on in horror. She knew that it was hopeless; it would be a miracle if Pascale did not sustain a serious injury. Pascale recovered quickly and leaping up onto his back wrapped her legs around his waist then holding on tightly, sank her teeth into his neck. Roaring with indignation, he swung round in an attempt to throw her off but she held on. Like a jockey riding a spirited mount, Pascale maintained her balance but it did not last for long. Reaching up, he grabbed a handful of hair and pulled her over his shoulder and tumbling through the air, she landed heavily against the steel table. Stars exploded inside her head and before she could respond, he was upon her. Picking her up, he dumped her roughly onto the table and held her down whilst he secured her right arm with a leather strap. Fighting back desperately she brought her knees up and kicked out forcing him back against the wall, then pulling at the strap with her left hand she failed to see the fist that slammed into the side of her head. Pascale jerked violently then lay still.

Kelly was shaking uncontrollably, the ferocity of the attack petrified her and moving behind the wooden rack, she sought sanctuary from what she feared the most.

Pascale remained still, slumped at an impossible angle across the table. He took a moment to recover then arranging her limbs, he tied her down using the straps and when he was finished, he stared murderously at Kelly. His face was puce with rage his chest rising and falling rapidly as he sucked in air between barred teeth. Kelly drew back against the wall fearful at what he might do next.

"Right," he said his voice steadier than she expected. "Shall we go?"

The relief that Kelly felt was overwhelming, she was not about to suffer the same fate but she was reluctant to leave the girl unconscious on the table. She could have suffered all manner of injury, but she had no choice. He marched her back to her cell where she collapsed to her knees and sobbed.

Libby stared at her from the lower bunk her face pale, her eyes huge with fear. She had heard the commotion and her imagination ran riot.

"Kelly," she cried then sliding from the mattress, threw herself down beside her.

"I'm okay, honestly I'm alright."

"But your blouse,"

Kelly explained what had happened, choosing not to mention that Pascale had been raped.

"What did she think she was doing?"

"It seems that Pascale can be rather aggressive once she becomes upset."

"Pascale," Libby replied, "Pascale Dominique?"

"Do you know her?"

"She is one of the models who occasionally works with Matt. What is going on?"

Kelly was stunned. "How well do you know her?"

"Well, I don't as such," Libby told her before going on to explain the professional relationship that existed between Matt and the people he worked with.

An alarm sounded in the command centre so racing along the corridor, he checked the data that appeared on the computer screen. Activating the perimeter cameras, he searched for the source of the intrusion and soon found what he was looking for. A pair of community officers were at the front of the building checking the boarded up windows and doors so tracking their progress, he watched as they called out to each other. It was obvious from their body language that they suspected nothing, this was merely a routine check. Nothing was out of place and he was satisfied they would be unable to breach the outer wall enclosing the rear of the building. The taxi used to abduct Pascale was hidden behind the huge gates leading into the courtyard; it would be unfortunate if they were to discover it. Watching closely, he was ready to deal with them if it became necessary.

Chapter Forty Five

MATT WAS ON HIS WAY to meet the writer who was going to produce the editorial for Veronique's magazine. It was Matt's job to provide information about the photo shoot, he would also go through and explain the images that he had prepared for the article. The terrible email that he received earlier that morning had shaken him to the core, but having shared it with DS Woods, he was now able to focus on his work and function with some degree of normality. Work was his saviour, without it, he would have gone mad with worry. His phone began to ring and he froze in the middle of the pavement. People dodged around him as he reached into his pocket. Reluctant to answer, he stared at the screen before he recognised the number then with a sigh of relief he pressed the receive button.

"Hello Matt," Julia said brightly and before he had chance to speak she went on. "Thank you for going to see Emilia Sykes yesterday, you really made an impression." She paused before adding. "The photos that you sent me are just perfect."

"Good, I'm glad you liked them. Emilia is such a charming person," he added, "and what a sense of style she has."

"Yes," Julia agreed. "We have never met but I've heard all about her."

Even with the photographs, the series that Libby was working on was incomplete. Julia would have to delay publishing the first article in the hope that once Libby returned she would finish the set.

"Listen," she said pushing her thoughts to the one side. "I've just had a telephone conversation with my friend and she has some interesting information."

"Okay, I'm listening."

"It concerns Libby but I don't want to discuss this on the phone. What say we meet up later for a glass of wine and a chat?" They arranged to meet after work at the usual place. The wine bar was close to both Veronique's boutique and the offices of *Fashion Today* so it was convenient for them both.

Veronique was standing on the pavement outside her shop talking with a couple of people as Matt approached so he slowed his pace.

"Matt," she called out when she spotted him. "Welcome."

They kissed cheeks continental style then in a cloud of expensive perfume, she led him to the office at the back of her shop.

"Jan is waiting to meet you," she told him and sitting down at her desk she reached for the telephone and spoke quickly in French. Matt was unable to catch what she said.

"Sit down," she said dropping the receiver back into its holder. "Jan won't be long, they are working upstairs," she explained. "We have turned part of the storeroom into a temporary office."

Shrugging off his coat, Matt did as he was told and made himself comfortable.

"I have told Jan nothing about the circumstances surrounding this job. It will be up to you to decide what to say."

Matt nodded his understanding but before he had time to reply, the door opened.

"Ah, Jan," Veronique said. "This is Matt our photographer. He will talk you through what is required."

Matt was surprised as he got to his feet. He was expecting to meet a female, but Jan was a very tall young man.

"I know what you are thinking," he smiled as they shook hands. "Jan is short for Johannes or John in English." He spoke with a South African accent. "My family were Dutch settlers, I come from Cape Town."

"Jan has worked for me before in Paris so is no stranger to our ways."

"I'm sure that things will be fine," he told them glancing down at Matt's briefcase. "Once I have my brief I can make a start."

"Make yourselves comfortable and I will order coffee before we begin."

She thought it important that the men get to know each other. It was her view that once the ice was broken they would work together more efficiently.

Matt discovered that Jan had recently been on an assignment in Monaco. He was covering a fashion show at the Royal Palace but his visit was cut short. He came to London at Veronique's request knowing nothing about the disappearance of Libby or Pascale. Veronique had been careful to keep him away from gossip. She thought that he would be uncomfortable if he were to discover that Libby, the writer he was about to replace was Matt's partner.

By the end of the meeting, Jan had everything that he needed to complete his editorial. Matt felt uneasy about handing over Libby's work, there was something final about it. She would be furious if she knew what he was doing. He chose to say nothing about past events but felt certain that Jan could sense that something was going on. Luckily, he was professional enough to accept the task without asking too many questions.

"Here is my card with my details," Matt said when they were finished. "Don't hesitate to contact me if you need more information."

"It's all good," Jan smiled, "you have done a fantastic job with the images."

Forty minutes later Matt arrived at the wine bar to find Julia already there. Sitting alone at a table, she was reading from a pile of papers laid out in front of her, but sensing his presence, she looked up.

"Matt," she cried then shuffling the papers into her bag, got to her feet.

Kissing his cheek affectionately, she watched as he dumped his coat and bag on to a vacant seat. He looked exhausted as he fell into a chair, the worry lines around his eyes seemed more pronounced.

"You have started without me," he said eyeing the bottle of wine standing open on the table.

"I anticipated your needs," she smiled. "One of your favourites I understand."

She poured wine into the glass reserved for him before topping up her own.

"Argentinian Malbec," he nodded his approval when he saw the label. "How do you know it's one of my favourites?"

"To tell you the truth I'm not sure." Shrugging her shoulders, she continued. "Libby must have told me."

Lifting his glass, he toasted her good health before savouring the rich, spicy flavours then he told her what he had been doing that afternoon. He needed to share with her his doubts about handing over Libby's work to a stranger.

"Libby will be back soon," she reassured him. She wanted to tell him that everything would be fine but she stopped herself. There was of course no guarantee that normality would be resumed.

Matt told her nothing about the photographs he received that morning or his conversation with the abductor.

"Right," Julia said having taken several sips from her glass. "My friend Fiona has managed to track the telephone call that you had this morning." She looked up at him and paused.

Matt shuffled in his seat, feeling awkward under her gaze but thankfully, Julia chose to ignore the fact that he had failed to tell her about it.

"The call was unfortunately not long enough for her to fix an exact location, however it originated from somewhere in Shoreditch."

"Really?" Matt said leaning forward, "so Libby could be somewhere close by then."

"Yes," she nodded, "or the abductor simply went there to make his call. He must realise that calls can be traced so maybe he decided to throw the police off the scent."

Matt thought about his conversation with DS Woods and DC James. This is how they knew that the man had made a call from his street.

"Did your friend say anything else?"

"She was reluctant to reveal too much, the police don't like it when people working for them leak information to the public."

Matt nodded his head.

"She has lent me a tracking device but it's useless until we can identify the next victim."

Matt paled at the thought of more of his friends suffering at the hands of this madman.

Julia remained silent as a group of noisy office workers passed by their table.

"I think that we should spend the weekend sleuthing around Shoreditch." Taking a sip from her glass, she waited for him to respond.

Matt raised his eyebrows, surprised at her suggestion but before he had chance to comment she anticipated his reservations.

"Come on Matt, we have to do something. Can't you telephone him, keep him talking long enough for Fiona to get a fix on his location?"

"No," he shook his head. "He turns the phone off after communicating so my calls go to voicemail. Don't you think I haven't tried that already?"

"Sorry Matt," she could see that he was hurt. "I'm sure you have tried everything but I just can't just sit back and do nothing. Fiona has assured me that the police are concentrating their efforts on the Shoreditch area."

Matt looked up so she went on.

"They have teams of officers out there searching."

"What do you think we can achieve on our own?"

"I don't know Matt but if Fiona could tell us where the police have already looked."

"I will get hold of a street map so we can make a plan."

Julia was one step ahead, reaching into her bag she produced a map and spread it out across the table.

"As you can see I have one already."

Coloured marks were dotted all over the proposed search area.

"I have highlighted a number of buildings that are undergoing refurbishment or are waiting to be developed." There were dots on the old railway station and a number of vacant pubs and warehouses nearby.

"What's this one?" he asked jabbing his finger at a pink dot.

"It's an old police station and courthouse. I believe it's going to be turned into a luxury hotel. Word has it that tunnels run beneath the road separating the police cells from the courthouse."

"That sounds interesting," Matt replied thinking about the cell like rooms in the photographs he had been sent.

They made their plans for the weekend oblivious to the fact that the stakes were about to be raised considerably.

Chapter Forty Six

DS WOODS WAS STUDYING HER notes and reaching for a pen ticked off the first three items from her list. The job of handling information coming in from the Tower Hamlets search teams had fallen to her, she was not entirely happy with that but it was of her own making. DCI Wyman had given her the go ahead to recruit officers from local police stations and now as co-ordinator, she was looking for patterns in their reports whilst planning the operation as necessary. Recent intelligence from the surveillance team ensured that the Shoreditch area search was stepped up but even with more officers on the ground, this had yet to yield results. The abductor's lair remained elusive and still there was no trace of the black taxi used to abduct Pascale Dominique.

Matthew Cunningham appeared on her list and unconsciously she circled his name several times with her pen. It was still her intention to interview him again, she was certain that he could tell them more even though he had presented them with another set of photographs. Looking up at the window that separated her office from the incident room, she failed to notice the men and women working there. Her mind was filled with the latest set of images. They were far more disturbing than anything she had seen before. This was evidence of imprisonment, physical and sexual assault and a host of other crimes against the women featured. Woods sighed and tapped her pen anxiously against her desktop. Again, she was reminded that in most cases like this, abduction and imprisonment lead to death and the last thing she wanted was to become involved in another murder case. Memories of a previous assignment involving the cellist Mia Ashton and other young musicians was still fresh in her mind.

Running her pen through his name, she relegated him to the bottom of her list. She would speak to him again, but that could wait. The next item included the names Charley Baker and Melissa Miles. She knew them to be models, colleagues of Pascale Dominique and they all featured in the first set of photographs handed in by Cunningham. If the abductor was working to a pattern then she regarded these women as potential victims. It was her view that they would need protection but Wyman would never agree to that. The best she could offer was advice so scribbling a note on her pad, she knew the ideal candidate for the job.

A Friday afternoon meeting was scheduled at Shoreditch police station. Representatives from the search teams would be there to share information and discuss their progress and Woods was going to take the opportunity to outline her plans for the week ahead.

The following item prompted her to check the details of her latest idea, these included notes printed from the Police National Computer system. Studying them carefully she realised that she needed more details so turning to her computer, she accessed the system for a more comprehensive record. She wanted to check all the addresses associated with absconders, particularly those with ties to the Tower Hamlets area. If their man was local, then maybe there would be something on the system, she had very little to go on but something might come of it. Several minutes later, she printed off the relevant information then gathering up her notes, including her draft plan for the following week she slipped them into a file before shoving it into her bag.

Suddenly DC James appeared at her door. "You asked me to make myself available for this afternoons meeting."

"Ah yes, however I have something else that I would like you to do."

The smile slipped from his face, he was obviously looking forward to an easy afternoon, it was Friday after all.

"Don't look so despondent," she said, "I'm sure you will find this task most agreeable." She told him about her concerns regarding Charley Baker and Melissa Miles. "I would like you to go and see them, make sure they are fully aware of the possible dangers. Don't alarm them, be tactful and informative."

His face brightened.

"Of course, if you would rather accompany me to the meeting I can find someone else to speak to the women."

"No, no, don't worry," he spluttered, "leave it to me. I'll make sure they understand our concerns and will insist they have the number to my hotline."

Woods knew that he would do his best to charm the women, she just hoped that he would not make a complete fool of himself, again.

Chapter Forty Seven

IT WAS ALMOST MEALTIME AND they could hear the sounds of the trolley as it trundled along the corridor. Both women stirred, they were lying on their beds silently contemplating the day ahead. Sliding her legs over the edge, Kelly dropped from the top bunk then reaching for the blanket, fashioned a shawl around her shoulders. She knew the drill, the flap in the door would slide across and he would peer in, but unexpectedly the door opened instead.

"Good morning ladies," he said amicably as if addressing old friends.

They both stared at him suspiciously but still Libby remained curled up on the bottom bunk and edged closer to the wall.

"I have something for you," he smiled at Kelly before stepping out into the corridor.

"Here," he said holding out her own blouse.

Reaching for it, she was surprised to discover that it was freshly laundered. Glancing at Libby, who was still wearing nothing but her coat, she was tempted to ask for more clothes but decided to remain silent for fear of reprisals.

He handed over plates of unappetising fast food that he obviously thought a wholesome meal, this was accompanied by mugs of lukewarm tea, but neither women felt brave enough to complain.

"I have a little job for you this afternoon," he said looking at Kelly then he left them to their meal.

They barely had time to finish eating before he returned.

"Come with me."

Doing as she was told Kelly could detect a change in his mood. He was no longer jovial, his features were decidedly severe and it frightened her. It was obvious where they were going, the door to the torture chamber stood open. She could hear nothing from inside and wondered what he had done with Pascale.

Standing back, he allowed her to enter then she froze, her eyes wide with disbelief. One of the walls had been decorated with huge photographs of her son. Some of the pictures featured her sister Caroline but it was clear that Callum was the primary subject. She stood for several seconds taking it all in and as her breath quickened her throat began to ache. She missed Callum terribly but was careful to mask her emotions. She had tried desperately to keep her son a secret but it seemed that he knew more about her than she imagined.

Callum looked happy enough, his little smiling face always brought sunshine to her life, but the longer she stared the more she missed her little boy. Her maternal longing was overpowering and she thought she might break down and weep but steeling herself, she would not give him the satisfaction of witnessing her pain.

Suddenly a groan brought her back to reality; Pascale was still there tied to the table.

"Are you okay?" Kelly asked moving closer.

"What do you think?" the girl snapped angrily. "Do I look alright to you?"

An ugly bruise had formed on the side of her face and the straps at her wrists only added to her previous wounds. Kelly could hardly believe that she had been left alone like this since the attack.

"Just undo these damn straps."

"I wouldn't do that if I were you."

The sound of his voice startled both women.

"Let me go," Pascale spat. "These straps are hurting me."

"You don't have to worry," he sneered as he moved alongside the table. "It won't last for much longer."

Something in his voice made Kelly shudder.

"What do you think of my display?" he asked watching her closely.

Kelly remained silent but her expression told him all that he needed to know. She had not yet seen the syringe in his hand but as he slipped the plastic cover from the needle, he lifted it into view.

"What is that?" Pascale cried out fearfully.

"It's alright, we call it the drug of war. You won't feel a thing."

From his waistband, he produced a long thin bladed knife and Pascale uttered something in French. Holding it by the blade, he watched as Kelly took a step backwards. He knew what she was thinking and he smiled then turning away, he secured the door.

"Open her blouse," he ordered.

Hardly daring to move, Kelly remained where she stood.

"Well," he snapped, "are you going to do as you are told?"

Slowly she edged towards the table and avoiding Pascale's pleading stare reached out and slowly began to unbutton her blouse. Pascale struggled, she swore in both French and English but it was no use. Suddenly he lashed out, Kelly was taking too long so slapping her hands aside, he grasped at the thin material and tore it open sending buttons skittering away across the floor. Pascale stopped struggling and looked murderously at them both then her huge dark eyes filled with tears. She hardly flinched as he pricked her skin with the needle and emptied the contents of the syringe into her arm.

"What was that?" Kelly asked looking down in anguish as the drug swiftly took hold.

"It's ketamine, a general anaesthetic. Best we spare her the agony of death."

Grasping at the edge of the table Kelly held on as her legs went weak.

"You know what to do," he said placing the knife across Pascale's flat stomach.

Kelly swallowed noisily as she stared at it.

"Just think about your son."

He appeared detached, inaccessible. It was as if he had seen this all before and it was just another mundane exercise but as he whispered, his voice was as smooth as the Devil tempting Eve with the sacred apple.

"Pick up the knife, you don't have long. The dose I have given her will only last for a few minutes."

"No, no, no," she whimpered.

Frozen to the spot she glanced down at Pascale. The girl looked serene, beautiful in sleep. Hers was the body that women craved, perfectly proportioned, smooth skinned and evenly tanned. How could she possibly destroy someone so exquisite?

"Think of Callum. How far will you go to keep him safe?"

She looked up at him again, her face full of hate and loathing. Slowly her fingers folded around the hilt and as she lifted the knife, she glanced hesitantly at the place between Pascale's breasts. Unlike the dummy she had practiced on the body laid out before her was soft, warm and full of life.

"Under her sternum and aim for the left shoulder," he reminded her as if this was just another training session.

Positioning the blade, Kelly felt her own heart pounding, beads of perspiration appeared on her brow and her hands began to shake.

"How much pain do you think your little boy could take?" he whispered then, delivering his killer blow, he said. "I would make you watch as I worked on him."

Kelly wanted nothing more than to plunge the knife into his chest but that would be a huge mistake. She would never get out of this cell, she would die here a slow and painful death along with Pascale. Libby would also perish before she was found. With these thoughts rushing through her head, her wrist jerked involuntarily and the blade slipped easily into Pascale. Kelly gasped in disbelief at what she had done and staggering backwards almost collapsed.

"You must remove the knife or the internal bleeding will be impeded. You don't want her to wake up and see what you have done."

Doing as she was told, Kelly took hold of the knife and closing her eyes tightly whispered a prayer before pulling it out.

There was no immediate change, a little blood oozed from the wound and the pulse in the side of Pascale's slender neck continued to beat. He had already told her that death could take up to three or four minutes, she just hoped that Pascale was suffering no pain and was unaware of what was happening.

Moving away on trembling legs, Kelly dropped the knife before collapsing to her knees then she wretched. A series of sobs followed before she vomited and tears streaked her face as realisation set in. She had murdered Pascale in order to save her son. How was she going to live with that, but faced with the same choice, what mother would do any differently?

Chapter Forty Eight

MONDAY MORNING BEGAN WELL ENOUGH but the moment she arrived at work Woods knew that something was wrong. A meeting was in progress in the incident room, DCI Wyman was on his feet and as soon as she appeared his comments began.

"Nice of you to join us Detective Sergeant Woods."

She stopped and stared at him from across the room. Pairs of eyes glanced away in awkward embarrassment and a hushed silence settled over the team.

"If someone had bothered to tell me that you had called a meeting I would have made an effort to come in earlier." She spotted DC James and glared at him coldly.

"You have no idea what's going on have you Sergeant?"

"Has something happened?" she replied, her stomach tightening.

Wyman made a show of sighing deeply.

"Your missing persons," he began but then he changed tack. "Have you heard from the abductor at all?"

"No, but he has been in contact with Matthew Cunningham. We know that's true because surveillance verified the fact, then Cunningham came forward with the information himself."

"So you personally have no idea of the abductor's mood?"

She looked at him and frowned. Why would she know that, did he think she had a personal hotline to the man himself?

"The latest set of photographs suggests an escalation of violence," she explained. "I strongly suspect that Pascale Dominique has been tortured and raped."

"Oh it's far worse than that DS Woods," he said firmly. "A body was found earlier this morning and it's likely to be one of your missing persons."

This was a shocking blow but she managed to remain calm. She was aware that the next step would probably be murder but was hoping to close in before it reached that stage.

"The victim was found by the owner of a shop in Piccadilly. SOCO are on their way to the scene now so I suggest you get over there pronto."

His attitude was full of unspoken recriminations and it made her feel awkward. Ordinarily she would have defended herself but in a room full of colleagues, it was neither the time nor place. DC James rose slowly to his feet, he

182

was mortified by her public humiliation and wanted no part of it. The boss was clearly unimpressed with their lack of progress and it left him feeling inadequate.

"I will remain the senior investigating officer on this case but for some reason the Chief wants you to lead."

Woods remained silent but nodded her understanding. Unfortunately, it would still mean reporting to him but at least she had the backing of the Chief. She realised that he would not have made that decision lightly. He must have gone through her work very carefully and no doubt would continue to scrutinise her closely. The pressure was beginning to build.

Woods had no memory of leaving the incident room. Her nerves were taut and her head was reeling. Clearly, there were no details about the victim but given the latest set of photographs, it was likely to be Pascale Dominique. The sound of footsteps coming up behind her disturbed her thoughts so glancing over her shoulder, she saw that it was James.

"You know where this place is?" she asked, her voice strained.

"Yes, I have the address."

In his hand, he clutched a scrap of paper.

"Look Sarge..."

"You drive," she snapped before he got any further. "Stop at the first coffee shop you see." Her caffeine levels were criminally low and with her mood on edge, she needed a boost.

SOCO was there when they arrived and a team of uniformed officers were busy securing the area. Woods stared out of the window as James brought the car to a stop, its nearside wheels bumping up on to the pavement. The shop was a pretty Georgian building situated in a narrow side street. She searched for CCTV cameras but found none, evidently they had not been installed this far from the main route. A screen had been erected in front of the window to the left of the entrance and as Woods climbed out of the car, she spotted an elegantly dressed woman talking to a couple of officers. Reaching onto her pocket, she took out her warrant card.

"Detective Sergeant Woods," she said formally, as she approached the group.

"Morning Sarge," one of the officers recognised her. "This is Miss Sykes, proprietor of the shop."

"Good morning, please call me Emilia." She sounded as smart as she looked, although understandably strained.

"Did you discover the body?" Woods immediately got down to business. She was not about to reveal her Christian name.

"I'm afraid I did," Emilia replied.

"Please describe what you saw."

"As soon as I arrived I knew that something was wrong. The window display had been tampered with."

Woods frowned and Emilia could see that she did not understand.

"The window," she said turning towards her shop, "has a mannequin displaying a wedding gown. The arrangement had been changed, the dress was the same, but the mannequin was different."

"How do you mean?"

"When I left on Saturday evening the mannequin had blonde hair but now we have a dark haired model standing in the window."

"I see," Woods replied. "Was the door forced, what about the alarm?"

"No, the door and alarm were just as I left them."

"When you entered the shop, did you touch the body?"

"I went in and picked up the mail then I turned on the lights but I didn't touch anything else." Emilia shuddered as she recalled her movements. "It's exactly as I found it."

Woods nodded her head gravely. The victim had dark hair, Libby Ellis was fair so it could not be her. The body had not yet been identified but Woods was fairly certain who she would find modelling the dress. The irony of it did not pass her by, wearing a wedding dress should be the highlight of a woman's life.

"Excuse me," Woods said after a moment and leaving Emilia with the officers went to speak to the Scene of Crime officer standing at the entrance of the shop. "Can I see the body?" she asked then as an afterthought she said. "I may be able to identify the victim."

"We are just waiting for the pathologist to arrive," he told her but then he saw the expression on her face. "I can take you in for a quick look but you will have to wear these."

Reaching into a plastic box on the pavement beside him, he pulled out a pack containing a paper suit and protective overshoes.

As soon as she entered the shop, Woods could see no evidence of a break in, the door was undamaged and to the casual observer everything appeared normal. The window display was impressive and the dress with its long train looked beautifully expensive but as she looked closer, Woods began to notice the finer details. The model was stiffly arranged, supported by something hidden beneath the folds of the dress. Her face was pale, devoid of make-up and her huge brown eyes stared lifelessly out onto the street. Her long dark hair was poorly arranged, partially hidden beneath a lacy veil and the dress was several sizes too big. An effort had been made to pin the excess material; no self-respecting bride would wish to look like this on her wedding day. Seeing through it all, Woods studied the face of the woman and from the pictures she had seen was satisfied that this was the body of Pascale Dominique.

Returning to the group outside the shop, she was not surprised to see DC James talking to Emilia Sykes who looked increasingly pale and drawn. Woods also noticed the way she was clutching her coat protectively around her. These were the classic symptoms of shock.

"Would you like to sit down?" Woods asked as she approached, sounding less businesslike than before.

"I must admit that I do feel a little wobbly."

"Is there somewhere nearby where you could get something hot to drink?"

"Yes," Emilia nodded, "there is a little cafe just around the corner."

Woods suggested that James accompany Emilia to the cafe where he could sit with her for a while and take a comprehensive statement.

It was not long before Patricia Fleming arrived. Woods knew her well. Pat was one of the senior pathologists from the Westminster Public Mortuary. She was also a good friend of her old boss DI Terry Ashton. The women exchanged warm greetings then Woods briefed her quickly with the basic details. Whilst she listened, Pat pulled on her protective clothing then lifting her bag and photographic equipment from the back of her car, she accompanied Woods towards the shop.

"White Lace and Promises," she said reading the sign above the door. "Great name for a bridal shop, great name for a song."

Just over an hour later, Pat had completed her initial assessment then turning to the members of her team indicated that the body could now be moved.

"I expect you want immediate answers on this one Izzy," she turned to face the detective.

"It would be helpful. The man who did this has two more women in captivity."

"Right," Pat nodded thoughtfully as she glanced at her watch. "Shall we say three thirty?"

James appeared with Emilia Sykes who now had a little more colour in her cheeks and her face lit up as she recognised someone standing just beyond the blue and white tape.

"Ben," she called out, delighted to see her brother.

185

Woods spoke to her briefly before Emilia left then as she moved towards the car, she noticed a black taxi parked further along the street.

Chapter Forty Nine

THE FIRST MATT KNEW ABOUT the grim discovery was when DS Woods telephoned him with the news. It was the least she could do; she did not want him to find out about the death of his colleague from media reports or a third party. It was important that he felt included, his continued help was invaluable besides, he was the only one in contact with the killer.

Matt was stunned, if he realised that Pascale would be killed he would never have agreed to help abduct her. He knew that Veronique would be devastated and was tempted to telephone her. Pascale was her prodigy, the daughter that she never had. She may have been awkward to work with but an affectionate bond existed between the two women. It was true that Pascale possessed a natural beauty and with careful nurturing, would have become one of Europe's top models.

Matt wondered what the implications would be regarding Libby. He was convinced that she would be released in exchange for Pascale, but he had been wrong. His phone began to ring and thinking that it was Veronique, he answered without checking the caller's identity.

"Cunningham."

Matt froze at the sound of his voice.

"I assume that you've heard the news."

Matt remained silent.

"Have you nothing to say?" the voice sneered.

"What have you done with Libby?" Matt asked unsteadily.

If the man was capable of murder then what else would he do. Matt was terrified to know the truth.

"Nothing, she is fit and well. I can assure you of that."

"When are you going to let her go?"

"Oh I don't know," he replied scornfully. "When I have finished with her I suppose."

Matt's stomach tightened as images of her tied helplessly to the wooden frame entered his head.

"What do you want from me?"

A demented chuckle sounded down the phone.

"It's not all about you."

"It damn well feels like it. Do you know what it's like to have someone you

187

love in the hands of someone like you?"

"Someone like me," he laughed again then he said. "Oh yes I think I do. You have no idea."

Matt gasped at his response.

"I have experienced loss." Becoming serious, he sounded bitter. "The frustration at knowing that things could have been very different if only your..."

Suddenly their conversation came to an abrupt end. Matt dropped the phone onto his desk and closing his eyes, massaged the sides of his head with his fingertips. He was completely lost, the shock of Pascale's death and his part in her abduction left him numb and he didn't know what to do next. Suddenly an email arrived then his phone began to ring again.

Ds Woods was at her desk going through CCTV images of the events leading up to the abduction of Pascale Dominique. She studied them again in the hope of finding something that she may have overlooked. The pictures of the taxi driver were impossible to make out. At best, they were distant, grainy shots with no definition, the camera angle providing only a darkened profile of a man hunched low in his seat. Woods sighed and pinched at the bridge of her nose. Something was gnawing at her but she could not make it out. She felt certain that the profile looked familiar but then she could be wrong. With a bit of imagination it could very easily be anyone.

Her telephone rang.

"Woods," she answered snatching it up.

"Hello," came a cheery voice. "It's Fiona from surveillance. I've just monitored another telephone call from Libby Ellis' phone to Matthew Cunningham."

"Did you manage to get a trace?"

"Yes, it was made from a coffee shop in Whitechapel. I will forward you the address."

"Good work Fiona," Woods said before ending the call.

Putting the CCTV images aside, she made a hasty call to DC James asking him to meet her at his car then, as she rushed along the corridor she telephoned Matthew Cunningham.

The cafe was located near the old Spitalfields Market and as usual, it was busy so there was nowhere to leave the car. Pulling across a bus lane, James scuffed the tyres against the kerb before coming to a stop.

"You can't leave it here," Woods told him.

"Well you can't go in there alone," he countered, shooting her a worried glance.

"The abductor will be gone by now, he's far too clever to hang around. You find a sensible place to park then meet me as soon as you can."

Before he could argue, Woods was out of the car. The cafe was just along the street and as she approached, she pulled out her warrant card. Once inside she discreetly flashed her ID to the barista who greeted her from behind the counter then Woods asked to speak to the manager. As she waited, she glanced around searching for a man dressed in a camouflage jacket but as suspected, he was no longer there.

"Hello." A rich deep voice invaded her thoughts.

Turning to face the counter Woods was pleasantly surprised to see a hand-some Asian man smiling back at her.

"My name is Detective Sergeant Woods," she said quietly in an attempt to avoid unwanted attention.

"I'm Ravinder Singh, manager and proprietor of this establishment."

"Mr Singh, just a few minutes ago we had a report that a man we are inter-ested in speaking to made a telephone call from this location." She described the abductor and Ravinder listened attentively.

"Yes, I remember the man, he was sitting just over there." He pointed towards a table at the window.

"Did he order a drink?" Woods asked.

"Yes, white coffee no sugar."

"Is that his cup?"

"Yes it is," his smile slipped. "We have not yet had chance to clear it away."

"Don't worry about that Mr Singh, I'm glad you didn't. Do you mind if I take the cup and saucer away with me?" She went on to explain that it might contain important DNA that would help with her investigation.

"Of course. Do you need something to put it in, a box or a bag perhaps?"

"No thank you, that won't be necessary. My colleague will be here shortly then we'll pop it into a sterile evidence bag."

She asked several more questions, happy to keep him talking then once she was finished she scanned the customers sitting at the tables and a profile caught her attention. At first she thought it was Matthew Cunningham but she was mistaken, it was a clergyman deep in conversation with an elderly woman. There was something significant about this man but her mind was blank, then suddenly her eyes widened with realisation.

The door banged opened and DC James appeared. He had been running so was out of breath. Standing in the doorway, he recovered quickly and glancing around the room, he spotted her. She was sitting alone at a table calmly sipping coffee from a white mug.

"What do you know?" he asked as he slipped into a chair opposite then eyeing the empty cup and saucer he asked. "Have you been entertaining someone?"

Woods filled him in with the developments then watched as he pulled a plastic bag and a pair of latex gloves from his pocket. Carefully he bagged the items before getting to his feet then he followed her to the door. Woods turned and smiled at Ravinder Singh before leaving. Suddenly her day was beginning to improve.

Chapter Fifty

KELLY WAS DEVASTATED AND STILL in shock. Libby did her best to comfort her but nothing could ease her pain. They had been left alone for most of the weekend, plenty of time for Kelly to contemplate her part in the death of Pascale and now she was convinced that she would go to hell for what she had done. Suddenly they heard a noise from outside in the corridor.

"Get up," he said as he pushed open the door.

In his hand, he held a camera and focusing the lens he peered through the viewfinder.

"Stand together," he urged as if arranging a holiday snap.

Doing as she was told, Kelly moved closer to Libby. She wondered why he was taking her picture. He had not done this before so why the sudden interest?

When he was done, he viewed his work on the little screen at the back of the camera and satisfied with the results, he left them with a tray of cold dry toast and mugs of bitter tasting orange juice.

Matt was still in his office, his mind reeling from recent events. He could not believe that Pascale was dead and battled with the guilt that threatened to consume him. The telephone call he had received from the abductor did nothing to help and when DS Woods called soon after, he could hardly focus on her questions. Things were beginning to happen, the police surveillance team were monitoring Libby's phone and he wondered if they were listening in on his conversations too. Would Julia's friend admit to this or would she keep it to herself? He would have to be careful when using his phone in future especially when talking to Julia.

He wondered how they had become involved in all this. What had happened to draw them in? They never strayed into the dark world of drugs, did not drink to excess or attend wild parties, they lived normal quiet lives and he could think of no one who bore them a grudge. Why would anyone want to abduct Libby? Pascale was dead and he hated himself for being so weak, but while the man had Libby he had no choice but do as he was told. Staring at his computer screen, he flicked through the latest images. They had arrived earlier and included a picture of Libby. She was standing with another woman in front of what looked like bunk beds. He had no idea who this woman was,

191

DS Woods had said nothing about other victims. Clearly, she was suffering the same treatment as Libby, they both looked exhausted and strained. The accompanying pictures were equally disturbing. They included shots of Charley Baker, Melissa Miles and Emilia Sykes. Matt knew that the man had pictures of Charley and Melissa but he was surprised to see photographs of Emilia Sykes. Obviously, the women were unaware of being photographed. These were surveillance shots rather than posed, the pictures of Emilia were from outside her shop.

Matt had no idea why they had been sent to him. What message were they supposed to convey? There was no accompanying note so all he could do was speculate. Was the man toying with him of was he really interested in these women. Matt shuddered at the thought. He could not bear to think of them as potential victims. It was true that both Charley and Melissa knew Pascale but where did Emilia fit in? Matt frowned as he searched for an answer and he groaned with frustration. Perhaps he was the link, he knew all of them but with one exception. Libby's companion was a stranger so that theory did not work. Maybe she was the key. He studied her picture again, probing his memory in an effort to recognise her but he was certain that he had never seen her before.

The sound of his phone vibrating against the desktop startled him and peering at the number on the tiny screen, he saw that it was DS Woods.

"Hello," he said expecting an update.

"Mr Cunningham, could you come to the station at your earliest convenience?" she asked. "I would like you to give a DNA sample. It's purely for elimination purposes."

Stunned at her request, he was not expecting that.

"Yes of course," he stuttered. "Would this afternoon be okay?" He may as well get it over with as soon as possible.

"That would be perfect. I won't be here myself but Detective Constable James will look after you."

The call ended leaving Matt staring at his phone. What evidence did they have he wondered and why would he need to be eliminated. Was this the real reason for him giving a DNA sample or was there something more? Surely, they could just ask him questions. It could only be relating to the abduction of Pascale. Having worked closely with her in the past he must have left his mark on some of her possessions, so maybe it was true and all they wanted to do was eliminate him from their inquires. He thought about the black taxi he had used to abduct her, but ruling it out he was confident that the abductor would have disposed of it by now. Questions turned relentlessly inside his head, but one thing was clear. He would have to be careful, the abductor must not know that he was going to visit the police station. Turning back to his computer he saved the images to a memory stick before shutting it down then collecting his coat from the peg beside the front door, he left the house.

The Metropolitan Police headquarters in London was bustling with activity. Matt had never set foot inside a police station until recently when reporting Libby missing and now his visits were becoming alarmingly regular. He had taken precautions when travelling into town, doing his best to shake off the man who might be following him and with a final glance over his shoulder made his way towards the main entrance.

Matt booked in with the officer on the desk who asked him to take a seat in the reception area, but he did not have to wait for long.

"Mr Cunningham," DC James said as he appeared and holding out his hand, he smiled. "Welcome to the madhouse."

Greetings over, he led Matt through a security door and into a small room.

"I think DS Woods explained that I need to take a DNA sample." He pointed to a chair and Matt sat down.

"It's nothing to worry about, just routine stuff."

A sealed plastic bag lay on the tabletop next to a piece of electrical equipment that resembled an oversized mobile phone. Ignoring Matt's startled gaze, James worked quickly taking the samples then he said.

"All we need to do now is take your fingerprints."

Matt looked increasingly worried. DS Woods had said nothing about this, they were being particularly thorough. James demonstrated how the equipment worked then Matt added his prints to the PNC along with his photograph.

"Your details will remain on the Police National Computer system for the duration of our investigation." James told him. "The file will then be deleted unless of course it's found that you were involved in any way and a criminal prosecution is brought against you. In that case the file will be retained for much longer."

James watched him closely as Matt nodded his understanding.

"Have there been any developments regarding Pascale?" Matt asked sounding a little uncertain.

"There will be a press release later today."

"I have received more images from the abductor." Matt told him and reaching into his pocket, produced the memory stick and handed it over.

"Was that after your communication with DS Woods this morning?" James asked reaching for the device.

"Yes, these arrived by email earlier this afternoon."

"Excuse me for just one minute," James said then getting to his feet, he left the room.

Several minutes later, he returned carrying a number of computer print-outs. Laying them out on the table, he handed back the memory stick.

"Is there anything that you can tell me about these images?"

Matt told him the names of the models and the location of each photograph. James nodded but made no comment, he had spoken to these women just the day before.

"This is Emilia Sykes," Matt said pointing to an image. "She is the owner of the bridal shop White Lace and Promises."

James knew this already.

"What was the reason for your meeting with Miss Sykes?"

Matt explained his assignment and how it was connected with the magazine *Fashion Today*.

"Clearly the man we are searching for followed you. Are you sure these pictures were taken on the same day that you were there."

"They must have been," Matt replied glancing at the photographs again.

"Why are you so sure?"

"I have images of Emilia dressed in the same clothes and I recognise the situation. I had stepped out of the shop to get some shots of the building and Emilia followed me out. The man who took these must have been further along the street."

"You didn't see anything then, a man with a camera perhaps?"

Suddenly Matt didn't like the way the conversation was going, James was beginning to sound suspicious.

"These have been taken using a zoom lens." Matt explained. "He was obviously some distance away and as my attention was focused on Emilia and the shop front it's unlikely that I would have noticed a man with a camera."

James grunted. "How can you be sure that these images were taken on the same day?" Still he wanted proof.

Leaning forward Matt pointed at a series of blurred numbers at the foot of the page.

"This is a time and date reference. I have photographs bearing the same information. If you check the computer image, this will show up more clearly."

James grunted again, annoyed at himself for not spotting the obvious.

"Clearly our man is interested in both Miss Baker and Ms Miles," James said recovering his composure. "Both women have been warned to be extra vigilant."

Matt nodded before saying. "I have no idea who this woman is." He tapped his finger on the photograph of Libby and the stranger.

"I can't reveal her name but I can tell you that she was abducted a few days before Libby."

Gathering up the prints, James got to his feet.

"Thank you for coming in Mr Cunningham. Your continued help is invaluable."

The men shook hands again, the interview clearly at an end.

Chapter Fifty One

DS WOODS WATCHED AS A mortuary technician wheeled a trolley into the post mortem room. She was sitting in a state of the art viewing area at the Westminster Public Mortuary where a live link TV monitor displayed the grim proceedings unfolding in the laboratory below. A communications link allowed her to speak directly to the pathologist involved and if she were to stand, she could look through thick glass panels and see the team at work below.

The body of Pascale Dominique was transferred carefully from the trolley to a stainless steel table. She was still dressed in the wedding gown but the veil covering her head had been removed.

Patricia Fleming entered what she affectionately called 'the cutting room' and glancing up at the viewing area said. "Izzy are you sitting comfortably?"

"Hello Pat," Woods replied speaking to the screen in front of her. "Ready when you are."

"Right," Pat nodded as she studied the body on the table, "then let us begin. We have a well nourished female who we know to be a French citizen by the name of Pascale Dominique."

She always outlined the facts for the record before touching the deceased. This allowed her to make initial observations and photographs could be taken from every angle.

"There is significant bruising to the right side of the face," Pat moved in for a closer look, probing the area with her fingertips before continuing. "The bruising extends beneath the hairline. I would say that these blunt trauma injuries are consistent with a blow from a fist. There are knuckle marks around the contusion."

Next, she checked Pascale's hands looking for defence wounds.

"Several nails on her right hand are broken," she paused, "her fingers and hands remain undamaged. She obviously made an attempt to fight off her attacker, but it could not have been a prolonged assault or there would be more significant injuries to her arms. There is however heavy bruising and abrasions to both wrists suggesting that restraints of some kind were used to hold her down. She must have struggled significantly to sustain these kinds of injuries."

Stepping back, Pat reached for what looked like a pair of gardening shears and Woods gasped as she cut into the expensive wedding dress. She hoped that Emilia Sykes had sufficient insurance to cover the loss.

Beneath the dress, Pascale was naked.

"Marks on her ankles are similar to those on her wrists and are consistent with being held down."

The technician moved in again with his camera.

Moving slowly along Pascale's shapely tanned legs, Pat continued her examination.

"There is evidence of sexual intercourse." Selecting an instrument from a tray, she moved in to collect a sample.

"Would you say that it was consensual Pat?" Woods asked but was sure that she already knew the answer.

"From the bruises, I would say not."

Again, photographs were taken.

"Can you please turn the body?" Pat turned to the assistants who were standing by.

The remains of the dress were removed as Pascale was placed on her front then Pat stepped forward again.

"There is bruising to her back and shoulders." Pat ran her fingers carefully along the spine before continuing. "The vertebrae seem to be in line but she made violent contact with something solid."

"Given the bruising to her face, would you say that she was held down and beaten or was she involved in a fight?"

Pat looked up at the camera.

"Either she was pushed up against a wall with some considerable force or was thrown to the ground where she landed awkwardly on her back."

Reaching for a syringe, Pat prepared to take a blood sample.

"To answer your earlier question, there are bruises to the small of her back and buttocks. I would say that she was brutally raped. She could of course have sustained these as she struggled but given the severity of the other injuries..."

Woods sighed deeply as she watched Pat draw blood up into the syringe and when she was finished she moved away leaving the assistants to turn Pascale onto her back again. Pat remained silent as she worked at a side bench. Distributing blood among several test tubes, she carried out a number of preliminary tests and when she was done, she looked up at the gallery.

"There are traces of ketamine in her blood."

"Ketamine," Woods replied. "Isn't that a general anaesthetic?"

"Yes," Pat nodded her head. "It's used in this country as a 'field anaesthetic', for example at a roadside traffic incident or similar situation."

Getting to her feet Woods moved to the glass screen and peered down at Pat.

"Would the military have access to this drug?"

"Sure," Pat replied looking up at her. "I believe it's sometimes known as 'the drug of war'."

"So it's used as a battlefield anaesthetic."

Pat did not answer but simply nodded her head as she moved back towards the table.

"Now we come to the chest wound."

Woods looked back at the screen as the camera zoomed in. It took her completely by surprise.

Pat measured and recorded what appeared to be a small abrasion just below the breastbone.

"It's a penetrating wound that has been sealed with surgical glue."

"Super glue?" Woods asked moving closer at the screen.

"Indeed, another reference to military medical tactics." Pat went on to explain. "The glue was used as a quick fix on the battlefield but it's been developed and is now widely used in general medical and surgical practice."

Reaching for a scalpel, she peeled away the glue that sealed the wound then with a probe plumbed its depths.

"I think we may have found the cause of death." She said staring into the camera. "I've seen this kind of injury before. It's a technique used by skilled knifemen."

"Like the military?" Woods interrupted.

"Possibly," Pat replied, unwilling to confirm her suspicions. "I will of course have to verify this but I would say the cause of death was a cardiac tamponade. The pericardium sac that surrounds the heart has been penetrated by something like a thin bladed knife, causing it to fill with blood resulting in death."

"So basically she was stabbed in the heart."

"Yes," Pat nodded. "You could say that."

"Summing up then," Woods continued. "Pascale received a severe beating, was held down against her will, then raped before being stabbed to death."

"Well essentially that's true. Her injuries and cause of death are consistent with your elementary hypothesis."

"Thank you Pat, one more question. Why was the wound sealed?"

"I would imagine so that blood wouldn't leak all over the wedding dress."

Woods nodded her head thoughtfully before saying. "Let me have your report as soon as you can."

She was not going to hang around. She had seen enough and had no wish to witness Pat yielding a scalpel. She wanted to get back to the station, see how SOCO was progressing with the black taxi.

Chapter Fifty Two

"Matt you look awful!" Julia said the moment he appeared at her office door.

Glancing at her, he said nothing. He knew Julia well enough to know that she was not afraid to say what she was thinking so lowering himself into a chair, he forgave her plain speaking and waited for her to continue.

"I know that our weekend of sleuthing came to nothing but at least it gave us the opportunity to become acquainted with the area." Her smile was less than genuine.

"It's just like everywhere else in this city," Matt replied his mood reflecting his crestfallen appearance, "overcrowded, noisy and dirty."

Searching for the abductors lair was going to be more of a task than she imagined but pushing her misgivings aside, she realised that she had to remain positive.

"That may be so but I have made a note of places that we should check in both Shoreditch and Whitechapel." She passed him a handwritten list.

Matt studied it with interest and thought it well researched. It consisted of a number of addresses that he recognised, these were mainly buildings no longer occupied or were undergoing restoration.

"Quite a few of those places I obtained from the police," Julia admitted and when Matt looked up, she went on. "My friend somehow managed to get hold of the information."

He dropped the paper onto her desk as if suddenly it was too hot to handle.

"I have no idea how she came by it and quite frankly I don't care."

Matt said nothing and she could see that he was uncomfortable with the arrangement.

"Oh come on Matt, as long as it helps us to find Libby."

"You are right of course but the police are not stupid." He thought of DC James' suspicious nature. "Your friend needs to be very careful if she is going to continue helping us."

The telephone on her desk rang and looking at him apologetically, she answered it. The ensuing conversation was laced with acronyms, abbreviations and technical talk reserved for the industry. Matt understood most of it as it was a language that Libby liked to use.

"Sorry about that," Julia said when she had finished. "Would you like some coffee?"

Thrown by her question Matt glanced around but could see no evidence of coffee making facilities. Julia watched him and smiled before making his mind up for him. Reaching for her phone, she ordered two mugs of strong coffee.

"I can check out some of these places during the week," he told her. "I'm on an assignment here in town for the next couple of days."

"We could meet up in the evenings if you like, have a look at a few together."

They discussed their commitments and Julia checked her diary before a firm plan was made. Her life was strictly ordered, she rarely left things to chance.

"So, it's agreed then," she said happily. "We'll meet up on Thursday evening to swap notes."

"The police must have already been to some of those locations," Matt said nodding at the list on the table, "but it won't do any harm to have another look. I can't imagine they would have spent time checking them out thoroughly, most of these places are pretty much derelict."

When their coffee arrived, Julia relaxed and changed the subject in an effort to lighten the mood.

He was sitting at his computer in his command centre reading the latest news stories on the internet. There was an announcement from DCI Wyman, the senior officer leading the investigation regarding the discovery of the body of fashion model Pascale Dominique. The article was brief, the barest of details being released to the media. There was however a photograph of Pascale smiling into the camera and an image of the shop front where her body was found.

Sitting back in his chair, he laughed silently. It was a stroke of pure genius arranging her in the window of the shop. The beautiful model on her final assignment, very apt he thought. It brought all the components together and linked Cunningham to the murder. The police must be suspicious, he knew both the victim and the owner of the shop. Flicking through the article, he could find no reference to the black taxi used to transfer her body. Surely, they must have discovered it by now.

Losing interest in the news items, he opened the file containing images of the women and scrolling through the collection, he studied them carefully. Charley Baker, Melissa Miles and now Emilia Sykes were his main interest.

They appeared to be of a similar age and he was attracted to them all. He particularly liked Emilia Sykes, she was an unexpected addition to his plan. He found her style refreshing, her tastes in colour drew her apart from the others. Unlike the models, she did not have to pose for the camera.

Which one should be his next victim? He sighed deeply as he considered the problem. They all knew Cunningham, he had worked with them all so a connection was firmly established. His mind wandered as he thought about Emilia again. How long would it be before she could re-open her shop? Would the discovery of a body in her window display coupled with the ongoing police investigation damage her business? He thought not, people were often drawn to the macabre. Looking at the images very carefully he zoomed in on each woman in turn. He would have to make a decision soon, come up with a plan that would draw one of them in. It was unfortunate that Pascale was such a hot head, if it wasn't for her turbulent nature she would still be alive. Murder had not been part of his plan, she had brought it upon herself and now it changed everything. Would Kelly do it again? His hold over her was infinitely stronger than that of Libby Ellis. The bond between mother and child was a powerful thing and he was satisfied that he could use this to his advantage.

Selecting an image of each woman, he created a new file then constructing a short email message, he attached the file. With that done, his smile widened as his finger hesitated over the send button.

Matt was still with Julia when the message arrived. Reaching into his pocket, he pulled out his phone and checked the screen before accessing his emails. Julia paused as she watched. From the expression on his face, she knew that it was another hostile communication but she had no idea how bad it was. Matt remained silent as his eyes moved rapidly over the images then he found the accompanying note.

"Is it from him?" Julia could wait no longer and as Matt looked up his expression made her gasp.

"What is it Matt. Is it Libby?"

Rising to her feet, she rushed to his side and reaching out, placed her hands on his shoulders. Matt, unable to read the message out, held his phone up so she could see for herself but his hand was shaking so badly that she had to steady it before she could read the words on the screen.

You are going to persuade one of these women to take the place of Pascale. It's your choice, you decide.

Julia gasped again and standing back, her arms dropped limply to her sides.

"Oh Matt," she whispered. "What are we going to do?"

"I don't know," he whimpered.

They could hardly take this to the police. The man had again made it quite clear that he would not tolerate any contact with the authorities. His mind was racing as he went over the message. The implications were huge, the consequences potentially disastrous. He was being drawn further into this nightmare and he had no idea how or when it would end. He had no control over the situation, he was a puppet dancing to the tune of a madman. How could he possibly make a choice, it was unthinkable. Charley was his favourite, she and Melissa were not just colleagues they were his friends. He hardly knew Emilia Sykes so she would have to be the one but the thought left him cold. How could he possibly betray any of these women?

Julia could see him struggling with his conscience and she knew what was going through his mind so pushing her emotions aside, she took control and began to think logically.

"You know Charley and Melissa well," she began with a statement rather than a question, which left Matt looking confused.

"You have worked with them both in the past so you must be familiar with their ways."

"Yes," he replied uncertainly then blinking rapidly he went on. "I have worked with them both but have got to know Charley better than Melissa."

Julia tapped her fingernail noisily on the tabletop as she considered her next question.

"How do you think they would feel about helping us?"

"What do you mean?" Matt stared at her blankly.

"Well, I have the communication wire or bug, whatever it's called." Reaching into her drawer, she pulled out the electronic listening device. "Fiona told me that this could be used by concealing it on the body or the little thing on the end could be placed inside a mobile phone or hidden under something in an office or another room."

Matt stared at it in horror as the implications of her suggestion took him completely by surprise.

"If one of those girls would be willing to let herself be abducted, we could use this thing to track her to his lair."

"No," Matt shook his head. "It's far too dangerous. You know what happened to Pascale."

"I don't think we have a choice. He has made it quite clear that one of

203

these women will be his next victim regardless of whether she is carrying this bug or not."

Matt realised that what she said was true but for the moment, he refused to believe it.

Chapter Fifty Three

THE BUILDINGS WERE CLUSTERED AROUND a small courtyard, security was tight, but it was not obvious that this small industrial site was home to scenes of crime officers and the police forensic unit in London. Some of the buildings had been set up as laboratories with no expense spared, the latest state of the art equipment installed. Here forensic scientists could carry out a whole range of experiments designed to help police with their investigations. Woods was interested in a building that resembled a mechanics workshop. Machinery that she did not recognise was set up on test benches and given the nature of the workshop, she thought they would be required to wear safety boots and glasses before entering but she was wrong. She and DC James were however required to put on overalls but these were the sterile type, they also had to wear hairnets and overshoes. Cross contamination was an issue that had to be avoided at all times, so preventative measures were firmly in place.

The taxi found in the street close to Emilia Sykes' shop now stood in the centre of the workshop. It was resting on axle stands, its wheels having been removed the debris from the tyres was now under scrutiny. It was amazing to think that fragments picked up in the grooves could be used to determine the vehicle's movements. There was very little left of the interior. The seats and lining were gone and when DC James stuck his head through the gap in the door, where the window should have been he was surprised to find nothing but an empty shell. Component parts lay spread over several benches, some items protected by plastic bags or sheeting as the ongoing work was carried out by highly skilled technicians.

"The vehicle was definitely used to convey the deceased," the senior officer in charge told Woods. "We have found DNA traces and fibres that could be a match for the coat she was wearing."

"Are those fibres in the lab?" Woods asked.

"Yes, our people are checking them out as we speak."

"We know the colour of her coat but I'll see if I can identify a manufacturer's label. What about the driver's compartment?"

"That is a little more problematic," he replied leading her towards a computer screen. "Clearly someone wanted to conceal their identity by wearing gloves."

Pulling up a series of diagrams, he showed her a number of indistinct fingerprints.

"These blotches indicate that gloves were worn by the last driver to use this vehicle. We have however managed to lift a number of other prints."

He touched a series of keys on the keyboard and the image changed.

"Here we have prints of a regular driver. All those working at the taxi firm have been identified and eliminated from our list."

He instructed the computer to use the prints stored on its system to make comparisons with those taken from the taxi.

"One set we have not yet managed to identify. There are not many so whoever they belong to was not a frequent driver of this vehicle."

"Can you access the PNC from here?"

"Yes of course," he replied, glancing at her curiously.

"We have just put some information onto the system so it's possible that you may not have seen it yet."

"What are we looking for?" he asked as he logged into the Police National Computer system.

"Search for Matthew Cunningham," Woods told him and watching the screen she waited for the information to appear.

"Right, here we are, Matthew Cunningham you say?"

She nodded her head and moved closer. The man beside her opened the file and selecting the fingerprint sample that DC James had taken he accessed the program by typing in a few commands then the computer began its analysis. They did not have to wait long before it revealed an answer.

"As you can see, the computer is coming up with a 70% match. We can't be certain because of the condition of the prints, but a 70% match is pretty conclusive. I would say without doubt that Matthew Cunningham was behind the wheel of this vehicle recently."

Woods smiled as she pictured the CCTV profile of the taxi driver at the time of Pascale's abduction and her suspicions were confirmed.

"Thank you," she said glancing at the officer. "This is just what I need. Could you send me your report as soon as you can?"

"Of course, we'll have a clearer picture of events once the lab has finished working with the samples."

Woods knew that could be a lengthy process but she had enough to be going on with so collecting James they made their way towards his car.

"It never ceases to amaze me just how much science can help with our investigations." James observed. "How did we ever manage before the days of fingerprinting and DNA analysis?"

"We wore deerstalker hats and went around peering through a magnifying glass."

James stared at her and laughed. This was a rare attempt at humour and he realised that it was the best he would get.

Climbing into the passenger seat, Woods pulled the seatbelt across her body and clipped it into place. "Drop me back at the yard," she told him as James got in beside her. "You can then go and find Matthew Cunningham."

James glanced at her in surprise before starting the engine.

"I want him brought in for questioning."

She realised the implications especially if the abductor was watching him, but it was a risk that she was willing to take.

The interview room was hot and airless, much warmer than outside so shrugging off his coat, Matt sat down at the steel-topped table. It was bolted to the floor, the chairs chained to its legs making it impossible to use them as a weapon. The WPC who escorted him from reception had left and he was now alone. Matt wondered what he was doing there. The unexpected arrival of DC James at his door had alarmed him at first but the detective assured him that it was safe. The house was not being watched, he had spent thirty minutes observing the street before making his move.

Suddenly the door opened and DS Woods entered followed by DC James. In her arms, she carried a file that she dropped noisily onto the table. The chains rattled as she pulled out a chair then she sat down.

"Thank you for coming in Mr Cunningham," she said formally acknowledging his presence. "It's time we had a little chat," she paused then fixed him with a stare. "This interview will be recorded." For the record, she announced the time, date and those present in the room. "Do you have something that you would like to share with us?" She asked calmly then sitting back in her chair, she folded her arms and waited.

"I received another message this morning." Matt told her handing over his phone.

DC James joined them at the table, he had been standing by the door. Sitting down beside Woods, they examined his phone together.

"He's now showing an interest in Emilia Sykes." James commented needlessly.

"Why do you think he is asking you to decide?" Woods asked once she had described for the tape what they were looking at.

"I can only assume that he likes to play mind games. He is manipulative and knows that I don't have a choice but carry out his demands."

"Is that what happened with Pascale Dominique?" She said, her eyes never leaving his face.

Matt, unable to hold her stare looked away. Did they suspect him of being involved or were they simply fishing for information.

"I don't know what you mean." He replied lamely.

"I'm showing Mr Cunningham CCTV images of a black taxicab." She read out the licence plate number for the benefit of the tape.

"It's a London cab. There must be thousands out there on the city streets."

Ignoring his comment Woods continued to lay out images in front of him.

"Do you recognise the woman in these pictures?"

"Yes of course, it's Pascale Dominique."

"Where do you think these were taken?"

He remained silent, clearly she was waiting on the pavement outside the Waldorf Hotel.

"Is that where you picked her up from?" DC James asked leaning forward.

"I still don't know what you mean." Matt replied.

"I'm now showing Mr Cunningham images of the taxi driver," Woods announced as she pushed them across the table.

"Do you deny that this is your profile?" she said firmly and when he failed to reply she went on. "You deliberately tried to conceal yourself by slouching down in the seat because you feared that Mademoiselle Dominique would recognise you." She stared at him intently waiting for a reaction.

Matt's stomach clenched uncomfortably and he shuffled in his seat. Although the images were blurred, he could hardly deny that he was the driver of the taxi that picked Pascale up from the hotel. They would of course have to prove that it was him and he was not about to make it easy for them. Libby's life depended on him communicating with the abductor, what use would he be stuck inside a police cell?

"You may as well tell us," she said. "We have evidence that puts you inside that cab and I'm sure that if we took samples from your coat they would match the fibres found on the driver's seat." She knew that was not entirely true but he would not know that.

Matt had no choice but tell them what happened the day Pascale disappeared. His heart was racing and he broke out in a sweat, a sure sign of his guilt.

"Before you say anything would you like us to contact a lawyer?"

"There is no need for that," Matt looked up at her and smiled grimly. "You clearly know what happened and are building a case against me."

"You have been helping us," Woods responded, her expression sincere. "We are not here to catch you out, you are an important link in this investigation, but if we are to find the man doing this we need your full co-operation." She paused and her expression softened further. "We also need you to continue liaising with him."

Thoughts whirled inside his head as he tried to sum up the situation. Could he trust them or would he be locked away the moment he revealed the truth. He could see the sense in what she was saying and in reality it hardly mattered what happened to him as long as Libby returned safely.

"Okay," he said his eyes flicking between the two detectives.

He told them about the threats and the ordeal of the failed attempt at drugging Pascale with Rohypnol. He left nothing out and when he was finished he slumped back in his chair totally deflated.

Chapter Fifty Four

THE PATHOLOGIST'S REPORT WAS WAITING for her when Woods returned to her office. DC James accompanied her to the door before heading off to find an unoccupied desk in the incident room but the moment she saw the report, she called him back.

"James, you might want to see this."

Taking her place behind the desk, she flipped open the buff coloured file and began to scan the introductory notes. Each section was clearly indexed and finding what she was looking for, she turned to the page.

"It was as Pat suspected," she said glancing up at him as he peering over her shoulder. "Cardiac Tamponade caused by a thin, smooth bladed knife."

Several photographs were included giving a graphic step by step account of the killer blow. These she put to one side as she searched through the file.

"Here we are."

It was a list of injuries that Pascale had sustained, each wound described in minute detail using both technical and medical terms. There was also a comprehensive paragraph relating to the rape.

"It says here that DNA samples have been recovered." James pointed to a paragraph and leaning closer he angled the file for a better look.

"If he is a military man and I'm convinced that he is, his service medical records should provide answers to many of our questions."

"We'll have to apply to the Home Office for that kind of information." James reminded her. "That could take months and Wyman won't be too impressed. There would be mountains of red tape to cut through."

Woods knew that what he said was true. Service records were confidential information guarded not only by the military but also by the Data Protection Act, but given this was a murder inquiry they could put forward an application.

"We have to find a way of identifying this man. The cup we took from the cafe provided a DNA sample that matches Pats findings; at least it confirms that the killer made a call from that location."

James could hear the frustration in her voice.

"There is nothing on our database that matches those DNA results, so our only hope is to get hold of his medical records."

"Without a name it will be an impossible task," James reminded her. "Do you really expect the MOD to simply hand over their records for our people to pick through while searching for a match?"

"No, you are right," Woods sighed loudly. "It's a crazy idea."

Unconsciously she began tapping her fingernail against the corner of her desk.

"I'm beginning to think that he's not a local man after all." She stopped tapping. "None of the reports about absconders seem to match the information we have already." She paused again. "The only real chance we have of getting close to him is through Matthew Cunningham. He is the only person apart from the victims to have had any form of contact with him. Without Cunningham we have nothing."

It galled her having to let him go especially after his confession. The fact that he helped kidnap Pascale, albeit under duress was enough to charge and hold him.

"I'll get on to the National Control Bureau, see if our friends at Interpol can help."

Woods looked up at him and this time was impressed. It was a brilliant idea and she wondered why she had not thought of it herself. Now they had something to work with maybe their colleagues across Europe could help.

Pacing restlessly along the corridor, he wondered what Cunningham had told the police. He was aware that he had been taken in for questioning; the small camera set up on a lamppost opposite his house confirmed this. The solar powered device produced an elongated view of the street leading to the main road. It was motion activated and became operational when someone approached Cunningham's front door. When this happened, it sent a sixty second video back to his computer in the command centre. He had installed the device recently to save having to spend long hours stationed outside the house.

He stopped pacing and smiled. It was such good fun manipulating Cunningham but then his thoughts turned to DS Woods. He had discovered that her Christian name was Isobel and slowly he was being drawn towards her. She was an attractive and formidable woman. In an effort to find out more about her he had studied some of her past cases and realised that she was not to be underestimated. Perhaps he should add her to his portfolio, it excited him to think that she could be his next victim. What fun he could have entertaining her in his torture chamber. The thought deserved further consideration.

He was going to spend some time with Libby Ellis; Cunningham would need further encouragement if he was to carry out his next assignment but that could wait. He had other business to attend to first so going into the command centre he reached for a camera and lenses then stuffing them into a bag, made his way out of the building.

DS Woods was driving to a scheduled meeting with the search teams at Shoreditch police station. Unfortunately, this was the wrong time to travel; the streets were crammed with commuters intent on leaving the city at the same time. Crawling along in her car, she drummed her fingers impatiently against the steering wheel and wished that she had begged a lift from a traffic car. At least they could have used 'blues and twos' to clear a path. It was an unorthodox trick used by certain crews when returning to the station at the end of their shift.

It was only a short distance from Westminster to Shoreditch and luckily, she had allowed sufficient time. The meeting was not due to start for another forty minutes. Moving forward slowly, the car in front stopped again so reaching into the passenger footwell, where she had dumped her bag, she pulled out her notes. May as well put the time to good use, she thought keeping an eye on the car ahead then she began to scan the notes that she intended to present at the meeting.

He was surprised at the amount of traffic clogging up the streets and wondered if there was something going on. Rush hour was usually manic but today it seemed even worse. Heading towards the tube station, he dodged the crowds moving in the same direction. Perhaps he should postpone his mission, it would be just as mad on the underground. He stopped and was jostled up against a shop window, then making up his mind he performed an about turn and glanced casually at the cars crawling past. Doing a double take, he could hardly believe his eyes. Detective Sergeant Woods was at the wheel of a car and if it wasn't for the fact that she was multi tasking she would have looked right at him. Instinctively he pushed back against the wall but then he realised that she had no idea what he looked like. None of them did apart from his captives and they were not about to broadcast his description.

Moving forward he kept pace with her car whilst remaining hidden by those around him. Occasionally she would pull ahead only to stop again and he would catch up. This was an amazing coincidence, he thought as he studied her from his position on the pavement. It was his plan to head for her place of work, wait for her to appear then use his camera to steal her image before attempting to follow her, but now his job was made easier. There was nowhere for her to go and on foot, keeping up with the car was not a problem. He guessed that she was heading for Shoreditch police station. It was a gamble that he was willing to take so glancing over his shoulder, he crossed the road between the cars before slipping into an alleyway that led to a series of shortcuts. He emerged close to the police station and had sufficient time to find a suitable spot from where he could observe her unseen and take his photographs.

Pulling up beside the kerb, Woods decided to avoid the small car park located behind the station. Climbing from the driver's seat, she reached in for her bag and notes before locking the door. Suddenly she felt uneasy so glancing over her shoulder she scanned the footpath. There was no one in the immediate vicinity so shrugging off her paranoia she chastised herself for being foolish.

Out of sight, he peered through the viewfinder and adjusting the lens focused in on DS Woods. He watched as she took in her surroundings. Her image was perfect and he could see her frown. For a moment, she appeared confused then as her expression changed, he clicked the shutter and the camera reacted soundlessly. He decided to wait for her to return to her car. He wanted to take her immediately, but he had not yet worked out a plan. It would be easy to overpower her but then there was a risk of being seen. There must be plenty of roadside cameras in the area, besides how would he put the blame onto Cunningham. It may be an ideal opportunity but without perfect planning this was not the right time.

Chapter Fifty Five

THE FOLLOWING DAY MATT LEFT his home early. It was the first of his two day assignment working with Charley.

"Cunningham is on the move." A police officer in an unmarked vehicle parked along the street spoke into his radio.

Not long ago Beadle and Hills relieved their colleagues who had been watching the house all night. DS Woods had arranged for twenty four hour surveillance, Cunningham had committed a serious crime that should have seen him behind bars, but she had allowed him to walk free. She knew that it was wrong and Cunningham should answer for the part he played in the Pascale Dominique murder, but she also realised that he was her only link with the man she was desperate to find. If the lines of communication were to stay open, then Cunningham would have to remain free. If Wyman discovered what she had done, she would undoubtedly be facing some very serious questions. Woods was convinced that she had made the right decision, as long as Cunningham remained on side he could answer for his crimes later.

"What do we have here?" Hills nudged his colleague and they watched as a man wearing a military style camouflage jacket appeared.

"Probably a neighbour heading for an early morning commute." Beadle replied before turning his attention to Cunningham who was now almost at the end of the street.

Starting the engine, he eased the car out of the parking space and cruised slowly between the tightly packed vehicles that lined the way.

"Don't you think he fits the description of Wood's murderer?"

"It's possible," Beadle murmured as he brought the car to a stop at the junction. "The description was a little vague though, but he is wearing a camo jacket."

Hills continued to watch as the man stepped out from between the parked cars then briefly, they made eye contact before he looked away and crossed the road.

He knew they were tailing Cunningham, he had seen them arrive earlier. The police were obviously becoming suspicious and he smiled, that was part of his plan and it was coming together nicely, but he would have to be careful. It wouldn't be difficult to lose these men so he continued to follow Cunningham who was heading for the tube station.

Hills was on the radio requesting more information as Beadle steered the car slowly along the main road.

"Can you give me a comprehensive description of DS Woods' suspect?"

"How do you mean?" came the reply.

"Well, average height, short dark hair, last seen wearing a camouflage jacket is hardly helpful."

"That's all we have I'm afraid."

"Great," Hills mumbled as he turned to Beadle. "So we stop and question every man we see fitting that description."

"Where did he go by the way?"

Craning his neck, Hills peered out of the rear window but the man who had been there just moments before was gone so the detectives turned their full attention to Cunningham.

Matt was fast approaching the station entrance when suddenly he stopped and did something that was completely out of character. Turning to a street vendor, he purchased a copy of a daily newspaper. He had never done this before but today he needed a distraction. His mind gave him no peace, images of Libby continued to fill his head, even the prospect of working with Charley did nothing to ease his anxiety.

Finding a seat on the half empty train, Matt unfolded his paper but he underestimated his ability to concentrate. Nothing that he could see interested him, individual words and grainy photographs stood out but he found it impossible to focus his mind. How could he possibly be expected to choose the next victim? Looking up he stared out of the window but all he could see was flashes of wall just inches from the carriage as it rumbled through the tunnel. The latest demand was outrageous and the more he thought about it the deeper he slipped into despondency. Libby's life hung in the balance and he couldn't bear the thought of her suffering further at the hands of this madman. Equally, the decision that he was expected to make was unimaginable.

Glancing at his newspaper, he turned the page and almost cried out in shock. The image of Emilia Sykes filled half the page, but looking closer he realised that he was mistaken. The article was about a backbench politician who uncannily resembled Emilia. Taking a deep breath, he closed his eyes and willed positive thoughts to enter his head but it was no good. Julia Peters' idea to convince one of the girls to be abducted whilst carrying the tracking device plagued him. The plan was outrageous and far too dangerous but she insisted it was the only way to locate the abductors lair. Maybe she was right, but he was not convinced, he wanted nothing to do with the plan. He had already sent Pascale to her death and could not bear the thought of doing it again. The madman had told him to make a choice, he was supposed to sacrifice one of his friends in an effort to keep Libby safe. What would she think knowing that he had played such an active part in this terrible crime?

The train slowed to a stop and as the doors slipped open, Matt got to his feet. Hoisting his equipment case over his shoulder, he stepped down onto the platform. The newspaper however remained on the seat that he had just vacated.

Beadle and Hills were covering both exits as the passengers emerged from the tunnels. Beadle stayed with the car whilst Hills struck out on foot. More people were arriving every second but Cunningham was easy enough to spot and Hills soon reported the sighting to his colleague. Beadle prepared to move the car but suddenly he saw something and reached for the radio.

"Hills, I have a visual on the man we saw earlier. I'm convinced it's him."

"Stand by," came the reply.

A few moments later Hills was back on the radio.

"He's just come into view. You are right he's our man and seems to be heading in the same direction as Cunningham. His camouflage jacket is doing very little to help him blend in with his surroundings."

"Well I can't see him anymore," Beadle laughed. "I'll bring the car round."

Outside the station, Matt turned right and joined the crowd ebbing like the tide along the pavement. He had no idea of the drama playing out behind him and keeping his head down continued to wrestle with his thoughts.

Beadle spotted his colleague standing on the pavement, but bringing the car to a standstill in the middle of a bus lane proved to be a mistake. A taxi driver blasted his horn noisily and yelled a few choice words and the man following Cunningham noticed the commotion. He then disappeared like a magician performing a stage trick.

Chapter Fifty Six

JAMES PRESENTED WOODS WITH THE prints he had taken from Matt's memory stick.

"This is evidence that Kelly Spencer is still alive."

"She was when these photos were taken," Woods reminded him.

His smile slipped as he nodded in agreement then he said. "Emilia Sykes appears to be his latest interest."

"So it seems," Woods replied as she spread the prints out over her desk. "Perhaps you should pay her a visit, warn her about his unwanted attention like you did with Charley Baker and Melissa Miles."

"Sounds good to me boss."

Woods knew that he would put up no objections.

"I wonder why he is showing us pictures of Kelly Spencer." James said thoughtfully.

"I suppose it's because he can. I guess he wants us to know how well he is taking care of her."

James studied the pictures again observing how unhappy and stressed the women looked. They were so pale and colourless the images may as well have been in monochrome. Suddenly the telephone on her desk rang.

"Hello, DS Woods." She spoke first then listened.

No sooner had the call ended the phone rang again so going through the same procedure she stared at James.

"Well, well, well," she said dropping the receiver into its cradle.

James waited expectantly.

"Our man has been spotted following Cunningham into the city this morning. The other call was from Shoreditch, they have come up with a possible address of an absconder in Bethnal Green."

"Do we know where Cunningham is now?" James asked.

"He is working with Charley Baker at a studio in town."

James pulled a face. He should have known that.

"Beadle and Hills are on location watching his every move. You go and see Emilia Sykes, make sure that she is aware of the situation and I'll check out Bethnal Green."

"Things are looking up," he smiled as he got to his feet.

"Maybe," Woods mumbled, her mind already elsewhere.

Turning to her computer, she opened her email account and found the message sent by Shoreditch. One of the officers on the search team had been trawling through the information she had forwarded, cross referencing it with the Royal Military Police files. He had come up with a name and address so checking a map of the area, she discovered that it was not far from Whitechapel. Switching back to the message she copied down the details before leaving her office.

Rita Morgan answered the door and smiled warmly as Woods introduced herself.

"Come in my dear. Don't mind the mess, I was just about to do some housekeeping."

Following the little grey haired woman along the hallway, Woods noticed that the walls were decorated with a floral scene that must have been popular in the 1970s. The carpet underfoot had seen better days but everything was clean, nothing seemed out of place. The living room was at the back of the house overlooking a small garden and as Woods glanced out through the window, she could see a vast collection of clay pots, each one bursting with spring colour.

"Sit yourself down."

Doing as she was told, Woods sank into an armchair beside a gas fire. The room was warm enough and thankfully, the fire was not on.

"Would you like a cup of tea dear?"

Woods was about to decline the offer but it seemed that no was not an option and a few minutes later Rita shuffled in from the kitchen carrying a tray laden with teapot, cups and saucers and a milk jug. There was no sugar, luckily Woods took her tea without.

"Now dear," Rita began as she settled into the chair next to a small table that separated them. "What's this all about?"

"I'm here to ask you some questions about your son."

"Oh him," Rita huffed as she poured tea from the pot. "I thought all that fuss was over with."

"What fuss might that be?" Leaning forward Woods reached for a cup and saucer.

"The Military Police went through all that business a few months ago."

"I'm not with the military," Woods explained. "I'm with the Metropolitan police."

"I know you are dear, I'm just saying that's all."

Obviously, Rita had no idea why she was there.

"I would like to know a little more about your son. It would help enormously with a case I'm working on." Sitting back, Woods smiled before taking a sip of tea. "Oh it's my favourite, Earl Grey with a dash of bergamot."

Rita studied her for a moment then she smiled and visibly relaxed. "I always have this brand of tea, it's my favourite too so I like to offer it to guests."

"Have you seen your son recently Mrs Morgan?" Woods asked, eager to get started.

"Dane, no. He hasn't been to see me since before."

"Before what?"

"Before his posting to Afghanistan. That was over a year ago now."

"What was he doing there?"

Woods knew that hostilities in that part of the world had ended and most of the troops had been withdrawn.

"It was the usual army stuff. A peace keeping mission or so he called it." Rita looked up at Woods and frowned. "Of course I think it was all whitewash, peace keeping my arse. He was sent there by the British Government to help force our way of thinking on some poor soul. It's what we did before in the days of the Empire."

Woods had no intention to become embroiled in a political debate on the role of the armed forces.

"So Dane was sent abroad." It was the first time she had used his name.

"Yes but he didn't stay there did he?"

"Do you know what happened to him or what he did in Afghanistan?"

"No, he wouldn't tell me anything. His messages were full of endearments, soppy stuff for his dear old mum."

"Do you still have his letters?"

"Letters?" Rita looked up and began to laugh. At first, the rattle began deep inside her chest then it rose with intensity until it enveloped her whole body. Tea slopped into the saucer from the cup she was holding before she placed it down on the table then probing with her fingers, she pulled a handkerchief from her sleeve and dabbed carefully at the corners of her eyes.

Woods looked on in amusement using the time to enjoy her tea.

"Letters dear?" Rita said when she had recovered sufficiently. "People don't write letters anymore you should know that, no he sent me messages via a computer. He used an ipad or tablet, whatever you call them. There was a time when his messages arrived regularly but since the Red Caps came calling with news that he had gone AWOL I've heard nothing."

Woods thought for a moment.

219

"What about Dane's father. Is he about?"

"Oh yes," Rita laughed again. "He's about alright."

"Does your son have any communication with him?"

"Well he might have." Rita replied then reaching for her tea, she drained the saucer first before taking a mouthful from the cup.

"It would be helpful to speak with your husband if that's possible."

"Be my guest." Rita replied, nodding her head towards the shelf above the fireplace.

Woods looked to where she was indicating and discovered a wooden urn with the name Percy Morgan and a date engraved onto a brass plate.

"He passed away months ago."

"Oh, I'm sorry to hear that." Woods shuffled uncomfortably in her chair.

"Don't be dear, there's no need to be sorry. Me and Percy spent most of our lives together." Leaning forward she lowered her voice before going on. "It's nice to have the house to myself, a bit of peace and quiet. It did seem strange at first though, but I've got used to it now."

Woods remained silent, waiting for Rita to continue.

"It was my Percy who insisted that Dane joined the army. Of course, I was not keen on the idea but what can you do, boys will be boys." She took another mouthful of tea before going on. "Dane seemed to enjoy what he was doing, but I say the army poisoned his mind."

"How do you mean Mrs Morgan?"

"Well, they showed my boy how to take a life then they sent him off to war. I swear that he was not the same when he came home from his first tour."

"Do you have a photograph of Dane?"

"Yes of course dear."

Reaching behind her, she produced a framed photograph from a table that stood to the right of the fireplace. Woods put her cup down before reaching forward and holding on to it carefully, she studied the face of the man in the picture. He was clean shaven, his head covered by a beret and he wore the stripes of a sergeant. There was nothing about him that she recognised from the grainy CCTV images. This could be their man but unfortunately, it was impossible to make a positive identification.

"How long have you lived here Mrs Morgan?"

"Forty years next month." Rita said proudly.

"So Dane lived here as a child."

"Oh yes, it was the only home he knew until he joined the army."

"Is there anyone else locally that I could talk to? Someone who might remember him from his childhood days."

"Oh I don't think so. Most people have either died or moved away especially the youngsters."

Woods nodded her understanding.

"I would imagine that this house is full of memories."

"Oh yes," Rita smiled happily.

"Can I ask," Woods said as something occurred to her. "Have you kept anything from Dane's childhood, a lock of hair for example of his milk teeth?"

"I have some of his teeth. Why do you ask?"

Chapter Fifty Seven

HIS MOOD WAS SOUR WHEN he returned. He had spent the day following Cunningham and not once did he get an opportunity to photograph the girl he was working with. It was impossible to get inside the studio without raising the alarm and with the police watching, it was not a good idea to try. Neither Cunningham nor the model had emerged and this only added to his frustration.

Libby and Kelly had remained locked in their cell for the whole time. He had given little thought to their wellbeing and Kelly was determined to let him know how she felt when he returned. Suddenly the door swung open and he stood there staring at them. They could see that he was in a foul mood so Kelly decided to remain silent.

"You," he snarled. "Get out of that flea pit."

Moving forward, he grabbed hold of Libby's arm and pulled her roughly from her bunk. She squealed and clutching at the metal frame for support remained frozen to the spot.

"Come with me."

She wanted to defy him, stay with Kelly in the safety of their cell but fearing reprisals she reluctantly followed him along the corridor. Instead of leading her toward the torture chamber, he turned the other way. She had never been this way before so was surprised at what she found. The last door on the left led to an improvised storeroom. The cell, originally designed to hold a single person, was fitted with shelves and stacked with all manner of dried and canned foods.

"Get something for you both to eat," he snapped before leaving her alone in the cramped space.

Reaching for a tray that lay abandoned on a shelf she moved along the rows looking at bags of rice, spaghetti, breakfast cereals, and packets of biscuits. On the shelf below, she found tins of soup, baked beans and fish. Selecting a can of tuna, she read the label noticing that the fish was in brine, she preferred spring water, but adding it to her tray, she could hardly be choosy. Without too much thought, she added a packet of biscuits and a family sized bag of crisps. Her choice was limited because he would hardly allow her to cook a proper meal, besides in her reduced state of shock Libby was unable to consider the ingredients for a healthy supper.

He returned carrying a bag of bread rolls, which he handed over before marching her back to her cell.

"I will bring you hot drinks later," he promised before closing the door loudly.

Returning to his command centre, he threw himself down in his chair then running his hands through his hair, he sighed loudly. Cunningham must have made his choice by now, so turning to his computer, he opened the file containing images of both Charley Baker and Melissa Miles. He had previously added shots of Emilia Sykes and now opening another folder, he selected the images of DS Woods before transferring them. Now with all the women featured in the same file, he went through them systematically noting their individual attributes. They were all good looking, the models in particular were naturally glamorous, but Emilia Sykes possessed a style that seemed unique. She may not be a model, but she was a stunner. Woods was older and seemed to have a harder edge to her character. This was hardly surprising given her profession. She reminded him of the female officers he had come across in the army. She would be more resourceful than the others, it would be interesting to find out just how capable she could be when put under pressure. She would be a worthy opponent. She reminded him of someone whose army training and arrogance had done nothing to avoid an agonising and savage death. This was something that he would rather not think about, so forcing these thoughts from his mind he concentrated on the women on the screen.

From Bethnal Green DS Woods went directly to the Westminster Public Mortuary. It might be late afternoon but she knew that Pat Fleming often remained at her office far beyond normal working hours.

"DS Woods to see Dr Fleming," holding out her warrant card Woods confirmed her identity.

"Do you have an appointment?" the receptionist asked.

"I'm afraid not," Woods made a face.

"That's not a problem. I'll just see if Dr Fleming is available." Pressing a button on a keyboard, the woman spoke into a tiny microphone that she wore on a wire around her neck and after a moment, she looked up. "Dr Fleming is currently in a meeting but it's due to finish in about ten minutes."

"Can I wait over there?" Woods indicated to a collection of easy chairs arranged around a little table.

"Of course. I'll let Dr Fleming know that you are here the moment she becomes available."

Taking a seat, Woods reached into her bag and pulled out her notebook then turning the pages, she found the notes that she had made earlier. She felt certain that Dane Morgan was the person she was looking for. Everything seemed to fit, he was a local man so must be familiar with the area, he was also a soldier who would have had access to military clothing and supplies. The use of Ketamine and adhesive to seal the wound in Pascale Dominique's chest underpinned the fact that he was a knowledgeable and inventive man but she had to discover more about Dane Morgan. The moment she was in front of a computer, she would request his military records. The only element of doubt that nagged at her was the fact that she could not identify him from the photograph that Rita had shown her. The CCTV images that she had as a reference were far too indistinct and she couldn't say with confidence that they were of the same man. She should have taken a picture of the photograph using her phone, show it to Ravinder Singh, owner of the coffee shop. He may have been able to confirm the ID.

"Izzy." A voice sounded from behind her and peering over her shoulder, Woods could see Pat hurrying across the foyer towards her.

"Pat, thank you for agreeing to see me." Woods said getting to her feet then the women embraced briefly.

"It's always a pleasure. You are far less dull than the vultures I have to deal with."

She dropped into a chair and crossed her legs before saying. "I've been stuck in a coroners meeting all afternoon."

"Poor you," Woods replied sympathetically before going on. "I've just had an interesting meeting myself." Rummaging in her bag she pulled out a small plastic evidence bag then holding it up she asked. "Can you extract DNA from this?"

Reaching forward Pat took hold of the bag and peered at its contents.

"A child's tooth."

"Yes, I need you to check it out."

Pat looked up seeking clarification.

"I'm convinced that it belongs to the man who murdered Pascale Dominique but I need you to confirm that."

"I take it that you don't have consent." She didn't need an answer, the look on Woods face told her all she wanted to know. "It's all rather unethical don't you think?"

"You don't need to worry about that. I'll take full responsibility if the proverbial hits the fan."

Staring at her, Pat raised her eyebrows.

"If you are worried about his rights, as far as I'm concerned he gave those up when he viciously raped and murdered Pascale Dominique."

"I will carry out these tests for you Izzy but be very careful how you use the results."

Woods was more than aware of the ethics surrounding protocols.

"I simply need you to confirm the identity of this man. There are at least two women to my knowledge whose lives depend on me catching him.

"I will have the results for you by tomorrow." Pat promised then she got to her feet. "I'll telephone you but now I'm afraid I have a report to write."

Unconsciously Woods glanced at her watch. "Me too," she grimaced. "I really appreciate this Pat, I owe you one as usual."

"The next bottle of bubbly is on you then."

They embraced again before going their separate ways.

Chapter Fifty Eight

JULIA KNEW THAT MATT WAS busy working with Charley. She was also aware of his reluctance to consider her scheme to help track down the abductor's lair but this did nothing to dampen her efforts. With his help or not she was determined to do whatever it took to find Libby and bring her abductor to justice.

Charley Baker was her first choice. She knew her quite well having interviewed her once for her magazine *Fashion Today*. She had produced an in depth article about a young woman working as a fashion model and knew that Charley possessed a dynamic and tenacious personality. Julia was convinced that she was the ideal candidate for the job but as Charley was with Matt, it would be impossible for them to meet and discuss her plan. Julia could wait no longer, her impetuous nature did not allow for caution. She could not understand why Matt was so reluctant to help find Libby. She knew that he was in contact with the abductor but was also aware of the threats that discouraged him from speaking to the police. This is why it was so important to launch their own investigation. Perhaps he was not telling her everything. Just how deeply was Matt involved she asked herself? Confident that she was doing the right thing she decided to press on with plan B.

From the pavement, Emilia looked up at the building that housed the offices of *Fashion Today*. Several companies shared the huge building but she couldn't help being impressed. The magazine was very popular and she knew that Julia Peters was the dynamic force behind the company in what was regarded as a highly competitive market. She wondered why Julia wanted to see her, she had been so insistent on the phone giving nothing away but promising to reveal all when they met. Naturally, Emilia was intrigued and could only think that it had something to do with the article that Libby Ellis was writing about her business.

The receptionist announced her arrival and directed Emilia to a lift that carried her to the floor that was home to *Fashion Today*. The doors slipped open allowing her access to a world that was very different to her own. The massive space was almost entirely open plan with banks of computer screens arranged in rows like trees in a forest. Portable dividers offered a degree of privacy to those working at the desks but most of the journalists, editors and other staff remained visible.

"Emilia." Julia spotted her the moment she arrived. "Welcome, it's so good of you to come at such short notice."

Emilia held out her hand as she advanced and they greeted each other formally. She had not met Julia before but they had spoken several times on the phone. Emilia was impressed by what she saw, she expected the owner of such a popular magazine to be formally dressed in a crisply cut suit, but Julia inhabited the other end of the fashion spectrum. Her thick, dark hair danced unruly around her shoulders and a pair of spectacles hung on a chain around her neck. Emilia wondered if these were functional or merely part of her outfit. She wore a heavy Arran cardigan over a pink blouse with a multi coloured skirt that ended just below her knees. Her tights were brightly coloured and on her feet were a pair of bright pink ballet slippers. She simply adored the woman's style.

"Let's go into my office."

Emilia followed her to the other end of the floor where Julia's office was situated. Inside it was cool, silent and tastefully furnished. In the centre of the room stood a huge antique desk and to one side, an informal area with easy chairs arranged around a glass topped coffee table. Beyond that was a door that led into a boardroom.

"Please make yourself comfortable." Julia indicated to one of the chairs. "Would you like some refreshment? Tea or coffee perhaps."

"Tea would be most welcome," Emilia replied as she slipped her coat from her shoulders.

"What a lovely dress," Julia said.

"Thank you. It's one of my own creations."

The simple 1950s utility dress boasted a floral print design that gave it a fresh and gentle appearance, quite the opposite of Julia's tastes. They chatted informally whilst they waited for their tea to arrive, Julia giving nothing away. The nature of their meeting would remain a mystery for just a little while longer as Julia used the time to get to know Emilia.

It wasn't long before a junior office clerk arrived with a tray and placing it down carefully on the table, she poured tea into two bone china cups before leaving.

"Right," Julia began once they were alone. "Down to business." She started by revealing the truth about Libby Ellis.

"Do the police know why she has been abducted?" Emilia was horrified at the news.

There had been nothing on the media channels and she wondered how

Julia was so well informed.

"No. There has been no ransom demand or anything like that and because of the nature of the case the police are reluctant to go public just yet."

She went on to explain that a line of communication existed between Matthew Cunningham and the abductor. Although Matt was working closely with the police, the abductor was using manipulative methods to prevent him from passing everything to the authorities.

"That's awful," Emilia gasped. "Poor Libby."

She listened to what Julia had to say, curious to know why she was telling her, but then realisation set in.

"Hold on a minute," she said suddenly, "the woman found dead in my shop. Where does she fit into all this?"

Julia had deliberately failed to mention Pascale Dominique, but Emilia was one step ahead. Julia had clearly underestimated her intelligence and would now have to think very carefully how to proceed. She could reveal nothing about Matt's involvement in the abduction.

"Pascale was abducted and murdered by the man holding Libby."

Emilia was hardly surprised by this admission but still it was shocking news. Detective Constable James had told her recently to be vigilant. He was clearly concerned and admitted that the killer may have taken an interest in her, he also told her that she was to report anything that she found unusual. He had revealed nothing about the connection between Pascale Dominique and Libby Ellis and now she began to wonder if Matthew Cunningham had unwittingly drawn her into this wretched business.

Julia could see what she was thinking and thought that now would be a good time to reveal her plan, but Emilia got in first asking the question that had been at the forefront of her mind since this discussion began.

"Why are you telling me this?"

"Matt and I are conducting an investigation of our own." She went on to tell her about their efforts to locate the abductor's lair.

"This is a serious police investigation," Emilia gasped. "Surely you can't just go messing with something like this. The lives of women are at stake here."

Julia explained their frustration at the lack of progress being made. She also told her about the surveillance device that Fiona had given them and their intention to recruit someone to help.

"Once we have our mole and everything is in place we can use it to track the abductor and then inform the police."

Emilia, hardly able take it all in stared at her in disbelief.

"I can't believe that you are actually considering a scheme as crazy as this. Surely the police would never allow it to happen."

"You are right they would not support something like this, but they have no idea what we are planning. I agree that it poses a risk but with the surveillance in place, I'm certain that whoever agrees to help will be safe enough. The moment we know where she is the police will launch a rescue mission."

Emilia shook her head. She realised now why Julia had invited her to this meeting.

"Surely you don't expect me to volunteer for such a foolish scheme."

Images of the dead model propped up in the window of her shop filled her with despair. She was appalled at how this man had been able to gain access to her property and do such a dreadful thing. She felt vulnerable enough knowing that he could be out there watching her, DC James' words of advice were hardly a comfort.

"I was hoping that you might agree to help us seeing as you know both Libby and Matt."

"I might know them but not well enough to risk my life. You have no right to ask me to do such a thing or anyone else for that matter. The police should know about what you are planning."

Getting to her feet, Emilia picked up her coat and headed for the door.

Chapter Fifty Nine

MATT WAS STANDING ON THE pavement outside the studio where he had spent the day working with Charley. The assignment was going well and support from the cosmetic company was surprisingly good. The team were willing to listen and discuss both Charley and Matt's ideas although they knew exactly what they wanted. Most of the promotion shots were done, so tomorrow would be an easy day.

Beadle and Hills remained in their car watching as Matt strode back and forth along the pavement. He seemed troubled and indecisive then suddenly he made up his mind and hurried away. This is not what the detectives expected.

"You turn the car round," Hills said as he climbed out of the passenger seat. "I'll pursue him on foot."

Matt stopped at a bus stop and glanced at his watch, he would not have to wait long. Next, he took the phone from his pocket and looked at his missed calls and messages. Most of them were from Julia and he wondered what could be so urgent. He did not want to speak to her just yet, he was going to do some sleuthing of his own. He told her during their previous meeting that he would do what he could during the early part of the week so dropping his phone back into his pocket, he thought about Charley. She had asked him to join her that evening at a presentation function of some kind, but he was in no mood for company so had declined her offer. Ordinarily Libby would accompany him to events like this.

The bus pulled into the stop and twenty minutes later, he arrived at his destination. Hills was on the same bus and when he got off, he melted into the crowd before calling Beadle on his radio. His colleague was some distance away struggling to overcome an increasing amount of traffic.

Matt found his way to the side street in Whitechapel where he had abandoned Pascale and standing in the road, he stared at the spot. Memories of her pleading for help choked him but after a moment, he managed to control his emotions. Choosing only to remember the good times, he realised they had worked surprisingly well together at Veronique's party. For a brief moment, something had developed between them and he wondered if it would have made a difference to their future working relationship. Unfortunately, he would never find out. Shaking his head sadly, he began to walk in the direction the taxi had taken. Julia had told him about an old police station and courthouse that she wanted to take a look at, but that was some distance away in Shoreditch.

Rows of Victorian terraces lined the streets many in a state of decay and across the road was a small open space. It looked as if it should have been occupied, whatever had stood there was now long gone, the site abandoned and overgrown. Next to that stood an old shop, its windows boarded, the entrance looking as if it had not been used in years. Graffiti, now known as urban art covered its crumbling walls, which made for a depressing canvas.

Hills watched from a distance, curious to know what Cunningham was doing there. Beadle was yet to appear, he was close by but still hemmed in by traffic. His radio provided him with a constant link to his colleague and if necessary, he could call for back up.

Matt followed the street with no clear indication of where he was going. He thought that being close to where Libby was being held would provide him with some kind of inspiration. Perhaps a stray emotion would reveal her secret location, but he was wrong. The neighbourhood seemed cold and unwelcoming so increasing his pace he headed back towards the main road. His phone began to ring so checking the screen he decided to answer the call.

"Julia, sorry I have not returned your calls but I have just finished work."

"Matt, I'm afraid that I have made a huge mistake." Without pausing for breath she told him about her disastrous meeting with Emilia Sykes.

"Whatever possessed you to do such a thing?" Matt was furious but with a huge effort managed to hide his anger.

"I am so sorry Matt. I was convinced that I was doing the right thing. If only she had agreed to help us, then we would be a lot closer to finding Libby."

"Listen Julia, we need to discuss this further." He did not want to talk about it on the phone.

Ignoring him, she went on. "I called her after she stormed out to apologise. I wanted to know if she intended going to the police, but she refused to talk to me."

"We would know by now if she had, you and I would be sitting in an interview room being grilled by DS Woods."

"Perhaps you could talk to her."

"Let's just leave it for now," he snapped then taking a deep breath, he continued. "I'm in Whitechapel at the moment checking out a few things, but we should meet up later."

Julia was full of good ideas and Matt appreciated her ongoing support but he was worried that if the abductor was to discover her involvement then she may also become a victim.

Their conversation ended and Matt continued on his way. He could hardly believe that Julia had gone behind his back, he was furious. She had made matters worse by attempting to persuade Emilia Sykes to help them. He did not like the idea of contacting Emilia himself, what could he possibly say to help diffuse the situation. He did however have the perfect excuse to pay her a visit. The photographs he had taken of her at her shop were really rather good. He had put together an advertising portfolio that he was certain would please her, but now was not the right time. She might see it as a bribe, a ploy to win her over so he decided to shelve the idea. Of course, there may be nothing to worry about, perhaps she would keep quiet and say nothing to the police, but that was unlikely. If he had been approached with a foolishly dangerous idea like this especially given the circumstances then he would not hesitate to inform the authorities.

His phone rang again so snatching it from his pocket he answered the call.

"Cunningham, have you made your decision yet?"

Matt's stomach lurched at the sound of his voice.

"How can you possibly expect me to make a choice?"

"I told you to come up with a name and I expect you to do as you are told."

"There is no way I'm going to condemn another young woman to torture and death," he snapped angrily.

Hills moved closer. Cunningham was involved in a heated conversation that may prove interesting so remaining out of sight he listened.

"This one might survive." There was a pause. "The French girl died because of her attitude."

"I can't do it." Matt groaned and closing his eyes, he slumped against the wall.

"Can't or won't?" the man hissed. "Do you want to see Libby again?"

"Of course," Matt opened his eyes at the sound of her name. "Why do you think I did what you wanted last time?"

"Well, from your negative attitude I just thought that maybe you had grown tired of her." He paused before going on. "I've seen the way you are with Charley Baker."

Matt was stunned and bristled at the accusation.

"Charley is merely a work colleague."

He regretted saying that, the moment it came out he knew that it was untrue. Charley was much more than that.

"Do you know where she is going tonight?"

"I have no idea."

"Oh I think you do." He saw through the lie immediately. "I'm outside the venue right now waiting for her to arrive."

Matt remained silent, his head reeling with confusion.

"I have made the decision for you," he whispered. "It's Charley I want and you are going to get her for me."

Before he had time to respond, the call ended leaving Matt staring at his phone. It was a full minute before his tortured mind began to function again. His hand was shaking badly as he went through his contact list but eventually he found the number he was looking for then he pressed the call button.

"Hello Charley, its Matt here."

"Hi Matt." She replied surprised at his call. "Are you okay?"

He was unsure how to begin. How could he warn her, would she take him seriously? He would have to be careful what he said because in his unsteady state of mind he could easily give himself away.

"Are you still going out tonight?" he heard himself say.

"Of course, I'm getting ready now." She was relaxing in a hot bath but was not about to admit to that.

"Where is the presentation being held?"

She told him the name of the venue but he was not familiar with it.

"Look, this might sound a little crazy but I've heard there's going to be some trouble later on tonight."

"What are you talking about Matt?"

Thinking on his feet, he struggled to find a plausible answer.

"A policeman friend told me that something might kick off in that area." He paused, hating himself for the lie. "I don't think you should go."

"I have to Matt, I have no choice. This is a work thing, a networking exercise that I can't afford to miss."

He understood what she was saying, he and Libby would jump at the chance of being seen at an event like this.

"What has any of this got to do with the presentation?"

"Look Charley, perhaps I'm wrong and you will be safe. I'm sure the authorities will deal with whatever might happen."

Matt realised that nothing short of a full confession would persuade her to stay at home and he was not about to take her into his confidence, not just yet anyway.

Fiona Richardson was still at work when the call was detected so reaching for her phone, she alerted DS Woods.

"The call was made just a few minutes ago from a location in central London."

She read out the address and Woods scribbled it down. Next, she got onto the traffic division and requested that a car be sent immediately to check it out. She gave a detailed description of the man she was looking for and when she was finished, she sat down at her desk and waited for a reply. Fifteen minutes later, she got it.

"Something is going on here tonight," the officer told her, explaining that it was a small theatre. "The staff are preparing for some kind of celebrity function."

"Did you see anyone matching the description of our man?"

"No, not yet. Our initial search came up with nothing but we'll have a scout around."

That meant they had established that a crime was not about to be committed so would widen their search. She hardly expected them to come up with anything, the man she wanted to speak to was far too clever for that, but police presence would be enough to send out a clear message. She wondered what linked Cunningham to the venue. Was something sinister going on or was it purely a coincidence. Reaching for her phone, she dialled his number.

"Mr Cunningham, its DS Woods."

"DS Woods, hello."

She could hear the uncertainty in his voice.

"You have just received a call from the abductor. Would you mind giving me the details of that conversation?"

Matt was relieved, he thought that she might be calling about Julia's disastrous meeting with Emilia Sykes.

"He asked me about a presentation event taking place this evening in the city."

"Why would he do that?"

Matt thought quickly. If he told her the truth then the police might provide Charley with the protection she needed, but if he did then the abductor would know that it had come from him. He made his decision.

"He asked me about Charley Baker and if she was attending the party."

"Did he indeed. Do you think that she might be in danger?"

"Yes I think that would be true."

234

Chapter Sixty

CUNNINGHAM WAS BECOMING A PROBLEM and would need another incentive to persuade him to carry out his next task. Striding purposefully along the corridor he threw open the door to the torture chamber then he set up his equipment and when he was finished he went to their cell.

"Get up and come with me." He said to Libby

Expecting nothing, she did as she was told. She had been to the storeroom before, but instead of turning right along the corridor he went the other way and sensing danger, she stopped but it was too late. Reaching out, he grabbed her arm and dragged her towards the torture chamber. Libby cried out as memories of the time before filled her with dread, she never wanted to go in there again, but resistance was futile.

The door stood open and as he threw her in, she stumbled and fell sprawling onto the floor. He was upon her immediately and forcing her arms behind her back, he secured her wrists with a cable tie before hauling her to her feet, then pushing her up against the wall, he held her there. This aggressive and assertive technique would subdue most people and Libby was no exception.

Turning her to face him, he snarled menacingly. Libby was terrified, his expression was murderous and she thought that she was about to die. Memories of what he had done to her before clouded her vision. Her worst nightmare had returned and as he released his grip, her legs were shaking so badly that she had to lean against the wall for support.

Quickly he set up a tri-pod and checked the video camera before securing it into position then after a few minor adjustments he peered through the viewfinder. He was satisfied with what he saw so standing back he pulled a balaclava over his head. Libby squealed involuntarily as he came towards her, he looked like the devil and in his hand, he held an evil looking blade.

"No..." her mouth worked pitifully as finally her legs gave way.

He caught her before she fell and pulling her upright held onto her tightly then he pressed the knife against her throat.

"Right," he said whispering into her ear. "You are going to say a few words clearly to the camera, do you understand?"

Libby was numb with shock and hardly able to respond as the razor sharp blade pierced her skin.

"Do you understand?" he hissed.

"Yes," she managed, her voice barely audible.

He told her what to say then made her repeat it. He insisted she do it again but louder this time and when she was finished, the blade burned deeper into her flesh. Blood oozed from the wound and tears rolled down her face then mercifully, she lost consciousness.

Dumping her onto the floor, he went to stand behind the camera. It had gone far better than he expected, Cunningham should be proud of her performance. Slipping the camera from its stand, he pulled off his balaclava before returning to where she lay then, reaching down he grabbed a handful of coat and dragged her back to her cell.

Going into his command centre, he wasted no time. Extracting the memory card from the camera, he inserted it into his computer and played back the short film before loading it onto a computer file. Once that was done, he attached it to an email and using software designed to block his details sent it to Cunningham.

Woods messaged James, he was not at his desk, but she needed to speak with him urgently. It was her intention to assemble a backup team and attend the presentation that evening. She had not yet worked out the details but the operation would need to be carried out covertly. She would have to inform the organisers but before that, she had to run it past DCI Wyman.

"DS Woods, it's always a pleasure to see you." He said unconvincingly as she entered his office.

"Sir," she began formally, "information has come our way that requires me to assemble a team and attend a presentation party this evening." She went on to explain the facts persuading him to support her decision to take an active role in the operation. To her surprise, he agreed.

"I'll see to the arrangements DS Woods, just make sure that no one gets hurt."

Woods returned to her office to find James waiting for her. She told him about the conversation she'd had with Matthew Cunningham before outlining her plan then, her phone began to ring.

"Izzy, its Pat Fleming."

"Pat, what do you have for me?" she knew that Pat was a busy woman and preferred not to stand on ceremony.

"The tooth you gave me to analyse contains the same DNA found on samples I took from the body of Pascale Dominique. It also matches those taken from the coffee cup."

"Thank you Pat, so now we can put a name to our killer."

"Glad to be of help Izzy. Just remember to be careful."

Ending the call, she looked up at James and smiled.

"We have an ID for the abductor. His name is Dane Morgan, a sergeant in the British Army. Records suggest that he's an absconder. We can now request his military records."

"I'll get onto it boss," James said and pausing by the door he turned to look at her. "Well done by the way, great work. We are now a step closer to catching this man."

Woods nodded but remained silent. It was one thing to identify him but quite another to run him to ground. Dane Morgan was an experienced soldier and not likely to come easily.

Matt abandoned his search for semi derelict buildings and returned home. He realised that he must attend the presentation, Charley would need his help before the night was through and he was determined to be there for her. Going into his office he turned on his computer, there was bound to be a number of messages needing his urgent attention. He was expecting a memo from Veronique with details of the upcoming trip to Rome. Whilst sorting through them another message arrived. It was anonymous, the sender having blocked their details. It was a video, but it could be a rogue message, a virus designed to destroy his files once opened. He was certain that the latest system he had downloaded would protect his computer, but he hesitated and sitting back in his chair, considered the consequences before making up his mind. Reaching for the mouse, he clicked on the file then watched as the video began to play.

The focal length of the lens changed and the picture blurred before it settled. Libby was standing with her back against the wall staring into the camera. Clearly, she was terrified. He got the impression that her wrists were tied but he could not see clearly. Suddenly a shadow passed over her as someone moved from behind the camera then she screamed. A man wearing dark clothing appeared beside her, his face covered with a balaclava. Matt was not fooled, he knew who he was immediately. He could not yet see the knife but suddenly it was there pressed against her throat. Matt clenched his fists in frustration and watched as the man pushed his face up against her ear and when Libby failed to respond the knife twitched against her skin. She cried out again before speaking in a wavering voice.

"Matt please help me. You must do whatever he wants, please Matt." The video ended abruptly with Libby falling to the floor.

Gripping at the arms of his chair Matt was speechless. Apart from a few photographs this was the first time he had seen her since she disappeared. The sound of her voice shocked him. Normally she was confident and upbeat, but suffering at the hands of this monster had completely broken her spirit. How would she ever recover from this?

The message was clear and it was several minutes before he could find the strength to move. He had been a fool to remain passive. He had carried out the man's wishes and committed a crime that no doubt he would have to answer for but Julia was right. The only way they were going to help Libby was to employ drastic measures of their own. Suddenly everything changed and he knew what had to be done, he just hoped they could pull it off without the loss of another life.

Chapter Sixty One

DS WOODS SWAPPED HER BADGE of authority for a supervisory role and was now busy organising temporary serving staff at The Old Opera House in central London. This was her cover for the evening, the only people to know her real identity were the members of her own team. Guests from the world of fashion, media and advertising were beginning to arrive along with a number of minor celebrities. Woods was not familiar with the charity sponsored event, but it was obviously an important evening for all those involved.

DC James was re-living his college days by mixing cocktails at the bar. This was a skill he'd perfected when a student and was now enjoying every minute of it. The detectives were wearing communication devices that not only allowed them to speak to each other but also to the backup team waiting patiently in vans nearby. Woods was determined that nothing should go wrong. At last, she had the opportunity to put a face to the name of Dane Morgan. If he should attempt to grab Charley Baker, then she would be ready for him.

Most of the guests had arrived and the event was about to get underway. The presenters were making their way to the stage, eager to announce the winners of the first category as a hush of anticipation descended over the audience.

DS Woods saw him first and before he had chance to recognise her she slipped back into the shadows, then speaking quietly into her microphone, she alerted James. Matt and Julia were amongst the last guests to arrive, the show was about to begin but Julia spotted the bar and steered Matt towards it.

"Isn't that just typical," she said tossing her head with indignation. "The moment we arrive, the bar staff disappear."

They waited for the man mixing cocktails to return but he was nowhere to be seen so they had to settle for sparkling wine from the tray of a passing waiter. On the way to their seats, Matt spotted Charley. She was sitting at a table close to the stage surrounded by a group of friends and she failed to notice him. He was happy with that, he didn't want to draw attention to himself or Julia.

Nominations for the first award were announced and the audience cheered as the winner got to her feet. Matt recognised her immediately as the director of a leading German fashion magazine and he wondered if Veronique was here. Julia obviously approved because she was clapping furiously and wearing a smile on her face.

Matt was certain that the abductor was not far away. Was he sitting in the audience or hiding somewhere behind the scenes? Unconsciously he checked the faces around them. He had not yet received his instructions. The abduction of Pascale had been well planned even though he had failed in his first attempt to kidnap her. What would he have to do this time he wondered? Thoughts rushed through his head and he found it difficult to concentrate on the presentation. Shocking images of Libby with the knife pressed against her throat were never far from his thoughts.

Julia was enjoying herself immensely, it was as if she had forgotten the task they had come to perform. She would rather have made a grand entrance, sneaking in unannounced was hardly her style.

DS Woods peered out over the audience. From her hiding place, she had a perfect view of Matthew Cunningham and Julia Peters who were sitting near the back of the auditorium. Occasionally she would recognise a celebrity but her focus was on the faces that she didn't know. Unfortunately, there was not a common blueprint of a criminal so Dane Morgan was unlikely to stand out. Now the show was underway her duties as supervisor were relaxed, her army of student waiting staff were now relaxing in a room set aside for them and would not be required until the interval.

DC James had swapped jobs, his position behind the bar was compromised, if Cunningham was to spot him then his cover would be blown. As far as he knew, Cunningham could be working with the abductor, waiting for his chance to approach Charley Baker.

The interval arrived and with over half the presentations complete the lights glowed brighter. Matt looked down at Charley, he had to get her alone, tell her everything, try to persuade her to help but for the moment she seemed content to remain with her friends. A waiter visited their table with a tray of drinks and as he watched, Matt became increasingly anxious. The abductor had still not made contact, maybe he was not there at all. Perhaps he was still in his lair tormenting Libby. Pushing these unwelcome thoughts aside, he shuffled in his seat.

"Let's get a drink," Julia suggested, "it looks as if you could do with one." She could sense his unease.

Rising to their feet, she wondered how he managed to keep it all together. She was convinced that if their roles were reversed she would have gone mad with worry.

Suddenly the phone in his pocket began to vibrate. He didn't need to check the screen, this was the call he was waiting for.

"How are you enjoying the show?" the hateful voice sneered.

"What have you done with Libby?" Matt demanded through clenched teeth.

"Ah, you found our little production entertaining then."

"If you've hurt her..."

"What are you going to do about it?" he replied sarcastically. "Libby is completely under my control and does exactly as she is told."

Matt shuddered and closing his eyes swallowed down his bile.

"Charley looks magnificent don't you think?" he paused before going on. "She will make a fine addition to my little collection."

"Where are you, why don't you show yourself?"

"Why would I want to do that? You have no idea of my appearance. I could be sitting right there beside you and you wouldn't have a clue."

Involuntarily Matt turned his head to peer at those around him and the sound of laughter on the other end of the phone annoyed him.

"You don't have to concern yourself, I am close by that's all you need to know."

Matt remained silent, it was pointless trying to reason with a madman.

"Down to business," he said as if directing a board meeting. "You need to dump your companion, three is definitely a crowd." He laughed again before outlining his plan and when he was finished, he said. "Do it Cunningham or the next time you see your Libby, she will be starring in a horror movie."

DS Woods was busy organising her waiting staff when she was told about the phone call.

"The signal came from your location." The voice in her earpiece informed her. "He is in there somewhere with you."

Woods thought for a moment. Was he in the audience or part of the crew working backstage? She eyed the people dashing around her and discounted the idea, they were all too young to be the abductor, she was looking for an older military man. The easiest place for him to conceal himself was in the audience. From a seat in the auditorium, he could keep an eye on Charley Baker. He was probably alone but could easily attach himself to a group, give the impression that he was in the company of friends. There were so many uncertainties, it was an impossible task to locate him in the crowd. Of one thing she was certain, he would not be wearing his camouflage jacket this evening.

Matt allowed Julia to lead him to the bar where she ordered drinks. Fortunately there were fewer people here than in the auditorium. Most people were taking advantage of the waiter service having pre ordered drinks delivered to their seats.

"Matt what are you doing here?"

He turned to see Charley standing behind him then she hugged him affectionately.

"I saw you as you were leaving your seats," she whispered in his ear.

Stepping to one side, he said. "I believe you have met Julia Peters from *Fashion Today* magazine."

"Yes of course," Charley smiled at Julia.

The women embraced briefly then exchanged small talk. Matt, grateful for the interaction, used the time to compose himself. He could hardly take her to a quiet corner and tell her what was going on. The abductor was most likely watching so he had to be careful.

"Don't tell me you are here to protect me from some nasty incident." Charley laughed and dug him in the ribs with her elbow. "What was your earlier phone call all about?"

"Look Charley, I can't explain now but you have to take this seriously. The threat is very real."

Charley could see that he was serious, she had never seen him like this before.

"I want you to meet Julia in the Ladies toilet in five minutes time. She will explain everything."

Charley nodded her head and her playful smile faded.

That was the best he could do. He hated the thought of Julia doing his dirty work but what choice did he have, Charley had to know the truth. Five minutes later, the women met. Luckily, the conveniences were empty, the presentations were about to resume and most people had returned to their seats.

"How did it go?" Matt whispered when at last Julia joined him.

"Fine, all sorted." She replied in a whisper. "She thinks very highly of you. I filled her in with the details and she agreed to help without hesitation."

Matt was stunned, he expected Charley to react in the same way as Emilia Sykes.

"She will meet you at the entrance when the show is over."

"Have you given her the device?"

"Yes," Julia nodded. "I have shown her how to use it."

Matt felt terrible. He was convinced that Charley had no idea what she was letting herself in for and he would not be able to forgive himself if anything happened to her. Thoughts of Pascale filled his head, but he had to remain strong. This may be their only chance to save Libby.

Chapter Sixty Two

DS WOODS ORDERED HER TEAM to watch the exits. Apart from the main entrance, there were two fire doors and a loading ramp at the rear of the building. This enabled stage sets to be delivered by way of a private access road leading from a side street. Officers covered all these points but their focus was the main entrance, this is where they would be needed most. Woods circulated a description of Dane Morgan with orders to look out for men leaving alone. All she had to go on was the photo she had seen but not yet having received his military records, information was still a little vague.

Charley was waiting as promised in the foyer. She had left her friends and was standing alone when she spotted Matt.

"Where is Julia?" she asked, her smile as radiant as ever.

"She is phoning for a taxi."

"Shouldn't we wait with her?"

"No, we are probably being watched. The madman will be close by so we should do nothing to arouse suspicion."

"Madman?" she looked at him questioningly.

"It's what I call the abductor."

"Right," her smile faded, "not to his face I hope. Shall we go?"

Linking her arm through his, they joined the crowds manoeuvring slowly towards the main doors. Cars were in position outside waiting for dignitaries to emerge. A few of the celebrities were showing off to the press who not wanting to miss a thing had gathered in a group on the pavement. Matt and Charley avoided this mass of bodies and slipped away unseen along the street. Charley, matching his stride glanced at him. His face was in darkness so she could not see the worry that creased his brow or the fine line of his lips. She could however feel the tension in his arm and sense his mood.

"I'm not happy with this," he told her when he realised she was looking at him.

"You don't have to worry Matt. You know that I would do anything to help you find Libby."

Matt grunted but remained silent. Would she be so keen if she had seen the photographs?

"Look," he stopped and turned towards her. "You really don't have to do this."

"Don't be silly Matt. I have already agreed to help besides I have the tracking device so you will know exactly where I am. Just make sure that you come and get me."

He stared at her sadly. She possessed a fresh look of innocence, but she was hardly naive. Situations that she had to deal with in her line of work helped to shape her personality and he knew that Charley was the type of girl who might just pull it off.

"Julia told you how to use the device?"

They resumed walking but slower this time. Matt wanted more time with her before handing her over.

"Did she tell you that it can be concealed inside a mobile phone?"

"She did but I have it hidden on my body."

She gazed up at him confidently then slipping her arm from his, began to rummage in her bag. Finding what she was looking for, she began her preparations.

"What are you doing?" he asked giving her a sideways look.

"I'm cutting my nails," she replied as if it was the natural thing to do whilst strolling along a darkened street. "I have to make it look as if I have been in a struggle and broken nails are a sure indication of that. We need to make it appear authentic or he might smell a rat."

Matt was amazed at her attention to detail, he would never have thought of that but she was right. To make it look right he was going to have to be rough with her.

The van was parked where he said it would be and they stopped walking then, turning to face him, she said.

"Let's do this."

Pulling away from him, she raised her voice.

"What do you mean get into the van. It doesn't belong to you."

Matt stared at her in shock, it was time to play his part, but he wanted nothing to do with this charade.

"Grab me," she whispered without moving her lips.

Reaching out he took her shoulders and pushed her against the side of the van.

"Take your hands off me," she said louder this time then she whispered. "Come on Matt, show some aggression."

Balling her fists, she struck him and each time she made contact she cried out with the effort.

The street may be empty but Matt was convinced that the abductor would be watching.

"Grip me harder," she continued, her performance faultless. "Hit me."

Dismayed at the thought, Matt knew what he had to do. In reality, it was the only way to subdue her. Charley screamed as he slammed his fist into the side of her face. Opening his hand at the last minute, he slapped her, knocking her head backwards with the force. The blow was not as hard as it could have been, but still she felt the sting of his palm against her cheek. Holding onto her roughly, he tore opened the rear doors and shoved her in, leaving her no time to react. He pretended to hit her again and Charley cried out before lying still.

Matt felt sickened as he pushed the doors shut and hurried away. Charley had played her part magnificently. He just hoped they could recover her before the abductor broke her spirit or worse.

Woods' team came up with nothing and when the last of the guests had gone, she checked every room in the building.

"The woman who accompanied Cunningham left in a taxi on her own." One of the officers informed her.

"What about Cunningham?"

"He left with Miss Baker."

"Did anyone see which way they went?" she snapped.

"The same way as everyone else," he replied pointing along the street. "They must have slipped into a side street because we lost sight of them."

Woods cursed. She had told the surveillance team watching Cunningham to stand down. She was convinced they would not be needed, he was not the threat here. Their focus was to identify the abductor.

"So no one saw what happened to Charley Baker?"

"Hopefully he saw her home safely."

Stepping away, Woods spoke quickly into her radio. She wanted to know if the young woman had returned home. Next, she turned to DC James.

"Let's go," she snapped. "We need to get to Cunningham's house, see if she ended up there." Consumed with dread, she felt certain that she already knew the answer.

Chapter Sixty Three

CHARLIE WAITED IN THE DARKNESS for what seemed like hours but in reality was less than ten minutes. The atmosphere inside the van seemed to close in around her and the chill from the thin metal sides made her shiver, even the hard wooden floor beneath her offered no comfort. This was a male domain that was completely alien to her, it undermined her confidence and she began to regret her decision to become involved. It was too late now; she could hardly open the doors and walk away besides helping to find Libby was the right thing to do. Closing her eyes, she pushed away her fears and pictured one of her favourite places. This was a technique that her mother had taught her years before and it always seemed to work.

Across the street, a man stepped from his hiding place and making his way cautiously across the road, he headed towards the van parked at the kerb. Opening the door, he climbed into the driver's seat and started the engine before glancing over his shoulder. He was disappointed, there was insufficient light for him to see, but he could smell her perfume and feel her presence. He grinned before checking the rear view mirror then he pulled away.

Probing with her fingers Charley sighed with relief, the tracking device was still in place. It was hard to believe that this tiny piece of equipment could save her life. Matt had assured her that he would be able to see where she was going and inform the police, this was a comforting thought.

The journey did not last for long and minutes later, the van bumped to a stop. The man got out and straining her ears Charley heard the sound of heavy gates swinging open. He climbed back into the van and it rolled forward before stopping for the last time. Switching off the engine, he climbed out and closed the gates.

"Get out," he snapped as the rear doors swung open.

Charley moved awkwardly encumbered by the folds of her dress and the snagging hazards of the rough wooden floor.

"Where am I?" she asked, sounding sufficiently dazed before putting her hand against the brick wall to steady herself.

Failing to answer her question, he studied her in the dim light that came from a solitary lamp above the door. Charley stared back at him but feeling anxious soon glanced away. They were in a small yard surrounded by high brick walls, the shadows looked foreboding and she got the impression this was a secure place.

"Where am I?" she asked again before taking a step backwards. "Who are you?"

"You don't need to know who I am," he hissed through clenched teeth. "You simply need to do as you are told."

Reaching out he grabbed a handful of her coat and dragged her roughly towards the open door. Charley screamed loudly and as the sound echoed around the walls, her fear became a reality.

"Take your hands off me."

Ignoring her complaints, he continued to manhandle her along a gloomy corridor. Charley realised that it would do no good to resist, he was a big man and she had nowhere to run then Matt's words came back to her. 'This is serious and I don't want you to do it.' Initially the prospect of danger excited her and she wanted to help, but now she was no longer so confident.

"Get in there."

With a final shove, he propelled her into a small room then the door slammed shut behind her. Suddenly alone, she took in her surroundings and shuddered. The air was cold and damp, her accommodation far from luxurious. The brick walls appeared solid enough and the rough concrete floor under foot only added to her discomfort. A cold draught swept in from beneath the door bringing with it the musty smell of decay. Along one wall was a narrow bed and in the corner a stainless steel toilet and small hand basin. Charley let out a moan as she realised that this was a prison cell and lowering herself down onto the thin mattress, she pulled her coat around her more tightly. Escape seemed impossible, she just hoped that the signal from the tracking device would find its way out. Suddenly her situation worsened as the light above the door went out plunging her into total darkness.

DS Woods got out of the car and running up the steps leading to the front door, pushed on the bell for longer than was necessary. DC James left the car in the road with the engine running and hurried after his colleague.

The door opened and Matt stared out at them.

"Is Miss Charley Baker here with you?" Woods asked urgently.

"No she isn't." Her question caught him by surprise. "I would imagine that she is at home. What's this all about?"

Matt, playing the innocent, had no idea how much they knew about the events of the evening.

"Will you come with us please Mr Cunningham?"

"Why, can't it wait until the morning?"

His reluctance to do as they asked was met by James staring back at him menacingly.

"We have reasons to believe that Miss Baker was abducted earlier." Woods informed him and edging closer she continued. "I also think that you had something to do with her disappearance."

"What, that's ridiculous," Matt gasped. "I don't know what you imagine I've done but Charley is at home. If she isn't then I have no idea where she is. I willingly gave you the details of the conversation I had with the abductor earlier so if she has gone then he has taken her." Words tumbled from his mouth, a desperate tirade designed to shake off her suspicions but hating himself he could hardly believe that he was telling so many untruths.

"Will you accompany us to the station Mr Cunningham?" Her tone laced with authority, she remained unmoved.

"Give me a minute will you."

"Leave the door open please sir," James said as Matt automatically tried to swing it shut.

Matt knew how his outburst must have sounded, he just hoped that it was more convincing than he was feeling.

"Get into the car please sir," James said as they escorted him from his home.

The interview room at the station was hot, stuffy and as brightly lit as an airport terminal. He was alone. The clock on the wall told him he had been there for fifteen minutes but it seemed much longer, the movement of the hands agonisingly slow. The detectives were using the time to review their strategy and to study the facts. This was a useful delaying tactic, leave the interviewee alone for a while to contemplate their fate. Woods received confirmation that Charley Baker was not at home. The officers attending had carried out a thorough search by entering her property.

Matt placed his elbows on the heavily marked table and rested his head in his hands. Thoughts of Charley and the madman would give him no peace. He should have logged onto a computer by now, it was crucial to initiate the tracking device, without it they would have no idea where Charley had been taken. The longer she was in captivity the more time he would have to carry out his threat. The madman had not been specific, but given the photographs he had seen of Libby and Pascale it did not take a vivid imagination to work out what he would do to her.

DS Woods and DC James appeared at the door and entering the room, they seated themselves at the table and the interview began.

"What have you done with Miss Charley Baker?" James was the first to speak.

The question caught him unawares and at first, Matt was unsure how to respond.

"I told you, I saw her to her car then she drove away."

"Why didn't she give you a lift home?"

"She offered but as I live in the opposite direction I declined. It was late and given the circumstances I was worried about her being out on her own."

"You attended the presentation with Ms Julia Peters. Why did she go home alone in a taxi?"

Again, the question surprised him. It was two o'clock in the morning and Matt was both physically and mentally exhausted. He was in no mood to play their game and come up with plausible answers to their questions.

"Look, Julia is an independent woman who prefers to make her own arrangements."

"You arrived together."

"Yes we did but that doesn't make it my responsibility to see her home." Matt regretted saying that and rubbing a hand over his face he looked down at the table. "As I said before, Julia likes her own space. Yes, we did arrive together and spent the evening in each other's company but that's as far as it went. Don't imagine there's more to it than that."

Glancing up, he saw the expression on Woods face. He was supposed to be grieving for Libby, clearly she was not impressed by him attending an event with another woman. He looked away again.

"Earlier you told us about the telephone conversation you had with the abductor. During that call he told you about his plans to kidnap Miss Baker?"

"Yes that's true," he replied wondering where the question was going.

"We also know that you received another call during the evening. Was that to arrange a place to meet so you could discuss the abduction?" James leaned across the table towards him.

"No, not at all," Matt looked up to return his stare. "I have never met him before. I have no idea what he looks like."

"What was the conversation about?" Woods asked this time.

"He taunted me about being able to see us both, myself and Charley that is. He repeated his intention to abduct her but I had no idea that his threat was imminent."

Woods was convinced that he was not telling the truth. If he was as fond of Charley as he made out then why didn't he warn her of the danger and see her home safely? Scribbling a note on her pad, she wondered what role Julia Peters played in all this.

"I'll tell you what I think happened this evening Mr Cunningham," James said leaning forward. "He contacted you with orders just like he did before with Pascale Dominique but this time you did exactly as you were told."

"That's not true." Matt hated himself for the deceit but he had to keep up the pretence.

He needed their help but it was dangerous. He couldn't stop thinking about the video. He had seen Libby cut with a knife, this clearly suggested an increased level of violence. He realised this was done to intimidate him, convince him to help abduct Charley, but what state was Libby in now? He worried about Charley, unless he could get to a computer, she would suffer the same fate. He just hoped that she was safe for now.

Chapter Sixty Four

SUDDENLY THE LIGHT WENT ON and covering her eyes with her hands, she waited for them to adjust before squinting at her watch. The time was eight thirty so slipping her legs over the side of the bed she groaned and sat up. After a moment, she got to her feet and smoothing the creases from her dress reached for her coat that she had used to cover herself during the night. Pulling it on she wrapped it tightly around herself before sitting down again then she looked around the room. Paint was peeling in clumps from the walls that were once a shade of light blue and buttermilk. Half way up the wall the colours merged, but with the passing of time and years of neglect had faded allowing the brickwork beneath to show through. The floor and ceiling were the same concrete grey, the floor worn smooth by the footsteps of those who came before her.

Charley wondered how long it would be before Matt organised a rescue. She had no idea where Libby was being kept but guessed that she must be locked in a similar cell. Suddenly there was a noise from the other side of the door then a flap shot open and he peered in.

"When are you going to let me out of here?" she demanded but her question went unanswered.

A mug and small plastic plate appeared through the flap, the plate held an apple and a couple of dry biscuits. Room service she thought so reaching for the items she sniffed cautiously at the contents of the mug. It seemed to contain lukewarm tea. There was no sugar and too much milk for her liking but it was all that was on offer. The flap closed noisily leaving her alone to eat her breakfast. Sometime later, he returned but this time the door opened and he entered.

"I trust you slept well," he began amiably then he said. "Come with me, we have work to do."

Charley followed him, glad to be out of the gloomy cell. Doors lined the corridor, each one firmly closed and she wondered if there were others locked away out of sight. He ushered her through an open door and into a larger cell. It was similar to the one she had just left, sparsely furnished with an old iron bed frame but this one had no mattress. In the corner was the customary stainless steel toilet and hand basin and high up on the wall was a tiny window, its glass blackened by time.

"Right," he said as Charley turned to face him. "I know that you are a model who likes to pose in front of the camera so I thought you might do the same for me."

"Why would I want to do that?"

"Well, it's what you do," he replied simply.

"Yes, but not just for anyone."

"I'm sure that you will do it for me."

"What makes you think that?"

"Because if you don't there will be consequences."

Charley swallowed noisily. Although he sounded calm, there was an underlying ruthlessness about him. The threat seemed very real and she realised that she would have to be careful. She had no choice but play along with his demands and hope that Matt would arrive soon to get her out of this mess.

"Good," he smiled sensing that she had made the right decision. "Take off your coat then we'll begin with a few shots of you wearing your party dress."

Alarm bells began to ring inside her head, but doing as he asked she slipped out of her coat. He left her alone for a few moments and when he returned he was carrying a professional digital camera.

Like Charley, Matt had spent the night in a cell. Sleep had been impossible as thoughts ran unbridled inside his head and now he was even more anxious than before. He simply had to get to a computer. The cell door opened suddenly and a uniformed officer appeared carrying a mug of tea.

"Best I can do I'm afraid sir," he said handing it over. "DS Woods will be with you shortly."

Matt sat on the edge of the bench-like bed and sipped at his tea. He realised that he had to remain calm, if he could only think straight then he was convinced that he could talk his way out of this. It was thirty minutes before the door opened again and he was escorted to the same interview room where he had spent most of the night. DS Woods and DC James were already there.

"Good morning Mr Cunningham," James greeted him with a friendly smile. "Nice of you to join us."

"Don't you people ever sleep?" Matt grunted. He was surprised to see them both looking so fresh.

Woods looked up and invited him to take a seat then the questioning began. They went over the same ground as before checking his answers against a transcript that lay on the table in front of them. Matt answered their questions cautiously but all he could think about was the tracking device. It was imperative that it was activated. With every passing moment, Charley's situation was becoming even more perilous. Woods could feel his anxiety, he was clearly not happy but she put it down to the stress that he was undeniably under and the fact that he had spent half the night in a police cell. She remained convinced that he was not telling her everything and while he persisted in hiding the truth, she would keep him under lock and key.

"I have a warrant here to search your home." She held up a document.

"You have already done that," he reminded her. "I gave you permission to do so, I also allowed you to remove documents and Libby's computer."

"Yes, you have been very helpful and I thank you for your co-operation, but things have moved on," she paused momentarily to study his reaction then she asked. "Is there anything that you would like to tell us Mr Cunningham?"

"I can assure you that I have told you everything."

"So there is nothing on your computer for example that you have failed to disclose."

The muscles in his face tightened as he thought about the photographs and the video that he had kept from them. They would also discover the tracking device app on his desktop.

"I have helped you in every way I can but you have to understand the threats this man has made should I speak to you."

"I am aware of that but you too must understand that these could be empty threats. A serious crime has taken place Mr Cunningham including the most shocking of all. You I'm afraid are implicated in a murder."

"No, you can't say that." Matt was stunned. "You know the circumstances surrounding my involvement."

"The fact is, you helped to send that young woman to her death and now I think you have done the same with Charley Baker."

Matt stared at her miserably his face twisting with torment. He was unsure of how to proceed. How long could he keep up the pretence? The longer he denied it the more dangerous it would be for Charley. He could only guess at how much they knew.

Suddenly there was a knock on the door and a WPC entered the room. DC James got to his feet and went to speak to her but Matt could not hear what was said. When he returned, James was wearing a smile.

"Well, well, well," he began. "Miss Emilia Sykes has just been in to make a statement."

He passed a sheet of paper to Woods who read it with interest.

"Good," he said checking the little screen on the back of the camera. "How about a few glamour shots?"

"What do you mean?" Charley looked up, her stomach tightening with apprehension.

"You know, underwear shots, topless perhaps."

She stared back at him incredulously.

"Don't tell me that you have never done that kind of thing before."

"I have modelled underwear before," she admitted hesitantly, "but never topless."

"There is a first time for everything," he said leering at her, "besides, you might enjoy it."

Placing his camera carefully on the floor at his feet, he took a step towards her.

"How dare you suggest such a thing," she replied backing away.

"Come on, it will be fun and something else to add to your CV."

Her mind was reeling as she assessed her chances. The door stood open but she would have to get past him first and there was not much room to manoeuvre. Even if she did manage to get out of the cell, where would she go?

"Take off your dress," he said calmly but the menace in his voice was unmistakable.

The only thing that she could do was face up to him.

"I'm certainly not going to take my clothes off for you."

Retribution was quick and suddenly he was upon her. Wrenching her arms up behind her back, he pushed her roughly against the wall.

"You will do as you are told," he hissed, his face close to hers.

Charley was sickened by the sudden violence. The pain in her arms was agonising and the weight of his body against hers made movement impossible. Like a butterfly caught in a spider's web, she was completely helpless.

Slowly releasing the pressure on her arms, he gripping the delicate fabric of her dress and tore open the fastenings. Charley cried out as he forced the material down over her shoulders and her head struck the abrasive brickwork. Flecks of dried paint stung her face and instinctively she closed her eyes.

Ignoring her discomfort, he tugged at the ruined material not stopping until it pooled around her ankles only then did he release his hold.

"Easy isn't it?" he grinned salaciously as he appraised her body then turning away he went to where he had left his camera. "Now stand where you were before."

255

She had no choice but do as he said so stepping over the remains of her dress she moved slowly across the room.

"Nice," he grinned as he watched, "quality underwear. Do you shop at Harrods?"

Ignoring his remark, she waited for him to take his photos.

Peering through the viewfinder, he adjusted the focus then began to click the shutter. Zooming in he recorded every detail then something caught his eye. Lowering the camera, he moved in for a better look. Something was pinned to the waistband of her panties.

Charley froze. He was staring at her curiously, his eyes flicking between her face and her body. She was convinced that he was about to strip away her underwear and closing her eyes she held her breath.

Reaching out slowly he took hold of the safety pin and unclipped a tiny disc-like object then holding it in the palm of his hand, he recognised it for what it was. Anger boiled up inside him like lava from a volcano and in a single movement, he knocked her sideways against the metal bed frame. Charley screamed as he grabbed a handful of her hair and jerking her head backwards, he hissed.

"What other dirty little tricks are you hiding?"

Every nerve in her body cried out as pain flowed through her like an electric current. Dodging his blows was impossible and all she could do was wait for the assault to stop. Letting go of her hair, he pushed her away before stepping back then he looked again at the device. He was enraged, but it was no use taking it out on the girl, he had not finished with her yet so dropping the little disc to the floor he crushed it underfoot.

Charley was distraught and could hardly believe that her only link with the outside world had been destroyed. With the tracking device gone, Matt would have no idea where she was. Her only hope was that he had already activated it and tracked her position.

Chapter Sixty Five

JULIA PETERS WAS SITTING IN an interview room. She had no idea that Matt was just along the corridor or that he had been there for most of the night. Several minutes later a detective and a female police officer joined her and taking their seats at the table, he introduced himself as Detective Constable John Bormann the woman however, remained silent.

Julia watched with interest as he placed a file on the table then he selected a typed document and began to read silently. She couldn't help being impressed by what she saw, John Bormann was an attractive man. Being close to him filled her with confidence and crossing her legs under the table her foot brushed against his knee. He made no attempt to move.

"So, Ms Peters," he began, eyeing her with sharp intelligent eyes, "how well do you know Miss Emilia Sykes?"

"Emilia," she frowned, "I don't know her that well. We have spoken several times on the telephone. Why do you ask?" She was not about to admit to their disastrous meeting.

Ignoring her question, he went on. "Would you say that you are on friendly terms?"

"Yes," Julia nodded her head. "There is no reason to believe otherwise."

She realised that Emilia must have reported her to the police but before she had time to put her thoughts in order, he asked another question.

"How well do you know Mr Matthew Cunningham?"

Playing down their relationship, she told him that Matt was the partner of her friend Libby Ellis. She explained how their professional relationship had steadily developed into a friendship and that's how she came to know Matt. Questions continued as every aspect of their relationship was examined and all the time Bormann made notes. His female colleague remained silent throughout and Julia smiled as she realised that her role was chaperone. She had no complaints about spending time alone with Bormann and as her fantasies threatened to take hold, she decided that it would be better to concentrate on the business at hand.

"Do you consider yourself an amateur detective Ms Peters?"

"I don't know what you mean." The question caught her off guard and sitting back in her chair, she folded her arms and studied him with amusement.

Staring back at her intently, Bormann scratched at the side of his face before going on.

"You seem to have taken it upon yourself to engage in a spot of detection, checking properties for example in the area of Whitechapel. Now why would you do that?" Tapping his pen annoyingly against the top of the table he waited for her to respond.

"I think you know very well why." She was convinced that he knew a lot more than he was letting on and was enjoying playing this silly game.

"Why don't you tell me." He stopped tapping and leaned forward expectantly.

"I have been looking for my friend," she admitted. "I thought that it might help with your investigation, you know, a little bit of public spirited assistance."

Bormann studied her for a moment then added to his notes and when he was finished he asked. "How far would you go to help your friend?"

"Detective," she was becoming tired with this war of words. "I think you have all the details so why don't we drop this charade and stop wasting each other's time."

He continued to stare at her. She was clearly a perceptive woman and he was in danger of underestimating her. The officer beside him stifled a grin and shot Julia a look of solidarity.

"Miss Sykes has made a very serious accusation," he began gravely, "and given your connection with Mr Cunningham I believe that you may be working together on some kind of vigilante plan."

"Okay!" Julia replied. It was no use denying the fact they were considering a plan of action. She had no idea just how much he knew but it seemed fool-hardy to deny the truth. "I did ask Emilia for her help and she had every right to refuse. I realise that what I asked of her was very dangerous and obviously she didn't like the sound of it."

"Where did you get the tracking device?"

Julia thought for a moment before answering. She had to be careful, she didn't want to incriminate Fiona.

"I found it on the internet. It was my intention to use it to help find out where Libby is being held. Matt of course was horrified and would have nothing to do with it. The idea of putting someone else in danger dismayed him but I really couldn't see any other way."

"Do you realise how serious this is?" he paused before going on. "The man we are searching for is extremely dangerous, in fact he is a murderer and you were expecting Miss Sykes to put her life at risk."

"I am aware of the dangers, Matt and I discussed it at length. We considered the risks and concluded that given the fact that we would be using a tracking device and with you responding quickly once we had the information, it would have been safe enough."

Bormann remained silent as he digested what she had just said then, as if making up his mind he asked.

"Did you give the device to Miss Charley Baker once you convinced her to help you?"

This surprised Julia, how could he know about that already? Matt was yet to contact her so she had no idea if he had activated the tracker. She had tried to speak to him earlier but strangely, her call went unanswered. It was then she began to suspect that something might have gone wrong.

"Is Matt Cunningham here?"

"Answer the question please Ms Peters."

"Yes, I gave the device to Charley."

Getting to his feet, Bormann hurried from the room.

Charley gasped as he tossed her onto the hard wooden frame. Her scalp burned from being dragged along by her hair and now as he secured her ankles and wrists her skin was chafed raw. At some point, she found herself alone. Her senses were spinning so fast that she was unaware of him leaving but now as she began to calm down she could hear sounds of distress coming from along the corridor.

Libby screamed as he pulled her from the cell that she shared with Kelly. She realised where they were going so fought back, but this only made matters worse. At the torture chamber door, she grabbed at the doorframe and held on tightly. This earned her another beating and unable to maintain her grip she collapsed under the rain of blows. When he was finished, he lifted her off her feet and dumped her onto a trolley where he tied her down. Next, he went to get Kelly.

Charley lifted her head and stared at the woman in utter amazement. The violence of the beating was shocking she had never experienced anything like this before.

"Libby," she called out in a voice reduced to a whisper by screaming.

Libby did not answer, her senses reeling, she did not hear Charley.

Kelly put up only a token resistance. It was foolish to try to fend him off, it was easier to accept his brutality, that way she might avoid serious injury. The blow to the side of her head sent her reeling and before she could react, her arms were pinioned above her head and her feet were lifted off the ground. Hanging helplessly, she could hardly breathe. The weight of her body suspended by her arms was slowly suffocating her and panicking only made it worse.

Looking at them in turn he smiled sadistically. His chest was heaving and it was an effort to think straight but his military training soon kicked in and he knew what he had to do. First, he would fetch his camera, the torture chamber had never been so full and he wanted to record the occasion. Next, he would have to consider the implications of the tracking device. Cunningham must have wired the girl; the police were unlikely to have been involved. He glanced at Libby and began to think of ways to punishing him.

He was safe enough for the moment. If the authorities were to storm the building, they would encounter a few surprises. This was a fortified strong room, once the door was closed and the security system locked down it would be almost impossible for them to gain access. Even if they did, it would be too late.

Using the time to fetch his camera he breathed deeply and now as he peered through the viewfinder his hands were no longer shaking. He took pictures of them all, focusing in on their pained and terrified expressions. It pleased him to know that these images would have far reaching consequences, Cunningham was bound to share them with the police. When he was finished, something else occurred to him.

"Oh yes," he said turning towards Charley, "where were we before we were so rudely interrupted?"

Her eyes flew open and she whimpered helplessly as he moved towards her.

"Topless photos that was it."

Chapter Sixty Six

"Do you know where Charley Baker is?"

Matt stared at her with eyes that burned with fatigue. The question had been put to him countless times and he was amazed at her ability to make it sound as if she was asking for the first time. Strangely, this was the only thing that he could answer truthfully and until he could access a computer, her whereabouts would remain a mystery.

"Right," she said and sitting up straighter, she took on an air of superiority. "I'm going to organise a search of your home and office. Your computer will be seized for analysis by our team of experts. You will remain in custody as I will want to talk to you again."

Matt was about to object when there was a loud knock on the door and a detective entered the room.

"DS Woods," he said urgently. "A word if you please."

Rising to her feet, she eyed Matt thoughtfully before moving away from the table. A muffled conversation took place at the back of the room and when she returned she looked at him stony faced.

"Tell me about the tracking device that you gave to Charley Baker yesterday evening."

Matt was unable to reply immediately. He frowned and tried to work out how they knew about the device then it all became clear.

"Mr Cunningham," she urged.

Sitting back in his chair, Matt realised that it could only have been Emilia Sykes, she must have reported her conversation with Julia. Running his hand through his hair, he rubbed at the stubble on his cheeks then making up his mind, he told them everything. There was little point in holding back, he had told so many lies that it was becoming difficult for him to think straight. Perhaps by telling them the truth, they would allow him access to a computer then he could activate the tracking device. When he was finished, Woods glared at him.

"Why all the lies?" James asked.

"Why do you think?" Matt replied. "Self preservation, protecting Libby, hoping that you would let me go so I could find out where he has taken Charley."

"You do realise that by wasting so much time you may have put her in even more danger."

Matt stared at James in desperation. He knew what he had done and was about to defend himself further, but it seemed pointless so he remained silent.

"Mr Cunningham," Woods fixed him with a cold stare. She was furious and barely able to control her emotions. "I am arresting you for the abduction of Pascale Dominique and Charley Baker..."

Her voice faded into the background as Matt realised that all was lost and he may never see Libby again.

Loading his photos onto the computer, he studied them with satisfaction. Charley Baker was an extraordinarily attractive young woman who seemed to glow even brighter when in front of a camera. The considerable pressure that she must be under did nothing to dampen her charm. This allowed him to get some splendid shots. Creating a separate folder, he labelled it with her name before saving the collection then he turned his attention to the others. There were several images of the women together. Kelly was hanging by her wrists, her face a picture of discomfort. He knew that he couldn't leave her like this indefinitely, then flashbacks of a time before entered his head. He had been part of a team tasked with storming an insurgent stronghold. Their mission, to rescue a number of prisoners being held there. The raid was considered a success even though they were unable to save the prisoners. Seven men had suffered unimaginable torture before being strung up by their wrists and left to suffocate. Kelly Spencer was experiencing the same treatment and he would soon have to cut her down.

Dismissing these images, he turned his thoughts to Cunningham. Using a 'Trojan Horse' to infiltrate his base was a daring move but the plan was doomed to failure from the start. He must think him a fool, did he really think that he would not find the device hidden in the girl's underwear. This was an ill conceived trick, he should have been more creative. Glancing at the computer screen, he decided on a plan of his own.

"Take a look boss," James called over his shoulder.

They had entered the house that Matt and Libby shared and now sitting at Matt's desk, he used the password provided to access the computer and soon found the latest shots of Libby.

"There is also a video." He clicked on the start button and they watched in shocked silence.

Woods was concerned. The conditions and unspeakable treatment that Libby was experiencing was clearly taking its toll. She appeared pale and drawn, her expression was that of a woman at the limit of her endurance.

"We need to get her out of there," James uttered emotionally as the video came to an end.

Woods couldn't help feeling sorry for Matthew Cunningham. He too must be under considerable pressure and was only doing what he thought best for the woman he loved, but she had no option. He had committed a serious crime and Wyman would expect her to do her duty.

"There is nothing else here," Woods remarked as she glanced around the office. She did not expect to find anything, the contents of his computer was her goal.

"Hang on," James said as suddenly another email arrived.

Moving to his side, she watched as he clicked on the message entitled 'Trojan Horse'. A series of thumbnail images appeared on the screen and enlarging each one in turn, they plotted a course of humiliation and torture. Charley Baker looked terrified and was clearly under duress. It became worse when they saw the images of her dressed in only her underwear. Woods swallowed noisily as James enlarged the final thumbnail. It showed all three women in what could only be described as a torture chamber.

"We need to track that email," Woods said, her voice unsteady. "Perhaps it will lead us to him."

James looked up at her doubtfully. "If I was sending images like this, I would use a program to conceal my address and internet service provider."

"Let's get this packed up and back to base where the experts can take a look at it."

Just over an hour later, a member of the Cybercrime Unit was powering up Matt's computer.

"We need to pinpoint the location of the machine that was used to send these messages." Woods told the officer.

"I'll see if I can trace the IP address," he replied. "Internet Protocol addresses are assigned to computers rather than people so I won't be able to tell you who is using it."

"I appreciate that," she replied then pulling out a chair, settled beside him. "I simply require its current location."

He glanced at her sideways and Woods missed the look of doubt that masked his face.

"The IP address probably won't give you that information," he paused to click on a series of commands. "It won't reveal a name or actual physical location."

"Would the Internet Service Provider be able to do that?"

"Yes, if we can furnish the ISP with the details, they should be able to give us the name and address of the registered user."

This was a positive step forward but still this information may not be enough.

"Ah," he said suddenly. "It's not as easy as that I'm afraid." Turning towards her, he gave Woods the bad news. "The user is employing a VPN, a Virtual Private Network software package designed to conceal the IP address and encrypt the internet traffic. Think of it as having your mail sent to a P.O. Box instead of your home."

"What can we do about that?"

"I have a few tricks that I can try but failing that we'll have to get onto the VPN supplier and request the details."

"Can you do that from what we have here?"

"Oh yes, it shouldn't be a problem. Leave it with me and I'll see what I can do."

Next, she asked him about the tracking device. "Perhaps we can approach this from a different direction?" she added hopefully.

"Let's see what he intended to use as a monitoring program." Running a search, he came up with a downloaded application. "This looks promising," he said. "All we have to do is run this bit of software and activate the tracking device."

Woods smiled and leaning closer watched as the program began to load up. A series of number chains floated across the screen then suddenly it went into standby mode. They waited patiently for what seemed an eternity, both watching but saying nothing.

"Strange," he remarked at last. "It appears to be struggling to run the initiation code."

They waited for a while longer before his fingers began to dance over the keyboard.

"We have several options open to us," he mumbled as he concentrated on the screen.

Working furiously, his frown deepened as one by one the commands failed then as he ran out of ideas, he turned to face Woods.

"It's no good, what we are searching for has either malfunctioned or it's been destroyed. Now, looking at the type of device I would say that it's unlikely to have failed."

"So it's been destroyed."

He stared at her for a few seconds before nodding his head.

"I would say so."

Woods shuddered as she thought of the women tied up in the torture chamber. The abductor must have discovered the tracking device. That made finding them even more urgent.

"Thank you for your help. Let me know the moment you hear from the internet people."

Chapter Sixty Seven

He LET HER DOWN SO that her feet were flat on the ground. Her arms were still pinioned above her head but now she could breathe more easily. Kelly glared at him hatefully, she was furious. What had she done to deserve treatment like this?

"Right ladies," he announced conversationally. "I have to go out for a while but I'll be back by supper time."

He glanced at Charley, leering at her lustfully before turning away then slamming the door he made his way along the corridor towards the command centre. Survey cameras set up around the perimeter of the building provided a view of what was going on outside so typing a command on the computer keyboard, the screen divided into several sections allowing him to use the cameras simultaneously. If something unusual caught his eye, he could zoom in for a closer look but everything seemed to be in order. The van used to abduct Charley was still parked in the old exercise yard hidden by high walls but he was taking nothing for granted. Manipulating the cameras, he scrutinised every section of the building including the pavements beyond. With the discovery of the tracking device, he would have to be cautious. If the authorities had used it to track Charley Baker then they could be waiting for him beyond the walls. This was the course of action that he would take if ordered to attack a building like this. Better to wait for the enemy to come to you because assaulting something as secure as a medieval fortress was a hazardous business. Sitting back in his chair, he stretched his arms above his head and sighed with satisfaction. The way ahead seemed clear so it was safe to leave the building.

Dane Morgan's military record was waiting for her when Woods returned to her office. It came in a sealed box file stamped 'Private and confidential'. Sliding the chair out from under her desk, she sat down and pulled the file towards her. She was tempted to wait for DC James to return before opening the box but he was away on an errand so would probably be some time so running her thumb under the ribbon she broke the seal.

Her first impression of Dane Morgan was that he was a good looking man. There were two photographs, in one he was dressed smartly in a British Army uniform and the other was a casual head and shoulders shot. The expression on his face displayed confidence and youthful expectation. Reading carefully through the notes she began to build up a character profile of the man she desperately wanted to find. Dane Morgan was a 'lifer'. Having signed up for twenty two years, he rose steadily through the ranks gaining the stripes of Sergeant in just under six years. His superiors described him as a responsible and capable leader. Woods was hoping to discover the reasons for his desertion. What could possibly have turned this respected man into a monster?

The telephone on her desk rang; it was DCI Wyman.

"I understand that you have made an arrest for the abduction of Pascale Dominique and Charley Baker."

"Yes sir, that's right."

"What about the third woman," he paused before coming up with her name.

"I don't believe that Mr Cunningham is responsible for the abduction of Kelly Spencer."

"She is part of your investigation though."

"Yes sir, she is but Cunningham isn't acting alone. We are still searching for his accomplice."

"Has he not made a full confession?"

"Yes he has but it's not as simple as that. Cunningham is merely the puppet, the man pulling his strings is still at large."

She went on to explain the complexities of her investigation and how it had developed since their last meeting.

"It sounds like you have everything under control DS Woods. Keep me informed will you?"

Putting the phone down, she stared at it for several moments. It was an odd conversation to have with the Senior Investigating Officer over the telephone. As SIO, Wyman should have called a meeting inviting everyone working on the case to attend. That way information could be shared and the team brought up to speed. He was definitely fishing she thought. She would have to be careful, Wyman would take the credit for all her work. Again, she wondered what she had done to upset him and sitting back in her chair, she chewed at her bottom lip. She really needed to speak to her old friend and colleague Terry Ashton, maybe he had heard of Simon Wyman and could shed some light on his hostile attitude. She knew that Terry and the Chief were old friends so it would do no harm to cosy up to him.

An hour later and she was no closer in discovering a revelation by reading between the lines of Dane Morgan's file. She must have missed something and would have to go through it again but the clock on the wall reminded her that her shift had ended forty minutes ago. She wanted to speak to Cunningham again and even considered staying on for another hour, but that could wait. Maybe another night in the cells will loosen his tongue further. James must have gone home, she was not aware that he had returned to the station and he had not phoned in. Closing the file, she locked it away in a desk drawer then reaching for her bag, she left the office.

Easing her car from its spot behind the building, Woods joined the traffic on the main road. Luckily, it was free flowing and even the traffic lights were in her favour. She didn't notice the little van that pulled out from the side of the road, it slotted neatly into line just two cars behind. Roadside cameras had not yet picked up on the fact that it was a stolen vehicle, the driver was careful, doing nothing to draw attention to himself.

Woods took a route out of the city and into the suburbs where the homes of middle class people were located. Most of the properties dated back to the 1950s and retained their pretty gardens, their owners preferring nature's barrier to shut out the bustle of the main street not far away. She occupied the upper floor of a large house having lived there alone for almost two years following the breakdown of a long term relationship. The accommodation consisted of a generous sized living room, dining room, study, plus a kitchen, bathroom with a walk in shower and three good sized double bedrooms. It was far too big for her but it suited her well enough. She adored the neighbourhood, it was a safe and quiet area.

The ground floor was currently unoccupied, the elderly lady who lived there had unfortunately passed away recently. She had owned the property for years before it became too much for her then the decision was made to convert it into two flats. Woods was her first tenant but now this agreement was under threat and at the mercy of those who were about to inherit the property.

Parking her car on the sweeping driveway, Woods entered the house by a private side door. A flight of stairs took her up to her own entrance and inserting the key into the lock, she pushed open the door and was greeted by the familiar scents of home.

Going into the living room, she took off her coat and dumped it along with her bag on the sofa then she went into the kitchen. A cup of tea was her first priority then she wanted to kick off her shoes and relax for a while in her favourite chair.

Driving slowly past the house he could just make out her car hidden behind some dark foliage. The drive swept in an arc across the front of the house and offered two access points onto the street. It was a detached property partially screened by trees and tall shrubs and because of its size, he guessed it stood on a large plot. There must be extensive grounds at the back of the house. He was unfamiliar with the area but that could easily be resolved. He could use his phone, log onto the internet and find out more but he decided to leave that for another day.

Parking the van further along the street, he remained behind the wheel whilst he considered his next move. Obviously, he would have to check the property, work out the best way to gain access. It was difficult to see from the road because of the shrubs and bushes but he got the impression that most of the house was in darkness, it seemed likely that DS Woods was home alone.

The road ahead was clear so leaving the van he made his way back along the footpath and using his military skills, moved swiftly and silently taking advantage of what cover he could find. At the entrance of the drive, he disappeared into the undergrowth. He was right, the entire front of the house was in darkness, this included the upstairs windows. Its size impressed him and he wondered if the house belonged to DS Woods. Perhaps her parents owned it, he thought and she still lived at home. This part of the house seemed unoccupied, he hoped that were true because an empty house would make his job that much easier.

Moving to the back of the property, he was careful to avoid setting off the security lights that surely must exist. Light came from just two windows on the first floor, but was not sufficient to spill out over the rear garden. If she remained on this side of the house then he could move his vehicle onto the drive undetected. Accessing the house would not be a problem and assuming she was alone he could overcome her then load her into the van. It couldn't be better.

Suddenly a car pulled onto the drive and he froze as the security lights came on. Pushing back deeper into the bushes, he was unable to see who it was but after a few moments, he heard voices.

"Terry thanks for coming over so promptly."

"It's been a while Izzy," he replied, "but I'm here now."

"Come in and welcome."

The door closed shutting out any thoughts of overpowering and making off with her. All he could do now was wait for another opportunity to present itself.

Chapter Sixty Eight

JULIA WAS SHAKEN. BEING ROUNDED up like a common criminal then interrogated by the police had unnerved her more than she cared to admit. Luckily, she had been let off with a caution for her part in their plan to recruit a mole, but she was certain that the police would come for her again.

"Fiona," she said clamping her phone to her ear.

"Hello Julia. What's up?" She could tell that something was wrong by the tone of her voice.

The noise of her surroundings had reached fever pitch so pushing her finger into her ear Julia tried to block it out. Perhaps it was not such a good idea to call Fiona from the wine bar at this time of day.

"I'm afraid the police know about the tracking device that you gave us."

"Oh and how did they find out about that?"

Julia relayed the story of the disastrous events involving Charley Baker.

"Matt is still with the police, I think he may have been arrested."

"Really," Fiona gasped. "How long has he been in custody?"

"It's been more that twenty four hours. Look, I told them that we got the device from the internet and I'm sure that's the story Matt will use. It's what we agreed if anything should go wrong. There is no way that he would mention your name so you don't have to worry."

Fiona gasped at the news. "So are you telling me that the device is not working?"

"My guess is that it's not. I don't think Matt had chance to activate it besides if the police had access to it then Charley would have been rescued by now."

"True," Fiona replied. She had heard nothing from her colleagues about the launch of a rescue mission. "I'll see if I can get a signal, I have the activation code. There may be something that I can do to help."

Their conversation continued for a while longer until it became impossible for them to hear each other so ending the call, Julia reached for her glass and gulped at her red wine.

Fiona was not surprised that something like this had happened. Helping friends was something that she tried to avoid especially if it might compromise her business or reputation but as she was already involved with the case and Julia was clearly in trouble, she had to do something. As long as the authorities remained unaware that she was passing on confidential information then she should be in the clear. There was always a chance that the tracking device would still work so logging onto her computer Fiona began to type. It was not long however before she came up with the same answers as the police. If the abductor had discovered the device then it was likely to have been destroyed. There was one other thing that she could try. Feeding the details into her computer, she instructed it to perform a series of actions. This was part of a spyware package developed by an old university friend some time ago. He was an electronics engineer researching into residual energy fields. He realised that every electrical component carried an electrical footprint that could be used to reveal its global position. He designed a computer program that in theory would detect these energy fields even if the component had been destroyed. Assuming some of its parts remained it should still be possible to detect even the weakest signal. This is how it was explained to her but in reality, she had no idea how something like this worked. If the device no longer existed then how could it give off a signal of any kind, especially if it was not activated in the first place?

Terry spoke proudly about his daughter Mia and her concerts with the Russian pianist Viktor Vasiliev. They were performing all over Europe. He also told her about Ben Sykes and his proposal of marriage.

"That's marvellous news," Woods enthused. "I'm so glad that things are finally going well for her. Mia has worked so hard to become a professional musician."

She didn't need to mention the terrible events that had threatened her future and almost took her life, but Terry knew what she was thinking. The murder case they had worked on together involved Mia and a number of young musicians. This was one of the reasons for him taking early retirement from the Force. The trauma of almost losing his daughter dictated the rest of his career and he set up her own personal security team, which he now managed.

"Have you ever come across someone called Simon Wyman?" she asked.

Terry laughed. "Of course, I remember him." His smile faded. "The rhyming detective we used to call him."

"The name has stuck, he's still known as that." She told him that Wyman had been his replacement after he left.

"You should keep a close eye on him," Terry warned, becoming serious.

"I'm more than aware of that." She went on to describe Wyman's apparent dislike for her. "I don't know why he is being so hateful towards me."

"That might be something to do with me I'm afraid." He looked at her ruefully.

"Allow me to pour you some more tea before you make a full confession."

Sitting back in his chair Terry watched her carefully. They had been colleagues for several years and over time had become good friends. Izzy got on well with Mia, they had socialised together on many occasions. If it wasn't for the age gap that existed between them their relationship might have developed further. Terry knew that Mia would have welcomed Izzy as stepmother, but it would never have worked so he kept their relationship professional.

"Right," she smiled at him before passing him a cup of tea. "Confess away."

"Well, just before I left I heard that a replacement would be brought in to fill my shoes. At first, I had no idea who this would be so I did a bit of digging and discovered that it was likely to be Simon Wyman. I've worked with him in the past and it didn't please me to think that you would be forced to spend time with a man like him. Naturally, I did everything I could to block the decision and get you the promotion that you deserve."

She frowned before saying. "I didn't know about this, I just assumed that you wouldn't be replaced."

"The Chief had other ideas. He thought that you might need more time before taking on the responsibilities of DI. Of course I argued your corner pointing out that you had passed the exams, had more than enough experience and was just waiting for a post to become available. I would have thought that my leaving would be the springboard that you needed."

"If the Chief was intending to bring Wyman in then surely he should have made his plans transparent."

"I agree, but I don't have all the answers."

"I can't believe that I didn't know about this."

"Maybe there is history between the Chief and Wyman. It does seem strange that he came in as a DCI when all that was required was a replacement DI."

"So this could be about rapid promotion then."

"Maybe, but there is something else that I think you should know." Terry sipped at his tea before going on. "I wouldn't go as far as to say that Wyman is a bent copper, but he does know how to manipulate the rules. He is not opposed to using the system for his own advantage."

"Are you suggesting that he's corrupt?"

"With the opportunities available to him here in the city..." He didn't need to go on.

They remained silent for a few moments and Izzy stared at him thoughtfully.

"I have no evidence of course but I am aware of his reputation." Terry said breaking the silence.

"So he's done this before then?"

"Let's just say that his reputation has not gone unnoticed amongst the criminal world."

She continued to stare at him and her eyes widened as she considered the implications. Terry watched her carefully, he had seen that look before.

"If he has deliberately manoeuvred his way in and has the Chief in his pocket then he must be stopped. Others need to know about him."

"Be very careful Izzy. I would imagine that he has studied your file thoroughly, especially if he considers you a threat. That's probably why he's out to discredit you."

Chapter Sixty Nine

THE FIRST THING FIONA DID when she arrived at work the following day was to check the details of the case that DS Woods was working on. Using her computer, she logged onto the system and confirmed that Matthew Cunningham had been arrested and was currently in custody. The notes also told her that Julia was held at the station for several hours before being released. Reading on, she found that the Cybercrime Unit was currently working on Matt's computer hoping to penetrate the codes used to activate the tracking device. There was nothing to indicate how well their search was going, but Fiona was confident that the device could not be tracked back to her. It was a common enough piece of equipment widely available on the internet or from a specialist supplier.

Her own efforts to track the device were ongoing. She had set up her home computer to tackle the problem and as soon as it found a solution, a signal would be sent to her phone. There was nothing more that she could do but be patient. She considered contacting her friend who had conceived the idea in the first place but he now lived and worked in sunny California. She had not spoken to him for many years so was reluctant to bother him now besides, he was bound to want to know why she was asking about something from their past. Staring thoughtfully out of the window she continued to think about her college days then, a noise broke her concentration and turning her head she saw DC James making his way towards her.

"Good morning," he smiled as he entered her office. "Start the day the way you mean to go on." Passing her one of the plastic cups that he was carrying he pulled up a chair and sat down.

Fiona studied him but remained silent. She wondered what he wanted but his expression gave nothing away.

"I didn't know if you take sugar," he continued and rummaging in his pocket, he pulled out packets of sugar and a plastic stirrer. "Hope you like it with milk."

She sniffed cautiously at the murky contents that resembled coffee but probably tasted nothing like the real thing.

"What do you want DC James?" She asked then sitting back in her chair, waited for the senseless banter that he obviously thought impressed her to continue.

"I want to talk to you about a tracking device."

Fiona's eyes widened, she was not expecting that. He sounded serious all of a sudden and she wondered if he knew about her part in supplying it.

"You must be quite an expert I should imagine having used this kind of equipment before." He eyed her expectantly before adding several packets of sugar to his coffee.

"Not as much as you might think," she replied, tugging nervously at a loose strand of hair.

"I was hoping that you could give me some information. There must be dozens of different types available on the market."

"Yes you are right there." She responded with a certain amount of relief.

Waiting as he stirred his coffee, she then got to her feet and turned towards a filing cabinet. She would have to think very carefully about what to say next. If he suspected that she was friends with Julia, he might ask some awkward questions.

"You might find this useful," she said handing him a glossy stock catalogue. "There are loads of different tracking devices in there."

Reaching out he took it from her and spent a moment leafing through the pages.

"What type of device would you buy from the internet?"

Clearly, he had no idea what Matthew Cunningham had given to Charley Baker.

"It would depend on the circumstances," she replied cautiously. "For example is it going to be used to track a vehicle or a person?"

Obviously, she knew the answer to his question but had to appear clueless. She told him what he wanted to know whilst playing down the extent of her technical knowledge. She was eager to conclude their conversation as at any moment she might unwittingly give herself away. She also wanted to discourage his advances. Clearly, he thought there was chance of a relationship developing between them but he was wrong. She simply did not fancy him.

"Kelly, are you okay?" Libby asked straining her neck to see over her shoulder.

They had been locked up for hours and she was concerned about her friend. From her position on the table it was almost impossible to see Kelly who was standing behind her, she had a better view of Charley. It had been bitterly cold during the night, but now in the grey light of dawn the temperature inside the cell was beginning to recover. Charley looked pale and exhausted, it was hardly surprising tied to the unforgiving wooden structure for hours on end.

Kelly chose not to answer. She was still traumatised over the part she had played in the death of Pascale. Libby was unaware that she was tied to the table on which the girl had died.

"Why is he doing this to us?" Charley groaned. "What is his obsession with nudity and ropes?"

"It's his way of humiliating us." Libby replied.

"But I don't understand. Locking us in these squalid little cells is bad enough, there is no need to keep us tied up like this."

Libby agreed but she also realised that he would not have so many photographic opportunities if they occupied different cells. This way was much more dramatic and had a greater impact on those receiving the images. Libby knew that he was sending copies to Matt but she wondered who would be receiving the photos of Charley.

"I'm sure it won't be much longer before the police arrive." Charley continued.

Her belief in Matt having activated the tracking device before it was destroyed helped to keep her spirits up. Libby hoped that it was true but kept her doubts to herself. Surely, help would have arrived by now if the device had done its job.

Suddenly the door opened and they became silent.

"Good morning Ladies," he said cheerfully as he marched in.

Walking slowly around the cell, he observed them all with satisfaction. Placing the bottle of water he was carrying down on the ground he stopped in front of Kelly. "I have a little job for you."

Lifting her chin, he looked at her and she glanced fearfully back at him then as her eyes darted towards Libby he smiled. He knew what she was thinking.

"No knives this time," he whispered, "not yet anyway." Then in a louder voice, he said. "It will be your job to look after both Libby and Charley."

He glanced at the women as he said their names and Kelly groaned with relief. Turning back towards her, he reached up and loosened the ropes holding her wrists then gently lowered her to the ground. Her legs and hips were numb from the effort of standing for so long in such an awkward position and her arms felt like dead weights. Blood rushed back into her hands making them tingle and choking back the discomfort, she worked through the stiffness flexing her fingers in turn.

"Your muscles will soon recover," he reassured her then stepping away, he moved towards the door.

He glanced at Charley and smiled. Pascale had been tied to the same rack but Charlie was nothing like the French girl. His smile soon faded as unwanted images of a time past forced their way into his mind.

"There is sufficient water here for you to share," he said, his voice sounding louder than was necessary. Reaching for the bottle, he held it up and continued. "I will bring more later along with some food."

"Can we have a blanket or something to cover Charley?" It was Kelly who spoke. "It gets awfully cold in here." There was nothing to lose by asking, he had probably made his mind up regarding their fate anyway.

"I will see what I can find," he said after a short pause. "It will however be a shame to cover such a magnificent body." He studied Charley for a while longer. "You see, I am watching you."

He pointed to a tiny camera situated on the wall just above the door.

"Now Kelly," he continued. "Don't be tempted to release your friends because if you so much as touch them I will know."

He moved to where she was sitting on the floor and nudged her with the toe of his boot.

"If you do as you are told then I might have a pleasant surprise for you, but if you don't then I will kill you."

His manic stare left her in no doubt that he would carry out his threat.

The thought that he was watching them disgusted Charley and she wondered if he was listening in on their conversations too. Following Libby's advice, she avoided making eye contact with him. His threat to kill Kelly shocked them all.

When he was gone, Kelly struggled to her feet.

"Take your time and be careful," Libby implored. "None of us are desperate for water so make sure you have recovered your strength before attempting to do anything."

Libby was concerned that if Kelly fell she might sustain an injury and they were in no position to help. It was several minutes before Kelly managed to unscrew the top then she helped both Libby and Charley to drink. Not long after that, the flap in the door opened and a thin grey blanket dropped to the floor.

Chapter Seventy

THE TELEPHONE AT HER ELBOW rang.

"DS Woods."

"It's Jon here from Cybercrime. I have managed to track the IP address that you requested to a location in Bethnal Green." He sounded pleased with himself as he read out the address.

Scribbling it down on a pad she fiddled with the end of her pen and her frown deepened. It was not quite what she was hoping for but it was another piece of the puzzle linking Rita Morgan's son to abduction and murder.

"The computer wouldn't necessarily be at that location?" she asked thinking out loud.

"Indeed not. It's merely the address where the internet provider is registered. The computer could be anywhere." Sensing that she wanted more he went on. "We can try to locate the machine by using GPS." He began to explain the process but it went over her head, so thanking him she ended the call.

Holding her head in her hands, she sighed. Had Rita Morgan told her the truth about having no contact with her son? Turning to her note pad, she jotted down a few more ideas. Questions to which she wanted answers filled the page and when there was no more room left, she reached for the file locked away in her drawer. An hour later DC James appeared.

"Ten minutes before we speak to Cunningham again boss," he reminded her.

Woods looked up at the clock on the wall. "Come in for a moment." She indicated to a chair. "This is Dane Morgan's military file," she told him and as he leaned forward for a closer look, she continued. "It says here that his final mission in Afghanistan was particularly harrowing. He lost a number of his close friends in a hand to hand battle with insurgents. Apparently he was leading a small group of men sent to prevent a female officer from falling into the hands of the enemy."

"I thought hostilities had ended in that part of the world."

"He was part of a peace keeping force working with the United Nations to help stabilise the area and train local forces to police the region."

"So what happened to the officer?"

"It says here that she was tortured and murdered," Woods glanced at him before going on. "That section of the report doesn't go into specific details, but if this is anything to go by then the troubles in that part of the world are clearly far from over."

James nodded his head gravely. "So, Morgan could be suffering from some kind of psychological disorder triggered by combat stress."

"Post Traumatic Stress Disorder." Woods confirmed with a nod of her head. "It mentions nothing about that here though." She tapped the file with her fingertip.

"I don't suppose it does," James replied dryly. "I guess the military are rather sensitive about admitting to that kind of thing. It's not a picture they want to project."

"I suppose you are right." She looked up at him again.

"PTSD is not an excuse for what he has done." James returned her stare. "There can be no justification for abduction and murder."

Woods glanced down at the file and managed to contain a shudder.

"At least now we are able to build up a clearer profile of the man doing this," she paused, then putting her thoughts in order she went on. "Get onto the MOD, see if you can find out more about Morgan's last mission. I want to know the name of his commanding officer in Afghanistan. I'm going to speak to his mother again." She looked up as something else occurred to her. "Didn't Kelly Spencer tell us that the father of her son is an army officer?"

"Yes she did," James confirmed. "Do you think there might be a connection?"

"I'm not sure," she shook her head. "I can't see where. The army is a huge organisation employing many thousands of people."

On her way to Bethnal Green, Woods called into the police station at Shoreditch. She wanted to speak to the co-ordinator heading up the search team.

"We have narrowed it down to this area of Whitechapel." He told her, indicating to a street map pinned to the wall.

Moving towards the map, she studied it for a few seconds before finding what she was looking for.

"What about here?" She prodded it with her finger before turning back towards him.

"The old magistrate's court and police station," he said as he realised where she was pointing. "I believe that is about to be turned into a luxury hotel." Dropping heavily into his chair, he reached for his computer keyboard and initiated a search. "Ah, here we are," he began reading. "Grade II listed building, baroque style architecture. They don't build them like that anymore." He smiled with appreciation as he eyed the images on the screen then he continued. "It says here that the court held some high profile cases in its day. The Kray twins were tried there."

Woods moved to stand behind him and staring at the screen she asked. "Has the building been searched?"

His fingers moved over the keyboard until he found the file he was looking for and when it opened, details of the search spilled out across the screen.

"Yes, officers from the Safer Network Team checked the building." He paused as he leaned closer. "That appears to have been several days ago."

"So only a cursory glance as they drove past then."

"It would have been more detailed than that." he replied defensively. "The officers were on foot."

"Did they enter the building?"

"That would have been impossible," he explained. "The whole place is sealed off with security safety fences and window boards in place to keep people out."

"Nothing out of the ordinary was reported?"

"No, if the officers had any concerns it would have been noted and acted upon immediately."

Woods accepted what he said and turned back towards the map.

"So the search area has been narrowed down to here." She swept her hand loosely over a section.

"Correct," he replied and sensing her frustration, went on quickly. "I don't think you appreciate the scale of this job. There are hundreds of old buildings out there ranging from industrial sites to railway arches many still in use as workshops or storage areas. With our limited resources I think we have done a sterling job so far."

"Yes," Woods agreed. "I'm not disputing that. Personally I am very grateful for your help." She moved away from the map. "I just have a feeling that this could be the place. You may have seen some of the photographs of the abducted women but I have studied them all closely. The rooms they are being held in could possibly be old police cells." She looked at him thoughtfully. "Do you have details of the owners? I assume a building like that could only belong to a large development company or consortium of some kind."

"I can find out." He promised.

Their meeting continued for a while longer as he updated her with the latest developments and when they were finished, Woods thanked him and his team for their ongoing support.

He watched as she emerged from the police station. It wasn't difficult to discover her movements, a quick phone call was all it took. Luckily, her lapdog was nowhere to be seen, she was alone so stepping from his hiding place, he kept pace with her from across the street. Moving between parked cars, he crossed the road and increasing his stride he closed the gap between them. DS Woods was an attractive woman, her shoulder length hair shone auburn in the sunlight and he smiled as he caught her scent on the breeze. She would make the perfect addition to his rapidly growing collection of women. It was his intention to break into her home and kidnap her, but snatching her from outside a police station in broad daylight was far more appealing.

Woods stopped beside her car and slipping her hand into the bag slung over her shoulder rummaged for the remote. Pressing the button, the car indicators flashed and the door locks released. She half turned as she opened the door but still did not notice him. He was not worried if she did, he would be upon her in seconds, overpowering her would be a simple task, she would have no chance to react.

One last check over his shoulder confirmed they were alone. The traffic that filled the street just moments earlier was gone so moving closer, he readied himself but as he was about to pounce, her phone began to ring.

"DS Woods," she said holding the phone to her ear.

Slipping into the driver's seat, she inserted the key into the ignition but did not start the engine then reaching for the door pulled it shut.

He stopped and waited as she continued with her conversation. Through the rear window, he could see her face reflected in the interior mirror. Her eyes were wide as if she had just heard something that had surprised her. It was then that he decided to make his move. Grasping the rear door, he pulled it open and flung himself into the car before jamming his finger hard into the back of her seat.

"Hey, what do you think you are doing?" Woods half turned, the phone still pressed to her ear.

"I have a weapon," he lied and pushing on with his advantage, he continued. "Be very careful what you do next."

Keeping his hand low and out of sight, he maintained the pressure into the back of her seat.

"Start the engine and drive," he hissed.

Woods glanced through the windscreen at the car in front and still holding onto her phone, made sure that DC James could hear what was going on. Pretending to have finished her call, she dropped the phone onto the passenger seat then glancing into the rear view mirror again, she looked into the cold dark eyes glaring back at her. She knew who he was, his distinctive camouflage jacket was a giveaway, but she recognised his face from the photos in his military file. Did he really have a weapon? There had been no mention of one from the previous abductions, but she could hardly afford to find out. She was certain that if he did have a gun pressed into the back of her seat he would not hesitate to use it.

"Dane," she locked eyes with him in the mirror. "This is not a good idea." If she could keep him talking, try to reason with him then maybe it would give James time to organise something.

"Do not attempt to escape. Start the engine then keep your hands where I can see them."

"Dane..."

"Shut up and move." The sound of his raised voice startled her and she cowered lower into her seat.

"If you don't do as I say I will leave you now and kill one of the hostages."

Woods could not allow that to happen, so biting down on her lower lip she started the engine and selected first gear. Going along with what he said was her only option. Suddenly he moved and grabbing the phone from the front seat dropped it out of the open window. Instinctively Woods turned her head and watched as it shattered against the hard surface of the road. A police car appeared, its occupants unaware of the drama unfolding in the parked car. Dane stared at the officers as they drove past then they were gone.

Chapter Seventy One

THE MOMENT THE LINE WENT dead DC James was on to Shoreditch.

"DS Woods has just been abducted by Dane Morgan." He shouted into the phone and they reacted in an instant.

The returning patrol car turned around and sped off in pursuit with sirens blaring but it was no good, Woods and her car were nowhere to be seen. Whilst that was going on James called Fiona in surveillance.

"Do you have a tracking device on DS Woods' car?"

"No, why would we? This isn't the secret service you know."

He explained what had just happened.

"My goodness," Fiona replied hardly able believe what he had just said. "You need to speak to PC Yearsley, get him to use CCTV and roadside cameras to search for her car."

"Tell him I'm on my way."

Running to the lift, he pressed the call button but it was stationary on an upper level, his only option was to use the stairs and several floors later, he burst into the surveillance suite.

"Yearsley we have a situation." Between gasps, he told him what had just happened.

"I can access the camera outside the station at Shoreditch." Responding immediately his fingers danced over the keyboard.

James, recovering from his exertions concentrated on the screen as a grainy image appeared. More finger tapping was required before the picture improved.

"She was taken about ten minutes ago." James told him and feeding this information into the computer, Yearsley used it as a starting point.

Once a timeline was established, both men watched as individual frames flashed rapidly across the screen. There was a slight delay between each shot and playing one after the other, the jerking images reminded James of an old black and white film show.

"There she is," Yearsley said as DS Woods appeared. "Her body language is relaxed," he observed, "she seems unconcerned."

"Maybe she is not aware of the danger at this point." James pointed out.

He accessed another camera further along the pavement and they watched as she made her way towards it but now they could see a man following along behind.

"That's him," James gasped and drawing closer to the screen, he continued. "This is our man alright, he is wearing a camouflage jacket."

They looked on helplessly as DS Woods stopped beside her car. She opened the driver's door and climbed in and in the next picture, Dane Morgan pulled opened the rear door and threw himself onto the back seat. A few moments later, the car pulled away from the kerb.

"Let's see where it went," Yearsley whispered as he shuffled closer to the keyboard then activating the multi-screen facility several views appeared at once.

At the end of the street, the car turned left onto Commercial Road and they tracked its progress as far as Leman Street then, as it turned into a side street it disappeared from view.

"Can you find it again?" James asked desperately as he stared at the empty screens.

"There are very few traffic cameras off the main street," Yearsley explained as his fingers worked the keyboard. "Some businesses in the backstreets will have security cameras set up to cover their own premises. These may of course overlook the road but I don't have access to those."

"Can you pull up a detailed street map of the area?" James tapped at the side of his face impatiently with his fingertips as he waited for the map to appear. "Where would he have taken her?" he asked himself.

He told her to keep driving and for twenty minutes, they cruised the backstreets before doubling back the way they had come. Woods realised they were close to the spot where the taxi used to abduct Pascale Dominique had stopped, CCTV had tracked it this far before losing sight of it. She was aware of him glancing over his shoulder, he must be fearful that they were being followed. Clearly, he was using the back streets to lose anyone that may be on their tale or attempting to track their progress. Woods wanted to disobey his orders, swing the car back towards the main road but she could still feel what she believed to be a weapon pressed up against the back of her seat. It was making her nervous, but maybe it was not a weapon at all. Did she have the courage to call his bluff? He was a large and powerful man and if she did anything to upset him, he might attack her and in the confines of the car, she would not be able to defend herself. Chewing nervously at her bottom lip, she checked the rear view mirror again. He was watching her intently and the amused expression on his face told her that he could read her mind.

"Do you really want to take a chance?" He goaded her, pushing harder against the back of her seat.

They had driven around so many corners that Woods was completely disorientated. She was unfamiliar with this part of London. Places that she had never seen before opened up in front of her and people that she had no desire to meet stood at the side of the road and stared as she swept past. He urged her on, bullying her to drive faster. She never broke the speed limits especially in a built up area like this and the concentration needed to keep the car from veering off the road left no room for plotting her escape. Any thoughts of throwing herself from the moving vehicle were forgotten.

"Turn left here," he growled, his face just inches from her ear and as the car swerved across the junction he held onto the back of her seat.

The road ahead widened then a large ornately designed building came into view.

"Slow down and stop close to that gate."

A high brick wall ran along the pavement and where it stopped a steel panelled security fence took its place. Wooden boards covering the windows gave the building an appearance of a secure prison. Woods realised this was the old Magistrates Court and Police Station. She had been right, this must be where he is holding the women. Silently she cursed herself for not having the building searched thoroughly days ago.

"Turn the engine off and give me the keys."

Slowly she did as he said whilst scanning her surroundings.

"Get out of the car."

Pushing open the door she steadied herself preparing to run, but the rear door opened trapping her between the car and the wall. She had to try something so pushing herself up against the brickwork, she attempted to squeeze past the driver's door, but it was impossible. Suddenly a crippling pain shot through her neck and shoulders and crying out she almost collapsed. Mercifully, he released his grip and the pain subsided.

"A few seconds more and you would have lost consciousness," he hissed.

Taking a deep breath, Woods rolled her shoulders tentatively in an effort to stave off the sensation of nausea.

"Move," he said and grasping her arm dragged her roughly along the wall towards the huge gate.

"Unlock the chain and don't forget," his fingers tensed against the nerves at the back of her neck and she stiffened.

There was no one around that she could rely on for help so leaning forward she took hold of the industrial sized padlock and used the key he had given her to unlock it. The heavy chain would have made an effective weapon, but one end was welded to the steel gatepost. This was just one of the many security measures left over from the days when prisoners waiting for their trial to begin were in residence. The gate was a solid mass that refused to move as she strained to push it open. She was convinced there must be another lock, but when he added his weight it swung open noisily on rusted hinges.

Woods took it all in immediately, the small exercise yard and the white van parked against the wall of the building. This must be the vehicle used to abduct Charley Baker.

"Get back into the car." Passing her the keys, he slipped in behind her. "Start the engine and park beside the van."

Reversing slowly, she lined the vehicle up with the opening then, allowing it to roll forward manoeuvred into the yard. The wheels had hardly stopped turning before he jumped out and she watched as he closed and secured the gate. Turning off the engine, she scanned her surroundings in the hope of finding a way out, but it was hopeless. The yard had been designed to contain desperate men and as she slumped in defeat, she realised that her bag was still slung over her shoulders. Slipping her hand into its depths, her fingers closed around her personal alarm. When activated it would to let off a piercing squeal and send a cloud of unpleasant vapour into the face of the attacker. This contained a dye that was invisible to the naked eye, but under ultra-violet light would show up on the attacker's skin and clothing. The alarm would also send a signal to her phone activating both a GPS position and a recording device that could help police to identify the attacker. Unfortunately, this would be of no use as her phone lay shattered on the road in Shoreditch. Woods hesitated she had just a few seconds to make up her mind. Would activating the alarm aid her escape or make matters worse?

Chapter Seventy Two

SHE WATCHED NERVOUSLY AS HE turned away from the heavy gates. These solid monuments of detainment, designed over one hundred and fifty years ago had confined the worst of the East End underworld whilst awaiting retribution at the courthouse next door. Her stomach tightened as realisation set in; there was no other way out.

Dane Morgan was sure of himself. His movements fluid and measured he was a man completely in control and when he glanced up his smile was lopsided. She had to do something, her fight or flight response had kicked in but there was nowhere to run. The only door that she could see led into the building and she really did not want to go that way. The only option left was to stand firm and fight. If she could overpower him and snatch the key from his pocket then maybe she could unlock the gate and escape into the street. This was not one of her better plans, in fact it was insane. How could she possibly expect to overpower a man like Dane Morgan? Her police training had equipped her with some basic self defence techniques designed to boost her confidence, but in reality facing a well built military man her chances of success were almost nonexistent. Her only hope was gripped tightly in the palm of her hand.

"Move," he grunted and moving his head indicated towards the door that she had seen earlier.

She made the mistake of taking her eyes off him and as he pushed up behind her, he shoved her forward. She almost stumbled but her reaction was immediate. Raising her right arm over her left shoulder, she pressed the button.

A piercing squeal assaulted her ears and as it bounced from the surrounding walls, a fine spray filled the space between them. He was blisteringly fast and turning away dropped to one knee but some of the atomised liquid splashed against his cheek sending a burning sensation into his right eye. Temporarily blinded, he held his breath and barred his teeth. Retribution was quick to follow. Reaching out he grabbed her arm then slipping his hands down over her hips he leaned forward and they both fell to the ground.

The force of the impact drove the air from her lungs and the alarm skittered away across the yard. Her ribcage almost collapsed as he crashed down on top of her and the palms of her hands stung as they slapped against the tarmac but still she held onto a slight advantage. Wriggling to one side, she twisted her hips in an effort to throw him off, but he was far too heavy.

He grunted the sound of a wild animal and maintaining his grip took the blows that rained down on his head and shoulders. She would not get away he was sure of that, all he had to do was wait for the burning sensation in his eyes to ease.

Her legs were trapped, it was almost impossible to move but somehow she managed to pull herself up into the sitting position. Her objective was to get the key to the gate so straining her muscles she reached out for his pocket and frantically began to explore with her fingertips.

His growl this time was louder. His right eye continued to burn madly and the other was half blinded with tears. He could feel her squirming beneath him, he knew what she wanted so releasing his grip he took hold of her arm and wrenched it backwards.

Pain exploded through her elbow and she cried out. Pounding his face with her free hand, her muscles cramped with the effort of maintaining an almost impossible position then screaming with frustration, she realised that she was losing this battle. She could do nothing to stop his fingers from sliding across her throat. He found the mark and applying pressure to the nerves in her neck her whole body tensed before darkness engulfed her.

Drifting up slowly from the pit of unconsciousness, she forced open her eyes and groaned. Her body ached, the pain running across her shoulders extended down her spine and into the small of her back. Blinking rapidly, she peered through the semi-darkness in an effort to make sense of her situation. Her wrists were bound, her arms pinioned above her head. She could not feel her fingers and the throbbing in her arms was becoming unbearable. She had to do something to relieve the growing discomfort so moving her feet, she discovered that she could stand upright. The pressure on her arms eased and the knot binding her wrists loosened allowing blood to flow back into her fingers.

The severity of her situation became apparent as her head began to clear. She had seen photographs of Libby Ellis hanging like this in a dingy cell. There were more disturbing images on Matthew Cunningham's computer that she could not allow herself to contemplate so pushing these unwelcome thoughts aside, she wondered how long she had been unconscious. From the angle of her wrists above her head, it was impossible to see the face of her watch. Her meeting at Shoreditch had ended just after midday and now she could sense that darkness was beginning to close in. Shuffling her feet, she angled her hips in an effort to find a more comfortable position. Pain was her constant companion and the ache in the small of her back was developing into something more serious. Her mind sharpened as she assessed her injuries. Luckily, no bones were broken but both her knees were sore, grazed when she fell to the ground and her hips ached with bruises.

Images of Libby Ellis and Charley Baker were never far from her thoughts, it was impossible to block them out completely. Dane Morgan was bound to appear with his camera then she realised that perhaps he had already taken his pictures when she was unconscious. The thought of her colleagues seeing her like this appalled her. Morgan would almost certainly send his pictures to Matthew Cunningham, whose computer had been set up at the station. Officers were scrutinising his files and would see the images the moment they arrived. Pushing this unsavoury prospect aside, she wondered how long it would be before DC James discovered where she was. He could access to her files and they had discussed everything regarding the case or had they? It was easy to share her theories with Terry Ashton but then she groaned as an element of doubt crept in.

The search for DS Woods continued well into the night involving dozens of officers from the Met and surrounding police stations. DC James was in Woods office scrutinising her notes. His shift had ended hours ago but not once did he consider abandoning his colleague. Working through her files, he had to come up with something. He was trying to piece together her day. What had she intended to do after her meeting at Shoreditch? He knew that she wanted to speak with Rita Morgan but she also planned to interview Matthew Cunningham again. What order had she decided on? He sighed and rubbing his fingers across his forehead looked up and stared blindly at the wall. It was all rather academic now. Everything changed the moment Morgan appeared. CCTV images confirmed that he had abducted her and if he kept to his usual pattern, photographic evidence would soon follow. He closed his eyes and wondered what horrors she was having to endure at that very moment.

Officers were standing by monitoring both Cunningham's computer and phone and the surveillance team were waiting to track any calls that might come in. Dane Morgan was unaware that Cunningham was in custody so would have no reason to avoid making contact with him.

Getting to his feet, James left the office and went into the incident room.

He had to find out where the women were being held. What did Morgan intend to do with them and why did he target DS Woods? He thought about Pascale Dominique and the details of her murder. The prospect of this happening to his colleague left him cold, but he had to remain calm. Earlier he had informed DCI Wyman about the situation. Wyman had promised to appoint a senior officer to take over and lead the case but that had not yet happened so he was currently in charge. This was a daunting prospect, he was hardly qualified to lead such an important case, but for the time being it was his responsibility to think logically. He would have to direct the team, step up his efforts to help solve the case before another woman was murdered.

Staring up at the street map pinned to the wall he studied the Whitechapel area. PC Yearsley had tracked her car as far as a side road running off the main thoroughfare, but had lost sight of it. Most of the old and abandoned buildings in this area had been checked but he could not help thinking that something significant had been missed.

Her mind would give her no peace. She thought about the post mortem report that Patricia Fleming had sent to her. It contained details of rape and torture. Pascale Dominique had suffered unthinkable torment at the hands of a lunatic. Woods groaned as she remembered the psychological profile of a serial killer. It often indicated a growing degree of disproportionate violence during the act of killing or in its aftermath. Brutal rape of the most obscene kind would be the most likely outcome. Pascale had undergone such treatment and she could expect nothing less. Woods shuddered as she tried without success to banish these thoughts from her mind. Her knowledge of the subject was complete, she had witnessed enough during her career to know exactly what to expect.

Dane Morgan, to her knowledge had only killed once; this hardly made him a serial killer. She barely knew the man so could not predict his mood. The only thing that gave her hope was that he was not presenting the characteristics associated with a serial killer. There was however no doubt, he was a dangerous man and things could change quickly. Dane Morgan had witnessed some atrocious experiences during his army career but surely, he was bound by the seven core values that formed the foundation of the army profession. Loyalty, Duty, Respect, Selfless service, Honour, Integrity and Personal courage are what soldiers learn during Basic Combat Training. They are expected to observe them every day and incorporate them into everything they do.

A noise from outside the door startled her and she stiffened. A bulkhead light came on above the door casting a dull light around the cell. Although hardly bright, it was sufficient to blind her temporarily and by the time her eyes adjusted Dane Morgan was standing there in front of her. His right eye was red rimmed and the skin across his cheek tender. This made him appear angry.

"So," he began, "you are back with us."

Woods remained silent and waited for him to continue.

"Not so brave now are you?"

"What do you expect? I can do nothing with my hands tied above my head."

He forced a smile and considered what to say next.

"I wonder how many of your rank would have come down here in the past to visit the felons they had put away."

"Why would they?" she frowned unable to understand where this was leading.

"Why indeed," he replied his smile more genuine this time. "At least now you have the opportunity to experience their suffering first hand."

"Oh I don't believe that," she snapped. "Do you really think that prisoners would have been subjected to torture?"

He stared at her but said nothing.

"Do I have to remain like this?"

"Oh yes, I think you do." He knew exactly what she was going through and her suffering excited him. He could see through her mask of bravery. She may be an officer of the Metropolitan Police Force but she was also a vulnerable young woman, as defenceless and pliable as the others in his torture chamber.

"Why should I cut you down?"

"Human decency springs to mind." This was her chance to appeal to his core values. "This is a violation of my rights and as a military man I would imagine you are aware of that."

"Don't you dare talk to me about human rights," he snarled. It surprised him to discover that she knew something about him, but he would have to pursue that later. "Do you realise that in most countries throughout the world human rights are none existent."

She glared at him and he could see that she was not convinced.

"It's something that I have experienced personally."

She waited for him to continue but his eyes glazed as memories clouded his vision.

"I can make things a lot more unpleasant for you," he said at last and reaching for a control box on the wall, he pressed a button.

A motor above her head began to whine and the rope binding her wrists tightened. The muscles in her arms strained as she tried to resist but the motor was far too powerful then pain surged through her body as her feet lifted off the ground.

"Let me down," she pleaded through clenched teeth as she swayed gently at the end of the rope.

Her muscles went into spasms and she almost passed out. Desperately clinging onto consciousness, she gasped for breath as the pressure across her chest became intense.

"Comfortable enough for you?" he chuckled dryly as he moved around her. The physical strain that she was suffering was obvious. "If you were to remain like this it would not be long before death would relieve you of your pain."

The sound of his voice faded in and out and it was all she could do to focus on what he was saying. He explained how she would gradually suffocate as the weight of her body suspended by her arms put increasing pressure on her diaphragm.

"You are young, fit and healthy so it may take a while. You will experience excruciating muscle spasms and severe cramps, it won't be pleasant, but I can assure you of the outcome."

"Let me down," she pleaded, her cheeks damp with tears.

It took a great effort to remain calm as she watched him walk away and taking small measured breaths, she squeezed her eyes shut and rode out her terror. Although her heart was pounding madly, she was cold, icy fingers of fear touched her skin and it was not long before her body began to shut down. The changes were subtle, her arms were already numb and now she could no longer feel her legs. Breathing was becoming increasingly more difficult and a huge amount of effort was required just to keep going. She could do nothing else, she had to continue breathing because without oxygen, everything would come to an end.

Suddenly he was there beside her. She could sense him, his shadow a spirit come to claim her soul. Blinking rapidly in an attempt to clear her vision she believed that if she could make eye contact with him she could appeal to his conscience but she was mistaken, he was no longer there.

Sometime later, she felt something tugging at her but hovering on the edge of darkness, she could be certain of nothing. A sound invaded her senses, the clicking of a camera then a deeper drone, the soft hum of a motor turning. Her feet touched cold concrete but she was unaware of movement. Her legs, unable to support her, folded uselessly and she collapsed to the ground. The iron band of pressure crushing her chest eased and she groaned with relief, her breath coming in short gasps as her limbs jerked helplessly. At least she was alive and on this occasion, pain was a sensation that she welcomed.

The camera continued to record the event, its constant clicking a sound that she could hear above the constant ringing in her ears. This annoyed her, surely he should be offering first aid, tending to her injuries, help to make more comfortable. Her chest rose and fell torturously as her lungs struggled to work. His camera was just inches from her heaving bosom and as she raised her head, her vision cleared. Looking up at him, she saw no compassion there, his expression was flushed with excitement and he was staring at her lewdly. It was then that she realised her blouse was gone, she was topless, her humiliation had begun.

Chapter Seventy Three

THE TELEPHONE ON THE DESK rang.

"DS Woods' office, DC James speaking."

"Dennis, it's Paul Goddard here from Cybercrime." Paul was one of the officers working on Matthew Cunningham's computer.

"We have just received an email from your man. You had better get up here and take a look."

Putting down the phone, James got to his feet. This was what he was waiting for but now the thought of seeing the message filled him with trepidation.

The computer was set up in a small windowless room not much larger than the desk it was placed on. There was just enough room for an operator's chair.

"Dennis, squeeze in if you can." Paul said as DC James appeared then he smiled lopsidedly. "You had better swing the door shut."

"You said we have a message from the abductor." James said as he turned to shut the door, then crouching down beside his colleague he faced the computer screen.

"Indeed we have. It came in about ten minutes ago." His fingers moved with practiced ease over the keyboard.

Holding his breath apprehensively, James knew what to expect but still his stress levels soared. Suddenly the screen filled with high resolution images that were disturbing and left very little to the imagination. DS Woods was hanging from her arms in a dull cell-like room. She appeared to have been in a fight, her clothing dishevelled, her expression twisted in agony. Paul scrolled slowly through the shocking collection, each image confirming unimaginable suffering, but it was the next photo that left both men stunned. Woods was lying on a concrete floor with her wrists still bound, but now she was topless.

"Bloody hell!" Paul whispered.

James looked on awkwardly, he did not want to see his colleague like this, but it was his job to look objectively at the scene. Distress and humiliation marred her face and with each new photo, any modesty that she had left was stripped away. Clearly, she knew what was happening and would understand the implications. James knew there was worse to come as thoughts of Pascale Dominique entered his mind.

"Has anyone else seen these?" he asked his voice an unsteady whisper.

"No," Paul shook his head.

"Let's keep it that way," James stared at him coldly. "I don't want to see copies of these pinned up all over the station. Don't even think about emailing them round to our colleagues."

"Would I do such a thing?" His grin left James in no doubt.

"I'm now going to see Wyman. He needs to know about this, but if I discover these have been distributed then I will know who to come looking for."

Paul could see that DC James was deadly serious and the childish grin slipped from his face.

Wyman studied the photo of DS Woods hanging from her arms and a grin of deadly satisfaction spread across his face.

"This is just the beginning," James told him and ignoring his expression he went on. "There is far worse to come I can assure you of that."

Wyman looked up. "What better incentive then to discover where DS Woods and the other women are being held."

James stared at his boss and felt the weight of the investigation settle firmly on his shoulders.

"You are best placed to move this forward," Wyman told him. "You worked closely with DS Woods, shared everything so I want you to take the lead." He paused as if waiting for a reaction then after a moment he continued. "You have the support of a good team."

"But sir," James responded. "I'm hardly qualified to lead a murder investigation."

"Don't worry DC James, I will appoint a DI to help take the strain just as soon as I can but in the meantime I expect you to do your duty."

James continued to stare at Wyman. There was so much that he wanted to say but he did not trust himself to remain civil so biting his tongue, he said nothing.

"I had better get on then sir," he moaned.

"Keep me informed DC James."

Moving zombie-like along the corridor James could hardly believe what his boss had just said. His decision was most unorthodox and above all, it was wrong. Obviously, something was going on between Wyman and DS Woods, he knew there was friction, but he didn't realise just how serious it had become. He considered taking this to the Chief, but it would be impossible to implicate Wyman in some kind of hostility towards Woods. He had no solid evidence and the Chief would probably write it off as a clash of personality.

Arriving at the incident room, he found a number of his colleagues already gathered there. They glanced at him as he appeared and he could feel the oppressive atmosphere that hung over them all. They were aware of the situation but would need updating with recent events.

"Can someone gather the rest of the team? I have some things to say."

Thirty minutes later the room was filled with detectives, only one officer was missing, DCI Wyman had declined an invitation to attend.

"As you are aware I have been tasked with taking this case forward."

A disapproving murmur went around the senior officers.

"Where is DCI Wyman?" someone called out.

"Good question," a chorus responded.

"As you are no doubt aware," James raised his voice and held his hands up in a gesture for silence. "Wyman and Woods are not on the best of terms. I have no idea what is going on between them but it need not concern us. We have more pressing things to think about and I will need all of your help and advice if we are going to bring this case to a satisfactory conclusion."

"Someone needs to inform the Chief. Wyman's lack of leadership leaves us all in a precarious position."

"I agree," James nodded. "Someone does need to inform the Chief but more importantly we have a job to do. We must pull together and focus on nothing else but this investigation. Not only are the lives of Kelly Spencer, Elizabeth Ellis and Charley Baker under threat, but now Detective Sergeant Isobel Woods has become the latest victim. One of our own is suffering unspeakably at the hands of a murderer and the only people capable of saving their lives are in this room. The longer we stand here bitching about senior officers the more these women will suffer."

Turning to face the street map hanging on the wall he began to go over the facts, cross referencing all the elements of the case. He pointed out the links that bound each victim together then he reminded them of Dane Morgan's movements.

"We know that Matthew Cunningham has been implicated in the disappearance of Pascale Dominique and Charley Baker, but I believe he's been drawn in and manipulated by Dane Morgan." Turning to the evidence board, he pointed at a photograph of the abductor. "I want to know what connects these two men. Cunningham says that he has no idea why he and Libby Ellis have been targeted and I am inclined to believe him."

"We know that Morgan sends images of his victims to Cunningham and taunts him with phone calls," DC Samantha Burkett announced as she got to her feet, "but does he know that Cunningham is in custody?"

"No," James replied, "and I want to keep it that way. If Morgan realises that we have Cunningham locked up then our only link will be lost."

"Don't you think that we should brief Cunningham," DC Burkett continued. "Morgan is sure to make contact with him soon so he will need to know how to respond."

James stared at her and wondered why he had not considered this himself. The shock of seeing DS Woods so distressed and the sudden responsibility of the case had thrown him completely, but now with the support of his colleagues his confidence levels were on the rise. He shared the photographs of Woods hanging helplessly in the cell but chose not to reveal the more humiliating shots. They had all seen the photos of the other women so could guess what was in store for their colleague.

Gradually a plan began to take shape and breaking up into smaller groups the detectives continued to work with renewed enthusiasm.

The women in the torture chamber froze as the door opened.

"Good morning Ladies," Morgan said brightly as he entered.

Charley watched as he looked her way, he hesitated but thankfully moved on. Libby refused to make eye contact with him as he paused beside her then he focused on Kelly who was huddled against the wall at the back of the cell. Turning back towards Libby, he stared down at her before asking.

"Are you comfortable enough?"

She did not respond so he continued.

"It's your lucky day," he smiled. "I'm going to release you from this position."

Libby looked up at him and frowned. This was completely unexpected, she had no idea what he had in mind, but then he looked away and spoke to Kelly.

"I have a little job for you. Will you please come with me?"

She glanced nervously at the table holding Libby.

"Don't worry," he laughed, "I don't intend to tie you down to that thing, not yet anyway."

Slowly Kelly rose to her feet and followed him from the cell.

Chapter Seventy Four

MATT WAS TAKEN FROM HIS cell to an interview room where he found DC James and a female police officer waiting.

"Thank you for joining us," James said as if greeting a colleague.

Gone was the cocksure and aggressive nature that Matt associated with the detective and studying him with increasing unease, Matt settled at the table.

"It's not Libby is it?"

Leaning forward on his elbows as if drawn by his distress, DC James replied. "No, there is nothing to worry about. As far as we are aware the situation remains unchanged."

Relief flooded Matt's face but he was still wary. What did DC James want from him?

"Things have however moved on a little," James began and shuffling uncomfortably in his seat, he told Matt about the abduction of DS Woods.

Matt sat in shocked silence as the story unfolded and lost for words, he listened as James went on.

"If the abductor follows the same pattern then we can expect him to make contact with you soon."

Matt eyed his phone. It was sitting on the table in a plastic evidence bag.

"Has he sent images?" he asked.

"Yes," James responded grimly but made no further comment.

Matt closed his eyes and sighed. "Is there anything I can do to help?" He opened his eyes and looked at the detectives.

James studied him from across the table, his expression neutral then after a short pause, he said. "I want you to have your phone and wait for him to call. When he does, on no account must he realise that you are in custody, he has to believe that nothing has changed. He must also believe that he is still in control." He smiled weakly. Dane Morgan was in fact leading the game and they were no closer in discovering where he was holding the women. These facts he kept to himself.

"We are of course monitoring his calls, each time he speaks with you we get a step closer, so you see how vital it is that we maintain contact with him." James realised this was not strictly true but he had to give Cunningham something positive. Fiona in surveillance was doing a great job; he was relying on her to come up with something that they could work with. He slipped the phone across the table. Reaching out Matt shook it from the bag and turned it on. He waited for the icons to settle on the screen before checking the battery life then he glanced at his messages. There was nothing important; Julia would have informed his immediate contacts about his situation and Veronique knew what was going on.

"I would like you to go up to the surveillance suite and work with the staff there. There is no need to keep you locked up in a cell. Fiona Richards is leading the team so will look after you. DC Burkett here show you the way."

The detective sitting beside James smiled as she got to her feet.

"If you would follow me sir," she indicated towards the door.

Matt hesitated before moving. If the abductor discovered that he was working with the police he would never see Libby again but he had no choice. It seemed that he was now one of the key players in the investigation.

Kelly cried out in astonishment when she saw the woman lying on the ground.

"Untie her and bring her to the other room." Leaving the cell door open, he disappeared from view.

Kelly wasted no time loosening the rope binding her wrists then gently she massaged warmth back into her swollen fingers. Bruises discoloured the woman's arms like unsightly tattoos but there was nothing that she could do about that. Gently she helped her to sit up and straightening out her legs, Kelly could see that her trousers were torn and her knees bloody.

"Thank you," Woods whispered as she moved then her face creased with pain as the muscles across her shoulders cramped.

"My name is Kelly," she spoke calmly and shuffling closer, began to work at the knots beneath her skin.

"Kelly Spencer?"

Sitting back, Kelly stopped what she was doing. "How do you know my name?"

"I'm a detective from the Met working on the abduction case. My name is Isobel Woods."

Kelly stared at Woods in disbelief then she found her voice. "What are you doing here like this?"

Woods smile turned sour as another bout of pain wracked her tortured body. "I guess I got too close," she groaned through clenched teeth.

"Do the police know about this place; are they coming to get us out?"

Woods shook her head sadly.

"No, I'm afraid that I'm the only one who knows where we are and I didn't get the opportunity to inform my colleagues."

Woods moved stiffly into a more comfortable position then, Kelly laying a hand on her shoulder said. "We need to find something to cover you with."

The remnants of her shredded blouse were strewn across the floor but Kelly spotted a black jacket thrown over the iron bedstead. Reaching for it, she helped Woods to put it on.

"He told me to take you to the 'torture chamber'." Kelly looked up as Woods eyes widened with alarm. "Don't worry, it's what we call the larger cell," she explained. "The others are there."

This did nothing to instil confidence but slowly Woods limped along the corridor counting the cell doors as they went. She noticed the sophisticated locking system on the wall beside one of the doors; a small touch pad and a minute camera lens completed the set-up.

"He told us that the door works by entering a password." Kelly whispered. "That little lens is part of a facial recognition system, the door won't open until he looks into the camera."

Woods could not understand why he needed such an elaborate system then stepping into the cell, she took a sharp intake of breath. Libby Ellis was secured to a table that would not look out of place in Pat Fleming's cutting room and Charley Baker was tied to an improvised wooden frame.

"So nice of you to join us."

The sound of his voice startled her and as she turned to face him, he smiled. The sophisticated locking system slipped into place with a heavy click when the door slammed shut then the keypad on the wall bleeped. Woods continued to watch as he approached the table where Libby lay.

"Would you like to get off this thing?" He asked amiably.

Libby stared up at him unsure of how to respond. What did he intend doing with her. Perhaps it would be best to remain where she was, but the decision was not hers to make. Reaching for the straps securing her ankles, he loosened them before stepping back then turning to Kelly, he said.

"Get over here and take over from me."

Before she had time to move, he reached into his pocket and produced a knife then he stepped towards Charley.

"You don't think I'm stupid enough to release her with you two standing behind me?"

Woods was reluctant to try anything, but it was her duty to help these women. She was in no condition to tackle him on her own, but with the help of both Libby and Kelly, maybe they could overpower him but they did not get the chance. Charley squealed as he placed the knife against her throat.

"Release Libby then put Detective Sergeant Woods in her place."

Kelly glanced at Woods who nodded her head almost imperceptibly then she began to undo the straps holding Libby's wrists. When Libby was free, she hobbled stiffly to the back of the cell where sinking to the ground she drew her knees up and hugged them tightly.

Against her better judgement, Woods climbed onto the table and allowed Kelly to strap her in place. Staring across the room at Morgan it was clear that if she refused to do as he said he would use the knife to harm or even kill Charley Baker.

When Kelly was finished, he moved away from Charley who wept with relief then standing over Woods, he gazing down at her and grinned with satisfaction.

"How does it feel to be totally helpless?" he studied her for a few seconds more before going on. "It must be hell for a woman of your rank, an officer with the power to issue orders and expect them to be carried out without question. "

The hatred in his voice was palpable and Woods realised that he was a man at odds with a system that he had once relied on. What had made him turn against authority she wondered? She had come across men like him before but not one as terrifying at Dane Morgan. How could she reason with a man like him, what psychological theories could she use to appeal to his better nature? She just hoped that it was not too late.

Suddenly he turned away and activated the lock and when the door swung opened, he simply left them alone.

Chapter Seventy Five

"WHEN THE CALL COMES IN try to keep him talking." Fiona reminded him. "We need him to stay on the line for as long as possible."

Matt had never met Fiona before but Julia had mentioned her on a number of occasions. She was the woman who supplied the tracking device that he had given to Charley.

"We are only able to discover where he is calling from when he hangs up; we've not yet been able to pinpoint his position in real time."

Matt could hardly believe that given the sophisticated equipment at her disposal they were unable to get to him before he finished his call.

"I assume that DS Woods passed on the activation code for the tracking device." He had to admit giving it to Charley in the hope they would discover where she had been taken.

"Yes she did." Fiona stopped what she was doing and swivelled her chair round to face him. She could hardly tell him that she always had the code but could not use it without implicating herself. If the police discovered that she had supplied the device then she would lose all credibility and probably be thrown into a cell. "Of course it was too late by then; he must have found and destroyed it."

She thought about the program running on her laptop at home. The Spyware package had not yet come up with anything and she was beginning to lose hope.

"I guess that you have no way of tracking Libby's phone using your system."

"As I said before, it only works when it's turned on. The abductor knows this and uses it at different locations."

"So he's deliberately giving the police the run around."

"Yes," Fiona nodded her head. "He's clever and knows exactly what he's doing."

"What about DS Woods' phone. Can't you track that?"

"Unfortunately it was destroyed when she was abducted."

Matt was silent for a moment then he lowered his voice and said.

"I know that it was you who supplied us with the tracking device."

Her eyes widened in alarm and glancing at her colleagues was relieved to see they were busy and didn't seem to be listening.

"Surely you have some other method of tracking it," he went on quietly.

"Not now that it's been destroyed." She studied him for a moment before making up her mind then she told him about the Spyware package running on her computer at home.

"The tracking device was tiny." Matt replied. "If it's been destroyed and component parts still exist, they must be microscopic."

"It doesn't matter how small the parts are, they will still give off a signal."

"Are you running this program on a laptop?"

Fiona nodded her head. "Yes, it's been going for several days now but with no results."

"Perhaps your computer is not powerful enough. Have you considered running it on another machine?"

"No not yet." She admitted. It had not occurred to her that her computer might not be up to the job.

"The computers here must be more than capable." He said looking round at the impressive array of technology.

"They don't like unauthorised software being introduced to the system."

"Surely your technical support team could give it the go ahead especially given the circumstances."

Fiona looked uncertain. "The program has never been released for general use, it's an experimental project developed by a friend of mine some years ago."

"My computer is in the building. If we could have access then we could use it to run the program."

"I doubt if DCI Wyman would allow that."

"Surely it's worth a try. We should speak to DC James."

Suddenly his phone began to ring and snatching it up he could see Libby's number displayed on the screen.

"It's him."

Fiona held up her hand preventing him from answering then, turning to her computer she pressed a series of keys before giving him the go ahead.

"Hello." He spoke into the phone.

"Cunningham, where have you been?"

His heart beat faster as he answered. "I'm away at the moment staying with friends."

"You're not at home?"

"No not for the next few days."

"Then why are there bottles of milk on your doorstep?"

Matt's mind was racing. "Bugger," he replied in an effort to sound genuine.

"I forgot to cancel my milk delivery."

"That's a silly thing to do. Milk bottles on your doorstep are a clear indication that you are not at home. Now what would a burglar make of that?"

Matt realised that he must be standing outside his house. Fiona had come to the same conclusion and reached for the phone on her desk.

"I assume that you have seen my latest photographs."

"Yes," Matt told him. Having not seen them himself, he knew they featured DS Woods.

"What do you think of the Detective Sergeant now?"

Matt didn't understand what he meant so remained silent.

"The great Metropolitan police force," he laughed. "Strip away the badge and what are you left with?" he laughed again. "I have exposed the woman beneath. Would you like to see more of DS Woods?"

Matt was shocked. "I'm not concerned about DS Woods. I want to know about Libby."

"Oh yes your woman. Well I can tell you that she is fine and if you continue to do as you are told then you might even get to see her again."

"What about Charley?"

"Now that was naughty of you. Fancy sending her in wired, I guess that was you. Surely she wouldn't have agreed to such a plan?"

Matt realised that he was toying with him.

"What are you going to do with her?"

He hardly wanted a detailed account, but if he could keep him talking then it might help track his position.

"There will of course be repercussions," he replied ignoring the question. "Let me think about it and get back to you."

The line went dead.

The nearest patrol car was diverted to the road where Matt lived. Parked cars lined both sides of the street but there was no one matching the description of Dane Morgan. They pulled up outside the address and turning to his colleague one of the officers said.

"DC James was right, milk bottles have been left on the step."

"The detectives at the Met are bloody geniuses!"

Dane Morgan watched from the shadows and his eyes narrowed suspiciously. How had the police managed to get there so quickly?

"Kelly, untie me then we can work out how to get out of here." Woods pleaded.

304

"I really can't do that," Kelly replied fearfully. "He made it quite clear that if I release anyone we will all suffer."

"How will he know?"

"There is a camera above the door. He's watching us."

Woods had not seen the tiny camera fixed to the wall.

"We could barricade the door, prevent him from coming in."

"If we do that then we will starve. He brings us food."

Woods realised that Kelly was right, upsetting the precarious balance of their situation could have terrible consequences.

"Who are you and why are you here?" Charley asked, her voice raised by stress.

"My name is Isobel. I'm a detective with the Metropolitan police." She went on to tell them about the ongoing investigation, using positive phrases to disguise their lack of progress.

"How long will it be before they get us out of here?"

Woods glanced at Charley before replying. "It won't be long, the investigation is nearing a critical stage, officers are very close to discovering our whereabouts."

"So they have no idea where we are." Libby gasped miserably.

"Very soon my colleagues will have the answers. Believe me, we will all get out of here." Testing the strength of the straps holding her down, Woods hoped that she was right. She had to keep their spirits up.

Morgan returned to his command centre and activated the camera overlooking the 'torture chamber'. He smiled with satisfaction as he looked down on the women. DS Woods was an unexpected bonus. He had not anticipated abducting a police officer that was never part of his plan. He wondered if her absence would have a significant impact on the police investigation, she seemed to be one of the leading detectives. He thought again about the patrol car arriving so quickly at Cunningham's house. Surely they could not have known that he was there, he wasn't on the phone long enough for them to track his position. It could have been a coincidence but he doubted it, he would have to be more careful.

Staring at the screen, he could see the women were talking. There was no audio system inside the cell so he had no idea what they were saying. Libby Ellis was still sitting on the floor at the back of the cell. She was harmless but he would have to restrain her. Getting to his feet, he went into the storeroom where he selected a pair of handcuffs.

Pushing open the door, he entered the cell and paused, the aroma of women made his nostrils flare and he stared at each of them in turn before settling on Woods. He was sorely tempted to torment her further, take more photos for Cunningham but that would have to wait. Going to where Libby was sitting he stopped in front of her.

"Get up," he snapped his voice filled with authority.

Doing as she was told Libby put up no resistance as he handcuffed her left wrist. Pushing her up against the wall, he secured the other end to a rusty water pipe then standing back, he admired his work before turning to Kelly.

"Follow me to the storeroom. You can pick up some supplies for yourself and your friends."

Woods observed his movements and mannerisms hoping to become familiar with his ways, she had to work out how to get through to him. Kelly had been here the longest and seemed to have his trust, perhaps she could help provide a psychological profile.

Kelly followed him out into the corridor and when they had gone, Charley let out a sigh of relief. Woods glanced at her, she could feel her pent up emotions and sympathised with her. Charley was a very striking young woman who even in her current situation oozed a sensuality that was bound to draw unwanted attention. Woods could hardly understand why Charley agreed to put herself in this situation. She must think very highly of Matthew Cunningham. Relying on the tracking system was foolhardy, she had obviously underestimated the situation and had no idea how unpleasant things could become. Thoughts turned over inside her head and she cursed herself for not observing the camera on the wall, errors like that could easily cost lives. Prioritising the tasks, she realised that the first thing she must do was asses the abilities of the women in the cell with her. Who could be relied on when the situation became critical?

Chapter Seventy Six

"WE KNOW THAT HE WAS outside Cunningham's house earlier today." DC James was on his feet addressing his colleagues in the incident room. "A Patrol car was on the scene soon after Morgan ended his call but he was nowhere to be seen. Why was that?"

"He must have been hiding somewhere." An answer came from one of the officers.

"He could have been mobile whilst on the phone and moved on once he had eyeballed the house." Another possible solution was voiced.

"He knew we were coming so buggered off smartly." No one laughed at this.

"All of these are credible ideas," James replied, "but I'm convinced he is playing games with us. He is a clever man that much we know from his army records. If he suspects that we have Cunningham in custody this might be his way of confirming it."

Everyone was staring at him, waiting for him to broaden his theory.

"He practically told Cunningham that he was standing outside his home, this leads me to believe that he is testing us. He must have known that if we were listening in on their conversation we would have our people heading for his location."

"Did Fiona confirm that Morgan was in that street at the time of the call? He could easily have discovered that Cunningham had not been home for some time by passing the house on an earlier occasion." DC Burkett sat down once she had made her point.

"Fiona was certain that Morgan was outside the house or at least in the street at the time he made the call."

This had far reaching implications. If they could pinpoint Morgan's position when he was making a call but still he remained elusive then it made their job even more difficult.

"I want the street where Cunningham lives searched for all possible hiding places. Does Morgan have access to another property close by? If he does then we need to know about it. If he makes another call from that location then I want to know exactly where to find him."

He paused for a moment as if something had just occurred to him then turning to the map he frowned. A concentration of coloured dots had been added to the map indicating the location of each call that Morgan had made and now another was placed in the street where Cunningham lived.

"As you can see, apart from these calls here," his hand swept over an area of suburbia several miles out, "the others are all grouped in and around Whitechapel." He turned to his colleagues before posing another question.

"Have there been any developments with finding DS Woods car?"

"Nothing yet. PC Yearsley is still trawling through CCTV and roadside camera footage. Patrols searching the area where she was last seen have come up with nothing. We do however have footage from a security camera belonging to a business. It shows her car briefly as it drove by. This confirms that she was in the backstreets." The detective gave James the name and address of the business.

"So, this puts her here," he said pointing at a road on the map then he studied the area thoughtfully.

"I interviewed the owner of the business," the officer continued. "He has local knowledge and tells me that Morgan and his victims couldn't possibly be holed up anywhere near there without someone knowing about it."

"He's got to be there somewhere," James replied. "Most of the calls are concentrated in this area."

Running his finger over the map, he traced a route from the main road following the back streets to where the business was located. "What are we missing?" he said thinking aloud. "There has to be something."

"We should tap into that local knowledge," DC Burkett suggested. "Make house to house calls if necessary."

"We hardly have the resources for that," James groaned at the enormity of the task. "The idea is sound," he admitted. "Perhaps we should make a list of places where the locals gather, pubs, clubs that kind of thing and hope they are not too hostile. I'll wager there are plenty of people around there who would run a mile if they saw us coming."

Laughter lightened the atmosphere in the room.

"I'm going to get mobile units to patrol this area of Whitechapel. If Morgan makes another call we need to be ready to pounce."

James was satisfied that progress was being made, each team had contributed valid ideas and a number of action plans had been agreed. The meeting was over and now he wanted to talk to Matthew Cunningham.

"DC Burkett, with me if you please."

"Why don't you ever call me Sam?" she asked as they walked along the corridor.

James glanced at her and frowned. "DS Woods would never allow me to call her Isobel."

"I'm not DS Woods am I?"

Matt was sitting at the table in interview room number one when the detectives arrived.

"We think that the abductor might be getting suspicious," James began as he settled at the table.

"Why do you say that?"

"I think he might suspect that you are in police custody."

"He gave me no reason to believe that during our conversation."

"He's playing a clever game. Has it ever occurred to you that he wanted to implicate you in his evil scheme and have you arrested?"

"Why would he do that?"

"I've no idea, but it's something that's been puzzling me for some time now."

"I have no idea who this man is, I'm certain that I've never come across him before."

"How can you be sure?"

"Well, he doesn't sound familiar and I just have a feeling that we have never met."

"Given the fact that he sends you photographs of the victims, is it possible that you might have come across him through work?" James realised that Morgan had a military background but he was making suggestions, fishing blindly for answers.

"No, he's definitely not a photographer."

"What makes you say that?"

"From the quality of his compositions for a start." Matt went on to highlight a dozen other reasons why he was not a professional photographer. "Fiona Richardson was telling me about some software that she has been running of her computer at home." He told them about the Spyware package.

"Why has she not come forward with this?" Burkett asked.

"It's not an official system, it's something that a friend of hers was developing whilst a student at university. Given the circumstances of the case, she thought it might be worth testing."

"We need to speak with Fiona." James said rising to his feet.

Chapter Seventy Seven

HE RETURNED TO HIS LAIR thinking that the police were closing in. Maybe it was time to finish what he had started. If Cunningham was in custody then he had achieved his objective, all he had to do now was tidy up. Before he could do that, he would need to carry out one more task. An incentive would be required in order to guarantee a result. Going into the command centre, he activated the camera and looked down on the women. Kelly was standing beside the detective deep in conversation, they had been locked up together for hours so what could they still have to talk about?

"I don't understand your involvement in all this." Woods said as she looked up at Kelly. "Both Libby and Charley know Matthew Cunningham. Pascale was also connected to him through work but I can find nothing that links you to him."

"Matthew Cunningham," Kelly repeated his name thoughtfully.

"I'm convinced that he is the link."

"That doesn't mean he's involved in this awful crime." Libby said defending her partner.

"Of course not, what I'm saying is that Matthew is as much a victim as the rest of us." Woods realised that Libby was unaware of his involvement in the disappearance of Pascale Dominique.

"The first time I heard his name was when Libby told me about him."

"Do you know of anything that might link you together?" Woods urged.

"No," Kelly shook her head. "I've never met him before. I didn't even know Libby or Charley until now. Pascale was here for only a short time so I didn't get to know her at all." Her eyes filled with tears as memories of what she had done surfaced.

Woods realised that Kelly must have witnessed the young woman's murder.

"Kelly," Libby called out softly. "We are here for you." Only she knew what had really happened.

"Cunningham," Kelly whispered, wiping her tears away with the back of her hand. "I used to know someone called Thomas Cunningham."

Libby looked up in surprise.

"Who is Thomas?" Woods asked softly as she noticed Libby's reaction.

"We were once close me and Thomas. We were supposed to be getting married." Turning away, Kelly began to pace the floor as memories that she had kept locked away began to escape.

"What happened?" Woods persisted after a several moments of silence.

Kelly stopped pacing and turned to face her. "It was when I told him that I was pregnant, that's when he up and left. I've not seen or heard from him since."

Libby groaned with shock. "Oh Kelly," she managed before her emotions made it impossible for her to go on. All she wanted to do was go to Kelly and hold her but she was chained to the pipe.

"Can you tell me about Thomas?" Woods continued with her questions. This had to be the link that she was looking for.

"Thomas is an officer in the British army and to be honest was far too good for me. I don't know what he saw in someone like me so I was hardly surprised when he left."

"Don't ever say that you are not good enough," Charley told her.

Ignoring her comment, Woods pressed on. "Callum is his son."

"How do you know about Callum?" Kelly exclaimed as she moved closer to Woods.

"When you disappeared we interviewed your sister Caroline. She is taking care of Callum. In fact it was something your son said that helped with our investigation."

"Thomas is Matt's brother." Libby told them suddenly.

Kelly stared at her in disbelief and Libby, shocked by the connection could hardly believe that he could be so cruel.

"Dane Morgan is a soldier," Woods told them before going on quickly. "Maybe these men know each other." She had asked James to get the name of Morgan's commanding officer in Afghanistan. Could they have served together? Her eyes narrowed. Why might that be significant?

He paused for a moment in anticipation of what he was about to do then, entering the password he peered into the camera before the door clicked open.

Kelly shrank away to the back of the cell where she stood beside Libby. She could sense danger and wanted no part of it. Standing in the doorway, Morgan glared at Woods. He was carrying a camera and she had little doubt as to what he had in mind. She struggled to focus on questions that might distract him, attempt to use psychology to dissuade him from making her situation worse but her brain refused to work.

Holding up his camera he peered at the little screen on the back and used the automatic focus to improve his view then once he was satisfied, he leered at her lecherously.

"Kelly," he growled. "Get over here." He watched menacingly as she moved slowly towards him.

"Unbutton her jacket."

She stared at him sourly.

"Do it," he hissed and given no choice, Kelly did as she was told.

She looked at Woods apologetically and saw the expression of defiance displayed clearly on the detective's face.

His camera recorded every detail and when he was finished, he stood back.

"Trousers," he murmured as he checked the shots on the little screen.

Kelly stared at him in disbelief.

"Look," he snapped. "It's simple, either you do as you are told or I will make things very unpleasant for Charley." Reaching out he grabbed the corner of the blanket covering the model and in a single movement exposed her semi naked body.

"No," Kelly cried as Charley squealed in terror.

"Remove her trousers."

Moving slowly, Kelly had no option but do as she was told. The atmosphere inside the room was charged, Charley was battling with a panic attack and Libby was crying silently. Kelly felt like a villain, she was still fully clothed and also had her freedom.

"Come on woman," he shouted, "tear them off."

It was proving difficult to complete the task. The trousers were torn at both knees and the fabric parted easily but still it was impossible to remove them completely. He growled in frustration and pushing Kelly aside, he produced a knife and moved in.

Woods remained still, it was the only way to avoid serious injury as the razor sharp knife cut away her clothing. Inside she was screaming with frustration and fury. How dare he subject her to such treatment? Almost naked, she could do nothing but lay there as he took more photos. Her greatest humiliation would come later when facing her colleagues knowing that everyone had seen these images. Her immediate future might be uncertain but she had to hold onto the belief that a rescue team were on their way and their ordeal would soon be over.

Moving around the table, he photographed her from every angle and when he was finished he looked down at her, his faced flushed with humour.

"The dangerously efficient detective reduced to a vulnerable wreck."

Charley wept silently as she watched him at work. Never in her wildest dreams could she imagine anything like this and she wondered how Isobel managed to remain so calm.

Stepping forward, Kelly asked. "Can I cover Charley?" she glanced at the blanket on the floor.

"Of course, I will be back later to take care of her."

The blanket offered little comfort but it was Kelly's touch that calmed Charley's frayed nerves.

DC James made his way back to the incident room. He had already requested a car to take Fiona home to collect the Spyware package. It was decided that the Cybercrime team would run the program on a standalone computer. His phone began to vibrate so reaching into his pocket he pulled it out.

"James," he spoke clearly.

"Dennis, it's Terry, Terry Ashton."

"DI Ashton," he replied, surprised to hear his voice. "Morning guv."

"Drop the DI bit will you, I'm no longer your guv."

"Sorry sir," it didn't seem right to use his Christian name. DI Ashton had been his senior officer and mentor when he worked for the Met and old habits were hard to break.

"Listen Dennis, I've heard about Izzy and I want to help. Can you meet me at the Richmond Hotel?" He wanted to know all about her abduction also, what the police were doing to find her.

"Yes of course."

The Richmond Hotel was a favourite haunt for the officers of the Met. A room was permanently set aside for their use, it was known by hotel staff as the Metropolitan bar. It provided a place where police business could be discussed in a relaxed and secure environment.

"When is your lunch break, perhaps we could meet up then?"

James almost laughed, lunch breaks had become a luxury that he could not afford, but today he would make an exception. He checked his watch before saying.

"If you can give me an hour I'll meet you then."

"Perfect," Ashton replied.

Twenty minutes later Fiona was back with the Spyware package and it wasn't long before it was up and running on a computer in the Cybercrime department.

"Keep me informed," James said. "I want to know the moment you have a result." He had no doubts that the system would work, Fiona wished that she shared his optimism.

When she returned to the surveillance suite, Fiona found Matthew nursing a cup of coffee. He looked lost and out of place, but when he looked up, his smile was genuine. She felt sorry for him, he was in an awkward position. Caught somewhere between police collaborator and felon, she knew that he was involved in the abduction of women but she also realised that he was himself a victim. Somehow, he had become embroiled in a game of manipulation completely against his will.

"DC James has got the Cybercrime people to run the Spyware program." She told him and visibly he appeared relieved. "They might have better luck with it but don't pin your hopes on a positive outcome."

His smile faded.

"I have no idea if it will actually work," she continued softly.

"We must cling to every scrap of hope," he mumbled in return.

His phone began to ring.

"It's him."

Running to her workstation, Fiona activated the tracking program before giving him the signal to answer.

"Cunningham, are you with the police?"

His heart missed a beat as he struggled for an answer.

"Why would you ask that?" he replied a little too quickly. "You told me quite clearly not to have contact with the authorities."

"Where are you now?"

"I'm with friends in Cambridge." It was all he could think of.

"Where in Cambridge?"

"I'm in a little cafe near to one of the colleges." He could remember going to one with Libby once.

"Let me speak to one of your friends."

He glanced at Fiona who stared back at him wide eyed then suddenly she held out her hand.

"Hello," she spoke confidently into the phone.

"Who are you, what is your name?"

"I'm Fiona, one of Matt's friends."

"Hello Fiona," he paused before going on. "Tell me, where are you?"

She hesitated, playing her part of a confused college friend.

"We are in a little cafe in Cambridge."

314

"What is it called and where are you located?"

Fiona frowned as she struggled to recall a place that she knew from her student days.

"The Red Brick cafe," she told him. "It's in Grange Road near Robinson College." Crossing her fingers, she hoped that it was still there.

"It's very quiet." He said suspiciously.

"It's what we call a study cafe. Students come here to work, it's a bit like a library."

He grunted and she was convinced that he did not believe her.

"Nice to speak to you Fiona, put me back onto Matt will you."

She passed him the phone.

"Cunningham, stand by to receive more photos. I think you might like this set."

The connection was terminated but before he went Matt was sure that he heard the cry of a child.

"Whitechapel again," Fiona said as a location appeared on her screen. "Brick Lane this time."

"He told me that he was sending more images."

Fiona looked up at him before saying. "We had better inform DC James."

James was standing next to Terry Ashton at the bar in the Richmond Hotel.

"The last time I was in here," Terry smiled, "we were celebrating the end of a murder case."

James was familiar with the job that almost claimed the life of Ashton's daughter. "Let's sit down," he gestured towards a couple of comfortable looking wingback chairs.

"Are you aware that Izzy and I spoke just the other evening?"

"No, I didn't know that." James admitted.

"We discussed the case, she also told me about the problems she is having with Wyman."

"Did she indeed," James looked at him gravely. "Something is going on between them." He felt unable to say more at this stage.

"How do you find Wyman, is he giving you the support that you need?"

James looked at him again sensing that Ashton already knew the answer.

"Just as I suspected." James didn't need to say anything. "Look, if it would help I could have a word with Brian Calvary."

"Surely that won't be necessary," he stuttered when Ashton mentioned the

Assistant Commissioner's name.

"If I thought that Wyman was deliberately putting Izzy's life at risk then I wouldn't hesitate."

"There are a number of irregularities in his dealings with the case." James admitted before going on with the details.

"With all respect to you Dennis, you are hardly senior enough to be running a case like this. There are protocols that must be followed; it should be headed up by a DI or even Wyman himself."

"True," James nodded. "Wyman is the SIO but we don't see much of him on the shop floor."

Terry nodded gravely before dropping the subject. He had heard enough to convince him that Brian Calvary should be informed.

"Izzy told me that the abductor, Dane Morgan is operating from somewhere in Whitechapel."

"Yes," James nodded, "but we are not sure where exactly."

"Izzy seems to think that the old police station and court house or whatever it's called is the place."

"All those buildings have been checked."

"Well that may be so but you know as well as I that searching every building thoroughly is an impossible task. If the place looks secure and unused then it's usually ticked off the list. You have to admit though, it would make an ideal hideout."

"The photos that I've seen could easily have been taken from inside an old police cell."

"Why not send a team in for a closer look. Do you know who owns the building?"

"I believe it's currently owned by a consortium of property developers. It's going to be converted into a hotel with some of the larger cells turned into luxury bedrooms."

Terry stared at him in amazement. He couldn't imagine paying to spend the night in an old police cell. "Tell me more about how Izzy was abducted."

James told him what he knew but it was precious little. He described seeing Morgan on CCTV as he approached her car then moments before they drove away her mobile phone was thrown onto the road.

Terry remained silent as he thought about what James had just told him. "If it were me running the case, I would contact the owners and get access to the old courthouse." He felt sure this is where they would find the women.

Chapter Seventy Eight

"Is Cunningham in police custody?" His face was so close that she could feel his breath hot against her cheek.

"No," she lied.

"Where is he?"

"I have no idea. Why would I know?"

He backed away slowly, glaring at her menacingly then he turned to face Libby and asked. "Why would Cunningham go to Cambridge?"

"Cambridge?" Libby stared back at him blankly.

"Who is Fiona?" He took a step towards her and Libby whimpered.

"I, I don't know," she replied in an unsteady voice.

"He said that he was with a friend called Fiona."

Libby shook her head. "I don't know who she is."

He stopped and thought for a moment before asking. "Does he have any links with Cambridge?"

"I don't think so," Libby whispered. She was terrified that if she said the wrong thing he would attack her again but then quite suddenly, he turned away and continued questioning Woods.

"Is Cunningham in police custody?" he asked again.

"No," she replied shaking her head.

"Why don't I believe you?"

Woods stared back at him in defiance but inside was shaking fearfully.

"I think that both you and Cunningham are being untruthful."

"If you are so convinced then why do you insist on asking me?" Keeping her voice even was a struggle but it was crucial to stand up to him and not display fear. The moment she broke down, he would have complete control and she must not allow that to happen.

"I simply want confirmation, I don't like to rely purely on conjecture." He asked her again. "Do you have Cunningham in custody?"

"No he is not."

Slowly he pulled the blanket covering Charley away leaving her exposed again then moving closer to Woods, he described in whispered tones what he would do to the young woman if she continued to deny the truth.

Woods gasped and turned her face away. How could she let him get away with this? His threats were horrifying and she had no doubt that he would carry them out. She glanced at Charley who looked terrified. Her training had not prepared her for something like this and she could think of nothing that would help disarm the situation.

Watching her closely he knew that he had won, but to underpin his victory he reached out for the only item of clothing that Charley had left and slipped his fingers under the flimsy fabric. She squirmed and whimpered as she tried to get away but the ropes holding her down restricted her movements.

"No," Woods pleaded, "don't do that."

"Is Cunningham in police custody?"

She knew that once confirmed, all communication with Cunningham would be severed and the police would have nothing more to go on. Closing her eyes, she also knew that she couldn't allow him to carry out his unspeakable threat. Charley did not deserve that.

"Yes," she whispered.

"What did you just say?" He snarled pulling the fabric tighter between his fingers.

"Yes, he is in police custody."

Leaving Charley alone, he moved to the foot of the table. Closing her eyes she waited for him to make his next move certain that he would make her pay for holding back the truth. For several excruciating moments, he simply remained there staring at her and breathing heavily. Libby and Kelly watched nervously both unable to move or react to the drama playing out in front of them. Suddenly he turned away and stormed out of the room slamming the door shut behind him.

DC James returned to headquarters accompanied by Terry Ashton. He was determined to share everything with his old colleague in the hope that he could provide some answers to their questions. If Wyman was unwilling to assign a more experienced officer to the investigation then he would unofficially appoint one himself.

"Dennis," DC Burkett said the moment he appeared.

"Sam," he replied using her Christian name for the first time. "This is Terry Ashton, he used to work here."

"Yes," she said moving towards them. "I've heard of you and I'm so pleased to meet you."

"My reputation precedes me," Terry grinned as he gripped her hand.

"Indeed it does. I'm Samantha, DC Sam Burkett."

James left them to get to know each other and went in search of a computer. He wanted to access his messages. After a while, Terry joined him in the incident room where he took his time to study the information on the evidence board.

"Paul Goddard from Cybercrime phoned earlier." Burkett told James when he had finished on the computer. "They have received another email from the abductor."

"We had better get up there then and take a look." He glanced at Terry. "Won't you join us?"

The officers of Cybercrime were surprised to see Terry, most of them knew him and were happy to see him again. James hung back as they greeted each other before reminding them of the purpose of their visit.

"The message came in about half an hour ago. Fiona also informed us that Morgan made another phone call telling Cunningham to expect an email."

"Have you opened it?" James asked.

"No, given the delicate nature of the earlier message I thought it best to wait for you."

They squeezed in to the tiny office where Cunningham's computer stood on a small table. It was tight but Goddard managed to sit down then accessing the message they waited.

DC Burkett breathed in sharply when the first image appeared. "This is appalling," she whispered.

Terry grunted, it was more serious than he anticipated. Seeing Izzy like this infuriated him but he managed to control his emotions.

"No one else must see these," James said once they had seen the rest. "Same as before, but this time I don't want Wyman to know about this."

Goddard glanced up but said nothing.

"Don't worry about Wyman," Terry growled. "I'll be taking care of him."

"Paul," one of his colleagues appeared at the door. "You really need to see this."

They followed him to the computer running the Spyware program. Fortunately, there was more space and they all gathered comfortably around the screen, which displayed a row of letters and numbers.

"A GPS reference," Paul said recognising the sequence. "All we need to do is run this through the computer to establish the location." He pressed a series of keys and the screen switched to a street map then Terry glanced at James.

"She was right all along." James whispered. "We need to get a team out there right now."

He bolted the door to the exercise yard and set up his defence system. If someone attempted to come in that way, they would get a nasty surprise. It was the only access to this side of the building. The doors and windows at the front were secure and there was a steel security fence surrounding the entrance. Anyone trying to get in would require heavy cutting equipment or keys to the locks. Security cameras covered the perimeter, these were linked directly to the computer in his command centre where the system would alert him to anyone trying to get in. Checking each camera in turn, he could see the white van and the detective's car still in the exercise yard. There was nothing he could do about that now besides what did it matter, he would be long gone before the authorities could catch him.

Accessing the camera in their cell, he checked on the women. Charley was covered by the blanket but the detective enjoyed no luxuries. He zoomed in and studied the curves of her body. She was an attractive woman, it would be a pity to destroy her. He thought about the French model. She was a lively one, it was her temper that sealed her fate. He could not resist having some fun with her before she went. He considered doing the same with the detective but chastised himself for allowing his mind to run wild. If he were to torture her in such a way then he would be no better than the rebels he had come across in Afghanistan. He regretted doing what he did to Pascale, it had been an unfortunate slip of discipline. Perhaps he should get a group photo, it would be a fitting trophy, a record of their time together. Reaching for his camera, he got to his feet and went to the torture chamber.

"Right Ladies," he said as if addressing a group of friends. "I want to get some more pictures." He raised the camera so they could see what he had in mind. "Kelly, perhaps you could stand beside Charley." He began to organise the women and as he moved around the cell, Woods observed him carefully. She had to say something, it was her duty to question him.

"Did you see action in Afghanistan?" she asked suddenly.

He stopped what he was doing and turned to face her. "Yes, I was in Afghan."

"Were you there for very long?"

"Long enough to discover what a hell hole it can be."

"So you were part of the peace keeping mission."

"Peace keeping," he laughed, "you have no idea."

"Why don't you tell me what it was like?"

"You think this is unpleasant?" He glanced around the cell. "If you were held by the rebels you would have been ripped apart by now and left to bake in the sun." Images of a female officer tied helplessly to an improvised wooden frame filled his head.

She noticed his pained expression and decided to dig deeper.

"Did you come across an officer by the name of Thomas Cunningham?"

His expression darkened. "Why do you ask?" he hissed through clenched teeth.

"I just wondered if he worked with you. Was he one of the officers in charge?"

"Cunningham was there," he nodded.

"Was he in command of your team?"

He stared at her through blurring vision as suppressed memories began to stir.

"Did you know that Thomas is Matthew Cunningham's brother?" she continued.

Kelly could sense danger so backed away slowly. She could not understand what Isobel was doing. Clearly, probing his past was upsetting him, it would only make matters worse.

Suddenly he snapped and struck out. The blow caught the side of her face forcing her head back violently against the hard stainless steel table. Spots floated in front of her eyes as she struggled to focus but the assault did not end there. Pain exploded across her chest and she held her breath as blow after blow rained down.

"Stop it, stop it." Charley cried, she was at breaking point and could take no more of his brutality.

"Leave her," Kelly moved up beside him and put her hand on his arm. "You don't have to do this."

He stared at her blindly, his eyes huge and dark and she thought that he might direct his aggression onto her. They had arrived at a standoff, him shaking with demented rage and she trembling with fear. Neither of them could back down then suddenly he roared ferociously and ran out leaving them stunned.

"Jesus!" Kelly said grasping Woods by the shoulders. "Are you okay?"

Woods stopped groaning and as her vision cleared, began to assess her pain. Her head was spinning mercilessly and her ribs had taken a beating.

"What do you think you were doing asking him all those questions?"

"I have to establish a motive. It's important to know why he is doing this."

"Even if it means getting us all killed?"

Suddenly he was back.

"Get out of my way." Pushing Kelly aside, he swept past.

In his hand, he carried a fold up tripod to which he attached a projector. Setting it up, he beamed a light against the wall where a test card projection appeared, then after making a few adjustments he turned it off and left.

"What's he doing now?" Kelly worried.

Several minutes later, they heard a noise coming form along the corridor. He appeared again this time pushing a trolley. He entered the cell then closing the door behind him the lock clicked into place. Kelly gasped in horror she had seen this before. The trolley held a tray containing a syringe and a thin bladed knife. He positioned it beside the table and reaching for Woods arm grinned down at her.

She watched horrified as he picked up the syringe. Pat Fleming had told her that Pascale was anesthetised using Ketamine, she had called it the 'drug of war'.

"Don't worry," he said when he saw the look on her face. "You won't feel a thing."

"You can't do this," she said trying to break his grip but her arm was trapped, she was unable to move.

"Who is going to stop me?" he hissed.

He pricked her arm with the needle and she felt the drug enter her bloodstream. It wasn't long before darkness hovered at the edges of her vision, muscles that had been tense before began to relax and she lost all feeling before slipping into unconsciousness. Her last thoughts were of Terry Ashton and her colleagues at the Met.

Chapter Seventy Nine

DC JAMES ASSEMBLED HIS TEAM before they set out for the old Magistrates Court and Police Station in Shoreditch. Close to Whitechapel, this was the area from where most of Morgan's phone calls had originated and as the car pulled to the side of the road, the first thing he saw was a fine looking building with graffitied boards at the windows. A steel security fence surrounded the entrance restricting much of the pathway and signs fixed to the fence informed the public that this was a building site although work had not yet begun.

James wasted no time, the moment the car stopped he climbed out. "Let's have a look round the back." Burkett and Ashton glanced at each other as they hurried after him.

They followed a high brick wall, which led them away from the main road and along a narrow side street. Buildings had gone up in the shadow of the wall sometime in the last century and Ashton studied them carefully. He could hardly imagine the open space that would have once surrounded the old courthouse when it was first constructed.

"This seems to be the only way in." The sound of James' voice interrupted Ashton's thoughts. "We need to see over the wall." Turning his back on the heavy wooden gate, James observed the buildings opposite searching for a window overlooking the yard but he was out of luck.

"We could call the fire brigade." Burkett suggested. "A long ladder would allow us a good view."

Craning his neck, James looked up and immediately discounted the idea. He did not possess a head for heights, he preferred to keep his feet firmly on the ground.

"I want someone down here with a drone," he said. "We can get an aerial view of the whole complex before planning our assault."

Pulling a phone from her pocket, Burkett moved away from the men before making her call. "They should be here within half an hour," she told them a few moments later.

"Good," James smiled. "That gives us time to poke around a bit first."

Returning to the front of the building, they found that someone had managed to remove the chain securing the steel fencing and stepping past the uniformed officer guarding the entrance, Ashton went to inspect the panels covering the windows. Nothing seemed to have been tampered with, the ornate double doors at the entrance were sealed and locked, it seemed that no one had used them for some time. Other members of the team were busy searching areas of grass and checking items of kit that construction workers had left in anticipation of starting work.

None of them observed the tiny security cameras set up on the corner of the building. One overlooked the main entrance and pathway while the other faced along the side street allowing a view of the rear gate. Both cameras had powerful zoom capabilities that provided Morgan with high resolution surveillance.

"The cells must be located at the back of the building," Ashton said. "It's no use going in through this way, we've got to get into that exercise yard."

"We'll need some heavy equipment if we are going to get through that gate," James nodded in agreement. "There must be access directly into the cells from the yard."

"Once the drone is here we'll get some answers." Ashton replied as they returned to the rear of the building. Seconds later, they heard the sound of Burkett running to catch up.

"The men with the drone have arrived." She told them as an unmarked van passed slowly.

It stopped beside the gate and two uniformed officers got out and introduced themselves before James explained what was required.

"This UAV will give you all the answers." One of the officers told him as he swung open the rear doors.

"UAV?" James frowned.

"Unmanned Aerial Vehicle."

"Oh, you mean the drone."

"This baby is not simply a drone," he explained as he lifted it carefully from the back of the van. "It's one of our technologically advanced Aeryon Skyrangers."

James was unimpressed. "Will it do the job?"

"This little fellow won't let you down."

Both men climbed into the back of the van and took up their positions, one in the pilot's seat the other at a computer screen. He would follow exactly what the UAV was seeing and record its progress.

The UAV was sitting on the road just metres from where they were standing and when it took off Ashton was amazed at how quiet it was. It rose effortlessly into the air, disappeared over the top of the wall and in seconds was beaming pictures back to the computer in the van.

"That's DS Woods' car," Burkett said recognising the vehicle the moment it appeared on the screen. A small white van was parked beside it.

"Can you zoom in on the licence plate?" James pulled his notebook from his pocket. "It's the vehicle used to abduct Charley Baker," he said moving closer. "Can you get a look inside?"

The pilot skilfully manoeuvred alongside the van then, dropping down to hover over the bonnet, they had a clear view through the windscreen.

"Nothing inside, the vehicle is empty."

He steered the UAV around the yard as the officer at the computer mapped details of its layout. Once that was done, he flew along the building before turning towards the door in the corner.

"It looks solid enough, no windows or bars but it seems to have a sheet steel cladding covering its surface."

"How do you know it's not made completely from steel?" Burkett asked.

"It's set into a timber frame," the officer told her. "I would expect to see a replacement steel door set into a steel frame. The keyhole suggests a mortice lock, the type found on old wooden doors."

"There is another key hole lower down," she pointed out.

"What about the windows?" James asked referring to the openings they had seen high up on the side of the building. "Any chance of a peek inside?"

"I'll do my best, but looking at the state of the glass."

Grime streaked the tiny windows and oxide from some of the steel bars stained the glass making it impossible to see through. One thing was clear however, there were no lights on inside the building and no signs of life.

"Sorry," the pilot glanced at James, "no can do."

"What about the gate. Can you get up close and have a look at the chain securing it?"

Turning away from the window the UAV swooped down towards the ground before coming to a stop in front of the gate. The camera focused and the optical zoom enlarged the area they were interested in.

"Close enough for you?"

The identification number of the padlock stood out clearly on the screen so the officer typed in a search command and the computer responded with the technical details.

"It's a high tensile lock so we can assume the chain will be the same."

"Whilst we are here, could you fly over the building and record every detail. I don't want our man escaping from some secret doorway on the roof."

"I'll let you know if we find anything interesting."

James stepped down from the van and checked his watch.

"Where are the 'heavy crew'?"

The 'heavy crew' carried a vast range of engineering equipment in their mobile workshop and could cope with almost any situation. They were often relied on to gain access into heavily reinforced entrances. He didn't have to wait long, they soon heard the sound of a lorry reversing into the street.

Ashton stood back with Burkett as James briefed the crew. He showed them the images of the lock and chain on the inside of the gate.

"We would normally access the chain and cut it using shears or a grinder." The man in charge told him. "We could use ladders to get over the wall and lower the equipment down."

"No time for that I'm afraid," James replied. "We potentially have hostages inside that building and time is becoming a crucial factor."

"Okay," the man nodded thoughtfully. "We'll use a hydraulic ram to force it open. The frame will either let go or the surrounding brickwork will collapse, either way you'll have access."

James agreed to this destructive method and men began to pull equipment from the back of the lorry then fifteen minutes later, they were ready to go. It wasn't long before the wooden frame splintered, sending the gate crashing to the ground. The detectives entered the yard followed by the heavy crew.

"Looks like you might need a hand with that door too."

The door was locked and would require more than a shoulder to force it open.

"We'll try the old fashioned method first," the man said and a few minutes later James stared wide eyed in amazement.

"Bloody hell!" he exclaimed. "It looks like an old medieval battering ram."

It took four men to heave the contraption into position and a lot of effort to get it in motion but as soon as it began to batter the door, the steel cladding buckled then the wooden frame gave way.

"I've seen everything now," James grinned as the men laid the ram to one side.

"I'll go in and clear away any debris," one of them said shining his torch into the darkened corridor.

James was happy to let him advance into the building, he must have done this many times before so was aware of the risks. Seconds later, he reappeared.

"All clear," he called happily.

James moved forward preparing to take charge but the man turned and disappeared inside the building.

"Shouldn't we wait for back up?" Burkett asked.

James was about to reply when suddenly there was a dull explosion.

"Bloody hell!" He exclaimed as smoke and dust billowed from the shattered doorway.

"Alan," one of the men called out and running towards the building, he directed a powerful light into the dust and smoke filled corridor. His colleague was lying just inside the door having staggered backwards before collapsing.

"Ambulance," he shouted before dropping to his knees.

Alan was unconscious. Blood soaked his overalls from a wound in his thigh but after a quick assessment, it was considered safe to move him. There seemed to be no immediate danger from fire or fumes but it was unclear what else might be waiting for them further along the corridor.

"Right," James said reacting to the situation. "Clearly we need SCO19 and a bomb disposal unit."

SCO19 was the Specialist Firearms Command. They would provide cover for the engineers who would deal with any other explosive devices.

"Right," Morgan said looking at Kelly. "You know what to do."

Unable to move, she stared at him in disbelief.

Turning to the trolley, he picked up the knife and placed it carefully on Woods stomach.

"Come on we don't have much time. You don't want her to wake up do you?"

Kelly remained fixed to the spot. The thought of going through this again horrified her.

"Perhaps you need persuading," he sneered and moving away, he went to the projector and beamed a live video against the wall.

Kelly stared in disbelief then she gasped, her face contorting with shock and rage. "Callum," she cried.

Her little boy looked terrified his eyes staring huge and dark from a face streaked with tears. She could hear him whimpering, the sound coming from a little speaker on the side of the projector.

"What have you done to him?" Kelly shrieked.

"Nothing yet," Morgan hissed, "but that can change. Do as you are told and he will be fine."

Kelly swallowed noisily, her eyes darting between her son and Woods.

"Why is he tied up?" She could see a metal strap around his wrist and a chain leading to the corner of the iron frame.

"Would you like to see what happens when I press this button?" Holding up what looked like a key fob he grinned.

"What is that?" she cried anxiously.

"When I activate this it sends a signal to an electrical transformer that releases a current into the bed frame."

He didn't need to say more, Kelly understood the implications and grinding her teeth in frustration, clenched her fists. She couldn't allow him to get away with this.

"A short burst is painful but not life threatening but a constant current would be fatal." He waved the device tauntingly in front of her face.

Rising up on the balls of her feet Kelly prepared to launch an attack but what good would that do? With a single blow, he could knock her to the ground then electrocute her son. Her chest heaved with sadness and frustration as she made her decision.

"Do as you are told and Callum will be fine."

Moving trance-like to the edge of the table where Woods was laying her head filled with miserable images of her son's suffering. She stopped and hesitated, reluctant to go on and as she reached for the knife, her fingers brushed against soft, warm skin. Woods stomach rose and fell gently as she breathed and Kelly trembled at the thought of ending her life. Her eyes were drawn to the spot between her breasts where the knife would slip effortlessly under bone just below the sternum.

"Think of your son," he whispered, his face just inches from her ear then reaching for her hand, he guided the point of the knife before going on. "All you have to do is push firmly and aim for the left shoulder."

Closing her eyes, she tried to ignore the ghost of Pascale lying in the same place on the table. The knife had slipped into her body so easily and Kelly groaned as the image refused to go away. How could she possibly do it again, taking a life was unthinkable. Forcing her eyes open, Kelly looked at the woman who so desperately wanted to help them. She appeared relaxed, serene almost, the lines of worry and stress gone from her face, her lips curved into a natural smile.

"Do it," he hissed as his fingers closed around the device.

Charley cried out at the sound of a child in distress and Libby stared wide eyed at the image projected onto the wall. Suddenly Kelly snapped, she could take no more. The sound of her child in agony triggered a reflex, an emotion that he had sorely underestimated. Striking out, she plunged the knife into his chest, stabbing repeatedly in a frenzied attempt to save her child.

Morgan staggered backwards, his face a mask of disbelief. The tripod supporting the projector crashed to the ground then falling against the frame holding Charley, he steadied himself. His fingers tightened around the device, but Kelly anticipated his actions and screaming with fury drove the point of the knife through his hand impaling it to the wooden frame. The device fell from his grip and she kicked it away across the floor.

He lunged forward with his free arm clawing at her face, but slowed by his wounds Kelly was able to pull the knife free. Staggering forward he wrapped his arms around her and lifting her off her feet squeezed. She tried desperately to wriggle free but his grip was firm, crushing her chest until it was impossible to breathe. Woods moaned, the effects of anaesthetic beginning to wear off, but she was not yet aware of events unfolding around her.

Releasing his grip, he reached for the knife but Kelly was ready. Holding it out of reach, she twisted away and bringing her outstretched arm round in an arc she used the momentum to drive the blade into his neck.

"You will never get out of here," he gasped, his fingers clawing at the hilt. "You are all going to die including your son."

He began to choke and unable to remove the blade collapsed to his knees, then slowly he pitched forward.

The women remained frozen for several moments unable to believe what had just happened. Kelly trembled uncontrollably as blood pooled around her feet. She had reached the limit of her endurance and as her overwrought muscles began to relax, she swayed drunkenly and almost collapsed.

The bomb disposal engineers sent a robot into the building to assess the way ahead as armed officers covered the windows. It was unlikely that Morgan would employ sniper tactics but they were taking no chances. Twenty minutes later, the robot returned.

"It's safe to enter," the officer in charge announced, "but caution is strongly advised."

His team led the way followed by the armed police officers leaving James, Burkett and Ashton to follow on behind. The corridor was oppressive and narrow, a typical Victorian penal block that offered no luxury. The first cell they came to displayed evidence of recent occupation.

"This must be where he strung them up and took his photos." James said eyeing the rope and winch system fixed to the roof above their heads.

Burkett moved slowly around this depressing space before stooping to pick up an item of clothing and running her fingers through the ruined material found no evidence of blood. She did however recognise the faint aroma of perfume clinging to the threads it belonged to Isobel Woods.

Leaving the cell, they moved further into the building passing a collection of dreary and identical rooms. Eventually they came to a door that not only looked different to the others it was locked.

"This is unusual." Ashton said looking at the digital keypad and camera fixed to the wall.

"Some kind of high tech locking system," Burkett remarked as she placed her hand against the cold surface of the door.

"It probably requires a coded password before it will open. It also appears to rely on facial or retinal recognition." He put his ear to the door but could hear nothing from within.

"This door is not original." James said stating the obvious. "Even the peephole is electronically controlled."

"DC James," the officer called out. "We have found some kind of command centre."

James rushed along the corridor passing the cell used as a storeroom, armed officers and engineers moved out of his way. The door to the command centre was open and passing through, the first thing he noticed was the computer sitting on the table.

"We have army kit here," the officer said as he went around the room but James was not interested, his focus was on the computer. Sitting down at the table, he prepared to access the machine but then a shout went up from further along the corridor.

"Sir, we have found something," a soldier appeared at the door. "A small child chained to a bed."

DC Burkett reacted immediately and following the man with James trailing behind, they went to investigate.

"It's Callum Spencer."

The child looked up at the sound of his name.

"Don't worry son, we'll soon have you out of here." James crouched down and took hold of the little boy's hand who smiled weakly as he recognised the detective.

Ashton remained in the command centre pressing a series of keys on the keyboard but the computer refused to give up its secrets.

"What are you looking for sir?" the officer asked when he returned.

"The cell door opens electronically so access must be controlled by this machine."

"Do you mind if I take a look? I'm not too bad with a computer." He smiled at the older man and Ashton, aware of his technical limitations, gladly stepped aside.

The young man sat down and soon had images scrolling across the screen.

"These are from inside the cell," he said over his shoulder and Ashton moved in for a closer look.

"That's Izzy," he gasped. "One of our colleagues," he explained as the officer glanced at him quizzically.

"What the hell has been going on in there?" he asked when he realised the woman tied to a stainless steel table was almost naked.

"Can you pan the camera around?" Ashton asked ignoring his question.

"No it seems to be fixed to the wall. I can zoom out, widen our field of view."

The picture became clearer as the camera zoomed out.

"Good Lord!" he exclaimed, "there's more."

Three other women appeared then they saw the body of a man on the floor.

"Is that a weapon in his neck?"

Ashton looked closer. This must be Dane Morgan the abductor, he thought. A woman was making her way around a wooden frame, loosening the ropes that held another victim down.

"Can you zoom in again on my colleague? Ashton was concerned for Izzy. He checked her body for fresh wounds. Her skin was discoloured with bruises and there were angry looking grazes at her knees. She was not moving but appeared to be breathing then he spotted the syringe sitting in a tray on a trolley beside her. He realised then that she must have been drugged.

"We have to get inside that cell."

"Did you say there is a security system controlling the door?"

"Yes," Ashton nodded. "It probably relies on a password and facial recognition."

"I'm afraid it goes further than that." The officer turned to look at him. "If this is to be believed," he nodded at the computer, "that door contains a complex explosive device."

James appeared. "What's this about an explosive device?"

"It's the door to the cell," Ashton told him.

"It seems to be rigged up to the security device." The officer said giving them the details. "I can only guess that it will detonate if the wrong code is entered or the sequence of input is disrupted."

"Bloody hell!" James groaned. "Can it be defused?"

"Looking at the complexity of the technology it would be tricky." He didn't want to say more without checking the door for himself.

Filing from the office, they retraced their steps along the corridor. The officer looked first at the way the door was constructed before turning his attentions to the touchpad and camera.

"It would be a disaster to tamper with this," he began. "The door appears to be constructed using high tensile steel so it would be very difficult to drill. The hinges are integral so we can't get at them. A thermal cutting process like oxy-gas or plasma would result in detonation so that leaves the electronics." He studied the touchpad again before shaking his head. "Any attempt at putting this out of action would trigger a signal between the computer and the door which is effectively the bomb." He looked up at them. "It's packed with explosives."

"Can't we approach it from the other direction," James asked. "We could take out the computer."

"No, that's impossible. If the computer goes off line or powers down or the program supporting it is tampered with then the bomb will detonate."

"Well let's hope we don't have a power cut then," James groaned. "So what you are saying is the only way to get inside that cell is by inputting the correct password and using the facial recognition device."

"I'm afraid so."

They returned to the command centre.

"What if we broke through the wall into the cell, couldn't we get the women out that way?"

Suddenly an alarm sounded on the computer and they visibly stiffened.

"Gentlemen," the officer said gravely as he studied the screen. "I'm afraid that the situation has become critical. There seems to be a timing device linked to the bomb. Your abductor set it up and it requires constant attention. He must have updated it recently but now it needs updating again." He tapped at the keyboard and a complicated timing device appeared on the screen. "We affectively have just under twenty minutes before the whole place goes up. I would say there is enough power in that bomb to take out this entire building."

"Can't you override it?" James asked his voice rising with stress.

"Not without a password."

"Not another bloody password!" he took a step backwards and rubbed a hand over his face before going on. "How long will it take to smash through the wall?"

"These old industrial bricks are extremely hard. There will also be some other kind of reinforcing within the wall. We don't have time to break through. We can't use a controlled explosion or ram the wall with a heavy vehicle because any kind of vibration might set off the bomb."

"Then we need to find the password and use the facial recognition device."

"I can probably work it out but first we have to clear this area." He called for his second in command.

"Evacuate the building and inform the authorities that we have an unexploded device on a timer. We have less than twenty minutes before it goes up so I want everyone within a hundred metres moved out, that includes those in the surrounding properties."

"Yes sir."

They realised that the man had an impossible task.

"We need to communicate with the women inside that cell," Ashton said. "Did you say the abductor uses a mobile phone to call Matthew Cunningham?"

"Yes," James replied.

"Well, I can't see a phone in here so maybe he has it on him."

"If he does it would be turned off. We need to find a way of getting the women to check his pockets and turn it on."

"Is there a gap under the door?" the officer said as his fingers danced hurriedly over the keyboard.

They both looked at him blankly.

"The solution is simple, write a note and slip it under the door."

The detectives rushed out, James reaching for his notebook as they went then he scribbled a note and pushed it under the door.

"We have to draw their attention to it," Ashton said.

"We'll have to rattle the door."

"You know what he said about vibrations."

"We don't have much choice, besides the clock is ticking."

"You get back to the command centre and activate the camera in the cell. We have to know when they spot the message."

Ashton remained by the door and gently began to tap with his knuckle increasing the pressure until he was hammering with his fist. Only then did the women inside the cell hear him.

"Terry, they have the message." James shouted.

Kelly read the note. "The police have found us. We need to check his pockets for a phone."

They looked at each other, reluctant to touch his body. Kelly groaned

333

before crouching down then running her hands over his pockets she found nothing. James watched from the command centre.

"I don't think he has a phone," he called to Ashton.

Scribbling another note, he told them they would have a password for the lock soon. He decided not to mention the bomb or the short time that was left. Meanwhile the officer continued to search the files on the computer and they all kept checking their watches.

Kelly almost cried with relief when she got the note informing her that they had found Callum and he was safe. He was being treated by paramedics and as a precaution would soon be on his way to hospital. Assisted by Charley, they loosened the straps holding Woods and realising that the police were probably watching, Kelly reached for the jacket that Woods had been wearing earlier but it was ruined. Removing her blouse, she covered the detective who was unsteady but sitting up. Libby remained secured to the pipe at the back of the cell. They would need a key to release her but unfortunately, Morgan did not have it on him.

"Right," the officer cried, "I've found the password."

"How do you know it's the right one?" James asked glancing at his watch again. They only had only six minutes left.

"It's the latest in a sequence and has not yet been used. I'm pretty sure it's the one."

"Let's hope you are right." James cried as they rushed from the room.

"Now, they have to be ready to use the face recognition system directly after inputting the password."

James wrote this down carefully explaining the sequence then he pushed the note under the door.

"Do they know that time is critical?" the officer asked.

"No, I didn't mention that but I guess they won't hang around."

Kelly retrieved the message and read it out. "We'll have to work together," she told them her eyes settling on the bloodied body on the floor. "We have to lift him up and hold his face against the camera."

"Do you think it will work?"

"It has to. Are you ready Isobel?"

She was not feeling her best but was willing to help. It would take a combined effort to lift and hold him upright so straining with the effort they tried to avoid slipping in the blood.

"Hold him steady while I enter the password," Kelly groaned. "Get ready to push his face up to the camera."

"Hold on," Woods croaked as she removed a smear of blood from his face then prising open one of his eyes that had closed she said. "Okay, go."

Kelly entered the eight figure password then stepping away from the touchpad she grabbed hold of Morgan and helped to guide his face towards the camera.

Ashton stood anxiously with the other men counting down the seconds. His muscles tensed as he got perilously close to zero then suddenly a loud crack split the air and the door swung open.

"Izzy," he exclaimed as she collapsed against the doorframe. Rushing forward he took her in his arms and hugged her then as the other women appeared he moved out of the way. James checked them quickly before sharing a smile with Charley.

The officer anxiously studied the security device on the wall. "It seems stable but let's not hang around."

James returned to the command centre where he found the key that would release Libby then he went back to help her.

"Is Matt okay?" she sobbed holding onto him tightly.

Whatever he had done, she would never stop loving him. Isobel had said that he was in police custody but she had no idea how much trouble he was in or how it would affect their future together. Would their lives ever be the same?

Chapter Eighty

TWO WEEKS LATER WOODS RETURNED to work. It was unusually quiet as she made her way through the building but she was thankful for that. DC Samantha Burkett was alone in the incident room and when Woods appeared, she squealed with delight.

"Izzy," getting to her feet she rushed to her side. "What are you doing here? We are not expecting you for another two weeks."

"Don't be daft," Woods smiled, "what would I do with myself?"

"It's so good to see you."

The women hugged affectionately then Burkett began to fill her in with recent events. Woods was shocked to find her office in such a mess. Clearly, her desk had become a dumping ground for reports and papers that should have been filed.

"How are you feeling?" Burkett asked, embarrassed at not asking earlier.

"I'm fine," she replied waving away her colleague's concern. "Honestly, no lasting effects."

Burkett wondered if that were true, then she said. "You have a loyal ally in Dennis James."

"What do you mean?" Woods looked up at her.

"If it wasn't for him taking over we might not have found you in time."

"I thought that Terry Ashton was responsible."

"It's true, his input was invaluable, but Dennis was amazing. He was completely dedicated to the task. He had no support from Wyman and was punching well above his weight." She paused then lowering her voice, she went on. "When the most unpleasant photos appeared on Cunningham's computer, Dennis made certain they went no further. You know what some of the men are like around here."

Woods shuddered, embarrassing images of this kind would have made her position at the Met impossible. She was an ambitious woman striving for success in a world still dominated by men and there were several who despised her and would stop at nothing to bring her down.

"He is solely responsible for protecting your modesty," Burkett whispered.

"And my career it seems." She had no idea that DC James thought so much of her.

They talked for a while longer before Burkett asked. "What became of Kelly Spencer?"

Easing back in her chair in an attempt to hide her discomfort she looked up at Burkett before replying. "After she was reunited with her son Callum, her sister Caroline insisted that she moved in with her for a while." Woods was aware that the women had bridges to rebuild and was glad that Kelly would have someone close to help her through the next few weeks. "Charley Baker spent a couple of days in hospital then I believe she joined her colleagues on an assignment in Rome. Of course Matthew Cunningham is unable to leave the country, the conditions of his bail would not allow that."

"I can't help feeling sorry for him," Burkett said. "He is such a nice man and was drawn in completely against his will."

A short while later Burkett left the office leaving Woods feeling uncomfortable. It was true that Cunningham had been manipulated by a madman but there was nothing that she could do to prevent him having to face the legal system. Woods sighed deeply then busied herself sorting out discarded reports, memos and notes. Glancing at a few, she got an idea of what had been going on in her absence. It was then she came across a military file that she had not seen before. Opening it up she began to read. The covering page informed her that it was from Captain Thomas Cunningham, Dane Morgan's commanding officer in Afghanistan. The report confirmed that Sergeant Morgan was sent out on what began as a simple rescue mission but developed into something far more serious. The report went on to say that Captain Cunningham had to make a number of very difficult decisions that effectively sealed the fate of Morgan and his men. The unstable political situation at the time could not be compromised by an aggressive British military strike against insurgents operating in the area. Sergeant Morgan and his men were left to cope in the field with no military back up. This unfortunate turn of events resulted in not only the tragic loss of a female officer but also the rescue party. Their bodies were recovered later from a remote mountain village but Morgan was never found. Attempts to locate him over the next few weeks drew a blank so he was reported as missing.

"He must have been seeking revenge," Woods whispered to herself. She had given this considerable thought over the last two weeks and concluded that his actions were not simply random attacks on women. Morgan was a man consumed by frustration and fury. The system that he had complete confidence in had let him down badly resulting in a deadly outcome that played on his mind. The only way that he could achieve some kind of relief was to target those closest to Captain Cunningham. It all began with the abduction Kelly Spencer, the mother of his child then his brother Matthew was drawn in.

Closing the file, she put it to one side then her thoughts turned to Matthew Cunningham again. He was no longer in police custody, bail had been granted and now he was at home with Libby Ellis. She realised that he too was a victim, manipulated by circumstances beyond his control, but a young woman had died as a direct result of his actions and that could not be ignored. The case was automatically referred to the Court Prosecution Service and there would be a trial. Woods would be called to give evidence but for Cunningham's sake, she hoped that the judgement would be lenient.

Burkett knocked on the door then entered carrying two mugs of coffee.

"You know that Wyman has gone?" she said placing a mug carefully on the desk.

Woods looked up in surprise so Burkett went on.

"An internal investigation is underway," she nodded with satisfaction. "It turns out that he is involved with a number of gangland bosses and drug dealers. He was running quite a racket. Apparently, that's why he came to London. He managed to bribe his way into the post in order to further his criminal activities."

"I had no idea." Woods replied.

"Terry Ashton insisted on taking this to the Chief, in fact he was instrumental in bringing Wyman down."

"Was he indeed?" Woods said remembering a conversation they had had recently. "Where is Wyman now?"

"He is in custody but no one knows where."

Woods shuffled in her seat and wondered what other surprises might be waiting for her.

"Izzy." James gasped as he pushed open the door, then recovering his composure he stuttered, "er, DS Woods, Guv."

Rising stiffly to her feet, Woods smiled. "Izzy will do for now." Moving around the desk, she embraced him before brushing her lips against his cheek.

James was amazed, she had never shown such affection before or allowed him to use her Christian name.

Suddenly the telephone on the desk began to ring and reaching for it, Burkett listened for a moment before passing it to Woods. "It's the Chief."

Chapter Eighty One

THE RICHMOND HOTEL APPEARED WARM and inviting as she stood on the pavement looking in through the window. Adjusting her jacket, she pulled her skirt straight before taking a deep breath then, pushing at the door, she went in.

"Good evening," she greeted the receptionist with a smile before heading towards the Metropolitan Bar.

A cheer went up the moment she appeared and her colleagues, eager to be the first to greet her, surged forward. Officially, this was the end of case celebration but it would always be remembered as her welcome back party. Woods, battered by the onslaught exchanged hugs and kisses then she raised a glass to everyone. Terry Ashton standing quietly at the back of the room waited as the crowd around her began to disperse then he moved up beside her.

"I want to be the first to congratulate you," he whispered his face flushed with pride.

"How do you know, it's not public knowledge yet?" she hugged him then realised that he was friends with Brian Calvary.

"Just think, someone is changing the nameplate on your office door as we speak and tomorrow morning everyone will know. Congratulations Detective Inspector Isobel Woods."

About your author

Kevin Marsh was born in Canterbury in 1961. He lived and went to school there attending the Technical College (now Canterbury College), as an apprentice sheet metal worker. During his five years of training he worked in a small local company with his father and brother. In 1981 he was married and moved to Whitstable, (his father's home town).

In 1999, work took him in a different direction and he began to study for a teaching certificate in further education. This led to a lecturing position at the college where he had been a student so many years before.

His first novel, The Belgae Torc, book 1 in the Torc Trilogy, was launched on 30th June 2012. Two more books followed to complete the trilogy then a change of genre produced several thrillers. Although the thrillers are stand alone, some of the favourite characters appear in each book.

He has recently retired from full time teaching and moved to the beautiful Kent countryside to focus on writing.

Other books by Kevin Marsh

The Torc Trilogy:
The Belgae Torc
The Gordian Knot
Cutting the Gordian Knot

Psychological Thriller:
The Witness

Thriller:
The Cellist

Website:
www.kevinmarshnovels.co.uk

Blog:
mynovelsandotherthings.blogspot.co.uk

CPSIA information can be obtained
at www.ICGtesting.com
Printed in the USA
LVHW050900241220
674974LV00009B/796